THE CLOISTER AND THE HEARTH

The Cloister
and the Hearth
Charles Reade

Illustrated by Paul Hardy

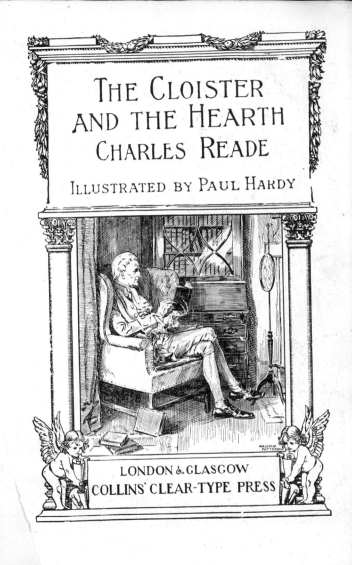

LONDON & GLASGOW
COLLINS' CLEAR-TYPE PRESS

PREFACE.

A SMALL portion of this tale appeared in *Once a Week*, July—September, 1859, under the title of "A Good Fight."

After writing it, I took wider views of the subject, and also felt uneasy at having deviated *unnecessarily* from the historical outline of a true story. These two sentiments have cost me more than a year's very hard labour, which I venture to think has not been wasted. After this plain statement I trust all who comment on this work will see that to describe it as a reprint would be unfair to the public and to me. The English language is copious, and, in any true man's hands, quite able to convey the truth ; viz., that one-fifth of the present work is a reprint, and four-fifths of it a new composition.

CHARLES READE.

The Cloister and the Hearth.

CHAPTER I.

NOT a day passes over the earth, but men and women of no note do great deeds, speak great words, and suffer noble sorrows. Of these obscure heroes, philosophers, and martyrs, the greater part will never be known till that hour, when many that are great shall be small, and the small great; but of others the world's knowledge may be said to sleep: their lives and characters lie hidden from nations in the annals that record them. The general reader cannot feel them, they are presented so curtly and coldly: they are not like breathing stories appealing to his heart, but little historic hailstones striking him but to glance off his bosom: nor can he understand them; for epitomes are not narratives, as skeletons are not human figures.

Thus records of prime truths remain a dead letter to plain folk; the writers have left so much to the imagination, and imagination is so rare a gift. Here, then, the writer of fiction may be of use to the public—as an interpreter.

There is a musty chronicle, written in tolerable Latin, and in it a chapter where every sentence holds a fact. Here is told, with harsh brevity, the strange history of a pair, who lived untrumpeted, and died unsung, four hundred years ago; and lie now, as unpitied, in that stern page, as fossils in a rock. Thus, living or dead, Fate is still unjust to them. For if I can but show you what lies below that dry chronicler's words, methinks you will correct the indifference of centuries, and give those two sore-tried souls a place in your heart—for a day.

It was past the middle of the fifteenth century; Louis XI. was sovereign of France; Edward IV. was wrongful king of England; and Philip "the Good," having by force and cunning dispossessed his cousin Jacqueline, and broken her heart, reigned undisturbed this many years in Holland, where our tale begins.

Elias, and Catherine his wife, lived in the little town of

Tergou. He traded, wholesale and retail, in cloth, silk, brown holland, and, above all, in curried leather, a material highly valued by the middling people, because it would stand twenty years' wear, and turn an ordinary knife, no small virtue in a jerkin of that century, in which folk were so liberal of their steel; even at dinner a man would leave his meat awhile, and carve you his neighbour, on a very moderate difference of opinion.

The couple were well-to-do, and would have been free from all earthly care, but for nine children. When these were coming into the world, one per annum, each was hailed with rejoicings, and the saints were thanked, not expostulated with; and when parents and children were all young together, the latter were looked upon as lovely little playthings invented by Heaven for the amusement, joy, and evening solace of people in business.

But as the olive-branches shot up, and the parents grew older, and saw with their own eyes the fate of large families, misgivings and care mingled with their love. They belonged to a singularly wise and provident people: in Holland reckless parents were as rare as disobedient children. So now when the huge loaf came in on a gigantic trencher, looking like a fortress in its moat, and, the tour of the table once made, seemed to have melted away, Elias and Catherine would look at one another and say, "Who is to find bread for them all when we are gone?"

At this observation the younger ones needed all their filial respect to keep their little Dutch countenances; for in their opinion dinner and supper came by Nature like sunrise and sunset, and, so long as that luminary should travel round the earth, so long *must* the brown loaf go round their family circle, and set in their stomachs only to rise again in the family oven. But the remark awakened the national thoughtfulness of the elder boys, and being often repeated, set several of the family thinking, some of them good thoughts, some ill thoughts, according to the nature of the thinkers.

"Kate, the children grow so, this table will soon be too small."

"We cannot afford it, Eli," replied Catherine, answering not his words, but his thought, after the manner of women.

Their anxiety for the future took at times a less dismal but more mortifying turn. The free burghers had their pride as well as the nobles; and these two could not bear that any of their blood should go down in the burgh after their decease.

So by prudence and self-denial they managed to clothe all the little bodies, and feed all the great mouths, and yet put by a small hoard to meet the future; and, as it grew, and grew, they felt a pleasure the miser hoarding for himself knows not.

One day the eldest boy but one, aged nineteen, came to his mother, and, with that outward composure which has so misled some persons as to the real nature of this people, begged her to intercede with his father to send him to Amsterdam, and place him with a merchant. "It is the way of life that likes me: merchants are wealthy; I am good at numbers; prithee, good mother, take my part in this, and I shall ever be, as I am now, your debtor."

Catherine threw up her hands with dismay and incredulity. "What! leave Tergou?"

"What is one street to me more than another? If I can leave the folk of Tergou, I can surely leave the stones."

"What! quit your poor father now he is no longer young?"

"Mother, if I can leave you, I can leave him."

"What! leave your poor brothers and sisters, that love you so dear?"

"There are enough in the house without me."

"What mean you, Richart? Who is more thought of than you? Stay! have I spoken sharp to you? Have I been unkind to you?"

"Never that I know of; and if you had, you should never hear of it from me. Mother," said Richart gravely, but the tear was in his eye, "it all lies in a word, and nothing can change my mind. There will be one mouth less for you to feed."

"There now, see what my tongue has done," said Catherine, and the next moment she began to cry. For she saw her first young bird on the edge of the nest trying his wings, to fly into the world. Richart had a calm, strong will, and she knew he never wasted a word.

It ended as Nature has willed all such discourse shall end: young Richart went to Amsterdam with a face so long and sad as it had never been seen before, and a heart like granite.

That afternoon at supper there was one mouth less. Catherine looked at Richart's chair and wept bitterly. On this Elias shouted roughly and angrily to the children, "Sit wider! can't ye: sit wider!" and turned his head away over the back of his seat awhile, and was silent.

Richart was launched; and never cost them another penny: but to fit him out and place him in the house of Vander Stegen, the merchant, took all the little hoard but one gold crown. They began again. Two years passed, Richart found a niche in commerce for his brother Jacob, and Jacob left Tergou directly after dinner, which was at eleven in the forenoon. At supper that day Elias remembered what had happened the last time; so it was in a low whisper he said, "Sit wider, dears!" Now until that moment, Catherine *would* not see the gap at table, for her daughter Catherine had besought her not to grieve to-night, and she had said, "No, sweetheart, I promise I will not, since it vexes my children." But when Elias whispered "Sit wider!" says she, "Ay! the table will soon be too big for the children: and you thought it would be too small;" and having delivered this with forced calmness, she put up her apron the next moment, and wept sore.

"'Tis the best that leave us," sobbed she; "that is the cruel part."

"Nay! nay!" said Elias, "our children are good children, and all are dear to us alike. Heed her not! What God takes from us still seems better than what He spares to us: that is to say, men are by nature unthankful —and women silly."

"And I say Richart and Jacob were the flower of the flock," sobbed Catherine.

The little coffer was empty again, and to fill it they gathered like ants. In those days speculation was pretty much confined to the card-and-dice business. Elias knew no way to wealth but the slow and sure one. "A penny saved is a penny gained," was his humble creed. All that was not required for the business and the necessaries of life went into the little coffer with steel bands and florid key. They denied themselves in turn the humblest luxuries, and then, catching one another's looks, smiled; perhaps with a greater joy than self-indulgence has to bestow. And so in three years more they had gleaned enough to set up their fourth son as a master-tailor, and their eldest daughter as a robemaker, in Tergou. Here were two more provided for: their own trade would enable them to throw work into the hands of this pair. But the coffer was drained to the dregs, and this time the shop too bled a little in goods if not in coin.

Alas! there remained on hand two that were unable to get their bread, and two that were unwilling. The unable ones were — 1, Giles, a dwarf, of the wrong sort, half stupidity, half malice, all head and claws and voice, run from by dogs and unprejudiced females, and sided with through thick and thin by his mother; 2, Little Catherine, a poor little girl that could only move on crutches. She lived in pain, but smiled through it, with her marble face and violet eyes and long silky lashes; and fretful or repining word never came from her lips. The unwilling ones were Sybrandt, the youngest, a ne'er-do-weel, too much in love with play to work, and Cornelis, the eldest, who had made calculations, and stuck to the hearth, waiting for dead men's shoes. Almost worn out by their repeated efforts, and, above all, dispirited by the moral and physical infirmities of those that now remained on hand, the anxious couple would often say, "What will become of all these when we shall be no longer here to take care of them?" But when they had said this a good many times, suddenly the domestic horizon cleared, and then they used still to say it, because a habit is a habit, but they uttered it half mechanically now, and added brightly and cheerfully, "But thanks to St. Bavon and all the saints, there's Gerard."

Young Gerard was for many years of his life a son apart and distinct; object of no fears and no great hopes. No fears; for he was going into the Church; and the Church could always maintain her children by hook or by crook in those days: no great hopes, because his family had no interest with the great to get him a benefice, and the young man's own habits were frivolous, and, indeed, such as our cloth merchant would not have put up with in any one but a clerk that was to be. His trivialities were reading and penmanship, and he was so wrapped up in them that often he could hardly be got away to his meals. The day was never long enough for him: and he carried ever a tinder-box and brimstone matches, and begged ends of candles of the neighbours, which he lighted at unreasonable hours —ay, even at eight of the clock at night in winter, when the very burgomaster was abed. Endured at home, his practices were encouraged by the monks of a neighbouring convent. They had taught him penmanship, and continued to teach him, until one day they discovered, in the middle of a lesson, that he was teaching them. They pointed this out to him in a merry way: he hung his head and blushed: he had suspected as much himself, but mistrusted his judgment in so delicate a matter. "But, my son," said an elderly monk, "how is it that you, to whom God has given an eye so true, a hand so subtle yet firm, and a heart to love these beautiful crafts—how is it you do not colour as well as write? A scroll looks but barren unless a border of fruit, and leaves, and rich arabesques surround the good words, and charm the sense as those do the soul and understanding; to say nothing of the pictures of holy men and women departed, with which the several chapters should be adorned, and not alone the eye soothed with the brave and sweetly-blended colours, but the heart lifted by effigies of the saints in glory. Answer me, my son."

At this Gerard was confused, and muttered that he had made several trials at illuminating, but had not succeeded well; and thus the matter rested.

Soon after this a fellow-enthusiast came on the scene in the unwonted form of an old lady. Margaret, sister and survivor of the brothers Van Eyck, left Flanders, and came to end her days in her native country. She bought a small house near Tergou. In course of time she heard of Gerard, and saw some of his handiwork: it pleased her so well that she sent her female servant, Reicht Heynes, to ask him to come to her. This led to an acquaintance: it could hardly be otherwise, for little Tergou had never held so many as two zealots of this sort before. At first the old lady damped Gerard's courage terribly. At each visit she fished out of holes and corners drawings and paintings, some of them by her own hand, that seemed to him unapproachable; but if the artist overpowered him, the woman kept his heart up. She and Reicht soon turned him inside out like a glove: among other things, they drew from him what the good monks had failed to hit upon, the reason why he did not illuminate, viz., that he could not afford the gold, the blue, and the red, but only the cheap earths; and that he was afraid to ask his mother to buy the choice colours, and was sure he should ask her in vain. Then Margaret Van Eyck gave him a little brush-gold, and some vermilion and ultramarine, and a piece of good vellum to lay them on. He almost adored her. As he left the house, Reicht ran after him with a

underrated the distance, and imprudently allowed her father to start too late in the day.

"No, no!" said the old man; "it is not the distance, it is the want of nourishment."

The girl put her arms round his neck with tender concern, but took that opportunity of whispering, "Father, a stranger—a young man!"

But it was too late. Gerard, with simplicity, and quite as a matter of course, fell to gathering sticks with great expedition. This done, he took down his wallet, out with the manchet of bread and the iron flask his careful mother had put up, and his everlasting tinder-box; lighted a match, then a candle-end, then the sticks; and put his iron flask on it. Then down he went on his stomach, and took a good blow: then looking up, he saw the girl's face had thawed, and she was looking down at him and his energy with a demure smile. He laughed back to her. "Mind the pot," said he, "and don't let it spill, for Heaven's sake: there's a cleft stick to hold it safe with;" and with this he set off running towards a corn-field at some distance.

Whilst he was gone, there came by, on a mule with rich purple housings, an old man redolent of wealth. The purse at his girdle was plethoric, the fur on his tippet was ermine, broad and new.

It was Ghysbrecht Van Swieten, the burgomaster of Tergou. He was old, and his face furrowed. He was a notorious miser, and looked one generally. But the idea of supping with the Duke raised him just now into manifest complacency. Yet at the sight of the faded old man and his bright daughter sitting by a fire of sticks, the smile died out of his face, and he wore a strange look of pain and uneasiness. He reined in his mule. "Why, Peter—Margaret," said he, almost fiercely, "what mummery is this?" Peter was going to answer, but Margaret interposed hastily, and said: "My father was exhausted, so I am warming something to give him strength before we go on." "What! reduced to feed by the roadside like the Bohemians," said Ghysbrecht, and his hand went into his purse: but it did not seem at home there; it fumbled uncertainly, afraid too large a coin might stick to a finger and come out.

At this moment who should come bounding up but Gerard. He had two straws in his hand, and he threw himself down by the fire, and relieved Margaret of the cooking part : then suddenly recognising the burgomaster, he coloured all over. Ghysbrecht Van Swieten started and glared at him, and took his hand out of his purse. "Oh!" said he bitterly, "I am not wanted," and went slowly on, casting a long look of suspicion on Margaret, and hostility on Gerard, that was not very intelligible. However, there was something about it that Margaret could read enough to blush at, and almost toss her head. Gerard only stared with surprise. "By St. Bavon, I think the old miser grudges us three our quart of soup," said he. When the young man put that interpretation on Ghysbrecht's strange and meaning look, Margaret was greatly relieved. and smiled gaily on the speaker.

Meantime Ghysbrecht plodded on, more wretched in his wealth than these in their poverty. And the curious thing is that the mule, the purple housings, and one half the coin in that plethoric purse, belonged not to Ghysbrecht Van Swieten, but to that faded old man and that comely girl, who sat by a roadside fire to be fed by a stranger. They did not know this ; but Ghysbrecht knew it, and carried in his heart a scorpion of his own begetting : that scorpion is remorse — the remorse that, not being penitence, is incurable, and ready for fresh misdeeds upon a fresh temptation.

Twenty years ago, when Ghysbrecht Van Swieten was a hard and honest man, the touchstone opportunity came to him, and he did an act of heartless roguery. It seemed a safe one. It had hitherto proved a safe one, though he had never felt safe. To-day he had seen youth, enterprise, and, above all, knowledge, seated by fair Margaret and her father on terms that look familiar and loving.

And the fiends are at his ear again.

CHAPTER II.

"The soup is hot," said Gerard.

"But how are we to get it to our mouths?" inquired the senior despondingly.

"Father, the young man has brought us straws." And Margaret smiled slily.

"Ay, ay!" said the old man ; "but my poor bones are

stiff, and indeed the fire is too hot for a body to kneel over with these short straws. St. John the Baptist, but the young man is adroit!"

For, while he stated his difficulty, Gerard removed it. He untied in a moment the knot on his breast, took his hat off, put a stone into each corner of it, then, wrapping his hand in the tail of his jerkin, whipped the flask off the fire, wedged it in between the stones, and put the hat under the old man's nose with a merry smile. The other tremulously inserted the pipe of rye-straw and sucked. Lo and behold, his wan, drawn face was seen to light up more and more, till it quite glowed; and as soon as he had drawn a long breath—

"Hippocrates and Galen!" he cried, "'tis a *soupe au vin* —the restorative of restoratives. Blessed be the nation that invented it, and the woman that made it, and the young man who brings it to fainting folk. Have a suck, my girl, while I relate to our young host the history and virtues of this his sovereign compound. This corrobora-tive, young sir, was unknown to the ancients : we find it neither in their treatises of medicine, nor in those popular narratives, which reveal many of their remedies, both in chirurgery and medicine proper. Hector, in the Ilias, if my memory does not play me false——"

[*Margaret.* "Alas! he's off."]

"——was invited by one of the ladies of the poem to drink a draught of wine; but he declined, on the plea that he was just going into battle, and must not take aught to weaken his powers. Now, if the *soupe au vin* had been known in Troy, it is clear that in declining *vinum merum* upon that score, he would have added in the next hexameter, 'But a *soupe au vin*, madam, I will degust, and gratefully.' Not only would this have been but common civility—a virtue no perfect commander is wanting in—but not to have done it would have proved him a shallow and improvident person, unfit to be trusted with the conduct of a war; for men going into a battle need sustenance and all possible support, as is proved by this, that foolish generals, bringing hungry soldiers to blows with full ones, have been defeated, in all ages, by inferior numbers. The Romans lost a great battle in the north of Italy to Hannibal, the Carthaginian, by this neglect alone. Now, this divine elixir gives in one moment force to the limbs and ardour to the spirits ;

and taken into Hector's body at the nick of time, would, by the aid of Phœbus, Venus, and the blessed saints, have most likely procured the Greeks a defeat. For, note how faint and weary and heart-sick I was a minute ago; well, I suck this celestial cordial, and now behold me brave as Achilles and strong as an eagle."

"Oh, father, now! an eagle, alack!"

"Girl, I defy thee and all the world. Ready, I say, like a foaming charger, to devour the space between this and Rotterdam, and strong to combat the ills of life, even poverty and old age, which last philosophers have called the *summum malum*. Negatur; unless the man's life has been ill-spent—which, by the bye, it generally has. Now for the moderns!"

"Father! dear father!"

"Fear me not, girl; I will be brief, unreasonably and unseasonably brief. The *soupe au vin* occurs not in modern science; but this is only one proof more, if proof were needed, that for the last few hundred years physicians have been idiots, with their chicken-broth and their decoction of gold, whereby they attribute the highest qualities to that meat which has the least juice of any meat, and to that metal which has less chemical qualities than all the metals. Mountebanks! dunces! homicides! Since, then, from these no light is to be gathered, go we to the chroniclers; and first we find that Duguesclin, a French knight, being about to join battle with the English—masters, at that time, of half France, and sturdy strikers by sea and land—drank, not one, but three *soupes au vin* in honour of the Blessed Trinity. This done, he charged the islanders; and, as might have been foretold, killed a multitude, and drove the rest into the sea. But he was only the first of a long list of holy and hard-hitting ones who have, by this divine restorative, been sustentated, fortified, corroborated, and consoled."

"Dear father, prithee add thyself to that venerable company ere the soup cools." And Margaret held the hat imploringly in both hands till he inserted the straw once more.

This spared them the "modern instances," and gave Gerard an opportunity of telling Margaret how proud his mother would be her soup had profited a man of learning.

"Ay! but," said Margaret, "it would like her ill to see her son give all and take none himself. Why brought you but two straws?"

"Fair mistress, I hoped you would let me put my lips to your straw, there being but two."

Margaret smiled and blushed. "Never beg that you may command," said she. "The straw is not mine, 'tis yours : you cut it in yonder field."

"I cut it, and that made it mine ; but, after that, your lip touched it, and that made it yours."

"Did it ? Then I will lend it you. There—now it is yours again : *your* lip has touched it."

"No, it belongs to us both now. Let us divide it."

"By all means ; you have a knife."

"No, I will not cut it—that would be unlucky. I'll bite it. There ! I shall keep my half : you will burn yours, once you get home, I doubt."

"You know me not. I waste nothing. It is odds but I make a hairpin of it, or something."

This answer dashed the novice Gerard, instead of provoking him, to fresh efforts, and he was silent. And now, the bread and soup being disposed of, the old scholar prepared to continue his journey. Then came a little difficulty : Gerard the adroit could not tie his ribbon again as Catherine had tied it. Margaret, after slily eyeing his efforts for some time, offered to help him ; for at her age girls love to be coy and tender, saucy and gentle, by turns, and she saw she had put him out of countenance but now. Then a fair head, with its stately crown of auburn hair, glossy and glowing through silver, bowed sweetly towards him ; and, while it ravished his eye, two white supple hands played delicately upon the stubborn ribbon, and moulded it with soft and airy touches. Then a heavenly thrill ran through the innocent young man, and vague glimpses of a new world of feeling and sentiment opened on him. And these new and exquisite sensations Margaret unwittingly prolonged : it is not natural to her sex to hurry aught that pertains to the sacred toilet. Nay, when the taper fingers had at last subjugated the ends of the knot, her mind was not quite easy, till, by a manœuvre peculiar to the female hand, she had made her palm convex, and so applied it with a gentle pressure to the centre of the knot— a sweet little coaxing hand-kiss, as much as to say, "Now be a good knot, and stay so." The palm-kiss was bestowed on the ribbon, but the wearer's heart leaped to meet it.

"There, that is how it was," said Margaret, and drew **back** to take one last keen survey of her work ; then

looking up for simple approval of her skill, received full
in her eyes a longing gaze of such ardent adoration,
as made her lower them quickly and colour all over.
An indescribable tremor seized her, and she retreated
with downcast lashes and tell-tale cheeks, and took her
father's arm on the opposite side. Gerard, blushing at
having scared her away with his eyes, took the other
arm; and so the two young things went downcast and
conscious, and propped the eagle along in silence.

They entered Rotterdam by the Schiedamze Poort; and,
as Gerard was unacquainted with the town, Peter directed
him the way to the Hoog Straet, in which the Stadthouse
was. He himself was going with Margaret to his cousin,
in the Ooster-Waagen Straet, so, almost on entering the
gate, their roads lay apart. They bade each other a
friendly adieu, and Gerard dived into the great town.
A profound sense of solitude fell upon him, yet the streets
were crowded. Then he lamented too late that, out of
delicacy, he had not asked his late companions who they
were and where they lived.

"Beshrew my shamefacedness!" said he. "But their
words and their breeding were above their means, and
something did whisper me they would not be known. I
shall never see her more. O weary world, I hate you
and your ways. To think I must meet beauty and
goodness and learning—three pearls of price—and never
see them more!"

Falling into this sad reverie, and letting his body go
where it would, he lost his way; but presently meeting
a crowd of persons all moving in one direction, he mingled
with them, for he argued they must be making for the
Stadthouse. Soon the noisy troop that contained the
moody Gerard emerged, not upon the Stadthouse, but
upon a large meadow by the side of the Maas; and
then the attraction was revealed. Games of all sorts
were going on: wrestling, the game of palm, the quintain,
legerdemain, archery, tumbling, in which art, I blush
to say, women as well as men performed, to the great
delectation of the company. There was also a trained
bear, who stood on his head, and marched upright, and
bowed with prodigious gravity to his master; and a
hare that beat a drum, and a cock that strutted on
little stilts disdainfully. These things made Gerard laugh
now and then; but the gay scene could not really enliven

it, for his heart was not in tune with it. So, hearing a young man say to his fellow that the Duke had been in the meadow, but was gone to the Stadthouse to entertain the burgomasters and aldermen and the competitors for the prizes, and their friends, he suddenly remembered he was hungry, and should like to sup with a prince. He left the river-side, and this time he found the Hoog Straet, and it speedily led him to the Stadthouse. But when he got there he was refused, first at one door, then at another, till he came to the great gate of the courtyard. It was kept by soldiers, and superintended by a pompous major-domo, glittering in an embroidered collar and a gold chain of office, and holding a white staff with a gold knob. There was a crowd of persons at the gate endeavouring to soften this official rock. They came up in turn like ripples, and retired as such in turn. It cost Gerard a struggle to get near him, and when he was within four heads of the gate, he saw something that made his heart beat; there was Peter, with Margaret on his arm, soliciting humbly for entrance.

"My cousin the alderman is not at home; they say he is here."

"What is that to me, old man?"

"If you will not let us pass in to him, at least take this leaf from my tablet to my cousin. See I have written his name: he will come out to us."

"For what do you take me? I carry no messages. I keep the gate."

He then bawled, in a stentorian voice, inexorably—

"No strangers enter here, but the competitors and their companies."

"Come, old man," cried a voice in the crowd, "you have gotten your answer; make way."

Margaret turned half round imploringly—

"Good people, we are come from far, and my father is old; and my cousin has a new servant that knows us not, and would not let us sit in our cousin's house."

At this the crowd laughed hoarsely. Margaret shrank as if they had struck her. At that moment a hand grasped hers—a magic grasp: it felt like heart meeting heart, or magnet steel. She turned quickly round at it, and it was Gerard. Such a little cry of joy and appeal came from her bosom, and she began to whimper prettily.

They had hustled her and frightened her, for one thing; and her cousin's thoughtlessness, in not even telling his servant they were coming, was cruel; and the servant's caution, however wise and faithful to her master, was bitterly mortifying to her father and her. And to her so mortified, and anxious and jostled, came suddenly this kind hand and face. "Hinc illæ lacrimæ."

"All is well now," remarked a coarse humorist; "she hath gotten her sweetheart."

"Haw! haw! haw!" went the crowd.

She dropped Gerard's hand directly, and turned round, with eyes flashing through her tears—

"I have no sweetheart, you rude men. But I am friendless in your boorish town, and this is a friend; and one who knows, what you know not, how to treat the aged and the weak."

The crowd was dead silent. They had only been thoughtless, and now felt the rebuke, though severe, was just. The silence enabled Gerard to treat with the porter.

"I am a competitor, sir."

"What is your name?" and the man eyed him suspiciously.

"Gerard, the son of Elias."

The janitor inspected a slip of parchment he held in his hand.

"Gerard Eliassoen can enter."

"With my company; these two?"

"Nay; those are not your company: they came before you."

"What matter? They are my friends, and without them I go not in."

"Stay without, then."

"That will I not."

"That we will see."

"We will, and speedily." And with this, Gerard raised a voice of astounding volume and power, and shouted, so that the whole street rang—

"Ho! Philip, Earl of Holland!"

"Are you mad?" cried the porter.

"Here is one of your varlets defies you."

"Hush, hush!"

"And will not let your guests pass in."

"Hush! murder! The Duke's there. I'm dead," cried the janitor, quaking.

Then suddenly trying to overpower Gerard's thunder, he shouted, with all his lungs—

"OPEN THE GATE, YE KNAVES! WAY THERE FOR GERARD ELIASSOEN AND HIS COMPANY! (The fiends go with him!)"

The gate swung open as by magic. Eight soldiers lowered their pikes half-way, and made an arch, under which the victorious three marched in triumphant. The moment they had passed, the pikes clashed together horizontally to bar the gateway, and all but pinned an abdominal citizen that sought to wedge in along with them.

Once past the guarded portal, a few steps brought the trio upon a scene of Oriental luxury. The courtyard was laid out in tables loaded with rich meats, and piled with gorgeous plate. Guests in rich and various costumes sat beneath a leafy canopy of fresh-cut branches fastened tastefully to golden, silver, and blue silken cords that traversed the area; and fruits of many hues, including some artificial ones of gold, silver, and wax, hung pendent, or peeped like fair eyes among the green leaves of plane-trees and lime-trees. The Duke's minstrels swept their lutes at intervals, and a fountain played red Burgundy in six jets that met and battled in the air. The evening sun darted its fires through those bright and purple wine spouts, making them jets and cascades of molten rubies; then passing on, tinged with the blood of the grape, shed crimson glories here and there on fair faces, snowy beards, velvet, satin, jewelled hilts, glowing gold, gleaming silver, and sparkling glass. Gerard and his friends stood dazzled, spell-bound. Presently a whisper buzzed round them, "Salute the Duke! Salute the Duke!" They looked up, and there on high, under the dais, was their sovereign, bidding them welcome with a kindly wave of the hand. The men bowed low, and Margaret curtsied with a deep and graceful obeisance. The Duke's hand being up, he gave it another turn, and pointed the new-comers out to a knot of valets. Instantly seven of his people, with an obedient start, went headlong at our friends, seated them at a table, and put fifteen many-coloured soups before them, in little silver bowls, and as many wines in crystal vases.

"Nay, father, let us not eat until we have thanked our good friend," said Margaret, now first recovering from all this bustle.

"Girl, he is our guardian angel."

Gerard put his face into his hands.

"Tell me when you have done," said he, "and I will reappear and have my supper, for I am hungry. I know which of us three is the happiest at meeting again."

"Me?" inquired Margaret.

"No: guess again."

"Father?"

"No."

"Then I have no guess which it can be;" and she gave a little crow of happiness and gaiety. The soup was tasted, and vanished in a twirl of fourteen hands, and fish came on the table in a dozen forms, with patties of lobster and almonds mixed, and of almonds and cream, and an immense variety of *brouets*, known to us as *rissoles*. The next trifle was a wild boar, which smelt divine. Why, then, did Margaret start away from it with two shrieks of dismay, and pinch so good a friend as Gerard? Because the Duke's *cuisinier* had been too clever; had made this excellent dish too captivating to the sight as well as taste. He had restored to the animal, by elaborate mimicry with burnt sugar and other edible colours, the hair and bristles he had robbed him of by fire and water. To make him still more enticing, the huge tusks were carefully preserved in the brute's jaw, and gave his mouth the winning smile that comes of tusk in man or beast; and two eyes of coloured sugar glowed in his head. St. Argus! what eyes! so bright, so bloodshot, so threatening —they followed a man and every movement of his knife and spoon. But, indeed, I need the pencil of Granville or Tenniel to make you see the two gilt valets on the opposite side of the table putting the monster down before our friends, with a smiling, self-satisfied, benevolent obsequiousness—for this ghastly monster was the flower of all comestibles—old Peter clasping both hands in pious admiration of it; Margaret wheeling round with horror-stricken eyes and her hand on Gerard's shoulder, squeaking and pinching; his face of unwise delight at being pinched, the grizzly brute glaring sulkily on all, and the guests grinning from ear to ear.

"What's to do?" shouted the Duke, hearing the signals of female distress. Seven of his people with a zealous start went headlong and told him. He laughed and said, "Give her of the beef-stuffing, then, and bring me Sir

Boar." Benevolent monarch! The beef-stuffing was his own private dish. On these grand occasions an ox was roasted whole, and reserved for the poor. But this wise as well as charitable prince had discovered, that whatever venison, hares, lamb, poultry, etc., you skewered into that beef cavern, got cooked to perfection, retaining their own juices and receiving those of the reeking ox. These he called his beef-stuffing, and took delight therein, as did now our trio; for, at his word, seven of his people went headlong, and drove silver tridents into the steaming cave at random, and speared a kid, a cygnet, and a flock of wild-fowl. These presently smoked before Gerard and company; and Peter's face, sad and slightly morose at the loss of the savage hog, expanded and shone. After this, twenty different tarts of fruits and herbs, and last of all, confectionery on a Titanic scale; cathedrals of sugar, all gilt and painted in the interstices of the bas-reliefs; castles with their moats, and ditches, imitated to the life; elephants, camels, toads; knights on horseback jousting; kings and princesses looking on; trumpeters blowing; and all these personages delicious eating, and their veins filled with sweet-scented juices: works of art made to be destroyed. The guests breached a bastion, crunched a crusader and his horse and lance, or cracked a bishop, cope, chasuble, crosier and all, as remorselessly as we do a caraway comfit; sipping, meanwhile, hippocras and other spiced drinks, and Greek and Corsican wines, while every now and then little Turkish boys, turbaned, spangled, jewelled, and gilt, came offering on bended knee golden troughs of rose-water and orange-water to keep the guests' hands cool and perfumed.

But long before our party arrived at this final stage, appetite had succumbed, and Gerard had suddenly remembered he was the bearer of a letter to the Princess Marie, and, in an undertone, had asked one of the servants if he would undertake to deliver it. The man took it with a deep obeisance: "He could not deliver it himself, but would instantly give it one of the Princess's suite, several of whom were about."

It may be remembered that Peter and Margaret came here not to dine, but to find their cousin. Well, the old gentleman ate heartily, and being much fatigued, dropped asleep, and forgot all about his cousin. Margaret did not remind him; we shall hear why.

Meantime, that cousin was seated within a few feet of them, at their backs, and discovered them when Margaret turned round and screamed at the boar. But he forbore to speak to them, for municipal reasons. Margaret was very plainly dressed, and Peter inclined to threadbare. So the alderman said to himself—

"'Twill be time to make up to them when the sun sets and the company disperses : then I will take my poor relations to my house, and none will be the wiser."

Half the courses were lost on Gerard and Margaret. They were no great eaters, and just now were feeding on sweet thoughts that have ever been unfavourable to appetite. But there is a delicate kind of sensuality, to whose influence these two were perhaps more sensitive than any other pair in that assembly—the delights of colour, music, and perfume, all of which blended so fascinatingly here.

Margaret leaned back and half closed her eyes, and murmured to Gerard : "What a lovely scene ! the warm sun, the green shade, the rich dresses, the bright music of the lutes and the cool music of the fountain, and all faces so happy and gay ! and then, it is to you we owe it."

Gerard was silent all but his eyes ; observing which—

"Now, speak not to me," said Margaret languidly ; "let me listen to the fountain : what are you a competitor for ?"

He told her.

"Very well ! You will gain one prize, at least."

"Which ? which ? Have you seen any of my work ?"

"I ?—no. But you will gain a prize."

"I hope so : but what makes you think so ?"

"Because you were so good to my father."

Gerard smiled at the feminine logic, and hung his head at the sweet praise, and was silent.

"Speak not," murmured Margaret. "They say this is a world of sin and misery. Can that be ? What is your opinion ?"

"No ! that is all a silly old song," explained Gerard. "'Tis a byword our elders keep repeating, out of custom : it is not true."

"How can you know ? You are but a child," said Margaret, with pensive dignity.

"Why, only look round! And then I thought I had lost you for ever; and you are by my side; and now the minstrels are going to play again. Sin and misery? Stuff and nonsense!"

The lutes burst out. The courtyard rang again with their delicate harmony.

"What do you admire most of all these beautiful things, Gerard?"

"You know my name? How is that?"

"White magic. I am a witch."

"Angels are never witches. But I can't think how you—"

"Foolish boy! was it not cried at the gate loud enough to deave one?"

"So it was. Where is my head? What do I admire most? If you will sit a little more that way, I'll tell you."

"This way?"

"Yes; so that the light may fall on you. There! I see many fair things here, fairer than I could have conceived; but the fairest of all, to my eye, is your lovely hair in its silver frame, and the setting sun kissing it. It minds me of what the Vulgate praises for beauty, '*An apple of gold in a network of silver*,' and oh, what a pity I did not know you before I sent in my poor endeavours at illuminating! I could illuminate so much better now. I could do everything better. There, now the sun is full on it, it is like an aureole. So our Lady looked, and none since her until to-day."

"Oh, fie! it is wicked to talk so. Compare a poor, coarse-favoured girl like me with the Queen of Heaven? Oh, Gerard! I thought you were a good young man." And Margaret was shocked apparently.

Gerard tried to explain. "I am no worse than the rest; but how can I help having eyes, and a heart—Margaret!"

"Gerard!"

"Be not angry now!"

"Now, is it likely?"

"I love you."

"Oh, for shame! you must not say that to me," and Margaret coloured furiously at this sudden assault.

"I can't help it. I love you. I love you."

"Hush, hush! for pity's sake! I must not listen to such words from a stranger. I am ungrateful to call you a stranger. Oh, how one may be mistaken! If I had known you were so bold——" And Margaret's bosom began to heave, and her cheeks were covered with blushes, and she looked towards her sleeping father, very much like a timid thing that meditates actual flight.

Then Gerard was frightened at the alarm he caused. "Forgive me," said he imploringly. "How could any one help loving you?"

"Well, sir, I will *try* and forgive you—you are so good in other respects; but then you must promise me never to say you—to say *that* again."

"Give me your hand then, or you don't forgive me."

She hesitated; but eventually put out her hand a very little way, very slowly, and with seeming reluctance. He took it, and held it prisoner. When she thought it had been there long enough, she tried gently to draw it away. He held it tight: it submitted quite patiently to force. What *is* the use resisting force? She turned her head away, and her long eyelashes drooped sweetly. Gerard lost nothing by his promise. Words were not heeded here; and silence was more eloquent. Nature was in that day what she is in ours; but manners were somewhat freer. Then, as now, virgins drew back alarmed at the first words of love; but of prudery and artificial coquetry there was little, and the young soon read one another's hearts. Everything was on Gerard's side; his good looks, her belief in his goodness, her gratitude; and opportunity: for at the Duke's banquet this mellow summer eve, all things disposed the female nature to tenderness: the avenues to the heart lay open; the senses were so soothed and subdued with lovely colours, gentle sounds, and delicate odours; the sun gently sinking, the warm air, the green canopy, the cool music of the now violet fountain.

Gerard and Margaret sat hand in hand in silence; and Gerard's eyes sought hers lovingly; and hers now and then turned on him timidly and imploringly; and presently two sweet unreasonable tears rolled down her cheeks, and she smiled deliciously while they were drying: yet they did not take long.

And the sun declined; and the air cooled; and the

fountain plashed more gently; and the pair throbbed in unison and silence, and this weary world looked heaven to them.

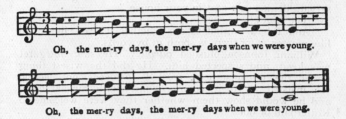

Oh, the mer-ry days, the mer-ry days when we were young.

Oh, the mer-ry days, the mer-ry days when we were young.

CHAPTER III.

A GRAVE, white-haired seneschal came to their table, and inquired courteously whether Gerard Eliassoen was of their company. Upon Gerard's answer, he said—

"The Princess Marie would confer with you, young sir; I am to conduct you to her presence."

Instantly all faces within hearing turned sharp round, and were bent with curiosity and envy on the man that was to go to a princess.

Gerard rose to obey.

"I wager we shall not see you again," said Margaret calmly, but colouring a little.

"That will you," was the reply: then he whispered in her ear, "This is my good princess; but you are my queen." He added aloud: "Wait for me, I pray you, I will presently return."

"Ay, ay!" said Peter, awaking and speaking at one and the same moment.

Gerard gone, the pair whose dress was so homely, yet they were with the man whom the Princess sent for, became "the cynosure of neighbouring eyes"; observing which, William Johnson came forward, acted surprise, and claimed his relations.

"And to think that there was I at your backs, and y̶ saw me not!"

"Nay, cousin Johnson, I saw you long syne," said Margaret coldly.

"You saw me, and spoke not to me?"

"Cousin, it was for you to welcome us to Rotterdam, as it is for us to welcome you at Sevenbergen. Your servant denied us a seat in your house."

"The idiot!"

"And I had a mind to see whether it was 'like maid like master': for there is sooth in bywords."

William Johnson blushed purple. He saw Margaret was keen, and suspected him. He did the wisest thing under the circumstances, trusted to deeds not words. He insisted on their coming home with him at once, and he would show them whether they were welcome to Rotterdam or not.

"Who doubts it, cousin? Who doubts it?" said the scholar.

Margaret thanked him graciously, but demurred to go just now: said she wanted to hear the minstrels again. In about a quarter of an hour Johnson renewed his proposal, and bade her observe that many of the guests had left. Then her real reason came out.

"It were ill manners to our friend; and he will lose us. He knows not where we lodge in Rotterdam, and the city is large, and we have parted company once already."

"Oh!" said Johnson, "we will provide for that. My young man, ahem! I mean my secretary, shall sit here and wait, and bring him on to my house: he shall lodge with me and with no other."

"Cousin, we shall be too burdensome."

"Nay, nay; you shall see whether you are welcome or not, you and your friends, and your friends' friends, if need be; and I shall hear what the Princess would with him."

Margaret felt a thrill of joy that Gerard should be lodged under the same roof with her; then she had a slight misgiving. "But if your young man should be thoughtless, and go play, and Gerard miss him?"

"He go play? He leave that spot where I put him, and bid him stay? Ho! stand forth, Hans Cloterman."

A figure clad in black serge and dark violet hose arose, and took two steps, and stood before them without moving a muscle: a solemn, precise young man, the very statue of gravity and starched propriety. At his aspect Margaret,

with gold ; and his mantle, too ; and it had a broad border, all pictures ; but, above all, his gloves ; you have no such gloves, mamma. They were embroidered and covered with jewels, and scented with such lovely scent ; I smelt them all the time he was giving me his blessing on my head with them. Dear old man ! I daresay he will die soon— most old people do—and then, sir, you can be bishop, you know, and wear——"

"Gently, Marie, gently : bishoprics are for old gentle-men ; and this is a young gentleman."

"Mamma ! he is not so very young."

"Not compared with you, Marie, eh ?"

"He is a good bigth, dear mamma ; and I am sure he is *good* enough for a bishop."

"Alas ! mademoiselle, you are mistaken."

"I know not that, Monsieur Gerard ; but I am a little puzzled to know on what grounds mademoiselle there pronounces your character so boldly."

"Alas ! mamma," said the Princess, "you have not looked at his face, then ; " and she raised her eyebrows at her mother's simplicity.

"I beg your pardon," said the Countess, "I have. Well, sir, if I cannot go quite so fast as my daughter, attribute it to my age, not to a want of interest in your welfare. A benefice will do to begin your career with ; and I must take care it is not too far from—what call you the place ? "

"Tergou, madam."

"A priest gives up much," continued the Countess ; "often, I fear, he learns too late how much ; " and her woman's eye rested a moment on Gerard with mild pity and half surprise at his resigning her sex, and all the heaven they can bestow, and the great parental joys : "at least, you shall be near your friends. Have you a mother ? "

"Yes, madam, thanks be to God ! "

"Good ! You shall have a church near Tergou. She will thank me. And now, sir, we must not detain you too long from those who have a better claim on your society than we have. Duchess, oblige me by bidding one of the pages conduct him to the hall of banquet ; the way is hard to find.

Gerard bowed low to the Countess and the Princess, and backed towards the door.

"I hope it will be a nice benefice," said the Princess to

him, with a pretty smile, as he was going out; then, shaking her head with an air of solemn misgiving, "but you had better have been Bishop of Liége."

Gerard followed his new conductor, his heart warm with gratitude: but ere he reached the banquet-hall a chill came over him. The mind of one who has led a quiet, uneventful life is not apt to take in contradictory feelings at the same moment and balance them, but rather to be over powered by each in turn. While Gerard was with the Countess, the excitement of so new a situation, the unlooked-for promise, the joy and pride it would cause at home, possessed him wholly; but now it was passion's turn to be heard again. What! give up Margaret, whose soft hand he still felt in his, and her deep eyes in his heart? resign her and all the world of love and joy she had opened on him to-day? The revulsion, when it did come, was so strong that he hastily resolved to say nothing at home about the offered benefice. "The Countess is so good," thought he, "she has a hundred ways of aiding a young man's fortune: she will not compel me to be a priest when she shall learn I love one of her sex: one would almost think she does know it, for she cast a strange look on me, and said, 'A priest gives up much, too much.' I daresay she will give me a place about the palace." And with this hopeful reflection his mind was eased; and, being now at the entrance of the banqueting-hall, he thanked his conductor, and ran hastily with joyful eyes to Margaret. He came in sight of the table—she was gone. Peter was gone too. Nobody was at the table at all; only a citizen in sober garments had just tumbled under it dead drunk, and several persons were raising him to carry him away. Gerard never guessed how important this solemn drunkard was to him: he was looking for "Beauty," and let the "Beast" lie. He ran wildly round the hall, which was now comparatively empty. She was not there. He left the palace: outside he found a crowd gaping at two great fanlights just lighted over the gate. He asked them earnestly if they had seen an old man in a gown and a lovely girl pass out. They laughed at the question. "They were staring at these new lights that turn night into day. They didn't trouble their heads about old men and young wenches, everyday sights." From another group he learned there was a Mystery being played under canvas hard by, and all the world gone to see it. This revived his hopes, and he went and saw the Mystery. In this representation divine personages, too sacred for me to name here, came clumsily down from heaven to talk sophistry with the cardinal Virtues, the nine Muses, and the seven deadly Sins, all present in human shape, and not unlike one another. To enliven which weary stuff, in rattled the Prince of the power of the air, and an imp that kept molesting him and buffeting him with a bladder, at each thwack of which the crowd were in ecstasies. When the Vices had uttered good store of obscenity and the Virtues twaddle, the celestials, including the nine Muses, went gingerly back to heaven one by one ; for there was but one cloud ; and two artisans worked it up with its supernatural freight, and worked it down with a winch, in full sight of the audience. These disposed of, the bottomless pit opened and flamed in the centre of the stage ; the carpenters and Virtues shoved the Vices in, and the Virtues and Beelzebub and his tormentor danced merrily round the place of eternal torture to the fife and tabor.

This entertainment was writ by the Bishop of Ghent for the diffusion of religious sentiment by the aid of the senses, and was an average specimen of theatrical exhibitions so long as they were in the hands of the clergy. But, in course of time, the laity conducted plays, and so the theatre, I learn from the pulpit, has become profane.

Margaret was nowhere in the crowd, and Gerard could not enjoy the performance ; he actually went away in Act 2, in the midst of a much-admired piece of dialogue, in which Justice out-quibbled Satan. He walked through many streets, but could not find her he sought. At last, fairly worn out, he went to a hostelry and slept till daybreak. All that day, heavy and heart-sick, he sought her, but could never fall in with her or her father, nor ever obtain the slightest clue. Then he felt she was false or had changed her mind. He was irritated now, as well as sad. More good fortune fell on him : he almost hated it. At last, on the third day, after he had once more been through every street, he said, "She is not in the town, and I shall never see her again. I will go home." He started for Tergou with royal favour promised, with fifteen golden angels in his purse, a golden medal on his bosom, and a heart like a lump of lead.

CHAPTER IV.

IT was near four o'clock in the afternoon. Eli was in the shop. His eldest and youngest sons were abroad. Catherine and her little crippled daughter had long been anxious about Gerard, and now they were gone a little way down the road, to see if by good luck he might be visible in the distance; and Giles was alone in the sitting-room, which I will sketch, furniture and dwarf included.

The Hollanders were always an original and leading people. They claim to have invented printing (wooden type), oil-painting, liberty, banking, gardening, etc. Above all, years before my tale, they invented cleanliness. So, while the English gentry, in velvet jerkins and chicken-toed shoes, trode floors of stale rushes, foul receptacle of bones, decomposing morsels, spittle, dogs, eggs, and all abominations, this hosier's sitting-room at Tergou was floored with Dutch tiles, so highly glazed and constantly washed that you could eat off them. There was one large window; the cross stone-work in the centre of it was very massive, and stood in relief, looking like an actual cross to the inmates, and was eyed as such in their devotions. The panes were very small and lozenge-shaped, and soldered to one another with strips of lead: the like you may see to this day in our rural cottages. The chairs were rude and primitive, all but the arm-chair, whose back, at right angles with its seat, was so high that the sitter's head stopped two feet short of the top. This chair was of oak, and carved at the summit. There was a copper pail, that went in at the waist, holding holy water, and a little hand-besom to sprinkle it far and wide; and a long, narrow, but massive oak table, and a dwarf sticking to its rim by his teeth, his eyes glaring, and his claws in the air like a pouncing vampire. Nature, it would seem, did not make Giles a dwarf out of *malice prepense;* she constructed a head and torso with her usual care; but just then her attention was distracted, and she left the rest to chance; the result was a human wedge, an inverted cone. He might justly have taken her to task in the terms of Horace:—

> " Amphora cœpit
> Institui ; currente rotâ cur urceus exit ? "

His centre was anything but his centre of gravity.

Bisected, upper Giles would have outweighed three lower Giles. But this very disproportion enabled him to do feats that would have baffled Milo. His brawny arms had no weight to draw after them ; so he could go up a vertical pole like a squirrel, and hang for hours from a bough by one hand like a cherry by its stalk. If he could have made a vacuum with his hands, as the lizard is said to do with its feet, he would have gone along a ceiling. Now, this pocket-athlete was insanely fond of gripping the dinner-table with both hands, and so swinging ; and then—climax of delight !—he would seize it with his teeth, and, taking off his hands, hold on like grim death by his huge ivories.

But all our joys, however elevating, suffer interruption. Little Kate caught Sampsonet in this posture, and stood aghast. She was her mother's daughter, and her heart was with the furniture, not with the 12mo gymnast.

"Oh, Giles ! how can you ? Mother is at hand. It dents the table."

"Go and tell her, little tale-bearer," snarled Giles. "You are the one for making mischief."

"Am I ?" inquired Kate calmly ; "that is news to me."

"The biggest in Tergou," growled Giles, fastening on again.

"Oh, indeed !" said Kate drily.

This piece of unwonted satire launched, and Giles not visibly blasted, she sat down quietly and cried.

Her mother came in almost at that moment, and Giles hurled himself under the table, and there glared.

"What is to do now ?" said the dame sharply. Then turning her experienced eyes from Kate to Giles, and observing the position he had taken up, and a sheepish expression, she hinted at cuffing of ears.

"Nay, mother," said the girl ; "it was but a foolish word Giles spoke. I had not noticed it at another time ; but I was tired and in care for Gerard, you know."

"Let no one be in care for me," said a faint voice at the door, and in tottered Gerard, pale, dusty, and worn out ; and amidst uplifted hands and cries of delight, curiosity, and anxiety mingled, dropped exhausted into the nearest chair.

Beating Rotterdam, like a covert, for Margaret, and the long journey afterwards, had fairly knocked Gerard up. But elastic youth soon revived, and behold him the centre of an eager circle. First of all they must hear about the prizes. Then Gerard told them he had been admitted to see the competitors' works, all laid out in an enormous hall, before the judges pronounced. "Oh, mother! oh, Kate! when I saw the goldsmiths' work, I had liked to have fallen on the floor. I thought not all the goldsmiths on earth had so much gold, silver, jewels, and craft of design and fracture. But, in sooth, all the arts are divine."

Then, to please the females, he described to them the reliquaries, feretories, calices, crosiers, crosses, pyxes, monstrances, and other wonders ecclesiastical, and the goblets, hanaps, watches, clocks, chains, brooches, etc., so that their mouths watered.

"But, Kate, when I came to the illuminated work from Ghent and Bruges, my heart sank. Mine was dirt by the side of it. For the first minute I could almost have cried; but I prayed for a better spirit, and presently I was able to enjoy them, and thank God for those lovely works, and for those skilful, patient craftsmen, whom I own my masters. Well, the coloured work was so beautiful I forgot all about the black and white. But, next day, when all the other prizes had been given, they came to the writing, and whose name, think you, was called first?"

"Yours," said Kate.

The others laughed her to scorn.

"You may well laugh," said Gerard, "but for all that, Gerard Eliassoen of Tergou was the name the herald shouted. I stood stupid; they thrust me forward. Everything swam before my eyes. I found myself kneeling on a cushion at the feet of the Duke. He said something to me, but I was so fluttered I could not answer him. So then he put his hand to his side, and did not draw a glaive and cut off my dull head, but gave me a gold medal; and there it is." There was a yell and almost a scramble. "And then he gave me fifteen great bright golden angels. I had seen one before, but I never handled one. Here they are."

"Oh, Gerard! oh, Gerard!"

"There is one for you, our eldest; and one for you, Sybrandt, and for you, Little Mischief; and two for thee, Little Lily, because God hath afflicted thee; and one for myself, to buy colours and vellum; and nine for her that nursed us all, and risked the two crowns upon poor Gerard's hand."

The gold drew out their characters. Cornelis and

Sybrandt clutched each his coin with one glare of greediness and another glare of envy at Kate, who had got two pieces. Giles seized his, and rolled it along the floor and gambolled after it. Kate put down her crutches and sat down, and held out her little arms to Gerard with a heavenly gesture of love and tenderness; and the mother, fairly benumbed at first by the shower of gold that fell on her apron, now cried out, "Leave kissing him, Kate; he is my son, not yours. Ah, Gerard! my boy! I have not loved you as you deserved."

Then Gerard threw himself on his knees beside her, and she flung her arms round him and wept for joy and pride, upon his neck.

"Good lad! good lad!" cried the hosier, with some emotion. "I must go and tell the neighbours. Lend me the medal, Gerard; I'll show it my good friend, Peter Buyskens; he is ever regaling me with how his son Jorian won the tin mug a-shooting at the butts."

"Ay, do, my man; and show Peter Buyskens one of the angels. Tell him there are fourteen more where that came from. Mind you bring it me back!"

"Stay a minute, father; there is better news behind," said Gerard, flushing with joy at the joy he caused.

"Better! better than this?"

Then Gerard told his interview with the Countess, and the house rang with joy.

"Now, God bless the good lady, and bless the Dame Van Eyck! A benefice? our son! My cares are at an end. Eli, my good friend and master, now we two can die happy whenever our time comes. This dear boy will take our place, and none of these loved ones will want a home or a friend."

From that hour Gerard was looked upon as the stay of the family. He was a son apart, but in another sense. He was always in the right, and nothing too good for him. Cornelis and Sybrandt became more and more jealous of him, and longed for the day he should go to his benefice: they would get rid of the favourite, and his reverence's purse would be open to them. With these views he co-operated. The wound love had given him throbbed duller and duller. His success and the affection and admiration of his parents made him think more highly of himself, and resent with more spirit Margaret's ingratitude and discourtesy. For all that, she had power

B 2

to cool him towards the rest of her sex, and now for every reason he wished to be ordained priest as soon as he could pass the intermediate orders. He knew the Vulgate already better than most of the clergy, and studied the rubric and the dogmas of the Church with his friends the monks ; and, the first time the bishop came that way, he applied to be admitted "exorcist," the third step in holy orders. The bishop questioned him, and ordained him at once. He had to kneel, and, after a short prayer, the bishop delivered to him a little MS. full of exorcisms, and said : "Take this, Gerard, and have power to lay hands on the possessed, whether baptised or catechumens !" and he took it reverently, and went home invested by the Church with power to cast out demons.

Returning home from the church, he was met by little Kate on her crutches.

"Oh, Gerard ! who, think you, hath sent to our house seeking you ?—the burgomaster himself."

"Ghysbrecht Van Swieten ? What would he with me ?"

"Nay, Gerard, I know not. But he seems urgent to see you. You are to go to his house on the instant."

"Well, he is the burgomaster : I will go . but it likes me not. Kate, I have seen him cast such a look on me as no friend casts. No matter ; such looks forewarn the wise. To be sure, he knows——"

"Knows what, Gerard ?"

"Nothing."

"Nothing ?"

"Kate, I'll go."

CHAPTER V.

GHYSBRECHT VAN SWIETEN was an artful man. He opened on the novice with something quite wide of the mark he was really aiming at. "The town records," said he, "are crabbedly written, and the ink rusty with age." He offered Gerard the honour of transcribing them fair.

Gerard inquired what he was to be paid.

Ghysbrecht offered a sum that would have just purchased the pens, ink, and parchment.

"But, burgomaster, my labour ? Here is a year's work."

"Your labour? Call your marking parchment labour? Little sweat goes to that, I trow."

"'Tis labour, and skilled labour to boot; and that is better paid in all crafts than rude labour, sweat or no sweat. Besides, there's my time."

"Your time? Why, what is time to you, at two-and-twenty?" Then fixing his eyes keenly on Gerard, to mark the effect of his words, he said: "Say, rather, you are idle grown. You are in love. Your body is with these chanting monks, but your heart is with Peter Brandt and his red-haired girl."

"I know no Peter Brandt."

This denial confirmed Ghysbrecht's suspicion that the caster-out of demons was playing a deep game.

"Ye lie!" he shouted. "Did I not find you at her elbow on the road to Rotterdam?"

"Ah!"

"Ah! And you were seen at Sevenbergen but t'other day."

"Was I?"

"Ay; and at Peter's house."

"At Sevenbergen?"

"Ay, at Sevenbergen."

Now, this was what in modern days is called a draw. It was a guess, put boldly forth as fact, to elicit by the young man's answer whether he had been there lately or not.

The result of the artifice surprised the crafty one. Gerard started up in a strange state of nervous excitement.

"Burgomaster," said he, with trembling voice, "I have not been at Sevenbergen these three years, and I know not the name of those you saw me with, nor where they dwelt; but, as my time is precious, though you value it not, give you good-day." And he darted out, with his eyes sparkling.

Ghysbrecht started up in huge ire; but he sank into his chair again.

"He fears me not. He knows something, if not all."

Then he called hastily to his trusty servant, and almost dragged him to a window.

"See you yon man?" he cried. "Haste! Follow him! But let him not see you. He is young, but old in craft. Keep him in sight all day. Let me know whither he goes, and what he does."

It was night when the servant returned.

" Well ? well ? " cried Van Swieten eagerly.

" Master, the young man went from you to Sevenbergen."
Ghysbrecht groaned.

" To the house of Peter the Magician."

CHAPTER VI.

"Look into your own heart and write !" said Herr Cant ;
and earth's cuckoos echoed the cry. Look into the Rhine
where it is deepest, and the Thames where it is thickest,
and paint the bottom. Lower a bucket into a well of self-
deception, and what comes up must be immortal truth,
mustn't it ? Now, in the first place, no son of Adam ever
reads his own heart at all, except by the habit acquired,
and the light gained, from some years' perusal of other
hearts ; and even then, with his acquired sagacity and
reflected light, he can but spell and decipher his own heart,
not read it fluently. Half way to Sevenbergen, Gerard
looked into his own heart, and asked it why he was going
to Sevenbergen. His heart replied without a moment's
hesitation, "We are going out of curiosity to know why
she jilted us, and to show her it has not broken our hearts ;
and that we are quite content with our honours and our
benefice *in prospectu*, and don't want her nor any of her
fickle sex."

He soon found out Peter Brandt's cottage ; and there
sat a girl in the doorway, plying her needle, and a stalwart
figure leaned on a long bow and talked to her. Gerard
felt an unaccountable pang at the sight of him. However,
the man turned out to be past fifty years of age, an old
soldier, whom Gerard remembered to have seen shoot at
the butts with admirable force and skill. Another minute
and the youth stood before them. Margaret looked up and
dropped her work, and uttered a faint cry, and was white
and red by turns. But these signs of emotion were swiftly
dismissed, and she turned far more chill and indifferent
than she would if she had not betrayed this agitation.

"What ! is it you, Master Gerard ? What on earth brings
you here, I wonder ? "

"I was passing by and saw you ; so I thought I would
give you good-day, and ask after your father."

"My father is well. He will be here anon."

"Then I may as well stay till he comes."

"As you will. Good Martin, step into the village and tell my father here is a friend of his."

"And not of yours?"

"My father's friends are mine."

"That is doubtful. It was not like a friend to promise to wait for me, and then make off the moment my back was turned. Cruel Margaret! you little know how I searched the town for you; how for want of you nothing was pleasant to me."

"These are idle words; if you had desired my father's company, or mine, you would have come back. There I had a bed laid for you, sir, at my cousin's, and he would have made much of you, and, who knows, I might have made much of you too. I was in the humour that day. You will not catch me in the same mind again, neither you nor any young man, I warrant me."

"Margaret, I came back the moment the Countess let me go; but you were not there."

"Nay, you did not, or you had seen Hans Cloterman at our table; we left him to bring you on."

"I saw no one there, but only a drunken man, that had just tumbled down."

"At our table? How was he clad?"

"Nay, I took little heed: in sad-coloured garb."

At this, Margaret's face gradually warmed; but presently, assuming incredulity and severity, she put many shrewd questions, all of which Gerard answered most loyally. Finally, the clouds cleared, and they guessed how the misunderstanding had come about. Then came a revulsion of tenderness, all the more powerful that they had done each other wrong; and then, more dangerous still, came mutual confessions. Neither had been happy since; neither ever would have been happy but for this fortunate meeting.

And Gerard found a MS. Vulgate lying open on the table, and pounced upon it like a hawk. MSS. were his delight; but before he could get to it, two white hands quickly came flat upon the page, and a red face came over them.

"Nay, take away your hands, Margaret, that I may see where you are reading, and I will read there, too, at home; so shall my soul meet yours in the sacred page. You will not? Nay, then I must kiss them away." And he kissed them so often, that for very shame they were fain to withdraw, and, lo! the sacred book lay open at

"An apple of gold in a network of silver."

"There, now," said she, "I had been hunting for it ever so long, and found it but even now—and to be caught!" and with a touch of inconsistency she pointed it out to Gerard with her white finger.

"Ay," said he, "but to-day it is all hidden in that great cap."

"It is a comely cap, I'm told by some."

"Maybe; but what it hides is beautiful."

"It is not: it is hideous."

"Well, it was beautiful at Rotterdam."

"Ay, everything was beautiful that day" (with a little sigh).

And now Peter came in, and welcomed Gerard cordially, and would have him to stay supper. And Margaret disappeared; and Gerard had a nice learned chat with Peter; and Margaret reappeared with her hair in her silver net, and shot a glance half arch, half coy, and glided about them, and spread supper, and beamed bright with gaiety and happiness. And in the cool evening, Gerard coaxed her out, and she objected, and came; and coaxed her on to the road to Tergou, and she declined, and came; and there they strolled up and down, hand in hand; and when he must go, they pledged each other never to quarrel or misunderstand one another again; and they sealed the promise with a long loving kiss, and Gerard went home on wings.

From that day Gerard spent most of his evenings with Margaret, and the attachment deepened and deepened on both sides, till the hours they spent together were the hours they lived; the rest they counted and underwent. And at the outset of this deep attachment all went smoothly. Obstacles there were, but they seemed distant and small to the eyes of hope, youth, and love. The feelings and passions of so many persons, that this attachment would thwart, gave no warning smoke to show their volcanic nature and power. The course of true love ran smoothly, placidly, until it had drawn these two young hearts into its current for ever.

And then——

CHAPTER VII.

ONE bright morning unwonted velvet shone, unwonted feathers waved, and horses' hoofs glinted and ran through the streets of Tergou, and the windows and balconies were studded with wondering faces. The French ambassador was riding through to sport in the neighbouring forest.

Besides his own suite, he was attended by several servants of the Duke of Burgundy, lent to do him honour and minister to his pleasure. The Duke's tumbler rode before him with a grave, sedate majesty, that made his more noble companions seem light, frivolous persons. But ever and anon, when respect and awe neared the oppressive, he rolled off his horse so ignobly and funnily, that even the ambassador was fain to burst out laughing. He also climbed up again by the tail in a way provocative of mirth, and so he played his part. Towards the rear of the pageant rode one that excited more attention still—the Duke's leopard. A huntsman, mounted on a Flemish horse of prodigious size and power, carried a long box fastened to the rider's loins by straps curiously contrived, and on this box sat a bright leopard crouching. She was chained to the huntsman. The people admired her glossy hide and spots, and pressed near, and one or two were for feeling her, and pulling her tail; then the huntsman shouted in a terrible voice, "Beware! At Antwerp one did but throw a handful of dust at her, and the Duke made dust of him."

"Gramercy!"

"I speak sooth. The good Duke shut him up in prison, in a cell under ground, and the rats cleaned the flesh off his bones in a night. Served him right for molesting the poor thing." There was a murmur of fear, and the Tergovians shrank from tickling the leopard of their sovereign.

But an incident followed that raised their spirits again. The Duke's giant, a Hungarian seven feet four inches high, brought up the rear. This enormous creature had, like some other giants, a treble, fluty voice of little power. He was a vain fellow, and not conscious of this nor any defect. Now it happened he caught sight of Giles sitting on the top of the balcony; so he stopped and began to make fun of him.

"Hollo! brother!" squeaked he, "I had nearly passed without seeing thee."

"*You* are plain enough to see," bellowed Giles in his bass tones.

"Come on my shoulder, brother," squeaked Titan, and held out a shoulder of mutton fist to help him down.

"If I do I'll cuff your ears," roared the dwarf.

The giant saw the homuncule was irascible, and played upon him, being encouraged thereto by the shouts of laughter. For he did not see that the people were laughing not at his wit, but at the ridiculous incongruity of the two voices—the gigantic feeble fife, and the petty deep, loud drum, the mountain delivered of a squeak, and the mole-hill belching thunder.

The singular duet came to as singular an end. Giles lost all patience and self-command, and being a creature devoid of fear, and in a rage to boot, he actually dropped upon the giant's neck, seized his hair with one hand, and punched his head with the other. The giant's first impulse was to laugh, but the weight and rapidity of the blows soon corrected that inclination.

"He! he! Ah! ha! hollo! oh! oh! Holy saints! here! help! or I must throttle the imp. I can't! I'll split your skull against the——" and he made a wild run backwards at the balcony. Giles saw his danger, seized the balcony in time with both hands, and whipped over it just as the giant's head came against it with a stunning crack. The people roared with laughter and exultation at the address of their little champion. The indignant giant seized two of the laughers, knocked them together like dumb-bells, shook them and strewed them flat (Catherine shrieked and threw her apron over Giles), then strode wrathfully away after the party. This incident had consequences no one then present foresaw. Its immediate results were agreeable. The Tergovians turned proud of Giles, and listened with more affability to his prayers for parchment. For he drove a regular trade with his brother Gerard in this article. Went about and begged it gratis, and Gerard gave him coppers for it.

On the afternoon of the same day, Catherine and her daughter were chatting together about their favourite theme —Gerard, his goodness, his benefice, and the brightened prospects of the whole family.

Their good luck had come to them in the very shape they would have chosen; besides the advantages of a benefice such as the Countess Charolois would not disdain to give, there was the feminine delight at having a priest, a holy man, in their own family. "He will marry Cornelis and Sybrandt: for they can wed (good housewives), now, if they will. Gerard will take care of you and Giles, when we are gone."

"Yes, mother, and we can confess to him instead of to a stranger," said Kate.

"Ay, girl! and he can give the sacred oil to your father and me, and close our eyes when our time comes."

"Oh, mother! not for many, many years, I do pray Heaven. Pray speak not of that, it always makes me sad. I hope to go before you, mother dear. No; let us be gay to-day. I am out of pain, mother, quite out of all pain; it does seem so strange; and I feel so bright and happy, that—— Mother, can you keep a secret?"

"Nobody better, child. Why, you know I can."

"Then I will show you something so beautiful. You never saw the like, I trow. Only Gerard must never know; for sure he means to surprise us with it; he covers it up so, and sometimes he carries it away altogether."

Kate took her crutches, and moved slowly away, leaving her mother in an exalted state of curiosity. She soon returned with something in a cloth, uncovered it, and there was a lovely picture of the Virgin, with all her insignia, and wearing her tiara over a wealth of beautiful hair, which flowed loose over her shoulders. Catherine, at first, was struck with awe.

"It is herself," she cried; "it is the Queen of Heaven. I never saw one like her to my mind before."

"And her eyes, mother: lifted to the sky, as if they belonged there, and not to a mortal creature. And her beautiful hair of burning gold."

"And to think I have a son that can make the saints live again upon a piece of wood!"

"The reason is, he is a young saint himself, mother. He is too good for this world; he is here to portray the blessed, and then to go away and be with them for ever."

Ere they had half done admiring it, a strange voice was heard at the door. By one of the furtive instincts of their sex, they hastily hid the picture in the cloth, though there was no need. And the next moment in came, casting his eyes furtively around, a man that had not entered the house this ten years—Ghysbrecht Van Swieten.

The two women were so taken by surprise, that they merely stared at him and at one another, and said "The burgomaster!" in a tone so expressive, that Ghysbrecht felt compelled to answer it.

"Yes! I own the last time I came here was not on a friendly errand. Men love their own interest—Eli's and mine were contrary. Well, let this visit atone the last. To-day I come on your business, and none of mine." Catherine and her daughter exchanged a swift glance of contemptuous incredulity. They knew the man better than he thought.

"It is about your son Gerard."

"Ay! ay! you want him to work for the town all for nothing. He told us."

"I come on no such errand. It is to let you know he has fallen into bad hands."

"Now Heaven and the saints forbid! Man, torture not a mother! Speak out, and quickly: speak ere you have time to coin falsehood: we know thee."

Ghysbrecht turned pale at this affront, and spite mingled with the other motives that brought him here. "Thus it is, then," said he, grinding his teeth, and speaking very fast. "Your son Gerard is more like to be father of a family than a priest: he is for ever with Margaret, Peter Brandt's red-haired girl, and loves her like a cow her calf."

Mother and daughter both burst out laughing. Ghysbrecht stared at them.

"What! you knew it?"

"Carry this tale to those who know not my son Gerard. Women are nought to him."

"Other women, mayhap. But this one is the apple of his eye to him, or will be, if you part them not, and soon. Come, dame, make me not waste time and friendly counsel: my servant has seen them together a score times, handed, and reading babies in one another's eyes like—you know, dame—you have been young too."

"Girl, I am ill at ease. Yea, I have been young, and know how blind and foolish the young are. My heart! he has turned me sick in a moment. Kate, if it should be true?"

"Nay, nay!" cried Kate eagerly. "Gerard might love a young woman: all young men do: I can't find what they see in them to love so; but if he did, he would let us know; he would not deceive us. You wicked man! No, dear mother, look not so! Gerard is too good to love a creature of earth. His love is for our Lady and the saints. Ah! I will show you the picture—there: if his heart was earthly, could he paint the Queen of Heaven like that— look! look!" and she held the picture out triumphantly, and, more radiant and beautiful in this moment of enthusiasm than ever dead picture was or will be, overpowered the burgomaster with her eloquence and her feminine proof of Gerard's purity. His eyes and mouth opened, and remained open: in which state they kept turning, face and all, as if on a pivot, from the picture to the women, and from the women to the picture.

"Why, it is herself," he gasped.

"Isn't it!" cried Kate, and her hostility was softened. "You admire it? I forgive you for frightening us."

"Am I in a madhouse?" said Ghysbrecht Van Swieten, thoroughly puzzled. "You show me a picture of the girl; and you say he painted it; and that is a proof he cannot love her. Why, they all paint their sweethearts, painters do."

"A picture of the girl?" exclaimed Kate, shocked. "Fie! this is no girl; this is our blessed Lady."

"No, no; it is Margaret Brandt."

"O blind! It is the Queen of Heaven."

"No; only of Sevenbergen village."

"Profane man! behold her crown!"

"Silly child! look at her red hair! Would the Virgin be seen in red hair? She who had the pick of all the colours ten thousand years before the world began."

At this moment an anxious face was insinuated round the edge of the open door: it was their neighbour Peter Buyskens.

"What is to do?" said he, in a cautious whisper. "We can hear you all across the street. What on earth is to do?"

"Oh, neighbour! What is to do? Why, here is the burgomaster blackening our Gerard."

"Stop!" cried Van Swieten. "Peter Buyskens is come in the nick of time. He knows father and daughter both. They cast their glamour on him."

"What! is she a witch too?"

"Else the egg takes not after the bird. Why is her father called the magician? I tell you they bewitched this very Peter here; they cast unholy spells on him, and cured him of the colic. Now, Peter, look and tell me who is that? and you, be silent, women, for a moment, if you can; who is it, Peter?"

"Well, to be sure!" said Peter, in reply; and his eye seemed fascinated by the picture.

"Who is it?" repeated Ghysbrecht impetuously.

Peter Buyskens smiled. "Why, you know as well as I do; but what have they put a crown on her for? I never saw her in a crown, for my part."

"Man alive! Can't you open your great jaws, and just speak a wench's name plain out to oblige three people?"

"I'd do a great deal more to oblige one of you than that, burgomaster. If it isn't as natural as life!"

"Curse the man! he won't, he won't—curse him!"

"Why, what have I done now?"

"Oh, sir!" said little Kate, "for pity's sake tell us; are these the features of a living woman, of—of—Margaret Brandt?"

"A mirror is not truer, my little maid."

"But is it she, sir, for very certain?"

"Why, who else should it be?"

"Now, why couldn't you say so at once?" snarled Ghysbrecht.

"I did say so, as plain as I could speak," snapped Peter; and they growled over this small bone of contention so zealously, that they did not see Catherine and her daughter had thrown their aprons over their heads, and were rocking to and fro in deep distress. The next moment Elias came in from the shop, and stood aghast. Catherine, though her face was covered, knew his footstep.

"That is my poor man," she sobbed. "Tell him, good Peter Buyskens, for I have not the courage."

Elias turned pale. The presence of the burgomaster in his house, after so many years of coolness, coupled with his wife's and daughter's distress, made him fear some heavy misfortune.

"Richart! Jacob!" he gasped.

"No, no!" said the burgomaster; "it is nearer home, and nobody is dead or dying, old friend."

"God bless you, burgomaster! Ah! something has gone off my breast that was like to choke me. Now, what is the matter?"

Ghysbrecht then told him all that he told the women, and showed the picture in evidence.

"Is that all?" said Eli, profoundly relieved. "What are ye roaring and bellowing for? It is vexing—it is angering; but it is not like death, nor even sickness. Boys will be boys. He will outgrow that disease: 'tis but skin-deep."

But when Ghysbrecht told him that Margaret was a girl of good character; that it was not to be supposed she would be so intimate if marriage had not been spoken of between them, his brow darkened.

"Marriage! that shall never be," said he sternly. "I'll stay that; ay, by force, if need be—as I would his hand lifted to cut his throat. I'd do what old John Koestein did t'other day."

"And what is that, in Heaven's name?" asked the mother, suddenly removing her apron.

It was the burgomaster who replied—

"He made me shut young Albert Koestein up in the prison of the Stadthouse till he knocked under. It was not long: forty-eight hours, all alone, on bread and water, cooled his hot stomach. 'Tell my father I am his humble servant,' says he, 'and let me into the sun once more—the sun is worth all the wenches in the world.'"

"Oh, the cruelty of men!" sighed Catherine.

"As to that, the burgomaster has no choice: it is the law. And if a father says, 'Burgomaster, lock up my son,' he must do it. A fine thing it would be if a father might not lock up his own son."

"Well, well! it won't come to that with me and my son. He never disobeyed me in his life: he never shall. Where is he? It is past supper-time. Where is he, Kate?"

"Alas! I know not, father."

"I know," said Ghysbrecht; "he is at Sevenbergen. My servant met him on the road."

Supper passed in gloomy silence. Evening descended—no Gerard! Eight o'clock came—no Gerard! Then the father sent all to bed, except Catherine.

"You and I will walk abroad, wife, and talk over this new care."

"Abroad, my man, at this time? Whither?"

"Why, on the road to Sevenbergen."

"Oh no; no hasty words, father. Poor Gerard! he never vexed you before.'

"Fear me not. But it must end; and I am not one that trusts to-morrow with to-day's work."

The old pair walked hand in hand; for, strange as it may appear to some of my readers, the use of the elbow to couples walking was not discovered in Europe till centuries after this. They sauntered on a long time in silence. The night was clear and balmy. Such nights, calm and silent, recall the past from the dead.

"It is a many years since we walked so late, my man," said Catherine softly.

"Ay, sweetheart, more than we shall see again.—(Is he never coming, I wonder?)"

"Not since our courting days, Eli."

"No. Ay, you were a buxom lass then."

"And you were a comely lad, as ever a girl's eye stole a look at. I do suppose Gerard is with her now, as you used to be with me. Nature is strong, and the same in all our generations."

"Nay, I hope he has left her by now, confound her, or we shall be here all night."

"Eli!"

"Well, Kate?"

"I have been happy with you, sweetheart, for all our rubs—much happier, I trow, than if I had—been—a—a—nun. You won't speak harshly to the poor child? One can be firm without being harsh."

"Surely."

"Have you been happy with me, my poor Eli?"

"Why, you know I have. Friends I have known, but none like thee. Buss me, wife!"

"A heart to share joy and grief with is a great comfort to man or woman. Isn't it, Eli?"

"It is so, my lass.

> 'It doth joy double,
> And halveth trouble,'

runs the byword. And so I have found it, sweetheart. Ah! here comes the young fool."

Catherine trembled, and held her husband's hand tight. The moon was bright, but they were in the shadow of some trees, and their son did not see them. He came singing in the moonlight, and his face shining.

CHAPTER VIII.

WHILE the burgomaster was exposing Gerard at Tergou, Margaret had a trouble of her own at Sevenbergen. It was a housewife's distress, but deeper than we can well conceive. She came to Martin Wittenhaagen, the old soldier, with tears in her eyes.

"Martin, there s nothing in the house, and Gerard is coming, and he is so thoughtless. He forgets to sup at home. When he gives over work, then he runs to me straight, poor soul; and often he comes quite faint. And to think I have nothing to set before my servant that loves me so dear."

Martin scratched his head. "What can I do?"

"It is Thursday; it is your day to shoot—sooth to say, I counted on you to-day."

"Nay," said the soldier, "I may not shoot when the Duke or his friends are at the chase; read else. I am no scholar." And he took out of his pouch a parchment with a grand seal. It purported to be a stipend and a licence given by Philip, Duke of Burgundy, to Martin Wittenhaagen, one of his archers, in return for services in the wars, and for a wound received at the Duke's side. The stipend was four merks yearly, to be paid by the Duke's almoner, and the licence was to shoot three arrows once a week, viz., on Thursday, and no other day, in any of the Duke's forests in Holland, at any game but a seven-year-old buck or a doe carrying fawn; proviso, that the Duke should not be hunting on that day, or any of his friends. In this case Martin was not to go and disturb the woods on peril of his salary and his head, and a fine of a penny.

Margaret sighed and was silent.

"Come, cheer up, mistress," said he; "for your sake I'll peril my carcass; I have done that for many a one that was not worth your forefinger. It is no such mighty risk either. I'll but step into the skirts of the forest here. It is odds but they drive a hare or a fawn within reach of my arrow."

"Well, if I let you go, you must promise me not to go far, and not to be seen; far better Gerard went supperless than ill should come to you, faithful Martin."

The required promise given, Martin took his bow and three arrows, and stole cautiously into the wood: it was scarce a furlong distant. The horns were heard faintly in the distance, and all the game was afoot. "Come," thought Martin, "I shall soon fill the pot, and no one be the wiser." He took his stand behind a thick oak that commanded a view of an open glade, and strung his bow, a truly formidable weapon. It was of English yew, six feet two inches high, and thick in proportion ; and Martin, broad-chested, with arms all iron and cord, and used to the bow from infancy, could draw a three-foot arrow to the head, and, when it flew, the eye could scarce follow it, and the bowstring twanged as musical as a harp. This bow had laid many a stout soldier low in the wars of the Hoecks and Cabbel-jaws. In those days a battlefield was not a cloud of smoke ; the combatants were few, but the deaths many ; for they saw what they were about, and fewer bloodless arrows flew than bloodless bullets now. A hare came cantering, then sat sprightly, and her ears made a capital V. Martin levelled his tremendous weapon at her : the arrow flew, the string twanged : but Martin had been in a hurry to pot her, and lost her by an inch : the arrow seemed to hit her, but it struck the ground close to her, and passed under her belly like a flash, and hissed along the short grass and disappeared. She jumped three feet perpendicular, and away at the top of her speed. "Bungler!" said Martin. A sure proof he was not a habitual bungler, or he would have blamed the hare. He had scarcely fitted another arrow to his string when a wood-pigeon settled on the very tree he stood under. "Aha!" thought he, "you are small, but dainty." This time he took more pains ; drew his arrow carefully, loosed it smoothly, and saw it, to all appearance, go clean through the bird, carrying feathers skyward like dust. Instead of falling at his feet, the bird, whose breast was torn, not fairly pierced, fluttered feebly away, and, by a great effort, rose above the trees, flew some fifty yards, and fell dead at last ; but where he could not see for the thick foliage.

"Luck is against me," said he despondingly. But he fitted another arrow, and eyed the glade keenly. Presently he heard a bustle behind him, and turned round just in time to see a noble buck cross the open, but too late to shoot at him. He dashed his bow down with an imprecation. At that moment a long, spotted animal glided swiftly across after the deer ; its belly seemed to touch the ground as it went. Martin took up his bow hastily: he recognised the Duke's leopard. "The hunters will not be far from her," said he, "and I must not be seen. Gerard must go supperless this night."

He plunged into the wood, following the buck and leopard, for that was his way home. He had not gone far when he heard an unusual sound ahead of him—leaves rustling violently, and the ground trampled. He hurried in the direction. He found the leopard on the buck's back, tearing him with teeth and claw, and the buck running in a circle and bounding convulsively, with the blood pouring down his hide. Then Martin formed a desperate resolution to have the venison for Margaret. He drew his arrow to the head, and buried it in the deer, who, spite of the creature on his back, bounded high into the air, and fell dead. The leopard went on tearing him as if nothing had happened.

Martin hoped that the creature would gorge itself with blood, and then let him take the meat. He waited some minutes, then walked resolutely up, and laid his hand on the buck's leg. The leopard gave a frightful growl, and left off sucking blood. She saw Martin's game, and was sulky and on her guard. What was to be done? Martin had heard that wild creatures cannot stand the human eye. Accordingly, he stood erect, and fixed his on the leopard: the leopard returned a savage glance, and never took her eye off Martin. Then Martin, continuing to look the beast down, the leopard, brutally ignorant of natural history, flew at his head with a frightful yell, flaming eyes, and jaws and claws distended. He had but just time to catch her by the throat, before her teeth could crush his face; one of her claws seized his shoulder and rent it, the other, aimed at his cheek, would have been more deadly still, but Martin was old-fashioned, and wore no hat, but a scapulary of the same stuff as his jerkin, and this scapulary he had brought over his head like a hood; the brute's claw caught in the loose leather. Martin kept her teeth off his face with great difficulty, and griped her throat fiercely, and she kept rending his shoulder. It was like blunt reaping-hooks grinding and tearing. The pain was fearful: but, instead of cowing the old soldier, it put his blood up, and he gnashed his teeth with rage almost as fierce as hers, and squeezed her neck with iron force. The two pair of eyes flared at one another—and now the man's were almost as furious as the brute's. She found he was throttling her, and made a wild attempt to free herself, in which she dragged his cowl all over his face and blinded him, and tore her claw out of his shoulder, flesh and all : but still he throttled her with hand and arm of iron. Presently her long tail, that was high in the air, went down. "Aha!" cried Martin joyfully, and griped her like death ; next, her body lost its elasticity, and he held a choked and powerless thing : he griped it still, till all motion ceased, then dashed it to the earth ; then, panting, removed his cowl : the leopard lay mute at his feet with tongue protruding and bloody paw ; and for the first time terror fell on Martin. "I am a dead man : I have slain the Duke's leopard." He hastily seized a few handfuls of leaves, and threw them over her ; then shouldered the buck, and staggered away, leaving a trail of blood all the way—his own and the buck's. He burst into Peter's house a horrible figure, bleeding and blood-stained, and flung the deer's carcass down.

"There—no questions," said he, "but broil me a steak on't ; for I am faint."

Margaret did not see he was wounded ; she thought the blood was all from the deer.

She busied herself at the fire, and the stout soldier stanched and bound his own wound apart ; and soon he and Gerard and Margaret were supping royally on broiled venison.

They were very merry ; and Gerard, with wonderful thoughtfulness, had brought a flask of Schiedam, and under its influence Martin revived, and told them how the venison was got ; and they all made merry over the exploit.

Their mirth was strangely interrupted. Margaret's eye became fixed and fascinated, and her cheek pale with fear. She gasped, and could not speak, but pointed to the window with trembling finger. Their eyes followed hers, and there in the twilight crouched a dark form with eyes like glow-worms.

It was the leopard.

While they stood petrified, fascinated by the eyes of green fire, there sounded in the wood a single deep bay. Martin trembled at it.

"They have lost her, and laid muzzled blood-hounds on her scent ; they will find her here, and the venison. Good-bye, friends, Martin Wittenhaagen ends here."

Gerard seized his bow, and put it into the soldier's hands.

"Be a man," he cried; "shoot her, and fling her into the wood ere they come up.   Who will know?"

More voices of hounds broke out, and nearer.

"Curse her!" cried Martin; "I spared her once; now she must die, or I, or both more likely;" and he reared his bow, and drew his arrow to the head.

"Nay! nay!" cried Margaret, and seized the arrow.   It broke in half: the pieces fell on each side the bow.   The air at the same time filled with the tongues of the hounds: they were hot upon the scent.

"What have you done, wench?   You have put the halter round my throat."

"No!" cried Margaret.   "I have saved you: stand back from the window, both!   Your knife, quick!"

She seized his long-pointed knife, almost tore it out of his girdle, and darted from the room.   The house was now surrounded with baying dogs and shouting men.

The glow-worm eyes moved not.

CHAPTER IX.

MARGARET cut off a huge piece of venison, and ran to the window, and threw it out to the green eyes of fire.   They darted on it with a savage snarl; and there was a sound of rending and crunching: at this moment, a hound uttered a bay so near and loud it rang through the house; and the three at the window shrank together.   Then the leopard feared for her supper, and glided swiftly and stealthily away with it towards the woods, and the very next moment horses and men and dogs came helter-skelter past the window, and followed her full cry.   Martin and his companions breathed again: the leopard was swift, and would not be caught within a league of their house. They grasped hands.   Margaret seized this opportunity, and cried a little; Gerard kissed the tears away.

To table once more, and Gerard drank to woman's wit: "'Tis stronger than man's force," said he.

"Ay," said Margaret, "when those she loves are in danger; not else."

To-night Gerard stayed with her longer than usual, and went home prouder than ever of her, and happy as a prince. Some little distance from home, under the shadow of some

trees, he encountered two figures : they almost barred his
way.

It was his father and mother.

Out so late ! what could be the cause ?

A chill fell on him.

He stopped and looked at them : they stood grim and
silent.   He stammered out some words of inquiry.

"Why ask ? " said his father ; "you know why we are
here."

"Oh, Gerard ! " said his mother, with a voice full of
reproach and yet of affection.

Gerard's heart quaked : he was silent.

Then his father pitied his confusion, and said to him—

"Nay, you need not to hang your head.   You are not
the first young fool that has been caught by a red cheek
and a pair of blue eyes."

"Nay, nay ! " put in Catherine, "it was witchcraft ;
Peter the Magician is well known for that."

"Come, Sir Priest," resumed his father, "you know
you must not meddle with women-folk.   But give us your
promise to go no more to Sevenbergen, and here all ends :
we won't be hard on you for one fault."

"I cannot promise that, father."

"Not promise it, you young hypocrite ! "

"Nay, father, miscall me not : I lacked courage to tell
you what I knew would vex you ; and right grateful am I
to that good friend, whoever he be, that has let you wot.
'Tis a load off my mind.   Yes, father, I love Margaret ;
and call me not a priest, for a priest I will never be.   I will
die sooner."

"That we shall see, young man.   Come, gainsay me no
more ; you will learn what 'tis to disrespect a father."

Gerard held his peace, and the three walked home in
gloomy silence, broken only by a deep sigh or two from
Catherine.

From that hour the little house at Tergou was no longer
the abode of peace.   Gerard was taken to task next day
before the whole family ; and every voice was loud against
him, except little Kate's, and the dwarf's, who was apt to
take his cue from her without knowing why.   As for
Cornelis and Sybrandt, they were bitterer than their father.
Gerard was dismayed at finding so many enemies, and
looked wistfully into his little sister's face : her eyes were
brimming at the harsh words showered on one who but

yesterday was the universal pet. But she gave him no encouragement: she turned her head away from him, and said—

"Dear, dear Gerard, pray to Heaven to cure you of this folly!"

"What, are you against me, too?" said Gerard sadly; and he rose with a deep sigh, and left the house, and went to Sevenbergen.

The beginning of a quarrel, where the parties are bound by affection though opposed in interest and sentiment, is comparatively innocent: both are perhaps in the right at first starting, and then it is that a calm, judicious friend, capable of seeing both sides, is a gift from Heaven. For, the longer the dissension endures, the wider and deeper it grows by the fallibility and irascibility of human nature: these are not confined to either side, and finally the invariable end is reached—both in the wrong.

The combatants were unequally matched: Elias was angry, Cornelis and Sybrandt spiteful; but Gerard, having a larger and more cultivated mind, saw both sides where they saw but one, and had fits of irresolution, and was not wroth, but unhappy. He was lonely, too, in this struggle. He could open his heart to no one. Margaret was a high-spirited girl: he dared not tell her what he had to endure at home; she was capable of siding with his relations by resigning him, though at the cost of her own happiness. Margaret Van Eyck had been a great comfort to him on another occasion; but now he dared not make her his confidant. Her own history was well known. In early life she had many offers of marriage; but refused them all for the sake of that art to which a wife's and mother's duties are so fatal: thus she remained single, and painted with her brothers. How could he tell her that he declined the benefice she had got him, and declined it for the sake of that which at his age she had despised and sacrificed so lightly?

Gerard at this period bade fair to succumb. But the other side had a horrible ally in Catherine, senior. This good-hearted but uneducated woman could not, like her daughter, act quietly and firmly: still less could she act upon a plan. She irritated Gerard at times, and so helped him; for anger is a great sustainer of the courage: at others, she turned round in a moment and made onslaughts on her own forces. To take a single instance out of many: one day that they were all at home, Catherine and all, Cornelis said: "Our Gerard wed Margaret Brandt? Why, it is hunger marrying thirst."

"And what will it be when you marry?" cried Catherine. "Gerard can paint, Gerard can write, but what can you do to keep a woman, ye lazy loon? Nought but wait for your father's shoon. Oh, we can see why you and Sybrandt would not have the poor boy to marry. You are afraid he will come to us for a share of our substance. And say that he does, and say that we give it him, it isn't yourn we part from, and mayhap never will be."

On these occasions Gerard smiled slily, and picked up heart; and temporary confusion fell on Catherine's unfortunate allies. But at last, after more than six months of irritation, came the climax. The father told the son, before the whole family, he had ordered the burgomaster to imprison him in the Stadthouse rather than let him marry Margaret. Gerard turned pale with anger at this, but by a great effort held his peace. His father went on to say, "And a priest you shall be before the year is out, nilly-willy."

"Is it so?" cried Gerard. "Then, hear me, all. By God and St. Bavon I swear I will never be a priest while Margaret lives. Since force is to decide it, and not love and duty, try force, father; but force shall not serve you, for the day I see the burgomaster come for me, I leave Tergou for ever, and Holland too, and my father's house, where it seems I have been valued all these years, not for myself, but for what is to be got out of me."

And he flung out of the room white with anger and desperation.

"There!" cried Catherine, "that comes of driving young folk too hard. But men are crueller than tigers, even to their own flesh and blood. Now, Heaven forbid he should ever leave us, married or single."

As Gerard came out of the house, his cheeks pale and his heart panting, he met Reicht Heynes: she had a message for him: Margaret Van Eyck desired to see him. He found the old lady seated grim as a judge. She wasted no time in preliminaries, but inquired coldly why he had not visited her of late: before he could answer, she said in a sarcastic tone, "I thought we had been friends, young sir-"

At this Gerard looked the picture of doubt and consternation.

"It is because you never told her you were in love," said Reicht Heynes, pitying his confusion.

"Silence, wench! Why should he tell us his affairs? We are not his friends: we have not deserved his confidence."

"Alas! my second mother," said Gerard, "I did not dare to tell you my folly."

"What folly? Is it folly to love?"

"I am told so every day of my life."

"You need not have been afraid to tell *my* mistress; she is always kind to true lovers."

"Madam—Reicht—I was afraid because I was told——"

"Well, you were told?"

"That in your youth you scorned love, preferring art."

"I did, boy; and what is the end of it? Behold me here a barren stock, while the women of my youth have a troop of children at their side, and grandchildren at their knee. I gave up the sweet joys of wifehood and motherhood for what? For my dear brothers. They have gone and left me long ago. For my art. It has all but left me too. I have the knowledge still, but what avails that when the hand trembles. No, Gerard; I look on you as my son. You are good, you are handsome, you are a painter, though not like some I have known. I will not let you throw your youth away as I did mine: you shall marry this Margaret. I have inquired, and she is a good daughter. Reicht here is a gossip. She has told me all about it. But that need not hinder *you* to tell me."

Poor Gerard was overjoyed to be permitted to praise Margaret aloud, and to one who could understand what he loved in her.

Soon there were two pair of wet eyes over his story; and when the poor boy saw that, there were three.

Women are creatures brimful of courage. Theirs is not exactly the same quality as manly courage; that would never do, hang it all; we should have to give up trampling on them. No; it is a vicarious courage. They never take part in a bull-fight by any chance; but it is remarked that they sit at one unshaken by those tremors and apprehensions for the combatants to which the male spectator— feeble-minded wretch! — is subject. Nothing can exceed the resolution with which they have been known to send forth men to battle : as some witty dog says, *Les femmes sont très braves avec la peau d'autrui.*

By this trait Gerard now profited. Margaret and Reicht were agreed that *a man* should always take the bull by the horns. Gerard's only course was to marry Margaret Brandt off-hand ; the old people would come to after a while, the deed once done. Whereas, the longer this misunderstanding continued on its present footing, the worse for all parties, especially for Gerard.

" See how pale and thin they have made him amongst them."

" Indeed you are, Master Gerard," said Reicht. " It makes a body sad to see a young man so wasted and worn.—Mistress, when I met him in the street to-day, I had liked to have burst out crying : he was so changed."

" And I'll be bound the others keep their colour ; eh, Reicht ? such as it is.'

" Oh, I see no odds in them."

" Of course not. We painters are no match for boors. We are glass, they are stone. We can't stand the worry, worry, worry of little minds ; and it is not for the good of mankind we should be exposed to it. It is hard enough, Heaven knows, to design and paint a masterpiece, without having gnats and flies stinging us to death into the bargain.**"**

Exasperated as Gerard was by his father's threat of violence, he listened to these friendly voices telling him the prudent course was rebellion. But though he listened, he was not convinced.

" I do not fear my father's violence," he said, " but I do fear his anger. When it came to the point he would not imprison me. I would marry Margaret to-morrow if that was my only fear. No ; he would disown me. I should take Margaret from her father, and give her a poor husband, who would never thrive, weighed down by his parent's curse. Madam ! I sometimes think if I could but marry her secretly, and then take her away to some country where my craft is better paid than in this ; and after a year or two, when the storm had blown over, you know, could come back with money in my purse, and say, ' My dear parents, we do not seek your substance, we but ask you to love us once more as you used, and as we have never ceased to love you '—but, alas ! I shall be told these are the dreams of an inexperienced young man."

The old lady's eyes sparkled.

"It is no dream, but a piece of wonderful common-sense in a boy; it remains to be seen whether you have spirit to carry out your own thought. There is a country, Gerard, where certain fortune awaits you at this moment. Here the arts freeze, but there they flourish, as they never yet flourished in any age or land."

"It is Italy!" cried Gerard. "It is Italy!"

"Ay, Italy! where painters are honoured like princes, and scribes are paid three hundred crowns for copying a single manuscript. Know you not that his Holiness the Pope has written to every land for skilful scribes to copy the hundreds of precious manuscripts that are pouring into that favoured land from Constantinople, whence learning and learned men are driven by the barbarian Turks?"

"Nay, I know not that; but it has been the dream and hope of my life to visit Italy, the queen of all the arts; oh, madam! But the journey, and we are all so poor."

"Find you the heart to go, I'll find the means. I know where to lay my hand on ten golden angels: they will take you to Rome: and the girl with you, if she loves you as she ought."

They sat till midnight over this theme. And, after that day, Gerard recovered his spirits, and seemed to carry a secret talisman against all the gibes and the harsh words that flew about his ears at home.

Besides the money she procured him for the journey, Margaret Van Eyck gave him money's worth. Said she, "I will tell you secrets that I learned from masters that are gone from me, and have left no fellow behind. Even the Italians know them not; and what I tell you now in Tergou you shall sell dear in Florence. Note my brother Jan's pictures: time, which fades all other paintings, leaves his colours bright as the day they left the easel. The reason is, he did nothing blindly, nothing in a hurry. He trusted to no hireling to grind his colours; he did it himself, or saw it done. His panel was prepared, and prepared again—I will show you how—a year before he laid his colour on. Most of them are quite content to have their work sucked up and lost, sooner than not be in a hurry. Bad painters are always in a hurry. Above all, Gerard, I warn you use but little oil, and never boil it:
c boiling it melts that vegetable dross into its very heart

which it is our business to clear away ; for impure oil is death to colour. No ; take your oil and pour it into a bottle with water. In a day or two the water will turn muddy : that is muck from the oil. Pour the dirty water carefully away, and add fresh. When that is poured away, you will fancy the oil is clear. You are mistaken. Reicht, fetch me *that!*" Reicht brought a glass trough with a glass lid fitting tight. "When your oil has been washed in bottle, put it into this trough with water, and put the trough in the sun all day. You will soon see the water turbid again. But mark, you must not carry this game too far, or the sun will turn your oil to varnish. When it is as clear as crystal, and not too luscious, drain carefully, and cork it up tight. Grind your own prime colours, and lay them on with this oil, and they shall live. Hubert would put sand or salt in the water to clear the oil quicker. But Jan used to say, 'Water will do it best ; give water time.' Jan Van Eyck was never in a hurry, and that is why the world will not forget *him* in a hurry."

This and several other receipts, *quæ nunc perscribere longum est*, Margaret gave him with sparkling eyes, and Gerard received them like a legacy from Heaven, so interesting are some things that read uninteresting. Thus provided with money and knowledge, Gerard decided to marry and fly with his wife to Italy. Nothing remained now but to inform Margaret Brandt of his resolution, and to publish the banns as quietly as possible. He went to Sevenbergen earlier than usual on both these errands. He began with Margaret ; told her of the Dame Van Eyck's goodness, and the resolution he had come to at last, and invited her co-operation.

She refused it plump.

"No, Gerard ; you and I have never spoken of your family, but when you come to marriage——" She stopped, then began again. "I do think your father has no ill-will to me more than to another. He told Peter Buyskens as much, and Peter told me. But so long as he is bent on your being a priest (you ought to have told me this instead of I you), I could not marry you, Gerard, dearly as I love you."

Gerard strove in vain to shake this resolution. He found it very easy to make her cry, but impossible to make her yield. Then Gerard was impatient and unjust.

"Very well !" he cried ; "then you are on their side, and

you will drive me to be a priest, for this must end one way
or another. My parents hate me in earnest, but my lover
only loves me in jest."

And with this wild, bitter speech, he flung away home
again, and left Margaret weeping.

When a man misbehaves, the effect is curious on a girl
who loves him sincerely. It makes her pity him. This, to
some of us males, seems anything but logical. The fault is
in our own eye; the logic is too swift for us. The girl
argues thus :— "How unhappy, how vexed, poor ——
must be ; *him* to misbehave ! Poor thing !"

Margaret was full of this sweet, womanly pity, when, to
her great surprise, scarce an hour and a half after he left
her, Gerard came running back to her with the fragments
of a picture in his hand, and panting with anger and grief.

"There, Margaret ! see ! see ! the wretches ! Look at
their spite ! They have cut your portrait to pieces."

Margaret looked, and sure enough, some malicious hand
had cut her portrait into five pieces. She was a good girl,
but she was not ice ; she turned red to her very forehead.

"Who did it ?"

"Nay, I know not. I dared not ask ; for I should hate
the hand that did it, ay, till my dying day. My poor
Margaret ! The butchers, the ruffians ! Six months'
work cut out of my life, and nothing to show for it
now. See, they have hacked through your very face ; the
sweet face that every one loves who knows it. Oh,
heartless, merciless vipers !"

"Never mind, Gerard," said Margaret, panting. "Since
this is how they treat you for my sake—Ye rob him of my
portrait, do ye ? Well, then, he shall have the face itself,
such as it is."

"Oh, Margaret !"

"Yes, Gerard ; since they are so cruel, I will be the
kinder : forgive me for refusing you. I will be your wife :
to-morrow, if it is your pleasure."

Gerard kissed her hands with rapture, and then her lips ;
and in a tumult of joy ran for Peter and Martin. They came
and witnessed the betrothal ; a solemn ceremony in those
days, and indeed for more than a century later, though now
abolished.

CHAPTER X.

THE banns of marriage had to be read three times, as in our days; with this difference, that they were commonly read on week-days, and the young couple easily persuaded the curé to do the three readings in twenty-four hours: he was new to the place, and their looks spoke volumes in their favour. They were cried on Monday at matins and at vespers; and, to their great delight, nobody from Tergou was in the church. The next morning they were both there, palpitating with anxiety, when, to their horror, a stranger stood up and forbade the banns, on the score that the parties were not of age, and their parents not consenting.

Outside the church door, Margaret and Gerard held a trembling and almost despairing consultation; but, before they could settle anything, the man who had done them so ill a turn approached, and gave them to understand that he was very sorry to interfere: that his inclination was to further the happiness of the young; but that in point of fact his only means of getting a living was by forbidding banns: what then? "The young people give me a crown, and I undo my work handsomely; tell the curé I was misinformed, and all goes smoothly."

"A crown! I will give you a golden angel to do this," said Gerard eagerly. The man consented as eagerly, and went with Gerard to the curé, and told him he had made a ridiculous mistake, which a sight of the parties had rectified. On this the curé agreed to marry the young couple next day at ten: and the professional obstructor of bliss went home with Gerard's angel. Like most of these very clever knaves, he was a fool, and proceeded to drink his angel at a certain hostelry in Tergou, where was a green devoted to archery and the common sports of the day. There, being drunk, he bragged of his day's exploit; and who should be there, imbibing every word, but a great frequenter of the spot, the ne'er-do-weel Sybrandt. Sybrandt ran home to tell his father his father was not at home; he was gone to Rotterdam to buy cloth of the merchants. Catching his elder brother's eye, he made him a signal to come out, and told him what he had heard.

There are black sheep in nearly every large family; and these two were Gerard's black brothers. Idleness is vitiating : waiting for the death of those we ought to love is vitiating ; and these two one-idead curs were ready to tear any one to death that should interfere with that miserable inheritance which was their thought by day and their dream by night. Their parents' parsimony was a virtue ; it was accompanied by industry, and its motive was love of their offspring ; but in these perverse and selfish hearts that homely virtue was perverted into avarice, than which no more fruitful source of crimes is to be found in nature.

They put their heads together, and agreed not to tell their mother, whose sentiments were so uncertain, but to go first to the burgomaster. They were cunning enough to see that he was averse to the match, though they could not divine why.

Ghysbrecht Van Swieten saw through them at once ; but he took care not to let them see through him. He heard their story ; and putting on magisterial dignity and coldness, he said—

"Since the father of the family is not here, his duty falleth on me, who am the father of the town. I know your father's mind ; leave all to me ; and, above all, tell not a woman a word of this, least of all the women that are in your own house : for chattering tongues mar wisest counsels."

So he dismissed them, a little superciliously : he was ashamed of his confederates.

On their return home they found their brother Gerard seated on a low stool at their mother's knee : she was caressing his hair with her hand, speaking very kindly to him, and promising to take his part with his father and thwart his love no more. The main cause of this change of mind was characteristic of the woman. She it was who in a moment of female irritation had cut Margaret's picture to pieces. She had watched the effect with some misgivings, and had seen Gerard turn pale as death, and sit motionless like a bereaved creature, with the pieces in his hands, and his eyes fixed on them till tears came and blinded them. Then she was terrified at what she had done ; and next, her heart smote her bitterly ; and she wept sore apart ; but, being what she was, dared not own it, but said to herself, "I'll not say a word, but I'll make it up to him." And her bowels yearned over her son, and her feeble violence died a natural death, and she was transferring her fatal alliance to Gerard when the two black sheep came in. Gerard knew nothing of the immediate cause; on the contrary, inexperienced as he was in the ins and outs of females, her kindness made him ashamed of a suspicion he had entertained that she was the depredator, and he kissed her again and again, and went to bed happy as a prince to think his mother was his mother once more at the very crisis of his fate.

The next morning, at ten o'clock, Gerard and Margaret were in the church at Sevenbergen, he radiant with joy, she with blushes. Peter was also there, and Martin Wittenhaagen, but no other friend. Secrecy was everything. Margaret had declined Italy. She could not leave her father; he was too learned and too helpless. But it was settled they should retire into Flanders for a few weeks until the storm should be blown over at Tergou. The curé did not keep them waiting long, though it seemed an age. Presently he stood at the altar, and called them to him. They went hand in hand, the happiest in Holland. The curé opened his book.

But ere he uttered a single word of the sacred rite, a harsh voice cried "Forbear!" And the constables of Tergou came up the aisle and seized Gerard in the name of the law. Martin's long knife flashed out directly.

"Forbear, man!" cried the priest. "What! draw your weapon in a church, and ye who interrupt this holy sacrament, what means this impiety?"

"There is no impiety, father," said the burgomaster's servant respectfully. "This young man would marry against his father's will, and his father has prayed our burgomaster to deal with him according to the law. Let him deny it if he can."

"Is this so, young man?"

Gerard hung his head.

"We take him to Rotterdam to abide the sentence of the Duke."

At this Margaret uttered a cry of despair, and the young creatures, who were so happy a moment ago, fell to sobbing in one another's arms so piteously, that the instruments of oppression drew back a step and were ashamed; but one of them that was good-natured stepped up under pretence of separating them, and whispered to Margaret—

"Rotterdam? it is a lie. We but take him to our Stadthouse."

They took him away on horseback, on the road to Rotterdam; and, after a dozen halts, and by sly detours, to Tergou. Just outside the town they were met by a rude vehicle covered with canvas. Gerard was put into this, and, about five in the evening, was secretly conveyed into the prison of the Stadthouse. He was taken up several flights of stairs and thrust into a small room lighted only by a narrow window, with a vertical iron bar. The whole furniture was a huge oak chest.

Imprisonment in that age was one of the high-roads to death. It is horrible in its mildest form; but in those days it implied cold, unbroken solitude, torture, starvation, and often poison. Gerard felt he was in the hands of an enemy.

"Oh, the look that man gave me on the road to Rotterdam. There is more here than my father's wrath. I doubt I shall see no more the light of day." And he kneeled down and commended his soul to God.

Presently he rose and sprang at the iron bar of the window, and clutched it. This enabled him to look out by pressing his knees against the wall. It was but for a minute; but in that minute he saw a sight such as none but a captive can appreciate.

Martin Wittenhaagen's back.

Martin was sitting, quietly fishing in the brook near the Stadthouse.

Gerard sprang again at the window, and whistled. Martin instantly showed that he was watching much harder than fishing. He turned hastily round and saw Gerard; made him a signal, and, taking up his line and bow, went quickly off.

Gerard saw by this that his friends were not idle: yet he had rather Martin had stayed. The very sight of him was a comfort. He held on, looking at the soldier's retiring form as long as he could; then falling back somewhat heavily, wrenched the rusty iron bar, held only by rusty nails, away from the stone-work just as Ghysbrecht Van Swieten opened the door stealthily behind him. The burgomaster's eye fell instantly on the iron, and then glanced at the window; but he said nothing. The window was a hundred feet from the ground; and if Gerard had a fancy for jumping out, why should he balk it? He brought a brown loaf and a pitcher of water, and set them on the chest in solemn silence. Gerard's first impulse was to brain him with the iron bar and fly down the stairs ; but the burgomaster seeing something wicked in his eye, gave a little cough, and three stout fellows, armed, showed themselves directly at the door.

"My orders are to keep you thus until you shall bind yourself by an oath to leave Margaret Brandt, and return to the Church, to which you have belonged from your cradle."

"Death sooner."

"With all my heart." And the burgomaster retired.

Martin went with all speed to Sevenbergen ; there he found Margaret pale and agitated, but full of resolution and energy. She was just finishing a letter to the Countess Charolois, appealing to her against the violence and treachery of Ghysbrecht.

"Courage !" cried Martin on entering. "I have found him. He is in the haunted tower, right at the top of it. Ay, I know the place : many a poor fellow has gone up there straight, and come down feet foremost."

He then told them how he had looked up and seen Gerard's face at a window that was like a slit in the wall.

"Oh, Martin ! how did he look ?"

"What mean you ? He looked like Gerard Eliassoen."

"But was he pale ?"

"A little."

"Looked he anxious ? Looked he like one doomed ?"

"Nay, nay ; as bright as a pewter pot."

"You mock me. Stay ! then that must have been at sight of you. He counts on us. Oh, what shall we do ? Martin, good friend, take this at once to Rotterdam."

Martin held out his hand for the letter.

Peter had sat silent all this time, but pondering, and yet, contrary to custom, keenly attentive to what was going on around him.

"Put not your trust in princes," said he.

"Alas ! what else have we to trust in ?"

"Knowledge."

"Well-a-day, father ! your learning will not serve us here."

"How know you that ? Wit has been too strong for iron bars ere to-day."

"Ay, father ; but Nature is stronger than wit, and she is

against us. Think of the height! No ladder in Holland might reach him."

"I need no ladder; what I need is a gold crown."

"Nay, I have money, for that matter. I have nine angels. Gerard gave them me to keep; but what do they avail? The burgomaster will not be bribed to let Gerard free."

"What do they avail? Give me but one crown, and the young man shall sup with us this night."

Peter spoke so eagerly and confidently, that for a moment Margaret felt hopeful; but she caught Martin's eye dwelling upon him with an expression of benevolent contempt.

"It passes the powers of man's invention," said she, with a deep sigh.

"Invention!" cried the old man. "A fig for invention. What need we invention at this time of day? Everything has been said that is to be said, and done that ever will be done. I shall tell you how a Florentine knight was shut up in a tower higher than Gerard's; yet did his faithful squire stand at the tower foot and get him out, with no other engine than that in your hand, Martin, and certain kickshaws I shall buy for a crown."

Martin looked at his bow, and turned it round in his hand, and seemed to interrogate it. But the examination left him as incredulous as before.

Then Peter told them his story, how the faithful squire got the knight out of a high tower at Brescia. The manœuvre, like most things that are really scientific, was so simple, that now their wonder was they had taken for impossible what was not even difficult.

The letter never went to Rotterdam. They trusted to Peter's learning and their own dexterity.

It was nine o'clock on a clear moonlight night; Gerard, senior, was still away; the rest of his little family had been some time abed.

A figure stood by the dwarf's bed. It was white, and the moonlight shone on it.

With an unearthly noise, between a yell and a snarl, the gymnast rolled off his bed and under it by a single unbroken movement. A soft voice followed him in his retreat.

C 2   "Why, Giles, are you afeard of me?"

At this, Giles's head peeped cautiously up, and he saw it was only his sister Kate.

She put her finger to her lips. "Hush! lest the wicked Cornelis or the wicked Sybrandt hear us." Giles's claws seized the side of the bed, and he returned to his place by one undivided gymnastic.

Kate then revealed to Giles that she had heard Cornelis and Sybrandt mention Gerard's name; and being herself in great anxiety at his not coming home all day, had listened at their door, and had made a fearful discovery. Gerard was in prison, in the haunted tower of the Stadthouse. He was there, it seemed, by their father's authority. But here must be some treachery; for how could their father have ordered this cruel act? He was at Rotterdam. She ended by entreating Giles to bear her company to the foot of the haunted tower, to say a word of comfort to poor Gerard, and let him know their father was absent, and would be sure to release him on his return.

"Dear Giles, I would go alone, but I am afeard of the spirits that men say do haunt the tower: but with you I shall not be afeard."

"Nor I with you," said Giles. "I don't believe there are any spirits in Tergou. I never saw one. This last was the likest one ever I saw; and it was but you, Kate, after all."

In less than half an hour Giles and Kate opened the house-door cautiously and issued forth. She made him carry a lantern, though the night was bright. "The lantern gives me more courage against the evil spirits," said she.

The first day of imprisonment is very trying, especially if to the horror of captivity is added the horror of utter solitude. I observe that in our own day a great many persons commit suicide during the first twenty-four hours of the solitary cell. This is doubtless why our Jairi abstain so carefully from the impertinence of watching their little experiment upon the human soul at that particular stage of it.

As the sun declined, Gerard's heart too sank and sank: with the waning light even the embers of hope went out. He was faint, too, with hunger; for he was afraid to eat the food Ghysbrecht had brought him; and hunger alone cows men. He sat upon the chest, his arms and his head drooping before him—a picture of despondency. Suddenly something struck the wall beyond him very sharply, and then rattled on the floor at his feet. It was an arrow; he saw the white feather. A chill ran through him—they meant then to assassinate him from the outside. He crouched. No more missiles came. He crawled on all fours, and took up the arrow: there was no head to it. He uttered a cry of hope: had a friendly hand shot it? He took it up, and felt it all over: he found a soft substance attached to it. Then one of his eccentricities was of grand use to him. His tinder-box enabled him to strike a light: it showed him two things that made his heart bound with delight, none the less thrilling for being somewhat vague. Attached to the arrow was a skein of silk, and on the arrow itself were words written.

How his eyes devoured them, his heart panting the while.

𝔚ell beloved, make fast the silk to thy knife and lower to us: but hold thine end fast: then count an hundred and draw up.

Gerard seized the oak chest, and with almost superhuman energy dragged it to the window: a moment ago he could not have moved it. Standing on the chest and looking down, he saw figures at the tower foot. They were so indistinct, they looked like one huge form. He waved his bonnet to them with trembling hand: then he undid the silk rapidly but carefully, and made one end fast to his knife, and lowered it till it ceased to draw. Then he counted a hundred. Then pulled the silk carefully up: it came up a little heavier. At last he came to a large knot, and by that knot a stout whipcord was attached to the silk. What could this mean? While he was puzzling himself Margaret's voice came up to him, low but clear. "Draw up, Gerard, till you see liberty." At the word Gerard drew the whipcord line up, and drew and drew till he came to another knot, and found a cord of some thickness take the place of the whipcord. He had no sooner begun to draw this up than he found that he had now a heavy weight to deal with. Then the truth suddenly flashed on him, and he went to work and pulled and pulled till the perspiration rolled down him: the weight got heavier and heavier, and at last he was well nigh exhausted: looking down, he saw in the moonlight a sight that revived him: it was as it were a great snake coming up to him out of the deep shadow cast by the tower. He gave a shout of joy, and a score more wild pulls, and lo! a stout new rope touched his hand: he hauled and hauled, and dragged the end into his prison, and instantly passed it through both handles of the chest in succession, and knotted it firmly; then sat for a moment to recover his breath and collect his courage. The first thing was to make sure that the chest was sound, and capable of resisting his weight poised in mid-air. He jumped with all his force upon it. At the third jump the whole side burst open, and out scuttled the contents—a host of parchments.

After the first start and misgiving this gave him, Gerard comprehended that the chest had not burst, but opened: he had doubtless jumped upon some secret spring. Still it shook in some degree his confidence in the chest's powers of resistance; so he gave it an ally: he took the iron bar and fastened it with the small rope across the large rope, and across the window. He now mounted the chest, and from the chest put his foot through the window, and sat half in and half out, with one hand on that part of the rope which was inside. In the silent night he heard his own heart beat.

The free air breathed on his face, and gave him the courage to risk what we must all lose one day—for liberty. Many dangers awaited him, but the greatest was the first getting on to the rope outside. Gerard reflected. Finally, he put himself in the attitude of a swimmer, his body to the waist being in the prison, his legs outside. Then holding the inside rope with both hands, he felt anxiously with his feet for the outside rope; and when he had got it, he worked it in between the palms of his feet, and kept it there tight: then he uttered a short prayer, and, all the calmer for it, put his left hand on the sill and gradually wriggled out. Then he seized the iron bar, and for one fearful moment hung outside from it by his right hand, while his left hand felt for the rope down at his knees; it was too tight against the wall for his fingers to get round it higher up. The moment he had fairly grasped it, he left the bar, and swiftly seized the rope with the right hand too; but in this manœuvre his body necessarily fell about a yard. A stifled cry came up from below.

Gerard hung in mid-air. He clenched his teeth, and nipped the rope tight with his feet and gripped it with his hands, and went down slowly, hand below hand. He passed by one huge rough stone after another. He saw there was green moss on one. He looked up and he looked down. The moon shone into his prison window: it seemed very near. The fluttering figures below seemed an awful distance. It made him dizzy to look down; so he fixed his eyes steadily on the wall close to him, and went slowly down, down, down.

He passed a rusty, slimy streak on the wall: it was some ten feet long. The rope made his hands very hot. He stole another look up.

The prison window was a good way off now.

Down—down—down—down.

The rope made his hands sore.

He looked up. The window was so distant, he ventured now to turn his eyes downward again; and there, not more than thirty feet below him, were Margaret and Martin, their faithful hands upstretched to catch him should he fall. He could see their eyes and their teeth shine in the moonlight. For their mouths were open, and they were breathing hard.

"Take care, Gerard! oh, take care! Look not down."

"Fear me not," cried Gerard joyfully, and eyed the wall, but came down faster.

In another minute his feet were at their hands. They seized him ere he touched the ground, and all three clung together in one embrace.

"Hush! away in silence, dear one."

They stole along the shadow of the wall.

Now, ere they had gone many yards, suddenly a stream of light shot from an angle of the building, and lay across their path like a barrier of fire, and they heard whispers and footsteps close at hand.

"Back!" hissed Martin. "Keep in the shade."

They hurried back, passed the dangling rope, and made for a little square projecting tower. They had barely rounded it when the light shot trembling past them, and flickered uncertainly into the distance.

"A lantern!" groaned Martin, in a whisper. "They are after us."

"Give me my knife," whispered Gerard. "I'll never be taken alive."

"No, no!" murmured Margaret; "is there no way out where we are?"

"None! none! But I carry six lives at my shoulder;" and, with the word, Martin strung his bow, and fitted an arrow to the string. "In war never wait to be struck: I will kill one or two ere they shall know where their death comes from:" then, motioning his companions to be quiet, he began to draw his bow, and, ere the arrow was quite drawn to the head, he glided round the corner ready to loose the string the moment the enemy should offer a mark.

Gerard and Margaret held their breath in horrible expectation: they had never seen a human being killed.

And now a wild hope, but half repressed, thrilled through Gerard, that this watchful enemy might be the burgomaster in person. The soldier, he knew, would send an arrow through a burgher or burgomaster, as he would through a boar in a wood.

But who may foretell the future, however near? The bow, instead of remaining firm, and loosing the deadly shaft, was seen to waver first, then shake violently, and the stout soldier staggered back to them, his knees knocking and his cheeks blanched with fear. He let his arrow fall, and clutched Gerard's shoulder.

"Let me feel flesh and blood," he gasped. "The haunted tower! the haunted tower!"

His terror communicated itself to Margaret and Gerard. They gasped rather than uttered an inquiry.

"Hush!" he cried, "it will hear you. *Up* the wall! it is going *up* the wall! Its head is on fire. *Up* the wall, as mortal creatures walk upon green sward. If you know a prayer, say it; for hell is loose to-night."

"I have power to exorcise spirits," said Gerard, trembling. "I will venture forth."

"Go alone, then!" said Martin; "I have looked on't once, and live."

CHAPTER XI.

THE strange glance of hatred the burgomaster had cast on Gerard, coupled with his imprisonment, had filled the young man with a persuasion that Ghysbrecht was his enemy to the death; and he glided round the angle of the tower, fully expecting to see no supernatural appearance, but some cruel and treacherous contrivance of a bad man to do him a mischief in that prison, his escape from which could hardly be known.

As he stole forth, a soft but brave hand crept into his; and Margaret was by his side, to share this new peril.

No sooner was the haunted tower visible, than a sight struck their eyes that benumbed them as they stood. More than half way up the tower, a creature with a fiery head, like an enormous glow-worm, was steadily mounting the wall: the body was dark, but its outline visible through the glare from the head, and the whole creature not much less than four feet long.

At the foot of the tower stood a thing in white, that looked exactly like the figure of a female. Gerard and Margaret palpitated with awe.

"The rope! the rope! It is going up the rope," gasped Gerard.

As they gazed, the glow-worm disappeared in Gerard's late prison, but its light illuminated the cell inside and reddened the window. The white figure stood motionless below.

Such as can retain their senses after the first prostrating effect of the supernatural are apt to experience terror in one of its strangest forms, a wild desire to fling themselves upon the terrible object. It fascinates them as the snake the bird. The great tragedian, Macready, used to render this finely in "Macbeth," at Banquo's second appearance. He flung himself with averted head at the horrible shadow. This strange impulse now seized Margaret. She put down Gerard's hand quietly, and stood bewildered; then, all in a moment, with a wild cry, darted towards the spectre. Gerard, not aware of the natural impulse I have spoken of, never doubted the evil one was drawing her to her perdition. He fell on his knees.

"Exorcizo vos. In nomine beatæ Mariæ, exorcizo vos."

While the exorcist was shrieking his incantations in extremity of terror, to his infinite relief he heard the spectre utter a feeble cry of fear. To find that hell had also its little weaknesses was encouraging. He redoubled his exorcisms, and presently he saw the ghastly shape kneeling at Margaret's knees, and heard it praying piteously for mercy.

Kate and Giles soon reached the haunted tower. Judge their surprise when they found a new rope dangling from the prisoner's window to the ground.

"I see how it is," said the inferior intelligence, taking facts as they came. "Our Gerard has come down this rope. He has got clear. Up I go, and see."

"No, Giles, no!" said the superior intelligence, blinded by prejudice. "See you not this is glamour? This rope is a line the evil one casts out to wile thee to destruction. He knows the weaknesses of all our hearts; he has seen how fond you are of going up things. Where should our Gerard procure a rope? how fasten it in the sky like this? It is not in nature. Holy saints, protect us this night, for hell is abroad."

"Stuff!" said the dwarf; "the way to hell is down, and this rope leads up. I never had the luck to go up such a long rope. It may be years ere I fall in with such a long rope all ready hung for me. As well be knocked on the head at once as never know happiness."

And he sprang on to the rope with a cry of delight, as a cat jumps with a mew on to a table where fish is. All the gymnast was on fire; and the only concession Kate could gain from him was permission to fasten the lantern on his neck first.

"A light scares the ill spirits," said she.

And so, with his huge arms, and his legs like feathers, Giles went up the rope faster than his brother came down it. The light at the nape of his neck made a glow-worm of him. His sister watched his progress with trembling anxiety. Suddenly a female figure started out of the solid masonry, and came flying at her with more than mortal velocity.

Kate uttered a feeble cry. It was all she could, for her tongue clove to her palate with terror. Then she dropped her crutches, and sank upon her knees, hiding her face and moaning—

"Take my body, but spare my soul!"

Margaret (panting). "Why, it is a woman!"

Kate (quivering). "Why, it is a woman!"

Margaret. "How you scared me!"

Kate. "I am scared enough myself. Oh! oh! oh!"

"This is strange! But the fiery-headed thing? Yet it was with you, and you are harmless! But why are you here at this time of night?"

"Nay, why are YOU?"

"Perhaps we are on the same errand? Ah! you are his *good* sister, Kate."

"And you are Margaret Brandt."

"Yea."

"All the better. You love him; you are here. Then Giles was right. He has won free."

Gerard came forward, and put the question at rest. But all further explanation was cut short by a horrible unearthly noise, like a sepulchre ventriloquising—

"PARCHMENT!—PARCHMENT!—PARCHMENT!"

At each repetition, it rose in intensity. They looked up, and there was the dwarf, with his hands full of parchments, and his face lighted with fiendish joy and lurid with diabolical fire. The light being at his neck, a more infernal "transparency" never startled mortal eye. With the word, the awful imp hurled parchment at the astonished heads below. Down came records, like wounded wild-ducks; some collapsed, others fluttering, and others spread out and wheeling slowly down in airy circles. They had hardly settled, when again the sepulchral roar was heard —"Parchment!—parchment!" and down pattered and sailed another flock of documents: another followed: they whitened the grass. Finally, the fire-headed imp, with his light body and horny hands, slid down the rope like a falling star, and (business before sentiment) proposed to his rescued brother an immediate settlement for the merchandise he had just delivered.

"Hush!" said Gerard; "you speak too loud. Gather them up, and follow us to a safer place than this."

"Will you not come home with me, Gerard?" said little Kate.

"I have no home."

"You shall not say so. Who is more welcome than you will be, after this cruel wrong, to your father's house?"

"Father! I have no father," said Gerard sternly. "He that was my father is turned my gaoler. I have escaped from his hands; I will never come within their reach again."

"An enemy did this, and not our father."

And she told him what she had overheard Cornelis and Sybrandt say. But the injury was too recent to be soothed. Gerard showed a bitterness of indignation he had hitherto seemed incapable of.

"Cornelis and Sybrandt are two ill curs that have shown

me their teeth and their heart a long while; but they could
do no more. My father it is that gave the burgomaster
authority, or he durst not have laid a finger on me, that am
a free burgher of this town. So be it, then. I was his son.
I am his prisoner. He has played his part. I shall play
mine. Farewell the burgh where I was born, and lived
honestly, and was put in prison. While there is another
town left in creation, I'll never trouble you again, Tergou."

"Oh, Gerard! Gerard!"

Margaret whispered her: "Do not gainsay him now.
Give his choler time to cool!"

Kate turned quickly towards her. "Let me look at your
face!" The inspection was favourable, it seemed, for she
whispered: "It is a comely face, and no mischief-maker's."

"Fear me not," said Margaret, in the same tone. "I
could not be happy without your love, as well as Gerard's."

"These are comfortable words," sobbed Kate. Then,
looking up, she said, "I little thought to like you so well.
My heart is willing, but my infirmity will not let me embrace
you."

At this hint, Margaret wound gently round Gerard's
sister, and kissed her lovingly.

"Often he has spoken of you to me, Kate; and often I
longed for this."

"You, too, Gerard," said Kate, "kiss me ere you go; for
my heart lies heavy at parting with you this night."

Gerard kissed her, and she went on her crutches home.
The last thing they heard of her was a little patient sigh.
Then the tears came and stood thick in Margaret's eyes.
But Gerard was a man, and noticed not his sister's sigh.

As they turned to go to Sevenbergen, the dwarf nudged
Gerard with his bundle of parchments, and held out a
concave claw.

Margaret dissuaded Gerard. "Why take what is not
ours?"

"Oh, spoil an enemy how you can."

"But may they not make this a handle for fresh
violence?"

"How can they? Think you I shall stay in Tergou
after this? The burgomaster robbed me of my liberty: I
doubt I should take his life for it, if I could."

"Oh, fie! Gerard."

"What! Is life worth more than liberty? Well, I can't
take his life, so I take the first thing that comes to hand."

He gave Giles a few small coins, with which the urchin was gladdened, and shuffled after his sister. Margaret and Gerard were speedily joined by Martin, and away to Sevenbergen.

CHAPTER XII.

GHYSBRECHT VAN SWIETEN kept the key of Gerard's prison in his pouch. He waited till ten of the clock ere he visited him; for he said to himself, "A little hunger sometimes does well; it breaks 'em." At ten he crept up the stairs with a loaf and pitcher, followed by his trusty servant well armed. Ghysbrecht listened at the door. There was no sound inside. A grim smile stole over his features. "By this time he will be as down-hearted as Albert Koestein was," thought he. He opened the door.

No Gerard.

Ghysbrecht stood stupefied.

Although his face was not visible, his body seemed to lose all motion in so peculiar a way, and then after a little he fell a-trembling so, that the servant behind him saw there was something amiss, and crept close to him and peeped over his shoulder. At sight of the empty cell, and the rope, and iron bar, he uttered a loud exclamation of wonder; but his surprise doubled when his master, disregarding all else, suddenly flung himself on his knees before the empty chest, and felt wildly all over it with quivering hands, as if unwilling to trust his eyes in a matter so important.

The servant gazed at him in utter bewilderment.

"Why, master, what is the matter?"

Ghysbrecht's pale lips worked as it he was going to answer; but they uttered no sound: his hands fell by his side, and he stared into the chest.

"Why, master, what avails glaring into that empty box? The lad is not there. See here! Note the cunning of the young rogue; he hath taken out the bar, and——"

"GONE! GONE! GONE!"

"Gone! What is gone? Holy saints! he is planet-struck."

"STOP THIEF!" shrieked Ghysbrecht, and suddenly turned on his servant and collared him, and shook him with rage. "D'ye stand there, knave, and see your master robbed? Run! fly! A hundred crowns to him that finds it me again. No, no! 'tis in vain. Oh, fool! fool! to leave that in the same room with him. But none ever found the secret spring before. None ever would but he. It was to be. It is to be. Lost! lost!" and his years and infirmity now gained the better of his short-lived frenzy, and he sank on the chest muttering "Lost! lost!"

"What is lost, master?" asked the servant kindly.

"House and lands and good name," groaned Ghysbrecht, and wrung his hands feebly.

"WHAT?" cried the servant.

This emphatic word, and the tone of eager curiosity, struck on Ghysbrecht's ear and revived his natural cunning.

"I have lost the town records," stammered he, and he looked askant at the man like a fox caught near a hen-roost.

"Oh, is that all?"

"Is't not enough? What will the burghers say to me? What will the burgh do?" Then he suddenly burst out again, "A hundred crowns to him who shall recover them; all, mind, all that were in this box. If one be missing, I give nothing."

"'Tis a bargain, master: the hundred crowns are in my pouch. See you not that where Gerard Eliassoen is, there are the pieces of sheepskin you rate so high?"

"That is true; that is true; good Dierich; good, faithful Dierich. All, mind, all that were in the chest."

"Master, I will take the constables to Gerard's house, and seize him for the theft."

"The theft? ay! good; very good. It is theft. I forgot that. So, as he is a thief now, we will put him in the dungeons below, where the toads are and the rats. Dierich, that man must never see daylight again. 'Tis his own fault; he must be prying. Quick, quick! ere he has time to talk, you know, time to talk."

In less than half an hour Dierich Brower and four constables entered the hosier's house, and demanded young Gerard of the panic-stricken Catherine.

"Alas! what has he done now?" cried she; "that boy will break my heart."

"Nay, dame, but a trick of youth," said Dierich. "He hath but made off with certain skins of parchment, in a frolic doubtless; but the burgomaster is answerable to the burgh for their safe keeping, so he is in care about them : as for the youth, he will doubtless be quit for a reprimand."

This smooth speech completely imposed on Catherine; but her daughter was more suspicious, and that suspicion was strengthened by the disproportionate anger and disappointment Dierich showed the moment he learned Gerard was not at home, had not been at home that night.

"Come away then," said he roughly. "We are wasting time." He added vehemently, "I'll find him if he is above ground."

Affection sharpens the wits, and often it has made an innocent person more than a match for the wily. As Dierich was going out, Kate made him a signal she would speak with him privately. He bade his men go on, and waited outside the door. She joined him.

"Hush !" said she; "my mother knows not. Gerard has left Tergou."

"How ?"

"I saw him last night."

"Ay ! Where ?" cried Dierich eagerly.

"At the foot of the haunted tower."

"How did he get the rope ?"

"I know not; but this I know; my brother Gerard bade me there farewell, and he is many leagues from Tergou ere this. The town, you know, was always unworthy of him, and when it imprisoned him, he vowed never to set foot in it again. Let the burgomaster be content, then. He has imprisoned him, and he has driven him from his birthplace and from his native land. What need now to rob him and us of our good name ?"

This might at another moment have struck Dierich as good sense; but he was too mortified at this escape of Gerard and the loss of a hundred crowns.

"What need had he to steal ?" retorted he bitterly.

"Gerard stole not the trash; he but *took* it to spite the burgomaster, who stole his liberty; but he shall answer to the Duke for it, he shall. As for these skins of parchment you keep such a coil about, look in the nearest brook or stye, and 'tis odds but you find them."

"Think ye so, mistress ?—think ye so ?" And Dierich's eyes flashed. "Mayhap you know 'tis so."

"This I know, that Gerard is too good to steal, and too wise to load himself with rubbish, going a journey."

"Give you good-day, then," said Dierich sharply. "The sheepskin you scorn, I value it more than the skin of any he in Tergou."

And he went off hastily on a false scent.

Kate returned into the house, and drew Giles aside.

"Giles, my heart misgives me; breathe not to a soul what I say to you. I have told Dirk Brower that Gerard is out of Holland, but much I doubt he is not a league from Tergou."

"Why, where is he, then?"

"Where should he be, but with her he loves? But if so, he must not loiter. These be deep and dark and wicked men that seek him. Giles, I see that in Dirk Brower's eye makes me tremble. Oh, why cannot I fly to Sevenbergen and bid him away? Why am I not lusty and active like other girls? God forgive me for fretting at His will; but I never felt till now what it is to be lame and weak and useless. But you are strong, dear Giles," added she coaxingly; "you are very strong."

"Yes, I am strong," thundered Perpusillus; then, catching sight of her meaning, "but I hate to go on foot," he added sulkily.

"Alas! alas! who will help me if you will not? Dear Giles, do you not love Gerard?"

"Yes, I like him best of the lot. I'll go to Sevenbergen on Peter Buyskens his mule. Ask you him, for he won't lend her me."

Kate remonstrated. The whole town would follow him. It would be known whither he was gone, and Gerard be in worse danger than before.

Giles parried this by promising to ride out of the town the opposite way, and not turn the mule's head towards Sevenbergen till he had got rid of the curious.

Kate then assented, and borrowed the mule. She charged Giles with a short but meaning message, and made him repeat it after her over and over, till he could say it word for word.

Giles started on the mule, and little Kate retired, and did the last thing now in her power for her beloved brother—prayed on her knees long and earnestly for his safety.

CHAPTER XIII.

GERARD and Margaret went gaily to Sevenbergen in the first flush of recovered liberty and successful adventure. But these soon yielded to sadder thoughts. Gerard was an escaped prisoner, and liable to be retaken and perhaps punished; and therefore he and Margaret would have to part for a time. Moreover, he had conceived a hatred to his native place. Margaret wished him to leave the country for a while, but at the thought of his going to Italy her heart fainted. Gerard, on the contrary, was reconciled to leaving Margaret only by his desire to visit Italy, and his strong conviction that there he should earn money and reputation, and remove every obstacle to their marriage. He had already told her all that the demoiselle Van Eyck had said to him. He repeated it, and reminded Margaret that the gold pieces were only given him to go to Italy with. The journey was clearly for Gerard's interest. He was a craftsman and an artist, lost in this boorish place. In Italy they would know how to value him. On this ground above all the unselfish girl gave her consent; but many tender tears came with it, and at that Gerard, young and loving as herself, cried bitterly with her, and often they asked one another what they had done, that so many different persons should be their enemies, and combine, as it seemed, to part them.

They sat hand in hand till midnight, now deploring their hard fate, now drawing bright and hopeful pictures of the future, in the midst of which Margaret's tears would suddenly flow, and then poor Gerard's eloquence would die away in a sigh.

The morning found them resigned to part, but neither had the courage to say when; and much I doubt whether the hour of parting ever would have struck.

But about three in the afternoon, Giles, who had made a circuit of many miles to avoid suspicion, rode up to the door. They both ran out to him, eager with curiosity.

"Brother Gerard," cried he, in his tremendous tones, "Kate bids you run for your life. They charge you with theft; you have given them a handle. Think not to explain. Hope not for justice in Tergou. The parchments you took, they are but a blind. She hath seen your death in the men's eyes: a price is on your head. Fly! For

Margaret's sake and all who love you, loiter not life away, but fly!"

It was a thunder-clap, and left two white faces looking at one another, and at the terrible messenger.

Then Giles, who had hitherto but uttered by rote what Catherine bade him, put in a word of his own.

"All the constables were at our house after you, and so was Dirk Brower. Kate is wise, Gerard. Best give ear to her rede, and fly."

"Oh yes, Gerard," cried Margaret wildly. "Fly on the instant. Ah! those parchments; my mind misgave me: why did I let you take them?"

"Margaret, they are but a blind: Giles says so. No matter: the old caitiff shall never see them again; I will not go till I have hidden his treasure where he shall never find it." Gerard then, after thanking Giles warmly, bade him farewell, and told him to go back and tell Kate he was gone. "For I shall be gone ere you reach home," said he. He then shouted for Martin; and told him what had happened, and begged him to go a little way towards Tergou, and watch the road.

"Ay!" said Martin, "and if I see Dirk Brower or any of his men, I will shoot an arrow into the oak-tree that is in our garden; and on that you must run into the forest hard by, and meet me at the weird hunter's spring. Then I will guide you through the wood."

Surprise thus provided against, Gerard breathed again. He went with Margaret, and while she watched the oak-tree tremblingly, fearing every moment to see an arrow strike among the branches, Gerard dug a deep hole to bury the parchments in.

He threw them in, one by one. They were nearly all charters and records of the burgh; but one appeared to be a private deed between Floris Brandt, father of Peter, and Ghysbrecht.

"Why, this is as much yours as his," said Gerard. "I will read this."

"Oh, not now, Gerard, not now," cried Margaret. "Every moment you lose fills me with fear; and see, large drops of rain are beginning to fall, and the clouds lower."

Gerard yielded to this remonstrance: but he put the deed into his bosom, and threw the earth in over the others, and stamped it down. While thus employed there came a flash of lightning, followed by a peal of distant thunder, and the rain came down heavily. Margaret and Gerard ran into the house, whither they were speedily followed by Martin.

"The road is clear," said he, "and a heavy storm coming on."

His words proved true. The thunder came nearer and nearer till it crashed overhead: the flashes followed one another close, like the strokes of a whip, and the rain fell in torrents. Margaret hid her face not to see the lightning. On this, Gerard put up the rough shutter and lighted a candle. The lovers consulted together, and Gerard blessed the storm that gave him a few hours more with Margaret. The sun set unperceived, and still the thunder pealed, and the lightning flashed, and the rain poured. Supper was set; but Gerard and Margaret could not eat: the thought that this was the last time they should sup together choked them. The storm lulled a little. Peter retired to rest. But Gerard was to go at peep of day, and neither he nor Margaret could afford to lose an hour in sleep. Martin sat a while, too; for he was fitting a new string to his bow, a matter in which he was very nice.

The lovers murmured their sorrows and their love beside him.

Suddenly the old man held up his hand to them to be silent.

They were quiet and listened, and heard nothing. But the next moment a footstep crackled faintly upon the autumn leaves that lay strewn in the garden at the back door of the house. To those who had nothing to fear such a step would have said nothing: but to those who had enemies it was terrible. For it was a foot trying to be noiseless.

Martin fitted an arrow to his string and hastily blew out the candle. At this moment, to their horror, they heard more than one footstep approach the other door of the cottage, not quite so noiselessly as the other, but very stealthily—and then a dead pause.

Their blood froze in their veins.

"Oh, Kate! oh, Kate! You said fly on the instant." And Margaret moaned and wrung her hands in anguish and terror and wild remorse for having kept Gerard.

"Hush, girl!" said Martin, in a stern whisper.

A heavy knock fell on the door.
And on the hearts within.

CHAPTER XIV.

As if this had been a concerted signal, the back door was struck as rudely the next instant. They were hemmed in. But at these alarming sounds Margaret seemed to recover some share of self-possession. She whispered, " Say he *was* here, but is gone." And with this she seized Gerard and almost dragged him up the rude steps that led to her father's sleeping-room. Her own lay next beyond it.

The blows on the door were repeated.

" Who knocks at this hour ? "

" Open, and you will see ! "

" I open not to thieves—honest men are all a-bed now."

" Open to the law, Martin Wittenhaagen, or you shall rue it."

" Why, that is Dirk Brower's voice, I trow. What make you so far from Tergou ? "

" Open, and you will know."

Martin drew the bolt, very slowly, and in rushed Dierich and four more. They let in their companion who was at the back door.

" Now, Martin, where is Gerard Eliassoen ? "

" Gerard Eliassoen ? Why, he was here but now ? "

" Was here ? " Dierich's countenance fell. " And where is he now ? "

" They say he has gone to Italy. Why, what is to do ? "

" No matter. When did he go ? Tell me not that he went in such a storm as this ! "

" Here is a coil about Gerard Eliassoen," said Martin contemptuously. Then he lighted the candle, and, seating himself coolly by the fire, proceeded to whip some fine silk round his bowstring at the place where the nick of the arrow frets it. " I'll tell you," said he carelessly. " Know you his brother Giles—a little misbegotten imp, all head and arms ? Well, he came tearing over here on a mule, and bawled out something. I was too far off to hear the creature's words, but only its noise. Anyway, he started Gerard. For as soon as he was gone, there was such crying and kissing, and then Gerard went away. They do tell me he has gone to Italy—mayhap you know where that is ; for I don't."

Dierich's countenance fell lower and lower at this account. There was no flaw in it. A cunninger man than Martin would perhaps have told a lie too many, and raised suspicion. But Martin did his task well. He only told the one falsehood he was bade to tell, and of his own head invented nothing.

"Mates," said Dierich, "I doubt he speaks sooth. I told the burgomaster how 'twould be. He met the dwarf galloping Peter Buyskens' mule from Sevenbergen. 'They have sent that imp to Gerard,' says he, 'so, then, Gerard is at Sevenbergen.' 'Ah, master!' says I, ''tis too late now. We should have thought of Sevenbergen before, instead of wasting our time hunting all the odd corners of Tergou for those cursed parchments that we shall never find till we find the man that took 'em. If he was at Sevenbergen,' quoth I, 'and they sent the dwarf to him, it must have been to warn him we are after him. He is leagues away by now,' quoth I. Confound that chalk-faced girl! she has outwitted us bearded men; and so I told the burgomaster, but he would not hear reason. A wet jerkin apiece, that is all we shall get, mates, by this job."

Martin grinned coolly in Dierich's face.

"However," added the latter, "to content the burgomaster, we will search the house."

Martin turned grave directly.

This change of countenance did not escape Dierich. He reflected a moment.

"Watch outside, two of you, one on each side of the house, that no one jump from the upper windows. The rest come with me."

And he took the candle and mounted the stairs, followed by three of his comrades.

Martin was left alone.

The stout soldier hung his head. All had gone so well at first: and now this fatal turn! Suddenly it occurred to him that all was not yet lost. Gerard must be either in Peter's room or Margaret's; they were not so very high from the ground. Gerard would leap out. Dierich had left a man below; but what then? For half a minute Gerard and he would be two to one, and in that brief space, what might not be done?

Martin then held the back door ajar and watched. The light shone in Peter's room. "Curse the fool!" said he, "is he going to let them take him like a girl?"

The light now passed into Margaret's bedroom. Still

no window was opened. Had Gerard intended to escape
that way, he would not have waited till the men were in
the room. Martin saw that at once, and left the door,
and came to the foot-stair and listened. He began to
think Gerard must have escaped by the window while all
the men were in the house. The longer the silence continued, the stronger grew this conviction. But it was
suddenly and rudely dissipated.

Faint cries issued from the inner bedroom—Margaret's.

"They have taken him," groaned Martin; "they have
got him."

It now flashed across Martin's mind that if they took
Gerard away, his life was not worth a button; and that,
if evil befell him, Margaret's heart would break. He cast
his eyes wildly round like some savage beast seeking an
escape, and in a twinkling formed a resolution terribly
characteristic of those iron times and of a soldier driven
to bay. He stepped to each door in turn, and imitating
Dirk Brower's voice, said sharply, "Watch the window!"
He then quietly closed and bolted both doors. He then
took up his bow and six arrows; one he fitted to his string,
the others he put into his quiver. His knife he placed
upon a chair behind him, the hilt towards him; and there
he waited at the foot of the stair with the calm determina-
tion to slay those four men, or be slain by them. Two, he
knew, he could dispose of by his arrows, ere they could
get near him, and Gerard and he must take their chance
hand-to-hand with the remaining pair. Besides, he had
seen men panic-stricken by a sudden attack of this sort.
Should Brower and his men hesitate but an instant before
closing with him, he should shoot three instead of two,
and then the odds would be on the right side.

He had not long to wait. The heavy steps sounded
in Margaret's room, and came nearer and nearer.

The light also approached, and voices.

Martin's heart, stout as it was, beat hard, to hear men
coming thus to their death, and perhaps to his; more likely
so than not: for four is long odds in a battlefield of ten
feet square, and Gerard might be bound perhaps, and
powerless to help. But this man, whom we have seen
shake in his shoes at a Giles-o'-lanthorn, never wavered
in this awful moment of real danger, but stood there, his
body all braced for combat, and his eye glowing, equally

ready to take life and lose it. Desperate game! to win which was exile instant and for life, and to lose it was to die that moment upon that floor he stood on.

Dierich Brower and his men found Peter in his first sleep. They opened his cupboards; they ran their knives into an alligator he had nailed to his wall; they looked under his bed: it was a large room, and apparently full of hiding-places, but they found no Gerard.

Then they went on to Margaret's room, and the very sight of it was discouraging—it was small and bare, and not a cupboard in it; there was, however, a large fireplace and chimney. Dierich's eye fell on these directly. Here they found the beauty of Sevenbergen sleeping on an old chest, not a foot high, and no attempt made to cover it; but the sheets were snowy white, and so was Margaret's own linen. And there she lay, looking like a lily fallen into a rut.

Presently she awoke, and sat up in the bed, like one amazed; then, seeing the men, began to scream faintly, and pray for mercy.

She made Dierich Brower ashamed of his errand.

"Here is a to-do," said he, a little confused. "We are not going to hurt you, my pretty maid. Lie you still, and shut your eyes, and think of your wedding-night, while I look up this chimney to see if Master Gerard is there."

"Gerard! in my room?"

"Why not? They say that you and he——"

"Cruel! you know they have driven him away from me —driven him from his native place. This is a blind. You are thieves; you are wicked men; you are not men of Sevenbergen, or you would know Margaret Brandt better than to look for her lover in this room of all others in the world. Oh, brave! Four great hulking men to come, armed to the teeth, to insult one poor honest girl! The women that live in your own houses must be naught, or you would respect them too much to insult a girl of good character."

"There! come away, before we hear worse," said Dierich hastily. "He is not in the chimney. Plaster will mend what a cudgel breaks; but a woman's tongue is a double-edged dagger, and a girl is a woman with her mother's milk still in her." And he beat a hasty retreat. "I told the burgomaster how 'twould be."

CHAPTER XV.

Where is the woman that cannot act a part? Where is she who will not do it, and do it well, to save the man she loves? Nature on these great occasions comes to the aid of the simplest of the sex, and teaches her to throw dust in Solomon's eyes. The men had no sooner retired than Margaret stepped out of bed, and opened the long chest on which she had been lying down in her skirt and petticoat and stockings, and night-dress over all; and put the lid, bed-clothes and all, against the wall: then glided to the door and listened. The footsteps died away through her father's room and down the stairs.

Now in that chest there was a peculiarity that it was almost impossible for a stranger to detect. A part of the boarding of the room had been broken, and Gerard being applied to make it look neater, and being short of materials, had ingeniously sawed away a space sufficient just to admit Margaret's *soi-disant* bed, and with the materials thus acquired he had repaired the whole room. As for the bed or chest, it really rested on the rafters a foot below the boards. Consequently, it was full two feet deep, though it looked scarce one.

All was quiet. Margaret kneeled and gave thanks to Heaven. Then she glided from the door and leaned over the chest, and whispered tenderly, "Gerard!"

Gerard did not reply.

She then whispered, a little louder, "Gerard, all is safe, thank Heaven! You may rise; but oh! be cautious!"

Gerard made no reply.

She laid her hand upon his shoulder—"Gerard!"

No reply.

"Oh, what is this?" she cried, and her hands ran wildly over his face and his bosom. She took him by the shoulders; she shook him; she lifted him; but he escaped from her trembling hands, and fell back, not like a man, but like a body. A great dread fell on her. The lid had been down. She had lain upon it. The men had been some time in the room. With all the strength of frenzy she tore him out of the chest. She bore him in her arms to the window. She dashed the window open. The sweet air came in. She laid him in it and in the moonlight. His face was the colour of ashes; his body was all limp and motionless. She felt his heart. Horror! it was as still as the rest! Horror of horrors! she had stifled him with her own body.

The mind cannot all at once believe so great and sudden and strange a calamity. Gerard, who had got alive into that chest scarce five minutes ago, how could he be dead?

She called him by all the endearing names that heart could think or tongue could frame. She kissed him, and fondled him, and coaxed him, and implored him to speak to her.

No answer to words of love, such as she had never uttered to him before, nor thought she could utter. Then the poor creature, trembling all over, began to say over that ashy face little foolish things that were at once terrible and pitiable.

"Oh, Gerard! I am very sorry you are dead. I am very sorry I have killed you. Forgive me for not letting the men take you; it would have been better than this. Oh, Gerard! I am very, very sorry for what I have done." Then she began suddenly to rave. "No! no! such things can't be, or there is no God. It is monstrous. How can my Gerard be dead? How can I have killed my Gerard? I love him. Oh, God! you know how I love him. He does not. I never told him. If he knew my heart, he would speak to me, he would not be so deaf to his poor Margaret. It is all a trick to make me cry out and betray him: but no! I love him too well for that. I'll choke first." And she seized her own throat, to check her wild desire to scream in her terror and anguish.

"If he would but say one word. Oh, Gerard! don't die without a word. Have mercy on me and scold me, but speak to me: if you are angry with me, scold me! curse me! I deserve it: the idiot that killed the man she loved better than herself. Ah! I am a murderess. The worst in all the world. Help! help! I have murdered him. Ah! ah! ah! ah! ah!"

She tore her hair, and uttered shriek after shriek, so wild, so piercing, they fell like a knell upon the ears of Dierich Brower and his men. All started to their feet, and looked at one another.

CHAPTER XVI.

MARTIN WITTENHAAGEN, standing at the foot of the stairs with his arrow drawn nearly to the head and his knife behind him, was struck with amazement to see the men come back without Gerard: he lowered his bow, and looked open-mouthed at them. They, for their part, were equally puzzled at the attitude they had caught him in.

"Why, mates, was the old fellow making ready to shoot at *us*?"

"Stuff!" said Martin, recovering his stolid composure; "I was but trying my new string. There! I'll unstring my bow, if you think that."

"Humph!" said Dierich suspiciously, "there is something more in you than I understand: put a log on, and let us dry our hides a bit ere we go."

A blazing fire was soon made, and the men gathered round it, and their clothes and long hair were soon smoking from the cheerful blaze. Then it was that the shrieks were heard in Margaret's room. They all started up, and one of them seized the candle, and ran up the steps that led to the bedrooms.

Martin rose hastily too, and being confused by these sudden screams, and apprehending danger from the man's curiosity, tried to prevent him from going there.

At this Dierich threw his arms round him from behind, and called on the others to keep him. The man that had the candle got clear away, and all the rest fell upon Martin; and after a long and fierce struggle, in the course of which they were more than once all rolling on the floor, with Martin in the middle, they succeeded in mastering the old Samson, and binding him hand and foot with a rope they had brought for Gerard.

Martin groaned aloud. He saw the man had made his way to Margaret's room during the struggle, and here was he powerless.

"Ay, grind your teeth, you old rogue," said Dierich, panting with the struggle. "You shan't use them."

"It is my belief, mates, that our lives were scarce safe while this old fellow's bones were free."

"He makes me think this Gerard is not far off," put in another.

"No such luck," replied Dierich. "Hollo, mates.

Jorian Ketel is a long time in that girl's bedroom. Best go and see after him, some of us."

The rude laugh caused by this remark had hardly subsided, when hasty footsteps were heard running along overhead.

"Oh, here he comes, at last. Well, Jorian, what is to do now up there?"

CHAPTER XVII.

JORIAN KETEL went straight to Margaret's room, and there, to his infinite surprise, he found the man he had been in search of, pale and motionless, his head in Margaret's lap, and she kneeling over him, mute now, and stricken to stone. Her eyes were dilated yet glazed, and she neither saw the light nor heard the man, nor cared for anything on earth, but the white face in her lap.

Jorian stood awestruck, the candle shaking in his hand.

"Why, where was he, then, all the time?"

Margaret heeded him not. Jorian went to the empty chest and inspected it. He began to comprehend. The girl's dumb and frozen despair moved him.

"This is a sorry sight," said he; "it is a black night's work: all for a few skins! Better have gone with us than so. She is past answering me, poor wench. Stop! let us try whether——"

He took down a little round mirror, no bigger than his hand, and put it to Gerard's mouth and nostrils, and held it there. When he withdrew it, it was dull.

"THERE IS LIFE IN HIM!" said Jorian Ketel to himself.

Margaret caught the words instantly, though only muttered, and it was as if a statue should start into life and passion. She rose, and flung her arms round Jorian's neck.

"Oh, bless the tongue that tells me so!" and she clasped the great rough fellow again and again, eagerly, almost fiercely.

"There, there! let us lay him warm," said Jorian; and in a moment he raised Gerard and laid him on the bed-clothes. Then he took out a flask he carried, and filled his hand twice with Schiedamze, and flung it sharply each time in Gerard's face. The pungent liquor
D co-operated with his recovery — he gave a faint sigh.

Oh, never was sound so joyful to human ear! She flew towards him, but then stopped, quivering for fear she should hurt him. She had lost all confidence in herself.

"That is right—let him alone," said Jorian; "don't go cuddling him as you did me, or you'll drive his breath back again. Let him alone: he is sure to come to. 'Tisn't like as if he was an old man."

Gerard sighed deeply, and a faint streak of colour stole to his lips. Jorian made for the door. He had hardly reached it, when he found his legs seized from behind.

It was Margaret! She curled round his knees like a serpent, and kissed his hand, and fawned on him. "You won't tell? You have saved his life; you have not the heart to thrust him back into his grave, to undo your own good work?"

"No, no! It is not the first time I have done you two a good turn; 'twas I told you in the church whither we had to take him. Besides, what is Dirk Brower to me? I'll see him hanged ere I'll tell him. But I wish you'd tell *me* where the parchments are! There are a hundred crowns offered for them. That would be a good windfall for my Joan and the children, you know."

"Ah! they shall have those hundred crowns."

"What! are the things in the house?" asked Jorian eagerly.

"No; but I know where they are; and by God and St. Bavon I swear you shall have them to-morrow. Come to me for them when you will, but come alone."

"I were mad else. What! share the hundred crowns with Dirk Brower? And now may my bones rot in my skin if I let a soul know the poor boy is here."

He then ran off, lest by staying longer he should excite suspicion, and have them all after him. And Margaret knelt, quivering from head to foot, and prayed beside Gerard, and for Gerard.

"What is to do?" replied Jorian to Dierich Brower's query; "why, we have scared the girl out of her wits. She was in a kind of fit."

"We had better all go and doctor her, then."

"Oh, yes! and frighten her into the churchyard. Her father is a doctor, and I have roused him, and set him to bring her round. Let us see the fire, will ye?"

His off-hand way disarmed all suspicion. And soon after the party agreed that the kitchen of the "Three Kings" was much warmer than Peter's house, and they departed, having first untied Martin.

"Take note, mates, that I was right, and the burgomaster wrong," said Dierich Brower, at the door; "I said we should be too late to catch him, and we were too late."

Thus Gerard, in one terrible night, grazed the prison and the grave.

And how did he get clear at last? Not by his cunningly contrived hiding-place, nor by Margaret's ready wit; but by a good impulse in one of his captors, by the bit of humanity left in a somewhat reckless fellow's heart, aided by his desire of gain. So mixed and seemingly incongruous are human motives, so shortsighted our shrewdest counsels.

They whose moderate natures or gentle fates keep them, in life's passage, from the fierce extremes of joy and anguish our nature is capable of, are perhaps the best, and certainly the happiest of mankind. But to such readers I should try in vain to convey what bliss unspeakable settled now upon these persecuted lovers. Even to those who have joyed greatly and greatly suffered, my feeble art can present but a pale reflection of Margaret's and Gerard's ecstasy.

To sit and see a beloved face come back from the grave to the world, to health and beauty, by swift gradations; to see the roses return to the loved cheek, love's glance to the loved eye, and his words to the loved mouth—this was Margaret's—a joy to balance years of sorrow. It was Gerard's to awake from a trance, and find his head pillowed on Margaret's arm; to hear the woman he adored murmur new words of eloquent love, and shower tears and tender kisses and caresses on him. He never knew, till this sweet moment, how ardently, how tenderly she loved him. He thanked his enemies. They wreathed their arms sweetly round each other, and trouble and danger seemed a world, an age, behind them. They called each other husband and wife. Were they not solemnly betrothed? And had they not stood before the altar together? Was not the blessing of Holy Church upon their union?—her curse on all who would part them?

But as no woman's nerves can bear with impunity so terrible a strain, presently Margaret turned faint, and sank on Gerard's shoulder, smiling feebly, but quite, quite unstrung. Then Gerard was anxious, and would seek assistance. But she held him with a gentle grasp, and implored him not to leave her for a moment. "While I can lay my hand on you, I feel you are safe, not else. Foolish Gerard! nothing ails me. I am weak, dearest, but happy, oh! so happy!"

Then it was Gerard's turn to support that dear head, with its great waves of hair flowing loose over him, and nurse her, and soothe her, quivering on his bosom, with soft, encouraging words and murmurs of love, and gentle caresses. Sweetest of all her charms is a woman's weakness to a manly heart.

Poor things! they were happy. To-morrow they must part. But that was nothing to them now. They had seen Death, and all other troubles seemed light as air. While there is life there is hope; while there is hope there is joy. Separation for a year or two, what was it to them, who were so young, and had caught a glimpse of the grave? The future was bright, the present was heaven: so passed the blissful hours.

Alas! their innocence ran other risks besides the prison and the grave. They were in most danger from their own hearts, and their inexperience, now that visible danger there was none.

CHAPTER XVIII.

GHYSBRECHT VAN SWIETEN could not sleep all night for anxiety. He was afraid of thunder and lightning, or he would have made one of the party that searched Peter's house. As soon as the storm ceased altogether, he crept downstairs, saddled his mule, and rode to the "Three Kings" at Sevenbergen. There he found his men sleeping, some on the chairs, some on the tables, some on the floor. He roused them furiously, and heard the story of their unsuccessful search, interlarded with praises of their zeal.

"Fool! to let you go without me," cried the burgomaster. "My life on't he was there all the time. Looked ye under the girl's bed?"

"No; there was no room for a man there."

"How know ye that, if ye looked not?" snarled Ghysbrecht. "Ye should have looked under her bed, and in it, too; and sounded all the panels with your knives. Come now, get up, and I shall show ye to search."

Dierich Brower got up, and shook himself: "If you find him, call me a horse and no man."

In a few minutes Peter's house was again surrounded.

The fiery old man left his mule in the hands of Jorian Ketel, and, with Dierich Brower and the others, entered the house.

The house was empty.

Not a creature to be seen, not even Peter. They went upstairs, and then suddenly one of the men gave a shout, and pointed through Peter's window, which was open. The others looked, and there, at some little distance, walking quietly across the fields with Margaret and Martin, was the man they sought. Ghysbrecht, with an exulting yell, descended the stairs, and flung himself on his mule; and he and his men set off in hot pursuit.

CHAPTER XIX.

GERARD, warned by recent peril, rose before daybreak, and waked Martin. The old soldier was astonished. He thought Gerard had escaped by the window last night. Being consulted as to the best way for him to leave the country and elude pursuit, he said there was but one road safe. "I must guide you through the great forest to a bridle-road I know of. This will take you speedily to a hostelry, where they will lend you a swift horse: and then a day's gallop will take you out of Holland. But let us start ere the folk here quit their beds."

Peter's house was but a furlong and a half from the forest. They started, Martin with his bow and three arrows, for it was Thursday; Gerard with nothing but a stout oak staff Peter gave him for the journey.

Margaret pinned up her kirtle and farthingale, for the road was wet. Peter went as far as his garden hedge with them, and then, with more emotion than he often bestowed on passing events, gave the young man his blessing.

The sun was peeping above the horizon as they crossed the stony field and made for the wood. They had crossed about half, when Margaret, who kept nervously looking back every now and then, uttered a cry, and, following her instinct, began to run towards the wood, screaming with terror all the way.

Ghysbrecht and his men were in hot pursuit.

Resistance would have been madness. Martin and Gerard followed Margaret's example. The pursuers gained slightly on them; but Martin kept shouting, "Only win the wood; only win the wood!"

They had too good a start for the men on foot, and their hearts bounded with hope at Martin's words, for the great trees seemed now to stretch their branches like friendly arms towards them, and their leaves like a screen.

But an unforeseen danger attacked them. The fiery old burgomaster flung himself on his mule, and, spurring him to a gallop, he headed not his own men only, but the fugitives. His object was to cut them off. The old man came galloping in a semicircle, and got on the edge of the wood, right in front of Gerard; the others might escape for aught he cared.

Margaret shrieked, and tried to protect Gerard by clasping him; but he shook her off without ceremony.

Ghysbrecht in his ardour forgot that hunted animals turn on the hunter; and that two men can hate, and two can long to kill the thing they hate.

Instead of attempting to dodge him, as the burgomaster made sure he would, Gerard flew right at him, with a savage, exulting cry, and struck at him with all his heart and soul and strength. The oak staff came down on Ghysbrecht's face with a frightful crash, and laid him under his mule's tail beating the devil's tattoo with his heels, his face streaming, and his collar spattered, with blood.

The next moment, the three were in the wood. The yell of dismay and vengeance that burst from Ghysbrecht's men at that terrible blow which felled their leader, told the fugitives that it was now a race for life or death.

"Why run?" cried Gerard, panting. "You have your bow; and I have this," and he shook his bloody staff.

"Boy!" roared Martin; "the GALLOWS! Follow me," and he fled into the wood. Soon they heard a cry like a pack of hounds opening on sight of the game. The men were in the wood, and saw them flitting amongst the trees. Margaret moaned and panted as she ran; and Gerard clenched his teeth, and grasped his staff. The next minute they came to a stiff hazel coppice. Martin dashed into it, and shouldered the young wood aside as if it were standing corn.

Ere they had gone fifty yards in it they came to four blind paths.

Martin took one. "Bend low," said he. And, half-creeping, they glided along. Presently their path was again intersected with other little tortuous paths. They took one of them. It seemed to lead back; but it soon took a turn, and, after a while, brought them to a thick pine grove, where the walking was good and hard. There were no paths here; and the young fir-trees were so thick, you could not see three yards before your nose.

When they had gone some way in this, Martin sat down; and, having learned in war to lose all impression of danger with the danger itself, took a piece of bread and a slice of ham out of his wallet, and began quietly to eat his breakfast.

The young ones looked at him with dismay. He replied to their looks.

"All Sevenbergen could not find you now. You will lose your purse, Gerard, long before you get to Italy; is that the way to carry a purse?"

Gerard looked, and there was a large triangular purse, entangled by its chains to the buckle and strap of his wallet.

"This is none of mine," said he. "What is in it, I wonder?" and he tried to detach it; but in passing through the coppice it had become inextricably entangled in his strap and buckle. "It seems loath to leave me," said Gerard, and he had to cut it loose with his knife. The purse, on examination, proved to be well provided with silver coins of all sizes, but its bloated appearance was greatly owing to a number of pieces of brown paper folded and doubled. A light burst on Gerard. "Why, it must be that old thief's; and see! stuffed with paper to deceive the world!"

The wonder was how the burgomaster's purse came on Gerard.

They hit at last upon the right solution. The purse must have been at Ghysbrecht's saddle-bow, and Gerard, rushing at his enemy, had unconsciously torn it away.

thus felling his enemy and robbing him, with a single gesture.

Gerard was delighted at this feat, but Margaret was uneasy.

"Throw it away, Gerard, or let Martin take it back. Already they call you a thief. I cannot bear it."

"Throw it away? give it him back? not a stiver! This is spoil lawfully won in battle from an enemy. Is it not, Martin?"

"Why, of course. Send him back the brown paper, an' you will; but the purse or the coin—that were a sin."

"Oh, Gerard!" said Margaret, "you are going to a distant land. We need the good-will of Heaven. How can we hope for that if we take what is not ours?"

But Gerard saw it in a different light.

"It is Heaven that gives it me by a miracle, and I shall cherish it accordingly," said this pious youth. "Thus the favoured people spoiled the Egyptians, and were blessed."

"Take your own way," said Margaret humbly; "you are wiser than I am. You are my husband," added she, in a low murmuring voice; "is it for me to gainsay you?"

These humble words from Margaret, who, till that day, had held the whip-hand, rather surprised Martin for the moment. They recurred to him some time afterwards, and then they surprised him less.

Gerard kissed her tenderly in return for her wife-like docility, and they pursued their journey hand in hand, Martin leading the way, into the depths of the huge forest. The farther they went, the more absolutely secure from pursuit they felt. Indeed, the townspeople never ventured so far as this into the trackless part of the forest.

Impetuous natures repent quickly. Gerard was no sooner out of all danger than his conscience began to prick him.

"Martin, would I had not struck quite so hard."

"Whom? Oh! let that pass; he is cheap served."

"Martin, I saw his gray hairs as my stick fell on him. I doubt they will not from my sight this while."

Martin grunted with contempt. "Who spares a badger for his gray hairs? The grayer your enemy is, the older; and the older the craftier; and the craftier the better for a little killing."

"Killing? Killing, Martin? Speak not of killing!" And Gerard shook all over.

"I am much mistook if you have not," said Martin cheerfully.

"Now Heaven forbid!"

"The old vagabond's skull cracked like a walnut, aha!"

"Heaven and the saints forbid it!"

"He rolled off his mule like a stone shot out of a cart. Said I to myself, 'There is one wiped out.'" And the iron old soldier grinned ruthlessly.

Gerard fell on his knees, and began to pray for his enemy's life.

At this Martin lost his patience. "Here's mummery. What! you that set up for learning, know you not that a wise man never strikes his enemy but to kill him? And what is all this coil about killing of old men? If it had been a young one, now, with the joys of life waiting for him—wine, women, and pillage! But an old fellow at the edge of the grave, why *not* shove him in? Go he must, to-day or to-morrow; and what better place for gray-beards? Now, if ever I should be so mischancy as to last so long as Ghysbrecht did, and have to go on a mule's legs instead of Martin Wittenhaagen's, and a back like this" (striking the wood of his bow), "instead of this" (striking the string), "I'll thank and bless any young fellow who will knock me on the head, as you have done that old shopkeeper; malison on his memory."

"Oh, culpa mea! culpa mea!" cried Gerard, and smote upon his breast.

"Look there!" said Martin to Margaret scornfully, "*he is a priest at heart still;* and when he is not in ire, St. Paul, what a milksop!"

"Tush, Martin!" cried Margaret reproachfully: then she wreathed her arms round Gerard, and comforted him with the double magic of a woman's sense and a woman's voice.

"Sweetheart!" murmured she, "you forget: you went not a step out of the way to harm him, who hunted you to your death. You fled from him. He it was who spurred on you. Then did you strike; but in self-defence and a single blow, and with that which was in your hand. Malice had drawn knife, or struck again and again. How often have men been smitten with staves not one but many blows, yet no lives lost! If, then, your enemy has fallen, it is through his own malice, not yours, and by the will of God."

"Bless you, Margaret; bless you for thinking so!"

2   "Yes; but, beloved one, if you have had the *misfortune*

to kill that wicked man, the more need is there that you fly with haste from Holland. Oh, let us on."

"Nay, Margaret," said Gerard. "I fear not man's vengeance, thanks to Martin here and this thick wood: only Him I fear whose eye pierces the forest, and reads the heart of man. If I but struck in self-defence, 'tis well; but if in hate, He may bid the avenger of blood follow me to Italy—to Italy? ay, to earth's remotest bounds."

"Hush!" said Martin peevishly. "I can't hear for your chat."

"What is it?"

"Do you hear nothing, Margaret; my ears are getting old."

Margaret listened, and presently she heard a tuneful sound, like a single stroke upon a deep ringing bell. She described it so to Martin.

"Nay, I heard it," said he.

"And so did I," said Gerard; "it was beautiful. Ah! there it is again. How sweetly it blends with the air. It is a long way off. It is before us, is it not?"

"No, no! the echoes of this wood confound the ear of a stranger. It comes from the pine grove."

"What! the one we passed?"

"The one we passed."

"Why, Martin, is this *anything*? You look pale."

"Wonderful!" said Martin, with a sickly sneer. "He asks me is it *anything*? Come, on, on! at anyrate, let us reach a better place than this."

"A better place—for what?"

"To stand at bay, Gerard," said Martin gravely; "and die like soldiers, killing three for one."

"What's that sound?"

"IT IS THE AVENGER OF BLOOD."

"Oh, Martin, save him! Oh, Heaven be merciful! What new mysterious peril is this?"

"GIRL, IT'S A BLOODHOUND."

CHAPTER XX.

THE courage, like the talent, of common men runs in a narrow groove. Take them but an inch out of that, and they are done. Martin's courage was perfect as far as it went. He had met and baffled many dangers in the course of his rude life, and these familiar dangers he could face with Spartan fortitude, almost with indifference; but he had never been hunted by a bloodhound, nor had he ever seen that brute's unerring instinct baffled by human cunning. Here then a sense of the supernatural combined with novelty to unsteel his heart. After going a few steps, he leaned on his bow, and energy and hope oozed out of him. Gerard, to whom the danger appeared slight in proportion as it was distant, urged him to flight.

"What avails it?" said Martin sadly; "if we get clear of the wood we shall die cheap; here, hard by, I know a place where we may die dear."

"Alas! good Martin," cried Gerard, "despair not so quickly; there must be some way to escape."

"Oh, Martin!" cried Margaret, "what if we were to part company? Gerard's life alone is forfeit. Is there no way to draw the pursuit on us twain and let him go safe?"

"Girl, you know not the bloodhound's nature. He is not on this man's track or that; he is on the track of blood. My life on't they have taken him to where Ghysbrecht fell, and from the dead man's blood to the man that shed it that cursed hound will lead them, though Gerard should run through an army or swim the Meuse." And again he leaned upon his bow, and his head sank.

The hound's mellow voice rang through the wood.

> "A cry more tunable
> Was never hallooed to, nor cheered with horn,
> In Crete, in Sparta, or in Thessaly."

Strange that things beautiful should be terrible and deadly. The eye of the boa-constrictor, while fascinating its prey, is lovely. No royal crown holds such a jewel; it is a ruby with the emerald's green light playing ever upon it. Yet the deer that sees it loses all power of motion, and trembles, and awaits his death; and even so, to compare hearing with sight, this sweet and mellow sound seemed to fascinate Martin Wittenhaagen. He stood uncertain, bewildered, and unnerved. Gerard was little better now Martin's last words had daunted him. He had struck an old man and shed his blood, and, by means of that very blood, blood's four-footed avenger was on his track. Was not the finger of Heaven in this?

Whilst the men were thus benumbed, the woman's brain was all activity. The man she loved was in danger.

"Lend me your knife," said she to Martin. He gave it her.

"But 'twill be little use in your hands," said he.

Then Margaret did a sly thing. She stepped behind Gerard, and furtively drew the knife across her arm, and made it bleed freely; then stooping, smeared her hose and shoes; and still as the blood trickled she smeared them; but so adroitly that neither Gerard nor Martin saw. Then she seized the soldier's arm.

"Come, be a man!" she said, "and let this end. Take us to some thick place, where numbers will not avail our foes."

"I am going," said Martin sulkily. "Hurry avails not; we cannot shun the hound, and the place is hard by;" then turning to the left, he led the way, as men go to execution.

He soon brought them to a thick hazel coppice, like the one that had favoured their escape in the morning.

"There," said he, "this is but a furlong broad, but it will serve our turn."

"What are we to do?"

"Get through this, and wait on the other side; then as they come straggling through, shoot three, knock two on the head, and the rest will kill us."

"Is that all you can think of?" said Gerard.

"That is all."

"Then, Martin Wittenhaagen, I take the lead; for you have lost your head. Come, can you obey so young a man as I am?"

"Oh yes, Martin," cried Margaret, "do not gainsay Gerard. He is wiser than his years."

Martin yielded a sullen assent.

"Do then as you see me do," said Gerard; and drawing his huge knife, he cut at every step a hazel shoot or two close by the ground, and, turning round, twisted them breast-high behind him among the standing shoots. Martin did the same, but with a dogged, hopeless air. When they had thus painfully travelled through the greater part of the coppice, the bloodhound's deep bay came nearer and nearer, less and less musical, louder and sterner.

Margaret trembled.

Martin went down on his stomach and listened.

"I hear a horse's feet."

"No," said Gerard; "I doubt it is a mule's. That cursed Ghysbrecht is still alive: none other would follow me up so bitterly."

"Never strike your enemy but to slay him," said Martin gloomily.

"I'll hit harder this time, if Heaven gives me the chance," said Gerard.

At last they worked through the coppice, and there was an open wood. The trees were large, but far apart, and no escape possible that way.

And now with the hound's bay mingled a score of voices, hooping and hallooing.

"The whole village is out after us," said Martin.

"I care not," said Gerard. "Listen, Martin. I have made the track smooth to the dog, but rough to the men, that we may deal with them apart. Thus the hound will gain on the men, and as soon as he comes out of the coppice we must kill him."

"The hound? There are more than one."

"I hear but one."

"Ay! but one speaks, the others run mute; but let the leading hound lose the scent, then another shall give tongue. There will be two dogs, at least, or devils in dogs' hides."

"Then we must kill two instead of one. The moment they are dead, into the coppice again, and go right back."

"That is a good thought, Gerard," said Martin, plucking up heart.

"Hush! the men are in the wood."

Gerard now gave his orders in a whisper.

"Stand you with your bow by the side of the coppice — there, in the ditch. I will go but a few yards to yon oak-tree, and hide behind it; the dogs will follow me, and, as they come out, shoot as many as you can, the rest will I brain as they come round the tree."

Martin's eye flashed. They took up their places.

The hooping and hallooing came closer and closer, and soon even the rustling of the young wood was heard, and every now and then the unerring bloodhound gave a single bay.

It was terrible! the branches rustling nearer and nearer, and the inevitable struggle for life and death coming on minute by minute, and that death-knell leading it. A trembling hand was laid on Gerard's shoulder. It made him start violently, strung up as he was.

"Martin says if we are forced to part company, make for that high ash-tree we came in by."

"Yes! yes! yes! but go back, for Heaven's sake! don't come here, all out in the open!"

She ran back towards Martin; but, ere she could get to him, suddenly a huge dog burst out of the coppice, and stood erect a moment. Margaret cowered with fear, but he never noticed her. Scent was to him what sight is to us. He lowered his nose an instant, and the next moment, with an awful yell, sprang straight at Gerard's tree, and rolled head-over-heels dead as a stone, literally spitted by an arrow from the bow that twanged beside the coppice in Martin's hand. That same moment out came another hound and smelt his dead comrade. Gerard rushed out at him; but ere he could use his cudgel, a streak of white lightning seemed to strike the hound, and he grovelled in the dust, wounded desperately, but not killed, and howling piteously.

Gerard had not time to despatch him: the coppice rustled too near: it seemed alive. Pointing wildly to Martin to go back, Gerard ran a few yards to the right, then crept cautiously into the thick coppice just as three men burst out. These had headed their comrades considerably: the rest were following at various distances. Gerard crawled back almost on all-fours. Instinct taught Martin and Margaret to do the same upon their line of retreat. Thus, within the distance of a few yards, the pursuers and pursued were passing one another upon opposite tracks.

A loud cry announced the discovery of the dead and the wounded hound. Then followed a babble of voices, still swelling as fresh pursuers reached the spot. The hunters, as usual on a surprise, were wasting time, and the hunted ones were making the most of it.

"I hear no more hounds," whispered Martin to Margaret, and he was himself again.

It was Margaret's turn to tremble and despair.

"Oh, why did we part with Gerard? They will kill my Gerard, and I not near him."

"Nay, nay! the head to catch him is not on their shoulders. You bade him meet us at the ash-tree?"

"And so I did. Bless you, Martin, for thinking of that. To the ash-tree!"

"Ay! but with less noise."

They were now nearly at the edge of the coppice, when suddenly they heard hooping and hallooing behind them. The men had satisfied themselves the fugitives were in the coppice, and were beating back.

"No matter," whispered Martin to his trembling companion. "We shall have time to win clear and slip out of sight by hard running. Ah!"

He stooped suddenly; for just as he was going to burst out of the brushwood, his eye caught a figure keeping sentinel. It was Ghysbrecht Van Swieten seated on his mule; a bloody bandage was across his nose, the bridge of which was broken; but over this his eyes peered keenly, and it was plain by their expression he had heard the fugitives rustle, and was looking out for them. Martin muttered a terrible oath, and cautiously strung his bow, then with equal caution fitted his last arrow to the string. Margaret put her hands to her face, but said nothing. She saw this man must die or Gerard. After the first impulse she peered through her fingers, her heart panting to her throat.

The bow was raised, and the deadly arrow steadily drawn to its head, when at that moment an active figure leaped on Ghysbrecht from behind so swiftly, it was like a hawk swooping on a pigeon. A kerchief went over the burgomaster, in a turn of the hand his head was muffled in it, and he was whirled from his seat and fell heavily upon the ground, where he lay groaning with terror; and Gerard jumped down after him.

"Hist, Martin! Martin!"

Martin and Margaret came out, the former openmouthed, crying, "Now fly! fly! while they are all in the thicket; we are saved."

At this crisis, when safety seemed at hand, as fate would have it, Margaret, who had borne up so bravely till now, began to succumb, partly from loss of blood.

"Oh, my beloved, fly!" she gasped. "Leave me, for I am faint."

"No! no!" cried Gerard. "Death together, or safety. Ah! the mule: mount her, you, and I'll run by your side."

In a moment Martin was on Ghysbrecht's mule, and Gerard raised the fainting girl in his arms and placed her on the saddle, and relieved Martin of his bow.

"Help! treason! murder! murder!" shrieked Ghysbrecht, suddenly rising on his hams.

"Silence, cur," roared Gerard, and trode him down again by the throat as men crush an adder.

"Now, have you got her firm? Then fly! for our lives! for our lives!"

But even as the mule, urged suddenly by Martin's heel, scattered the flints with his hind hoofs ere he got into a canter, and even as Gerard withdrew his foot from Ghysbrecht's throat to run, Dierich Brower and his five men, who had come back for orders, and heard the burgomaster's cries, burst roaring out of the coppice on them.

CHAPTER XXI

SPEECH is the familiar vent of human thoughts: but there are emotions so simple and overpowering, that they rush out not in words, but in eloquent sounds. At such moments man seems to lose his characteristics, and to be merely one of the higher animals; for these, when greatly agitated, ejaculate, though they cannot speak.

There was something terrible, and truly animal, both in the roar of triumph with which the pursuers burst out of the thicket on our fugitives, and the sharp cry of terror with which these latter darted away. The pursuers' hands clutched the empty air, scarce two feet behind them, as they fled for life. Confused for a moment, like lions that miss their spring, Dierich and his men let Gerard and the mule put ten yards between them. Then they flew after with uplifted weapons. They were sure of catching them; for this was not the first time the parties had measured speed. In the open ground they had gained visibly on the three this morning, and now, at last, it was a fair race again, to be settled by speed alone. A hundred yards were covered in no time. Yet still there remained these ten yards between the pursuers and the pursued.

This increase of speed since the morning puzzled Dierich Brower. The reason was this. When three run in company, the pace is that of the slowest of the three. From Peter's house to the edge of the forest Gerard ran Margaret's pace; but now he ran his own; for the mule was fleet, and could have left them all far behind. Moreover, youth and chaste living began to tell. Daylight grew imperceptibly between the hunted ones and the hunters. Then Dierich made a desperate effort, and gained two yards; but in a few seconds Gerard had stolen them quietly back. The pursuers began to curse.

Martin heard, and his face lighted up. "Courage, Gerard! courage, brave lad! they are straggling."

It was so. Dierich was now headed by one of his men, and another dropped into the rear altogether.

They came to a rising-ground, not sharp, but long; and here youth, and grit, and sober living told more than ever.

Ere he reached the top, Dierich's forty years weighed him down like forty bullets. "Our cake is dough," he gasped. "Take him dead, if you can't alive;" and he left running, and followed at a foot's pace. Jorian Ketel tailed off next; and then another, and so, one by one, Gerard ran them all to a standstill, except one who kept on staunch as a blood-hound, though losing ground every minute. His name, if I am not mistaken, was Eric Wouverman. Followed by him, they came to a rise in the wood, shorter, but much steeper than the last.

"Hand on mane!" cried Martin.

Gerard obeyed, and the mule helped him up the hill faster even than he was running before.

At the sight of this manœuvre Dierich's man lost heart; and, being now full eighty yards behind Gerard, and rather more than that in advance of his nearest comrade, he pulled up short, and, in obedience to Dierich's order, took down his crossbow, levelled it deliberately, and just as the trio were sinking out of sight over the crest of the hill, sent the bolt whizzing among them.

There was a cry of dismay; and, next moment, as if a thunderbolt had fallen on them, they were all lying on the ground, mule and all.

CHAPTER XXII.

THE effect was so sudden and magical, that the shooter himself was stupefied for an instant. Then he hailed his companions to join him in effecting the capture, and himself set off up the hill; but, ere he had got half way, up rose the figure of Martin Wittenhaagen with a bent bow in his hand.

Eric Wouverman no sooner saw him in this attitude than he darted behind a tree, and made himself as small as possible. Martin's skill with that weapon was well known, and the slain dog was a keen reminder of it.

Wouverman peered round the bark cautiously: there was the arrow's point still aimed at him. He saw it shine. He dared not move from his shelter.

When he had been at peep-bo some minutes, his companions came up in great force.

Then, with a scornful laugh, Martin vanished, and presently was heard to ride off on the mule.

All the men ran up together. The high ground commanded a view of a narrow but almost interminable glade.

They saw Gerard and Margaret running along at a prodigious distance; they looked like gnats; and Martin galloping after them *ventre à terre*.

The hunters were outwitted as well as outrun. A few words will explain Martin's conduct. We arrive at causes by noting coincidences; yet, now and then, coincidences are deceitful. As we have all seen a hare tumble over a briar just as the gun went off, and so raise expectations, then dash them to earth by scudding away untouched, so the burgomaster's mule put her foot in a rabbit-hole at or about the time the crossbow bolt whizzed innocuous over her head: she fell and threw both her riders. Gerard caught Margaret, but was carried down by her weight and impetus; and, behold, the soil was strewed with dramatis personæ.

The docile mule was up again directly, and stood trembling. Martin was next, and, looking round, saw there was but one in pursuit; on this he made the young lovers fly on foot, while he checked the enemy as I have recorded.

He now galloped after his companions, and when after a long race he caught them, he instantly put Gerard and Margaret on the mule, and ran by their side till his breath failed, then took his turn to ride, and so in rotation. Thus the runner was always fresh, and long ere they relaxed their speed all sound and trace of them was hopelessly lost to Dierich and his men. These latter went crestfallen back to look after their chief and their winged bloodhound.

CHAPTER XXIII.

LIFE and liberty, while safe, are little thought of : for why ? they are matters of course. Endangered, they are rated at their real value. In this, too, they are like sunshine, whose beauty men notice not at noon when it is greatest, but towards evening when it lies in flakes of topaz under shady elms. Yet it is feebler then ; but gloom lies beside it, and contrast reveals its fire. Thus Gerard and Margaret, though they started at every leaf that rustled louder than its fellows, glowed all over with joy and thankfulness as they glided among the friendly trees in safety and deep tranquil silence, baying dogs and brutal voices yet ringing in their mind's ears.

But presently Gerard found stains of blood on Margaret's ankles.

" Martin ! Martin ! help ! they have wounded her : the crossbow ! "

" No, no ! " said Margaret, smiling to reassure him ; " I am not wounded, nor hurt at all."

" But what is it, then, in Heaven's name ? " cried Gerard, in great agitation.

" Scold me not, then ! " and Margaret blushed.

" Did I ever scold you ? "

" No, dear Gerard. Well, then, Martin said it was blood those cruel dogs followed ; so I thought if I could but have a little blood on my shoon, the dogs would follow me instead, and let my Gerard wend free. So I scratched my arm with Martin's knive—forgive me ! Whose else could I take ? Yours, Gerard ? Ah, no. You forgive me ? " said she beseechingly, and lovingly, and fawningly, all in one.

" Let me see this scratch first," said Gerard, choking with emotion. " There, I thought so. A scratch ? I call it a cut—a deep, terrible, cruel cut."

Gerard shuddered at sight of it.

" She might have done it with her bodkin," said the soldier. " Milksop ! that sickens at sight of a scratch and a little blood."

" No, no. I could look on a sea of blood, but not on hers. Oh, Margaret ! how could you be so cruel ? "

Margaret smiled with love ineffable. " Foolish Gerard," murmured she, " to make so much of nothing." And she flung the guilty arm round his neck. "As if I would not give all the blood in my heart for you, let alone a few drops from my arm." And with this, under the sense of his recent danger, she wept on his neck for pity and love: and he wept with her.

"And I must part from her," he sobbed; "we two that love so dear—one must be in Holland, one in Italy. Ah me! ah me! ah me!"

At this Margaret wept afresh, but patiently and silently. Instinct is never off its guard, and with her unselfishness was an instinct. To utter her present thoughts would be to add to Gerard's misery at parting, so she wept in silence.

Suddenly they emerged upon a beaten path, and Martin stopped.

"This is the bridle-road I spoke of," said he, hanging his head; "and there away lies the hostelry."

Margaret and Gerard cast a scared look at one another.

"Come a step with me, Martin," whispered Gerard. When he had drawn him aside, he said to him in a broken voice, "Good Martin, watch over her for me! She is my wife; yet I leave her. See, Martin! here is gold—it was for my journey; it is no use my asking her to take it—she would not; but you will for her, will you not? Oh, Heaven! and is this all I can do for her? Money? But poverty is a curse. You will not let her want for anything, dear Martin? The burgomaster's silver is enough for me."

"Thou art a good lad, Gerard. Neither want nor harm shall come to her. I care more for her little finger than for all the world; and were she nought to me, even for thy sake would I be a father to her. Go with a stout heart, and God be with thee going and coming." And the rough soldier wrung Gerard's hand, and turned his head away, with unwonted feeling.

After a moment's silence he was for going back to Margaret; but Gerard stopped him. "No, good Martin; prithee, stay here behind this thicket, and turn your head away from us, while I—oh, Martin! Martin!"

By this means Gerard escaped a witness of his anguish at leaving her he loved, and Martin escaped a piteous sight. He did not see the poor young things kneel and renew before Heaven those holy vows cruel men had interrupted. He did not see them cling together like one, and then try to part, and fail, and return to one another, and cling again, like drowning, despairing creatures. But he heard Gerard sob and sob, and Margaret moan.

At last there was a hoarse cry, and feet pattered on the hard road.

He started up, and there was Gerard running wildly, with both hands clasped above his head, in prayer, and Margaret tottering back towards him with palms extended piteously, as if for help, and ashy cheek and eyes fixed on vacancy.

He caught her in his arms, and spoke words of comfort to her; but her mind could not take them in; only at the sound of his voice she moaned and held him tight, and trembled violently.

He got her on the mule, and put his arm round her, and so, supporting her frame, which, from being strung like a bow, had now turned all relaxed and powerless, he took her slowly and sadly home.

She did not shed one tear, nor speak one word.

At the edge of the wood, he took her off the mule, and bade her go across to her father's house. She did as she was bid.

Martin to Rotterdam. Sevenbergen was too hot for him.

Gerard, severed from her he loved, went like one in a dream. He hired a horse and a guide at the little hostelry, and rode swiftly towards the German frontier. But all was mechanical; his senses felt blunted; trees and houses and men moved by him like objects seen through a veil. His companion spoke to him twice, but he did not answer. Only once he cried out savagely, "Shall we never be out of this hateful country?"

After many hours' riding they came to the brow of a steep hill; a small brook ran at the bottom.

"Halt!" cried the guide, and pointed across the valley. "Here is Germany."

"Where?"

"On t'other side of the bourn. No need to ride down he hill, I trow."

Gerard dismounted without a word, and took the burgomaster's purse from his girdle: while he opened it, "You will soon be out of this hateful country," said his guide, half sulkily; "mayhap the one you are going to will like you no better: anyway, though it be a church you have robbed, they cannot take you, once across that bourn."

These words at another time would have earned the speaker an admonition or a cuff. They fell on Gerard now like idle air. He paid the lad in silence, and descended the hill alone. The brook was silvery; it ran murmuring over little pebbles that glittered, varnished by the clear water; he sat down and looked stupidly at them. Then he drank of the brook; then he laved his hot feet and hands in it; it was very cold: it waked him. He rose, and, taking a run, leaped across it into Germany. Even as he touched the strange, land he turned suddenly and looked back. "Farewell, ungrateful country!" he cried. "But for *her* it would cost me nought to leave you for ever, and all my kith and kin, and—the mother that bore me, and—my playmates, and my little native town. Farewell, fatherland—welcome the wide world! omne solum for—ti p—p—at—ri—a." And with these brave words in his mouth he drooped suddenly with arms and legs all weak, and sat down and sobbed bitterly upon the foreign soil.

When the young exile had sat a while bowed down, he rose and dashed the tears from his eyes like a man; and, not casting a single glance more behind him, to weaken his heart, stepped out into the wide world.

His love and heavy sorrow left no room in him for vulgar misgivings. Compared with rending himself from Margaret, it seemed a small thing to go on foot to Italy in that rude age.

All nations meet in a convent. So, thanks to his good friends the monks, and his own thirst of knowledge, he could speak most of the languages needed on that long road. He said to himself, "I will soon be at Rome: the sooner the better now."

After walking a good league, he came to a place where four ways met. Being country roads, and serpentine, they had puzzled many an inexperienced neighbour passing from village to village. Gerard took out a little dial Peter had given him, and set it in the autumn sun, and by this compass steered unhesitatingly for Rome—inexperienced as a young swallow flying south; but, unlike the swallow, wandering south alone.

CHAPTER XXIV.

Not far on this road he came upon a little group. Two men in sober suits stood leaning lazily on each side of a horse, talking to one another. The rider, in a silk doublet and bright green jerkin and hose, both of English cloth, glossy as a mole, lay flat on his stomach in the afternoon sun, and looked an enormous lizard. His velvet cloak (flaming yellow) was carefully spread over the horse's loins.

"Is aught amiss?" inquired Gerard.

"Not that I wot of," replied one of the servants.

"But your master, he lies like a corpse. Are ye not ashamed to let him grovel on the ground?"

"Go to; the bare ground is the best cure for his disorder. If you get sober in bed, it gives you a headache; but you leap up from the hard ground like a lark in spring. Eh, Ulric?"

"He speaks sooth, young man," said Ulric warmly.

"What, is the gentleman drunk?"

The servants burst into a hoarse laugh at the simplicity of Gerard's question. But suddenly Ulric stopped, and, eyeing him all over, said very gravely, "Who are you, and where born, that know not the Count is ever drunk at this hour?" And Gerard found himself a suspected character.

"I am a stranger," said he, "but a true man, and one that loves knowledge; therefore ask I questions, and not for love of prying."

"If you be a true man," said Ulric shrewdly, "then give us trinkgeld for the knowledge we have given you."

Gerard looked blank, but putting a good face on it, said, "Trinkgeld you shall have, such as my lean purse can spare, an' if you will tell me why ye have ta'en his cloak from the man and laid it on the beast:"

Under the inspiring influence of coming trinkgeld, two solutions were instantly offered Gerard at once: the one was, that should the Count come to himself (which, being a seasoned toper, he was apt to do all in a minute), and find his horse standing sweating in the cold, while a cloak lay idle at hand, he would fall to cursing, and peradventure to laying on; the other, more pretentious, was, that a horse is a poor milksop, which, drinking nothing but water, has to be cockered up and warmed outside; but a master, being a creature ever filled with good beer, has a store of inward heat that warms him to the skin, and renders a cloak a mere shred of idle vanity.

Each of the speakers fell in love with his theory, and, to tell the truth, both had taken a hair or two of the dog that had bitten their master to the brain: so their voices presently rose so high, that the green sot began to growl instead of snoring. In their heat they did not notice this.

Ere long the argument took a turn that sooner or later was pretty sure to enliven a discussion in that age. Hans, holding the bridle with his right hand, gave Ulric a sound cuff with his left; Ulric returned it with interest, his right hand being free; and at it they went, ding dong, over the horse's mane, pommelling one another, and jagging the poor beast, till he ran backward, and trode with iron heel upon a promontory of the green lord; he, like the toad stung by Ithuriel's spear, started up howling, with one hand clapped to the smart and the other tugging at his hilt. The servants, amazed with terror, let the horse go; he galloped off whinnying, the men in pursuit of him crying out with fear, and the green noble after them, volleying curses, his naked sword in his hand, and his body rebounding from hedge to hedge in his headlong but zigzag career down the narrow lane.

"In which hurtling" Gerard turned his back on them all, and went calmly south, glad to have saved the four tin farthings he had got ready for trinkgeld, but far too heavy-hearted even to smile at their drunken extravagance.

The sun was nearly setting, and Gerard, who had now for some time been hoping in vain to find an inn by the way, was very ill at ease. To make matters worse, black clouds gathered over the sky.

Gerard quickened his pace almost to a run.

It was in vain: down came the rain in torrents, drenched the bewildered traveller, and seemed to extinguish the very sun—for his rays, already fading, could not cope with this new assailant. Gerard trudged on, dark, and wet, and in an unknown region. "Fool! to leave Margaret," said he.

Presently the darkness thickened.

He was entering a great wood. Huge branches shot across the narrow road, and the benighted stranger groped his way in what seemed an interminable and inky cave with a rugged floor, on which he stumbled and stumbled as he went.

On, and on, and on, with shivering limbs, and empty stomach, and fainting heart, till the wolves rose from their lairs and bayed all round the wood.

His hair bristled; but he grasped his cudgel, and prepared to sell his life dear.

There was no wind; and his excited ear heard light feet patter at times over the newly fallen leaves, and low branches rustle with creatures gliding swiftly past them.

Presently in the sea of ink there was a great fiery star close to the ground. He hailed it as he would his patron saint. "CANDLE! a CANDLE!" he shouted, and tried to run; but the dark and rugged way soon stopped that. The light was more distant than he had thought. But at last, in the very heart of the forest, he found a house, with lighted candles and loud voices inside it. He looked up to see if there was a sign-board. There was none. "Not an inn, after all," said he sadly. "No matter; what Christian would turn a dog out into this wood to-night?" and with this he made for the door that led to the voices. He opened it slowly, and put his head in timidly. He drew it out abruptly, as if slapped in the face, and recoiled into the rain and darkness.

He had peeped into a large but low room, the middle of which was filled by a huge round stove, or clay oven, that reached to the ceiling; round this wet clothes were drying—some on lines, and some more compendiously, on rustics. These latter habiliments, impregnated with the wet of the day, but the dirt of a life, and lined with what another foot traveller in these parts calls "rammish clowns," evolved rank vapours and compound odours inexpressible, in steaming clouds.

In one corner was a travelling family, a large one: thence flowed into the common stock the peculiar sickly smell of neglected brats. Garlic filled up the interstices of the air. And all this with closed window, and intense heat of the central furnace, and the breath of at least forty persons.

They had just supped.

Now Gerard, like most artists, had sensitive organs, and the potent effluvia struck dismay into him. But the rain lashed him outside, and the light and the fire tempted him in.

He could not force his way all at once through the
palpable perfumes ; but he returned to the light again and
again, like the singed moth. At last he discovered that
the various smells did not entirely mix, no fiend being
there to stir them round. Odour of family predominated
in two corners ; stewed rustic reigned supreme in the
centre ; and garlic in the noisy group by the window. He
found, too, by hasty analysis, that of these the garlic
described the smallest aërial orbit, and the scent of reeking rustic darted farthest—a flavour as if ancient goats,
or the fathers of all foxes, had been drawn through a
river, and were here dried by Nebuchadnezzar.

So Gerard crept into a corner close to the door. But
though the solidity of the main fetors isolated them somewhat, the heat and reeking vapours circulated, and made
the walls drip : and the home-nurtured novice found something like a cold snake wind about his legs, and his head
turn to a great lump of lead ; and next, he felt like choking,
sweetly slumbering, and dying, all in one.

He was within an ace of swooning, but recovered to a
deep sense of disgust and discouragement ; and settled to
go back to Holland at peep of day. This resolution formed,
he plucked up a little heart ; and, being faint with hunger,
asked one of the men of garlic whether this was not an inn
after all ?

"Whence come you, who know not 'The Star of the
Forest'?" was the reply.

"I am a stranger ; and in my country inns have aye a
sign."

"Droll country yours ! What need of a sign to a public-
house—a place that every soul knows?"

Gerard was too tired and faint for the labour of argument ; so he turned the conversation, and asked where he
could find the landlord.

At this fresh display of ignorance, the native's contempt
rose too high for words. He pointed to a middle-aged
woman seated on the other side of the oven ; and, turning
to his mates, let them know what an outlandish animal
was in the room. Thereat the loud voices stopped, one by
one, as the information penetrated the mass ; and each
eye turned, as on a pivot, following Gerard and his every
movement, silently and zoologically.

The landlady sat on a chair an inch or two higher than
the rest, between two bundles. From the first, a huge

heap of feathers and wings, she was taking the downy plumes, and pulling the others from the quills, and so filling bundle two — littering the floor ankle-deep, and contributing to the general stock a stuffy little malaria, which might have played a distinguished part in a sweet room, but went for nothing here. Gerard asked her if he could have something to eat.

She opened her eyes with astonishment. "Supper is over this hour and more."

"But I had none of it, good dame."

"Is that my fault? You were welcome to your share for me."

"But I was benighted, and a stranger; and belated sore against my will."

"What have I to do with that? All the world knows 'The Star of the Forest' sups from six till eight. Come before six, ye sup well; come before eight, ye sup as pleases Heaven; come after eight, ye get a clean bed, and a stirrup cup, or a horn of kine's milk, at the dawning."

Gerard looked blank. "May I go to bed, then, dame?" said he sulkily; "for it is ill sitting up wet and fasting, and the byword saith, 'He sups who sleeps.'"

"The beds are not come yet," replied the landlady. "You will sleep when the rest do. Inns are not built for *one*."

It was Gerard's turn to be astonished. "The beds were not come! what, in Heaven's name, did she mean?" But he was afraid to ask; for every word he had spoken hitherto had amazed the assembly, and zoological eyes were upon him—he felt them. He leaned against the wall, and sighed audibly.

At this fresh zoological trait, a titter went round the watchful company.

"So this is Germany," thought Gerard; "and Germany is a great country by Holland. Small nations for me."

He consoled himself by reflecting it was to be his last, as well as his first, night in the land. His reverie was interrupted by an elbow driven into his ribs. He turned sharp on his assailant, who pointed across the room. Gerard looked, and a woman in the corner was beckoning him. He went towards her gingerly, being surprised and irresolute, so that to a spectator her beckoning finger seemed to be pulling him across the floor with a gut-line.

When he had got up to her, "Hold the child," said she, in a fine hearty voice; and in a moment she plumped the bairn into Gerard's arms.

He stood transfixed, jelly of lead in his hands, and sudden horror in his elongated countenance.

At this ruefully expressive face, the lynx-eyed conclave laughed loud and long.

"Never heed them," said the woman cheerfully; "they know no better; how should they, bred an' born in a wood?" She was rummaging among her clothes with the two penetrating hands, one of which Gerard had set free. Presently she fished out a small tin plate and a dried pudding; and resuming her child with one arm, held them forth to Gerard with the other, keeping a thumb on the pudding to prevent it from slipping off.

"Put it in the stove," said she; "you are too young to lie down fasting."

Gerard thanked her warmly. But on his way to the stove, his eye fell on the landlady. "*May* I, dame?" said he beseechingly.

"Why not?" said she.

The question was evidently another surprise, though less startling than its predecessors.

Coming to the stove, Gerard found the oven door obstructed by "the rammish clowns." They did not budge. He hesitated a moment. The landlady saw, calmly put down her work, and coming up, pulled a hircine man or two hither, and pushed a hircine man or two thither, with the impassive countenance of a housewife moving her furniture. "Turn about is fair play," she said; "ye have been dry this ten minutes and better."

Her experienced eye was not deceived; Gorgonii had done stewing, and begun baking. Debarred the stove, they trundled home, all but one, who stood like a table, where the landlady had moved him to, like a table. And Gerard baked his pudding; and getting to the stove, burst into steam.

The door opened, and in flew a bundle of straw.

It was hurled by a hind with a pitchfork. Another and another came flying after it, till the room was like a clean farm-yard. These were then dispersed round the stove in layers, like the seats in an arena, and in a moment the company was all on its back.

The beds had come.

Gerard took out his pudding, and found it delicious. While he was relishing it, the woman who had given it him, and who was now abed, beckoned him again. He went to her bundle side. "She is waiting for you," whispered the woman. Gerard returned to the stove, and gobbled the rest of his sausage, casting uneasy glances at the landlady, seated silent as fate amid the prostrate multitude. The food bolted, he went to her, and said, "Thank you kindly, dame, for waiting for me."

"You are welcome," said she calmly, making neither much nor little of the favour; and with that began to gather up the feathers. But Gerard stopped her. "Nay, that is my task;" and he went down on his knees, and collected them with ardour. She watched him demurely.

"I wot not whence ye come," said she, with a relic of distrust; adding, more cordially, "but ye have been well brought up; y' have had a good mother, I'll go bail."

At the door she committed the whole company to Heaven, in a formula, and disappeared. Gerard to his straw in the very corner—for the guests lay round the sacred stove by seniority, *i.e.*, priority of arrival.

This punishment was a boon to Gerard; for thus he lay on the shore of odour and stifling heat, instead of in mid-ocean.

He was just dropping off, when he was awakened by a noise; and lo! there was the hind remorselessly shaking and waking guest after guest, to ask him whether it was he who had picked up the mistress's feathers.

"It was I," cried Gerard.

"Oh, it was you, was it?" said the other, and came striding rapidly over the intermediate sleepers. "She bade me say, 'One good turn deserves another,' and so here's your night-cap," and he thrust a great oaken mug under Gerard's nose.

"I thank her, and bless her: here goes—ugh!" and his gratitude ended in a wry face; for the beer was muddy, and had a strange, medicinal twang new to the Hollander.

"Trinke aus!" shouted the hind reproachfully.

"Enow is as good as a feast," said the youth Jesuitically.

The hind cast a look of pity on this stranger who left liquor in his mug. "Ich brings euch," said he, and drained it to the bottom.

And now Gerard turned his face to the wall, and pulled

up two handfuls of the nice clean straw, and bored in them with his finger, and so made a scabbard, and sheathed his nose in it. And soon they were all asleep; men, maids, wives, and children, all lying higgledy-piggledy, and snoring in a dozen keys like an orchestra slowly tuning; and Gerard's body lay on straw in Germany, and his spirit was away to Sevenbergen.

When he woke in the morning, he found nearly all his fellow-passengers gone. One or two were waiting for dinner, nine o'clock; it was now six. He paid the landlady her demand, two pfenning, or about an English halfpenny, and he of the pitchfork demanded trinkgeld, and getting a trifle more than usual, and seeing Gerard eye a foaming milk-pail he had just brought from the cow, hoisted it up bodily to his lips. "Drink your fill, man," said he, and on Gerard offering to pay for the delicious draught, told him in broad patois that a man might swallow a skinful of milk, or a breakfast of air, without putting hand to pouch. At the door Gerard found his benefactress of last night, and a huge-chested artisan, her husband.

Gerard thanked her, and in the spirit of the age offered her a creutzer for her pudding.

But she repulsed his hand quietly. "For what do you take me?" said she, colouring faintly; "we are travellers and strangers the same as you, and bound to feel for those in like plight."

Then Gerard blushed in his turn and stammered excuses.

The hulking husband grinned superior to them both.

"Give the vixen a kiss for her pudding, and cry quits," said he, with an air impartial, judge-like and Jove-like.

Gerard obeyed the lofty behest, and kissed the wife's cheek. "A blessing go with you both, good people," said he.

"And God speed you, young man!" replied the honest couple; and with that they parted, and never met again in this world.

The sun had just risen: the raindrops on the leaves glittered like diamonds. The air was fresh and bracing, and Gerard steered south, and did not even remember his resolve of overnight.

Eight leagues he walked that day, and in the afternoon

came upon a huge building with an enormous arched gateway and a postern by its side.

"A monastery!" cried he joyfully; "I go no farther lest I fare worse." He applied at the postern, and on stating whence he came and whither bound, was instantly admitted and directed to the guest chamber, a large and lofty room, where travellers were fed and lodged gratis by the charity of the monastic orders. Soon the bell tinkled for vespers, and Gerard entered the church of the convent, and from his place heard a service sung so exquisitely, it seemed the choir of heaven. But one thing was wanting, Margaret was not there to hear it with him, and this made him sigh bitterly in mid-rapture. At supper, plain but wholesome and abundant food, and good beer, brewed in the convent, were set before him and his fellows, and at an early hour they were ushered into a large dormitory, and, the number being moderate, had each a truckle bed, and for covering, sheepskins dressed with the fleece on; but previously to this a monk, struck by his youth and beauty, questioned him, and soon drew out his projects and his heart. When he was found to be convent bred, and going alone to Rome, he became a personage, and in the morning they showed him over the convent, and made him stay and dine in the refectory. They also pricked him a route on a slip of parchment; and the prior gave him a silver guilden to help him on the road, and advised him to join the first honest company he should fall in with, "and not face alone the manifold perils of the way."

"Perils?" said Gerard to himself.

That evening he came to a small straggling town where was one inn; it had no sign; but being now better versed in the customs of the country, he detected it at once by the coats of arms on its walls. These belonged to the distinguished visitors who had slept in it at different epochs since its foundation, and left these customary tokens of their patronage. At present it looked more like a mausoleum than a hotel. Nothing moved nor sounded either in it or about it. Gerard hammered on the great oak door: no answer. He hallooed: no reply. After a while he hallooed louder, and at last a little round window, or rather hole in the wall, opened, a man's head protruded cautiously, like a tortoise's from its shell, and eyed Gerard stolidly, but never uttered a syllable.

"Is this an inn?" asked Gerard, with a covert sneer.

The head seemed to fall into a brown study; eventually it nodded, but lazily.

"Can I have entertainment here?"

Again the head pondered and ended by nodding, but sullenly, and seemed a skull overburdened with catch-penny interrogatories.

"How am I to get within, an't please you?"

At this the head popped in, as if the last question had shot it; and a hand popped out, pointed round the corner of the building, and slammed the window.

Gerard followed the indication, and after some research discovered that the fortification had one vulnerable part, a small low door on its flank. As for the main entrance, that was used to keep out thieves and customers, except once or twice in a year, when they entered together, *i.e.*, when some duke or count arrived in pomp with his train of gaudy ruffians.

Gerard, having penetrated the outer fort, soon found his way to the stove (as the public room was called from the principal article in it), and sat down near the oven, in which were only a few live embers that diffused a mild and grateful heat.

After waiting patiently a long time, he asked a grim old fellow with a long white beard, who stalked solemnly in, and turned the hour-glass, and then was stalking out, when supper would be. The grisly Ganymede counted the guests on his fingers—"When I see thrice as many here as now." Gerard groaned.

The grisly tyrant resented the rebellious sound. "Inns are not built for one," said he; "if you can't wait for the rest, look out for another lodging."

Gerard sighed.

At this the graybeard frowned.

After a while company trickled steadily in, till full eighty persons of various conditions were congregated, and to our novice the place became a chamber of horrors; for here the mothers got together and compared ringworms, and the men scraped the mud off their shoes with their knives and left it on the floor, and combed their long hair out, inmates included, and made their toilet, consisting generally of a dry rub. Water, however, was brought in ewers. Gerard pounced on one of these, but at sight of the liquid contents

"Gerard struck at him with all his heart." *Page* 102.

lost his temper, and said to the waiter, "Wash you first your water, and then a man may wash his hands withal."

"An it likes you not, seek another inn !"

Gerard said nothing, but went quietly, and courteously besought an old traveller to tell him how far it was to the next inn.

"About four leagues."

Then Gerard appreciated the grim pleasantry of th' unbending sire.

That worthy now returned with an armful of wood, and counting the travellers, put on a log for every six, by which act of raw justice the hotter the room the more heat he added. Poor Gerard noticed this little flaw in the ancient man's logic, but carefully suppressed every symptom of intelligence, lest his feet should have to carry his brains four leagues farther that night.

When perspiration and suffocation were far advanced, they brought in the tablecloths ; but oh, so brown, so dirty, and so coarse ; they seemed like sacks that had been worn out in agriculture and come down to this, or like shreds from the mainsail of some worn-out ship. The Hollander, who had never seen such linen even in nightmare, uttered a faint cry.

"What is to do ?" inquired a traveller. Gerard pointed ruefully to the dirty sackcloth. The other looked at it with lack lustre eye, and comprehended nought.

A Burgundian soldier with his arbalest at his back came peeping over Gerard's shoulder, and, seeing what was amiss, laughed so loud that the room rang again ; then slapped him on the back and cried, " Courage ! le diable est mort."

Gerard stared : he doubted alike the good tidings and their relevancy ; but the tones were so hearty, and the arbalestrier's face, notwithstanding a formidable beard, was so gay and genial that he smiled, and after a pause said drily, " Il a bien fait : avec l'eau et linge du pays on allait le noircir à ne se reconnaître plus."

"Tiens, tiens !" cried the soldier, " v'là qui parle le Français, peu s'en faut," and he seated himself by Gerard, and in a moment was talking volubly of war, women, and pillage, interlarding his discourse with curious oaths, at which Gerard drew away from him more or less.

E Presently in came the grisly servant, and counted them

all on his fingers superciliously, like Abraham telling sheep ; then went out again, and returned with a deal trencher and deal spoon to each.

Then there was an interval. Then he brought them a long mug apiece made of glass, and frowned. By and by he stalked gloomily in with a hunch of bread apiece, and exit with an injured air. Expectations thus raised, the guests sat for nearly an hour balancing the wooden spoons, and with their own knives whittling the bread. Eventually, when hope was extinct, patience worn out, and hunger exhausted, a huge vessel was brought in with pomp, the lid was removed, a cloud of steam rolled forth, and behold some thin broth with square pieces of bread floating. This, though not agreeable to the mind, served to distend the body. Slices of Strasbourg ham followed, and pieces of salt fish, both so highly salted that Gerard could hardly swallow a mouthful. Then came a kind of gruel, and, when the repast had lasted an hour and more, some hashed meat highly peppered ; and the French and Dutch being now full to the brim with the above dainties, and the draughts of beer the salt and spiced meats had provoked, in came roasted kids, most excellent, and carp and trout fresh from the stream. Gerard made an effort and looked angrily at them, but "could no more," as the poets say. The Burgundian swore by the liver and spike-staff of the good centurion the natives had outwitted him. Then turning to Gerard he said, " Courage, l'ami, le diable est mort," as loudly as before, but not with the same tone of conviction. The canny natives had kept an internal corner for contingencies, and polished the kids' very bones.

The feast ended with a dish of raw animalcula in a wicker cage. A cheese had been surrounded with little twigs and strings ; then a hole made in it and a little sour wine poured in. This speedily bred a small but numerous vermin. When the cheese was so rotten with them that only the twigs and string kept it from tumbling to pieces and walking off quadrivious, it came to table. By a malicious caprice of fate, cage and menagerie were put down right under the Dutchman's organ of self-torture. He recoiled with a loud ejaculation, and hung to the bench by the calves of his legs.

" What is the matter ? " said a traveller disdainfully. " Does the good cheese scare ye ? Then put it hither, in the name of all the saints ! "

"Cheese!" cried Gerard, "I see none. These nauseous reptiles have made away with every bit of it."

"Well," replied another, "it is not gone far. By eating of the mites we eat the cheese to boot."

"Nay, not so," said Gerard. "These reptiles are made like us, and digest their food and turn it to foul flesh even as we do ours to sweet: as well might you think to chew grass by eating of grass-fed beeves, as to eat cheese by swallowing these uncleanly insects."

Gerard raised his voice in uttering this, and the company received the paradox in dead silence, and with a distrustful air, like any other stranger, during which the Burgundian, who understood German but imperfectly, made Gerard Gallicise the discussion. He patted his interpreter on the back. "C'est bien, mon gars : plus fin que toi n'est pas bête," and administered his formula of encouragement ; and Gerard edged away from him ; for next to ugly sights and ill odours, the poor wretch disliked profaneness.

Meantime, though shaken in argument, the raw reptiles were duly eaten and relished by the company, and served to provoke thirst—a principal aim of all the solids in that part of Germany. So now the company drank *garausses* all round, and their tongues were unloosed, and oh, the Babel ! But above the fierce clamour rose at intervals, like some hero's war-cry in battle, the trumpet-like voice of the Burgundian soldier shouting lustily, "Courage, camarades, le diable est mort !"

Entered grisly Ganymede holding in his hand a wooden dish with circles and semicircles marked on it in chalk. He put it down on the table and stood silent, sad, and sombre, as Charon by Styx waiting for his boatload of souls. Then pouches and purses were rummaged, and each threw a coin into the dish. Gerard timidly observed that he had drunk next to no beer, and inquired how much less he was to pay than the others.

"What mean you?" said Ganymede roughly. "Whose fault is it you have not drunken? Are all to suffer because one chooses to be a milksop? You will pay no more than the rest, and no less."

Gerard was abashed.

"Courage, petit, le diable est mort," hiccoughed the soldier, and flung Ganymede a coin.

"You are as bad as he is," said the old man peevishly ;

"you are paying too much;" and the tyrannical old Aristides returned him some coin out of the trencher with a most reproachful countenance. And now the man whom Gerard had confuted an hour and a half ago awoke from a brown study, in which he had been ever since, and came to him and said, "*Yes;* but the honey is none the worse for passing through the bees' bellies."

Gerard stared. The answer had been so long on the road he hadn't an idea what it was an answer to. Seeing him dumbfoundered, the other concluded him confuted, and withdrew calmed.

The bedrooms were upstairs, dungeons with not a scrap of furniture except the bed, and a male servant settled inexorably who should sleep with whom. Neither money nor prayers would get a man a bed to himself here; custom forbade it sternly. You might as well have asked to monopolise a see-saw. They assigned to Gerard a man with a great black beard. He was an honest fellow enough, but not perfect; he would *not* go to bed, and *would* sit on the edge of it telling the wretched Gerard by force, and at length, the events of the day, and alternately laughing and crying at the same circumstances, which were not in the smallest degree pathetic or humorous, but only dead trivial. At last Gerard put his fingers in his ears, and lying down in his clothes, for the sheets were too dirty for him to undress, contrived to sleep. But in an hour or two he awoke cold, and found that his drunken companion had got all the feather bed; so mighty is instinct. They lay between two beds; the lower one hard and made of straw, the upper soft and filled with feathers light as down. Gerard pulled at it, but the experienced drunkard held it fast mechanically. Gerard tried to twitch it away by surprise, but instinct was too many for him. On this he got out of bed, and kneeling down on his bedfellow's unguarded side, easily whipped the prize away and rolled with it under the bed, and there lay on one edge of it, and curled the rest round his shoulders. Before he slept he often heard something grumbling and growling above him, which was some little satisfaction. Thus Instinct was outwitted, and victorious Reason lay chuckling on feathers, and not quite choked with dust.

At peep of day Gerard rose, flung the feather bed upon his snoring companion, and went in search of milk and air.

A cheerful voice hailed him in French : "What ho! you are up with the sun, comrade."

"He rises betimes that lies in a dog's lair," answered Gerard crossly.

"Courage, l'ami! le diable est mort," was the instant reply. The soldier then told him his name was Denys, and he was passing from Flushing in Zealand to the Duke's French dominions ; a change the more agreeable to him, as he should revisit his native place, and a host of pretty girls who had wept at his departure, and should hear French spoken again. "And who are you, and whither bound?"

"My name is Gerard, and I am going to Rome," said the more reserved Hollander, and in a way that invited no further confidences.

"All the better; we will go together as far as Burgundy."

"That is not my road."

"All roads take to Rome."

"Ay, but the shortest road thither is my way."

"Well, then, it is I who must go out of my way a step for the sake of good company, for thy face likes me, and thou speakest French, or nearly."

"There go two words to that bargain," said Gerard coldly. "I steer by proverbs too. They do put old heads on young men's shoulders. 'Bon loup mauvais compagnon, dit le brebis ;' and a soldier, they say, is near akin to a wolf."

"They lie," said Denys ; "besides, if he is, 'les loups ne se mangent pas entre eux.'"

"Ay, but, sir soldier, I am not a wolf; and thou knowest, 'à bien petite occasion se saisit le loup du mouton.'"

"Let us drop wolves and sheep, being men ; my meaning is, that a good soldier never pillages—a comrade. Come, young man, too much suspicion becomes not your years. They who travel should learn to read faces ; methinks you might see lealty in mine sith I have seen it in yourn. Is it yon fat purse at your girdle you fear for?" (Gerard turned pale.) "Look hither!" and he undid his belt, and poured out of it a double handful of gold pieces, then returned them to their hiding-place. "There is a hostage for you," said he ; "carry you that, and let us be comrades," and handed him his belt, gold and all.

Gerard stared. "If I am over prudent, you have not

enow." But he flushed, and looked pleased at the other's trust in him.

"Bah! I can read faces; and so must you, or you'll never take your four bones safe to Rome."

"Soldier, you would find me a dull companion, for my heart is very heavy," said Gerard, yielding.

"I'll cheer you, mon gars."

"I think you would," said Gerard sweetly; "and sore need have I of a kindly voice in mine ear this day."

"Oh! no soul is sad alongside me. I lift up their poor little hearts with my consigne: 'Courage, tout le monde, le diable est mort.' Ha! ha!"

"So be it, then," said Gerard. "But take back your belt, for I could never trust by halves. We will go together as far as Rhine, and God go with us both!"

"Amen!" said Denys, and lifted his cap. "En avant!"

The pair trudged manfully on, and Denys enlivened the weary way. He chatted about battles and sieges, and things which were new to Gerard; and he was one of those who *make* little incidents wherever they go. He passed nobody without addressing him. "They don't understand it, but it wakes them up," said he. But whenever they fell in with a monk or priest, he pulled a long face, and sought the reverend father's blessing, and fearlessly poured out on him floods of German words in such order as not to produce a single German sentence. He doffed his cap to every woman, high or low, he caught sight of, and with eagle eye discerned her best feature, and complimented her on it in his native tongue, well adapted to such matters; and at each carrion crow or magpie, down came his cross-bow, and he would go a furlong off the road to circumvent it; and indeed he did shoot one old crow with laudable neatness and despatch, and carried it to the nearest hen-roost, and there slipped in and set it upon a nest. "The good-wife will say, 'Alack, here is Beelzebub ahatching of my eggs.'"

"No, you forget he is dead," objected Gerard.

"So he is, so he is. But she doesn't know that, not having the luck to be acquainted with me, who carry the good news from city to city, uplifting men's hearts."

Such was Denys in time of peace.

Our travellers towards nightfall reached a village: it was a very small one, but contained a place of entertainment.

They searched for it, and found a small house with barn and stables. In the former was the everlasting stove, and the clothes drying round it on lines, and a traveller or two sitting morose. Gerard asked for supper.

"Supper? We have no time to cook for travellers; we only provide lodging, good lodging for man and beast. You can have some beer."

"Madman, who, born in Holland, sought other lands!" snorted Gerard in Dutch. The landlady started.

"What gibberish is that?" asked she, and crossed herself with looks of superstitious alarm. "You can buy what you like in the village, and cook it in our oven; but, prithee, mutter no charms nor sorceries here, good man; don't ye now, it do make my flesh creep so."

They scoured the village for food, and ended by supping on roasted eggs and brown bread.

At a very early hour their chambermaid came for them. It was a rosy-cheeked old fellow with a lanthorn.

They followed him. He led them across a dirty farm-yard, where they had much ado to pick their steps, and brought them into a cow-house. There, on each side of every cow, was laid a little clean straw, and a tied bundle of ditto for a pillow. The old man looked down on this his work with paternal pride. Not so Gerard. "What, do you set Christian men to lie among cattle?"

"Well, it is hard upon the poor beasts. They have scarce room to turn."

"Oh! what, it is not hard on us then?"

"Where is the hardship? I have lain among them all my life. Look at me! I am four score, and never had a headache in all my born days—all along of lying among the kye. Bless your silly head, kine's breath is ten times sweeter to drink nor Christians'. You try it!" and he slammed the bedroom door.

"Denys, where are you?" whined Gerard.

"Here, on her other side."

"What are you doing?"

"I know not; but, as near as I can guess, I think I must be going to sleep. What are you at?"

"I am saying my prayers."

"Forget me not in them!"

"Is it likely? Denys, I shall soon have done: do not go to sleep, I want to talk."

"Despatch then! for I feel—augh—like—floating in the sky—on a warm cloud."

"Denys!"

"Augh! eh! hollo! is it time to get up?"

"Alack, no. There, I hurried my orisons to talk; and look at you, going to sleep! We shall be starved before morning, having no coverlets."

"Well, you know what to do."

"Not I, in sooth."

"Cuddle the cow."

"Thank you."

"Burrow in the straw then. You must be very new to the world to grumble at this. How would you bear to lie on the field of battle on a frosty night, as I did t'other day, stark naked, with nothing to keep me warm but the carcass of a fellow I had been and helped kill?"

"Horrible! horrible! Tell me all about it! Oh, but this is sweet."

"Well, we had a little battle in Brabant, and won a little victory, but it cost us dear; several arbalestriers turned their toes up, and I among them."

"Killed, Denys? come now!"

"Dead as mutton. Stuck full of pike-holes till the blood ran out of me, like the good wine of Mâcon from the trodden grapes. It is right bounteous in me to pour the tale in minstrel phrase, for—augh—I am sleepy. Augh—now where was I?"

"Left dead on the field of battle, bleeding like a pig; that is to say, like grapes, or something; go on, prithee go on, 'tis a sin to sleep in the midst of a good story."

"Granted. Well, some of those vagabonds, that strip the dead soldier on the field of glory, came and took every rag off me; they wrought me no further ill, because there was no need."

"No; you were dead."

"C'est convenu. This must have been at sundown; and with the night came a shrewd frost that barkened the blood on my wounds, and stopped all the rivulets that were running from my heart, and about midnight I awoke as from a trance."

"And thought you were in heaven?" asked Gerard eagerly, being a youth inoculated with monkish tales.

"Too frost-bitten for that, mon gars; besides, I heard the wounded groaning on all sides, so I knew I was in the old place. I saw I could not live the night through without cover. I groped about shivering and shivering; at last one did suddenly leave groaning. 'You are sped,' said I, so made up to him, and true enough he was dead, but warm, you know. I took my lord in my arms, but was too weak to carry him, so rolled with him into a ditch hard by; and there my comrades found me in the morning properly stung with nettles, and hugging a dead Fleming for the bare life."

Gerard shuddered. "And this is war; this is the chosen theme of poets and troubadours, and Reden Ryckers. Truly was it said by the men of old, *dulce bellum inexpertis.*"

"Tu dis?"

"I say—oh, what stout hearts some men have!"

"N'est-ce pas, p'tit? So after that sort—thing—this sort thing is heaven. Soft—warm—good company, comradancow—cou'age—diable—m—ornk!"

And the glib tongue was still for some hours.

In the morning Gerard was wakened by a liquid hitting his eye, and it was Denys employing the cow's udder as a squirt.

"Oh, fie!" cried Gerard, "to waste the good milk;" and he took a horn out of his wallet. "Fill this! but indeed I see not what right we have to meddle with her milk at all."

"Make your mind easy! Last night la camarade was not nice; but what then, true friendship dispenses with ceremony. To-day we make as free with her."

"Why, what did she do, poor thing?"

"Ate my pillow."

"Ha! ha!"

"On waking I had to hunt for my head, and found it down in the stable gutter. She ate our pillow from us, we drink our pillow from her. A votre santé, madame; et sans rancune;" and the dog drank her milk to her own health.

"The ancient was right, though," said Gerard. "Never have I risen so refreshed since I left my native land. Henceforth let us shun great towns, and still lie in a convent or a cowhouse; for I'd liever sleep on fresh straw, than on linen well washed six months agone; and the breath of kine it is sweeter than that of Christians, let alone the garlic, which men and women folk affect, but cowen abhor from, and so do I, St. Bavon be my witness!"

2   The soldier eyed him from head to foot: "Now but for

that little tuft on your chin I should take you for a girl ; and by the finger-nails of St. Luke, no ill-favoured one neither."

These three towns proved types and repeated themselves with slight variations for many a weary league ; but even when he could get neither a convent nor a cowhouse, Gerard learned in time to steel himself to the inevitable, and to emulate his comrade, whom he looked on as almost superhuman for hardihood of body and spirit.

There was, however, a balance to all this veneration.

Denys, like his predecessor Achilles, had his weak part, his very weak part, thought Gerard.

His foible was "woman."

Whatever he was saying or doing, he stopped short at sight of a farthingale, and his whole soul became occupied with that garment and its inmate till they had disappeared ; and sometimes for a good while after.

He often put Gerard to the blush by talking his amazing German to such females as he caught standing or sitting indoors or out, at which they stared ; and when he met a peasant girl on the road, he took off his cap to her and saluted her as if she was a queen ; the invariable effect of which was, that she suddenly drew herself up quite stiff like a soldier on parade, and wore a forbidding countenance.

"They drive me to despair," said Denys. "Is that a just return to a civil bonnetade ? They are large, they are fair, but stupid as swans."

"What breeding can you expect from women that wear no hose ? " inquired Gerard ; "and some of them no shoon? They seem to me reserved and modest, as becomes their sex, and sober, whereas the men are little better than beer-barrels. Would you have them brazen as well as hoseless ? "

"A little affability adorns even beauty," sighed Denys.

"Then let them alone, sith they are not to your taste," retorted Gerard. "What, is there no sweet face in Burgundy that would pale to see you so wrapped up in strange women ? "

"Half a dozen that would cry their eyes out."

"Well then ! "

"But it is a long way to Burgundy."

"Ay, to the foot, but not to the heart. I am there, sleeping and waking, and almost every minute of the day."

"In Burgundy ? Why, I thought you had never——"

"In Burgundy?" cried Gerard contemptuously. "No, in sweet Sevenbergen. Ah! well-a-day! well-a-day!"

Many such dialogues as this passed between the pair on the long and weary road, and neither could change the other.

One day about noon they reached a town of some pretensions, and Gerard was glad, for he wanted to buy a pair of shoes; his own were quite worn out. They soon found a shop that displayed a goodly array, and made up to it, and would have entered it, but the shopkeeper sat on the door-step taking a nap, and was so fat as to block up the narrow doorway; the very light could hardly struggle past his "too, too solid flesh," much less a carnal customer.

My fair readers, accustomed, when they go shopping, to be met half way with nods, and becks, and wreathed smiles, and waved into a seat, while almost at the same instant an eager shopman flings himself half across the counter in a semicircle to learn their commands, can best appreciate this mediæval Teuton, who kept a shop as a dog keeps a kennel, and sat at the exclusion of custom snoring like a pig.

Denys and Gerard stood and contemplated this curiosity; emblem, permit me to remark, of the lets and hindrances to commerce that characterised his epoch.

"Jump over him!"

"The door is too low."

"March through him!"

"The man is too thick."

"What is the coil?" inquired a mumbling voice from the interior; apprentice with his mouth full.

"We want to get into your shop."

"What for, in Heaven's name??!!!"

"Shoon, lazy bones!"

The ire of the apprentice began to rise at such an explanation. "And could ye find no hour out of all the twelve to come pestering us for shoon, but the one little, little hour my master takes his nap, and I sit down to my dinner, when all the rest of the world is full long ago?"

Denys heard, but could not follow the sense. "Waste no more time talking their German gibberish," said he; "take out thy knife and tickle his fat ribs."

"That will I not," said Gerard.

'Then here goes: I'll prong him with this."

Gerard seized the mad fellow's arm in dismay, for he had been long enough in the country to guess that the whole town would take part in any brawl with the native against a stranger. But Denys twisted away from him, and the cross-bow bolt in his hand was actually on the road to the sleeper's ribs; but at that very moment two females crossed the road towards him; he saw the blissful vision, and instantly forgot what he was about, and awaited their approach with unreasonable joy.

Though companions, they were not equals, except in attractiveness to a Burgundian cross-bow man; for one was very tall, the other short, and, by one of those anomalies which society, however primitive, speedily establishes, the long one held up the little one's tail. The tall one wore a plain linen coif on her head, a little grogram cloak over her shoulders, a gray kirtle, and a short farthingale or petticoat of bright red cloth, and feet and legs quite bare, though her arms were veiled in tight linen sleeves.

The other a kirtle broadly trimmed with fur, her arms in double sleeves, whereof the inner of yellow satin clung to the skin; the outer, all befurred, were open at the inside of the elbow, and so the arm passed through and left them dangling. Velvet head-dress, huge purse at girdle, gorgeous train, bare legs. And thus they came on, the citizen's wife strutting, and the maid gliding after, holding her mistress's train devoutly in both hands, and bending and winding her lithe body prettily enough to do it. Imagine (if not pressed for time) a bantam, with a guinea-hen stepping obsequious at its stately heel.

This pageant made straight for the shoemaker's shop. Denys louted low: the worshipful lady nodded graciously, but rapidly, having business on hand, or rather on foot; for in a moment she poked the point of her little shoe into the sleeper, and worked it round in him like a gimlet, till with a long snarl he woke. The incarnate shutter rising and grumbling vaguely, the lady swept in and deigned him no further notice. He retreated to his neighbour's shop, the tailor's, and sitting on the step, protected it from the impertinence of morning calls. Neighbours should be neighbourly.

Denys and Gerard followed the dignity into the shop, where sat the apprentice at dinner; the maid stood outside with her insteps crossed, leaning against the wall, and tapping it with her nails.

"Those, yonder," said the dignity briefly, pointing with an imperious little white hand to some yellow shoes gilded at the toe. While the apprentice stood stock still, neutralised by his dinner and his duty, Denys sprang at the shoes, and brought them to her; she smiled, and calmly seating herself, protruded her foot, shod, but hoseless, and scented. Down went Denys on his knees, and drew off her shoe, and tried the new ones on the white skin devoutly. Finding she had a willing victim, she abused the opportunity, tried first one pair and then another, then the first again, and so on, balancing and hesitating for about half an hour, to Gerard's disgust, and Denys's weak delight. At last she was fitted, and handed two pair of yellow and one pair of red shoes out to her servant. Then was heard a sigh. It burst from the owner of the shop : he had risen from slumber, and was now hovering about, like a partridge near her brood in danger. "There go all my coloured shoes," said he, as they disappeared in the girl's apron.

The lady departed : Gerard fitted himself with a stout pair, asked the price, paid it without a word, and gave his old ones to a beggar in the street, who blessed him in the market-place, and threw them furiously down a well in the suburbs. The comrades left the shop, and in it two melancholy men, that looked, and even talked, as if they had been robbed wholesale.

"My shoon are sore worn," said Denys, grinding his teeth : "but I'll go barefoot till I reach France, ere I'll leave my money with such churls as these."

The Dutchman replied calmly, "They seem indifferent well sewn."

As they drew near the Rhine, they passed through forest after forest, and now for the first time ugly words sounded in travellers' mouths, seated around stoves. "Thieves !" "black gangs !" "cut-throats !" etc.

The very rustics were said to have a custom hereabouts of murdering the unwary traveller in these gloomy woods, whose dark and devious windings enabled those who were familiar with them to do deeds of rapine and blood undetected, or, if detected, easily to baffle pursuit.

Certain it was, that every clown they met, carried, whether for offence or defence, a most formidable weapon ; a light axe with a short pike at the head, and a long slender handle of ash or yew, well seasoned. These the natives could all throw with singular precision, so as to make the point strike an object at several yards' distance, or could slay a bullock at hand with a stroke of the blade. Gerard bought one and practised with it. Denys quietly filed and ground his bolt sharp, whistling the whilst; and, when they entered a gloomy wood, he would unsling his cross-bow and carry it ready for action; but not so much like a traveller fearing an attack, as a sportsman watchful not to miss a snap shot.

One day, being in a forest a few leagues from Düsseldorf, as Gerard was walking like one in a dream, thinking of Margaret, and scarce seeing the road he trode, his companion laid a hand on his shoulder, and strung his cross-bow with glittering eye. "Hush!" said he, in a low whisper that startled Gerard more than thunder. Gerard grasped his axe tight, and shook a little: he heard a rustling in the wood hard by, and at the same moment Denys sprang into the wood, and his cross-bow went to his shoulder, even as he jumped. Twang! went the metal string; and after an instant's suspense he roared, "Run forward, guard the road, he is hit! he is hit!"

Gerard darted forward, and as he ran a young bear burst out of the wood right upon him; finding itself intercepted, it went upon its hind legs with a snarl, and though not half grown, opened formidable jaws and long claws. Gerard, in a fury of excitement and agitation, flung himself on it, and delivered a tremendous blow on its nose, with his axe, and the creature staggered; another, and it lay grovelling, with Gerard hacking it.

"Hollo! stop! you are mad to spoil the meat."

"I took it for a robber," said Gerard, panting. "I mean, I had made ready for a robber, so I could not hold my hand."

"Ay, these chattering travellers have stuffed your head full of thieves and assassins; they have not got a real live robber in their whole nation. Nay, I'll carry the beast; bear thou my cross-bow."

"We will carry it by turns then," said Gerard, "for 'tis a heavy load: poor thing, how its blood drips. Why did we slay it?"

"For supper and the reward the bailie of the next town shall give us."

"And for that it must die, when it had but just begun to live; and perchance it hath a mother that will miss it sore this night, and loves it as ours love us; more than mine does me."

"What, know you not that his mother was caught in a pitfall last month, and her skin is now at the tanner's? and his father was struck full of cloth-yard shafts t'other day, and died like Julius Cæsar, with his hands folded on his bosom, and a dead dog in each of them?"

But Gerard would not view it jestingly: "Why, then," said he, "we have killed one of God's creatures that was all alone in the world—as I am this day, in this strange land."

"You young milksop," roared Denys, "these things must not be looked at so, or not another bow would be drawn nor quarel fly in forest nor battlefield. Why, one of your kidney consorting with a troop of pikemen should turn them to a row of milk-pails; it is ended, to Rome thou goest not alone, for never wouldst thou reach the Alps in a whole skin. I take thee to Remiremont, my native place, and there I marry thee to my young sister, she is blooming as a peach. Thou shakest thy head? ah! I forgot; thou lovest elsewhere, and art a one-woman man, a creature to me scarce conceivable. Well, then, I shall find thee, not a wife, nor a leman, but a friend; some honest Burgundian who shall go with thee as far as Lyons; and much I doubt that honest fellow will be myself, into whose liquor thou hast dropped sundry powders to make me love thee; for erst I endured not doves in doublet and hose. From Lyons, I say, I can trust thee by ship to Italy, which being by all accounts the very stronghold of milksops, thou wilt there be safe; they will hear thy words, and make thee their duke in a twinkling."

Gerard sighed: "In sooth I love not to think of this Düsseldorf, where we are to part company, good friend."

They walked silently, each thinking of the separation at hand; the thought checked trifling conversation, and at these moments it is a relief to do something, however insignificant. Gerard asks Denys to lend him a bolt. "I have often shot with a long-bow, but never with one of these!"

"Draw thy knife and cut this one out of the cub," said Denys slily.

"Nay, nay, I want a clean one."

Denys gave him three out of his quiver.

Gerard strung the bow, and levelled it at a bough that had fallen into the road at some distance. The power of the instrument surprised him; the short but thick steel bow jarred him to the very heel as it went off, and the swift steel shaft was invisible in its passage; only the dead leaves, with which November had carpeted the narrow road, flew about on the other side of the bough.

"Ye aimed a thought too high," said Denys.

"What a deadly thing! no wonder it is driving out the long-bow—to Martin's much discontent."

"Ay, lad," said Denys triumphantly, "it gains ground every day, in spite of their laws and their proclamations to keep up the yewen bow, because, forsooth, their grandsires shot with it, knowing no better. You see, Gerard, war is not pastime. Men will shoot at their enemies with the hittingest arm and the killingest, not with the longest and missingest."

"Then these new engines I hear of will put both bows down; for these with a pinch of black dust, and a leaden ball, and a child's finger, shall slay you Mars and Goliath, and the Seven Champions."

"Pooh! pooh!" said Denys warmly; "petrone nor harquebuss shall ever put down Sir Arbalest. Why, we can shoot ten times while they are putting their charcoal and their lead into their leathern smoke belchers, and then kindling their matches. All that is too fumbling for the field of battle; there a soldier's weapon needs be aye ready, like his heart."

Gerard did not answer, for his ear was attracted by a sound behind them. It was a peculiar sound, too, like something heavy, but not hard, rushing softly over the dead leaves. He turned round with some little curiosity. A colossal creature was coming down the road at about sixty paces distance.

He looked at it in a sort of calm stupor at first, but the next moment he turned ashy pale.

"Denys!" he cried. "Oh, God! Denys!"

Denys whirled round.

It was a bear as big as a cart-horse.

It was tearing along with its huge head down, running on a hot scent.

The very moment he saw it Denys said in a sickening whisper—

"THE CUB!"

Oh! the concentrated horror of that one word, whispered hoarsely, with dilating eyes! For in that syllable it all flashed upon them both like a sudden stroke of lightning in the dark—the bloody trail, the murdered cub, the mother upon them, *and it.* DEATH.

All this in a moment of time. The next, she saw them. Huge as she was, she seemed to double herself (it was her long hair bristling with rage): she raised her head big as a bull's, her swine-shaped jaws opened wide at them, her eyes turned to blood and flame, and she rushed upon them, scattering the leaves about her like a whirlwind as she came.

"Shoot!" screamed Denys, but Gerard stood shaking from head to foot, useless.

"Shoot, man! ten thousand devils, shoot! too late! Tree! tree!" and he dropped the cub, pushed Gerard across the road, and flew to the first tree and climbed it, Gerard the same on his side; and as they fled, both men uttered inhuman howls like savage creatures grazed by death.

With all their speed one or other would have been torn to fragments at the foot of his tree; but the bear stopped a moment at the cub.

Without taking her bloodshot eyes off those she was hunting, she smelt it all round, and found, how her Creator only knows, that it was dead, quite dead. She gave a yell such as neither of the hunted ones had ever heard, nor dreamed to be in nature, and flew after Denys. She reared and struck at him as he climbed. He was just out of reach.

Instantly she seized the tree, and with her huge teeth tore a great piece out of it with a crash. Then she reared again, dug her claws deep into the bark, and began to mount it slowly, but as surely as a monkey.

Denys's evil star had led him to a dead tree, a mere shaft, and of no very great height. He climbed faster than his pursuer, and was soon at the top. He looked this way and that for some bough of another tree to spring to. There was none; and if he jumped down, he knew the bear would be upon him ere he could recover the fall, and make short work of him. Moreover, Denys was little used to turning his back on danger, and his blood was rising at being hunted. He turned to bay.

"My hour is come," thought he. "Let me meet death like a man." He kneeled down and grasped a small shoot to steady himself, drew his long knife, and clenching his teeth, prepared to job the huge brute as soon as it should mount within reach.

Of this combat the result was not doubtful.

The monster's head and neck were scarce vulnerable for bone and masses of hair. The man was going to sting the bear, and the bear to crack the man like a nut.

Gerard's heart was better than his nerves. He saw his friend's mortal danger, and passed at once from fear to blindish rage. He slipped down his tree in a moment, caught up the cross-bow, which he had dropped in the road, and running furiously up, sent a bolt into the bear's body with a loud shout. The bear gave a snarl of rage and pain, and turned its head irresolutely.

"Keep aloof!" cried Denys, "or you are a dead man."

"I care not;" and in a moment he had another bolt ready and shot it fiercely into the bear, screaming, "Take that! take that!"

Denys poured a volley of oaths down at him. "Get away, idiot!"

He was right: the bear finding so formidable and noisy a foe behind him, slipped growling down the tree, rending deep furrows in it as she slipped. Gerard ran back to his tree and climbed it swiftly. But while his legs were dangling some eight feet from the ground, the bear came rearing and struck with her fore paw, and out flew a piece of bloody cloth from Gerard's hose. He climbed, and climbed; and presently he heard as it were in the air a voice say, "Go out on the bough!" He looked, and there was a long massive branch before him shooting upwards at a slight angle: he threw his body across it, and by a series of convulsive efforts worked up it to the end.

Then he looked round panting.

The bear was mounting the tree on the other side. He heard her claws scrape, and saw her bulge on both sides of the massive tree. Her eye not being very quick, she reached the fork and passed it, mounting the main stem. Gerard drew breath more freely. The bear either heard him, or found by scent she was wrong: she paused; presently she caught sight of him. She eyed him steadily, then quietly descended to the fork.

Slowly and cautiously she stretched out a paw and tried the bough. It was a stiff oak branch, sound as iron.

Instinct taught the creature this: it crawled carefully out on the bough, growling savagely as it came.

Gerard looked wildly down. He was forty feet from the ground. Death below. Death moving slow but sure on him in a still more horrible form. His hair bristled. The sweat poured from him. He sat helpless, fascinated, tongue-tied.

As the fearful monster crawled growling towards him, incongruous thoughts coursed through his mind. Margaret: the Vulgate, where it speaks of the rage of a she-bear robbed of her whelps—Rome—Eternity.

The bear crawled on. And now the stupor of death fell on the doomed man; he saw the open jaws and bloodshot eyes coming, but in a mist.

As in a mist he heard a twang: he glanced down; Denys, white and silent as death, was shooting up at the bear. The bear snarled at the twang, but crawled on. Again the cross-bow twanged, and the bear snarled, and came nearer. Again the cross-bow twanged; and the next moment the bear was close upon Gerard, where he sat, with hair standing stiff on end, and eyes starting from their sockets, palsied. The bear opened her jaws like a grave, and hot blood spouted from them upon Gerard as from a pump. The bough rocked. The wounded monster was reeling; it clung, it stuck its sickles of claws deep into the wood; it toppled, its claws held firm, but its body rolled off, and the sudden shock to the branch shook Gerard forward on his stomach with his face upon one of the bear's straining paws. At this, by a convulsive effort, she raised her head up, up, till he felt her hot fetid breath. Then huge teeth snapped together loudly close below him in the air, with a last effort of baffled hate. The ponderous carcass rent the claws out of the bough, then pounded the earth with a tremendous thump. There was a shout of triumph below, and the very next instant a cry of dismay, for Gerard had swooned, and, without an attempt to save himself, rolled headlong from the perilous height.

CHAPTER XXV.

DENYS caught at Gerard, and somewhat checked his fall; but it may be doubted whether this alone would have saved him from breaking his neck, or a limb. His best friend now was the dying bear, on whose hairy carcass his head and shoulders descended. Denys tore him off her. It was needless. She panted still, and her limbs quivered, but a hare was not so harmless; and soon she breathed her last; and the judicious Denys propped Gerard up against her, being soft, and fanned him. He came to by degrees, but confused, and feeling the bear all around him, rolled away, yelling.

"Courage," cried Denys, "le diable est mort."

"Is it dead? quite dead?" inquired Gerard from behind a tree; for his courage was feverish, and the cold fit was on him just now, and had been for some time.

"Behold," said Denys, and pulled the brute's ear playfully, and opened her jaws and put in his head, with other insulting antics; in the midst of which Gerard was violently sick.

Denys laughed at him.

"What is the matter now?" said he; "also, why tumble off your perch just when we had won the day?"

"I swooned, I trow."

"But *why*?"

Not receiving an answer, he continued, "Green girls faint as soon as look at you, but then they choose time and place. What woman ever fainted up a tree?"

"She sent her nasty blood all over me. I think the smell must have overpowered me. Faugh! I hate blood."

"I do believe it potently."

"See what a mess she has made me!"

"But with her blood, not yours. I pity the enemy that strives to satisfy you."

"You need not to brag, Maître Denys; I saw you under the tree, the colour of your shirt."

"Let us distinguish," said Denys, colouring; "it is permitted to tremble *for a friend*."

Gerard, for answer, flung his arms round Denys's neck in silence.

"Look here," whined the stout soldier, affected by this little gush of nature and youth, "was ever aught so like a woman? I love thee, little milksop—go to. Good! behold him on his knees now. What new caprice is this?"

"Oh, Denys, ought we not to return thanks to Him who has saved both our lives against such fearful odds?" And Gerard kneeled, and prayed aloud. And presently he found Denys kneeling quiet beside him, with his hands across his bosom, after the custom of his nation, and a face as long as his arm. When they rose, Gerard's countenance was beaming.

"Good Denys," said he, "Heaven will reward thy piety."

"Ah, bah! I did it out of politeness," said the Frenchman. "It was to please thee, little one. C'est égal : 'twas well and orderly prayed, and edified me to the core while it lasted. A bishop had scarce handled the matter better; so now our evensong being sung, and the saints enlisted with us—marchons."

Ere they had taken two steps, he stopped. "By the bye, the cub!"

"Oh, no, no!" cried Gerard.

"You are right. It is late. We have lost time climbing trees, and tumbling off 'em, and swooning, and vomiting, and praying; and the brute is heavy to carry. And now I think on't, we shall have papa after it next; these bears make such a coil about an odd cub. What is this? you are wounded! you are wounded!"

"Not I."

"He is wounded: miserable that I am!"

"Be calm, Denys. I am not touched; I feel no pain anywhere."

"You? you only feel when another is hurt," cried Denys, with great emotion; and throwing himself on his knees, he examined Gerard's leg with glistening eyes.

"Quick! quick! before it stiffens," he cried, and hurried him on.

"Who makes the coil about nothing now?" inquired Gerard composedly.

Denys's reply was a very indirect one.

"Be pleased to note," said he, "that I have a bad heart. You were man enough to save my life, yet I must sneer at you, a novice in war. Was not I a novice once myself? Then you fainted from a wound, and I thought you swooned for fear, and called you a milksop. Briefly, I have a bad tongue and a bad heart."

"Denys!"

"Plait-il?"

"You lie."

"You are very good to say so, little one, and I am eternally obliged to you," mumbled the remorseful Denys.

Ere they had walked many furlongs, the muscles of the wounded leg contracted and stiffened, till presently Gerard could only just put his toe to the ground, and that with great pain.

At last he could bear it no longer.

"Let me lie down and die," he groaned, "for this is intolerable."

Denys represented that it was afternoon, and the nights were now frosty; and cold and hunger ill companions; and that it would be unreasonable to lose heart, a certain great personage being notoriously defunct. So Gerard leaned upon his axe, and hobbled on; but presently he gave in, all of a sudden, and sank helpless in the road.

Denys drew him aside into the wood, and to his surprise gave him his cross-bow and bolts, enjoining him strictly to lie quiet, and if any ill-looking fellows should find him out and come to him, to bid them keep aloof; and should they refuse, to shoot them dead at twenty paces. "Honest men keep the path; and, knaves in a wood, none but fools do parley with them." With this he snatched up Gerard's axe, and set off running—not, as Gerard expected, towards Düsseldorf, but on the road they had come.

Gerard lay aching and smarting; and to him Rome, that seemed so near at starting, looked far, far off, now that he was two hundred miles nearer it. But soon all his thoughts turned Sevenbergen-wards. How sweet it would be one day to hold Margaret's hand, and tell her all he had gone through for her! The very thought of it, and her, soothed him; and in the midst of pain and irritation of the nerves he lay resigned, and sweetly, though faintly, smiling.

He had lain thus more than two hours, when suddenly there were shouts; and the next moment something struck a tree hard by, and quivered in it.

He looked, it was an arrow.

He started to his feet. Several missiles rattled among the boughs, and the wood echoed with battle-cries. Whence they came he could not tell, for noises in these huge woods are so reverberated, that a stranger is always at fault as to their whereabout; but they seemed to fill the whole air. Presently there was a lull; then he heard the fierce galloping of hoofs; and still louder shouts and cries arose, mingled with shrieks and groans; and, above all, strange and terrible sounds, like fierce claps of thunder, bellowing loud, and then dying off in cracking echoes; and red tongues of flame shot out ever and anon among the trees, and clouds of sulphurous smoke came drifting over his head. And all was still.

Gerard was struck with awe. "What will become of Denys?" he cried. "Oh, why did you leave me? Oh, Denys, my friend! my friend!"

Just before sunset Denys returned, almost sinking under a hairy bundle. It was the bear's skin.

Gerard welcomed him with a burst of joy that astonished him.

"I thought never to see you again, dear Denys. Were you in the battle?"

"No. What battle?"

"The bloody battle of men, or fiends, that raged in the wood a while agone;" and with this he described it to the life, and more fully than I have done.

Denys patted him indulgently on the back.

"It is well," said he; "thou art a good limner; and fever is a great spur to the imagination. One day I lay in a cart-shed with a cracked skull, and saw two hosts manœuvre and fight a good hour on eight feet square, the which I did fairly describe to my comrade in due order, only not so gorgeously as thou, for want of book learning."

"What, then, you believe me not? when I tell you the arrows whizzed over my head, and the combatants shouted and——"

"May the foul fiends fly away with me if I believe a word of it."

Gerard took his arm and quietly pointed to a tree close by.

"Why, it looks like—it is—a broad arrow, as I live!" And he went close, and looked up at it.

"It came out of the battle. I heard it, and saw it."

"An English arrow."

"How know you that."

"Marry, by its length. The English bowmen draw the bow to the ear, others only to the right breast. Hence the

English loose a three-foot shaft, and this is one of them, perdition seize them! Well, if this is not glamour, there has been a trifle of a battle. And if there has been a battle in so ridiculous a place for a battle as this, why then 'tis no business of mine, for my Duke hath no quarrel hereabouts. So let's to bed," said the professional. And with this he scraped together a heap of leaves, and made Gerard lie on it, his axe by his side. He then lay down beside him, with one hand on his arbalest, and drew the bear-skin over them, hair inward. They were soon as warm as toast, and fast asleep.

But long before the dawn Gerard woke his comrade.

"What shall I do, Denys, I die of famine?"

"Do? why, go to sleep again incontinent: qui dort dîne."

"But I tell you I am too hungry to sleep," snapped Gerard.

"Let us march, then," replied Denys, with paternal indulgence.

He had a brief paroxysm of yawns; then made a small bundle of bear's ears, rolling them up in a strip of the skin, cut for the purpose; and they took the road.

Gerard leaned on his axe, and, propped by Denys on the other side, hobbled along, not without sighs.

"I hate pain," said Gerard viciously.

"Therein you show judgment," replied papa smoothly.

It was a clear, starlight night; and soon the moon rising revealed the end of the wood at no great distance: a pleasant sight, since Düsseldorf they knew was but a short league farther.

At the edge of the wood they came upon something so mysterious that they stopped to gaze at it, before going up to it. Two white pillars rose in the air, distant a few paces from each other; and between them stood many figures, that looked like human forms.

"I go no farther till I know what this is," said Gerard, in an agitated whisper. "Are they effigies of the saints, for men to pray to on the road? or live robbers waiting to shoot down honest travellers? Nay, living men they cannot be, for they stand on nothing that I see. Oh! Denys, let us turn back till daybreak; this is no mortal sight."

Denys halted, and peered long and keenly. "They are men," said he at last. Gerard was for turning back all the more.

"But men that will never hurt us, nor we them. Look not to their feet for that they stand on!"

"Where, then, i' the name of all the saints?"

"Look over their heads," said Denys gravely.

Following this direction, Gerard presently discerned the outline of a dark wooden beam passing from pillar to pillar; and, as the pair got nearer, walking now on tiptoe, one by one dark snake-like cords came out in the moonlight, each pendent from the beam to a dead man, and tight as wire.

Now as they came under this awful monument of crime and wholesale vengeance a light air swept by, and several of the corpses swung, or gently gyrated, and every rope creaked. Gerard shuddered at this ghastly salute. So thoroughly had the gibbet, with its sickening load, seized and held their eyes, that it was but now they perceived a fire right underneath, and a living figure sitting huddled over it. His axe lay beside him, the bright blade shining red in the glow. He was asleep.

Gerard started, but Denys only whispered, "Courage, comrade, here is a fire."

"Ay! but there is a man at it."

"There will soon be three;" and he began to heap some wood on it that the watcher had prepared; during which the prudent Gerard seized the man's axe, and sat down tight on it, grasping his own, and examining the sleeper. There was nothing outwardly distinctive in the man. He wore the dress of the country-folk, and the hat of the district, a three-cornered hat called a Brunswicker, stiff enough to turn a sword cut, and with a thick brass hatband. The weight of the whole thing had turned his ears entirely down, like a fancy rabbit's in our century; but even this, though it spoiled him as a man, was nothing remarkable. They had of late met scores of these dog's-eared rustics. The peculiarity was, this clown watching under a laden gallows. What for?

Denys, if he felt curious, would not show it; he took out two bears' ears from his bundle, and running sticks through them, began to toast them. "'Twill be eating coined money," said he; "for the burgomaster of Düsseldorf had given us a rix-dollar for these ears, as proving the death of their owners; but better a lean purse than a lere stomach."

"Unhappy man!" cried Gerard, "could you eat food *here?*"

"Where the fire is lighted there must the meat roast, and where it roasts there must it be eaten; for nought travels worse than your roasted meat."

"Well, eat thou, Denys, an thou canst! but I am cold and sick; there is no room for hunger in my heart after what mine eyes have seen," and he shuddered over the fire. "Oh! how they creak! and who is this man, I wonder? what an ill-favoured churl!"

Denys examined him like a connoisseur looking at a picture, and in due course delivered judgment. "I take him to be of the refuse of that company, whereof these (pointing carelessly upward) were the cream, and so ran their heads into danger."

"At that rate, why not stun him before he wakes?" and Gerard fidgeted where he sat.

Denys opened his eyes with humorous surprise. "For one who sets up for a milksop you have the readiest hand. Why should two stun one? tush! he wakes: note now what he says at waking, and tell me."

These last words were hardly whispered when the watcher opened his eyes. At sight of the fire made up, and two strangers eyeing him keenly, he stared, and there was a severe and pretty successful effort to be calm: still a perceptible tremor ran all over him. Soon he manned himself, and said gruffly, "Good-morrow." But at the very moment of saying it he missed his axe, and saw how Gerard was sitting upon it, with his own laid ready to his hand. He lost countenance again directly. Denys smiled grimly at this bit of by-play.

"Good-morrow!" said Gerard quietly, keeping his eye on him.

The watcher was now too ill at ease to be silent. "You make free with my fire," said he; but he added in a somewhat faltering voice, "you are welcome."

Denys whispered Gerard. The watcher eyed them askant.

"My comrade says, sith we share your fire, you shall share his meat."

"So be it," said the man warmly. "I have half a kid hanging on a bush hard by, I'll go fetch it;" and he arose with a cheerful and obliging countenance, and was retiring.

Denys caught up his cross-bow, and levelled it at his head. The man fell on his knees.

Denys lowered his weapon, and pointed him back to his

place. He rose and went back slowly and unsteadily, like one disjointed ; and sick at heart as the mouse, that the cat lets go a little way, and then darts and replaces.

"Sit down, friend," said Denys grimly, in French.

The man obeyed finger and tone, though he knew not a word of French.

"Tell him the fire is not big enough for more than three. He will take my meaning."

This being communicated by Gerard, the man grinned ; ever since Denys spoke he had seemed greatly relieved. "I wist not ye were strangers," said he to Gerard.

Denys cut a piece of bear's ear, and offered it with grace to him he had just levelled cross-bow at.

He took it calmly, and drew a piece of bread from his wallet, and divided it with the pair. Nay, more, he winked and thrust his hand into the heap of leaves he sat on (Gerard grasped his axe ready to brain him), and produced a leathern bottle holding full two gallons. He put it to his mouth, and drank their healths, then handed it to Gerard ; he passed it untouched to Denys.

"Mort de ma vie !" cried the soldier, "it is Rhenish wine, and fit for the gullet of an archbishop. Here's to thee, thou prince of good fellows, wishing thee a short life and a merry one ! Come, Gerard, sup ! sup ! Pshaw, never heed them, man ! they heed not thee. Natheless, did I hang over such a skin of Rhenish as this, and three churls sat beneath a-drinking it, and offered me not a drop, I'd soon be down among them."

"Denys ! Denys !"

"My spirit would cut the cord, and womp would come my body amongst ye, with a hand on the bottle, and one eye winking, t'other——"

Gerard started up with a cry of horror and his fingers to his ears, and was running from the place, when his eye fell on the watcher's axe. The tangible danger brought him back. He sat down again on the axe with his fingers in his ears.

"Courage, l'ami, le diable est mort !" shouted Denys gaily, and offered him a piece of bear's ear, put it right under his nose as he stopped his ears. Gerard turned his head away with loathing. "Wine !" he gasped. "Heaven knows I have much need of it, with such companions as thee and——"

He took a long draught of the Rhenish wine : it ran

glowing through his veins, and warmed and strengthened his heart, but could not check his tremors whenever a gust of wind came. As for Denys and the other, they feasted recklessly, and plied the bottle unceasingly, and drank healths and caroused beneath that creaking sepulchre and its ghastly tenants.

"Ask him how they came here," said Denys, with his mouth full, and pointing up without looking.

On this question being interpreted to the watcher, he replied that treason had been their end, diabolical treason and priestcraft. He then, being rendered communicative by drink, delivered a long, prosy narrative, the purport of which was as follows. These honest gentlemen who now dangled here so miserably were all stout men and true, and lived in the forest by their wits. Their independence and thriving state excited the jealousy and hatred of a large portion of mankind, and many attempts were made on their lives and liberties; these the Virgin and their patron saints, coupled with their individual skill and courage, constantly baffled. But yester eve a party of merchants came slowly on their mules from Düsseldorf. The honest men saw them crawling, and let them penetrate near a league into the forest, then set upon them to make them disgorge a portion of their ill-gotten gains. But alas! the merchants were no merchants at all, but soldiers of more than one nation, in the pay of the Archbishop of Cologne: haubergeons had they beneath their gowns, and weapons of all sorts at hand; natheless, the honest men fought stoutly, and pressed the traitors hard, when lo! horsemen, that had been planted in ambush many hours before, galloped up, and with these new diabolical engines of war, shot leaden bullets, and laid many an honest fellow low, and so quelled the courage of others that they yielded them prisoners. These being taken red-handed, the victors, who with malice inconceivable had brought cords knotted round their waists, did speedily hang, and by their side the dead ones, to make the gallanter show. "That one at the end was the captain. He never felt the cord. He was riddled with broad arrows and leaden balls or ever they could take him: a worthy man as ever cried 'Stand and deliver!' but a little hasty, not much: stay! I forgot; he is dead. Very hasty, and obstinate as a pig. That one in the buff jerkin is the lieutenant, as good a soul as ever lived: he was hanged alive. This one here, I never could abide ; no (not that one ; that is Conrad, my bosom friend) ; I mean this one right overhead in the chicken-toed shoon ; you were always carrying tales, ye thief, and making mischief ; you know you were ; and, sirs, I am a man that would rather live united in a coppice than in a forest with backbiters and tale-bearers : strangers, I drink to you." And so he went down the whole string, indicating with the neck of the bottle, like a showman with his pole, and giving a neat description of each, which though pithy was invariably false ; for the showman had no real eye for character, and had misunderstood every one of these people.

"Enough palaver !" cried Denys. "Marchons ! Give me his axe : now tell him he must help you along."

The man's countenance fell, but he saw in Denys's eye that resistance would be dangerous ; he submitted. Gerard it was who objected. He said, "Y pensez-vous ? to put my hand on a thief, it maketh my flesh creep."

"Childishness ! all trades must live. Besides, I have my reasons. Be not you wiser than your elder."

"No. Only if I am to lean on him I must have my hand in my bosom, still grasping the haft of my knife."

"It is a new attitude to walk in ; but please thyself."

And in that strange and mixed attitude of tender offices and deadly suspicion the trio did walk. I wish I could draw them : I would not trust to the pen.

The light of the watch-tower at Düsseldorf was visible as soon as they cleared the wood, and cheered Gerard. When, after an hour's march, the black outline of the tower itself and other buildings stood out clear to the eye, their companion halted and said gloomily, "You may as well slay me out of hand as take me any nearer the gates of Düsseldorf town."

On this being communicated to Denys, he said at once, "Let him go then, for in sooth his neck will be in jeopardy if he wends much farther with us." Gerard acquiesced as a matter of course. His horror of a criminal did not in the least dispose him to active co-operation with the law. But the fact is, that at this epoch no private citizen in any part of Europe ever meddled with criminals but in self-defence, except, by the bye, in England, which, behind other nations in some things, was centuries before them all in this.

The man's personal liberty being restored, he asked

for his axe. It was given him. To the friends' surprise he still lingered. Was he to have nothing for coming so far out of his way with them?

"Here are two batzen, friend."

"And the wine, the good Rhenish?"

"Did you give aught for it?"

"Ay! the peril of my life."

"Hum! what say you, Denys?"

"I say it was worth its weight in gold. Here, lad, here be silver groschen, one for every acorn on that gallows tree; and here is one more for thee, who wilt doubtless be there in due season."

The man took the coins, but still lingered.

"Well! what now?" cried Gerard, who thought him shamefully overpaid already. "Dost seek the hide off our bones?"

"Nay, good sirs, but you have seen to-night how parlous a life is mine. Ye be true men, and your prayers avail; give me then a small trifle of a prayer, an't please you; for I know not one."

Gerard's choler began to rise at the egotistical rogue; moreover, ever since his wound he had felt gusts of irritability. However, he bit his lip and said, "There go two words to that bargain; tell me first, is it true what men say of you Rhenish thieves, that ye do murder innocent and unresisting travellers as well as rob them?"

The other answered sulkily, "They you call thieves are not to blame for that; the fault lies with the law."

"Gramercy! so 'tis the law's fault that ill men break it?"

"I mean not so; but the law in this land slays an honest man if he do but steal. What follows? he would be pitiful, but is discouraged herefrom; pity gains him no pity, and doubles his peril: an he but cut a purse his life is forfeit; therefore cutteth he the throat to boot, to save his own neck. dead men tell no tales. Pray then for the poor soul who by bloody laws is driven to kill or else be slaughtered; were there less of this unreasonable gibbeting on the highroad, there should be less enforced cutting of throats in dark woods, my masters."

"Fewer words had served," replied Gerard coldly. "I asked a question, I am answered," and suddenly doffing his bonnet—

"'Obsecro Deum omnipotentem, ut, quâ cruce jam pendent isti quindecim latrones fures et homicidæ, in eâ homicida fur et latro tu pependeris quam citissime, pro publica salute, in honorem justi Dei cui sit gloria, in æternum, Amen.'"

"And so good-day."

The greedy outlaw was satisfied at last. "That is Latin," he muttered, "and more than I bargained for." So indeed it was.

And he returned to his business with a mind at ease. The friends pondered in silence the many events of the last few hours.

At last Gerard said thoughtfully, "That she-bear saved both our lives—by God's will."

"Like enough," replied Denys; "and talking of that, it was lucky we did not dawdle over our supper."

"What mean you?"

"I mean they are not all hanged; I saw a refuse of seven or eight as black as ink around our fire."

"When? when?"

"Ere we had left it five minutes."

"Good Heavens! and you said not a word."

"It would but have worried you, and had set our friend a-looking back, and mayhap tempted him to get his skull split. All other danger was over; they could not see us, we were out of the moonshine, and indeed, just turning a corner. Ah! there is the sun; and here are the gates of Düsseldorf. Courage, l'ami, le diable est mort!"

"My head! my head!" was all poor Gerard could reply.

So many shocks, emotions, perils, horrors, added to the wound, his first, had tried his youthful body and sensitive nature too severely.

It was noon of the same day.

In a bedroom of "The Silver Lion" the rugged Denys sat anxious, watching his young friend.

And he lay raging with fever, delirious at intervals, and one word for ever on his lips—

"Margaret!—Margaret!—Margaret!"

CHAPTER XXVI.

It was the afternoon of the next day. Gerard was no longer light-headed, but very irritable and full of fancies; and in one of these he begged Denys to get him a lemon to suck. Denys, who from a rough soldier had been turned by tender friendship into a kind of grandfather, got up hastily, and bidding him set his mind at ease, "lemons he should have in the twinkling of a quart pot," went and ransacked the shops for them.

They were not so common in the North as they are now, and he was absent a long while, and Gerard getting very impatient, when at last the door opened. But it was not Denys. Entered softly an imposing figure; an old gentleman in a long sober gown trimmed with rich fur, cherry-coloured hose, and pointed shoes, with a sword by his side in a morocco scabbard, a ruff round his neck not only starched severely, but treacherously stiffened in furrows by rebatoes, or a little hidden framework of wood; and on his head a four-cornered cap with a fur border; on his chin and bosom a majestic white beard. Gerard was in no doubt as to the vocation of his visitor, for, the sword excepted, this was familiar to him as the full dress of a physician. Moreover, a boy followed at his heels with a basket, where phials, lint, and surgical tools rather courted than shunned observation. The old gentleman came softly to the bedside, and said mildly and *sotto voce*, "How is't with thee, my son?"

Gerard answered gratefully that his wound gave him little pain now; but his throat was parched, and his head heavy.

"A wound! they told me not of that. Let me see it. Ay, ay, a good clean bite. The mastiff had sound teeth that took this out, I warrant me;" and the good doctor's sympathy seemed to run off to the quadruped he had conjured, his jackal.

"This must be cauterised forthwith, or we shall have you starting back from water, and turning somersaults in bed under our hands. 'Tis the year for raving curs, and one hath done your business; but we will baffle him yet. Urchin, go heat thine iron."

"But, sir," edged in Gerard, "''twas no dog, but a bear."

"A bear! Young man," remonstrated the senior severely, "think what you say; 'tis ill jesting with the man of art who

PAVLHARDY

"They caroused beneath that creaking sepulchre."

brings his gray hairs and long study to heal you. A bear, quotha! Had you dissected as many bears as I, or the tithe, and drawn their teeth to keep your hand in, you would know that no bear's jaw ever made this foolish, trifling wound. I tell you 'twas a dog, and, since you put me to it, I even deny that it was a dog of magnitude, but neither more nor less than one of these little furious curs that are so rife, and run devious, biting each manly leg, and laying its wearer low, but for me and my learned brethren, who still stay the mischief with knife and cautery."

"Alas, sir! when said I 'twas a bear's jaw; I said, 'A bear:' it was his paw, now."

"And why didst not tell me that at once?"

"Because you kept telling me instead."

"Never conceal aught from your leech, young man," continued the senior, who was a good talker, but one of the worst listeners in Europe. "Well, it is an ill business. All the horny excrescences of animals, to wit, claws of tigers, panthers, badgers, cats, bears, and the like, and horn of deer, and nails of humans, especially children, are imbued with direst poison. Y'had better have been bitten by a cur, *whatever you may say*, than gored by bull or stag, or scratched by bear. However, shalt have a good biting cataplasm for thy leg; meantime keep we the body cool: put out thy tongue!—good!—fever. Let me feel thy pulse: good!—fever. I ordain flebotomy, and on the instant."

"Flebotomy! that is blood-letting: humph! Well, no matter, if 'tis sure to cure me, for I will not lie idle here." The doctor let him know that flebotomy was infallible, especially in this case.

"Hans, go fetch the things needful; and I will entertain the patient meantime with reasons."

The man of art then explained to Gerard that in disease the blood becomes hot and distempered and more or less poisonous; but a portion of this unhealthy liquid removed, Nature is fain to create a purer fluid to fill its place. Bleeding, therefore, being both a cooler and a purifier, was a specific in all diseases, for all diseases were febrile, whatever empirics might say.

"But think not," said he warmly, "that it suffices to bleed; any paltry barber can open a vein (though not all can close it again). The art is to know what vein to
F empty for what disease. T'other day they brought me

one tormented with earache. I let him blood in the right thigh, and away flew his earache. By the bye, he has died since then. Another came with the toothache. I bled him behind the ear, and relieved him in a jiffy. He is also since dead as it happens. I bled our bailiff between the thumb and forefinger for rheumatism. Presently he comes to me with a headache and drumming in the ears, and holds out his hand over the basin; but I smiled at his folly, and bled him in the left ankle sore against his will, and made his head as light as a nut."

Diverging then from the immediate theme after the manner of enthusiasts, the reverend teacher proceeded thus—

"Know, young man, that two schools of art contend at this moment throughout Europe. The Arabian, whose ancient oracles are Avicenna, Rhazes, Albucazis; and its revivers are Chauliac and Lanfranc; and the Greek school, whose modern champions are Bessarion, Platinus, and Marsilius Ficinus, but whose pristine doctors were medicine's very oracles, Phœbus, Chiron, Æsculapius, and his sons Podalinus and Machaon, Pythagoras, Democritus, Praxagoras, who invented the arteries, and Dioctes, *qui primus urinæ animum dedit.* All these taught orally. Then came Hippocrates, the eighteenth from Æsculapius, and of him we have manuscripts; to him we owe 'the vital principle.' He also invented the bandage, and tapped for water on the chest; and above all he dissected; yet only quadrupeds, for the brutal prejudices of the pagan vulgar withheld the human body from the knife of science. Him followed Aristotle, who gave us the aorta, the largest blood-vessel in the human body."

"Surely, sir, the Almighty gave us all that is in our bodies, and not Aristotle, nor any Grecian man," objected Gerard humbly.

"Child! of course He gave us the thing; but Aristotle did more, he gave us the name of the thing. But young men will still be talking. The next great light was Galen; he studied at Alexandria, then the home of science. He, justly malcontent with quadrupeds, dissected apes, as coming nearer to man, and bled like a Trojan. Then came Theophilus, who gave us the nerves, the lacteal vessels, and the pia mater."

This worried Gerard. "I cannot lie still and hear it said that mortal man bestowed the parts which Adam our father took from Him, who made him of the clay, and us his sons."

"Was ever such perversity?" said the doctor, his colour rising. "Who is the real donor of a thing to man? he who plants it secretly in the dark recesses of man's body, or the learned wight who reveals it to his intelligence, and so enriches his mind with the knowledge of it? Comprehension is your only true possession. Are you answered?"

"I am put to silence, sir."

"And that is better still; for garrulous patients are ill to cure, especially in fever: I say, then, that Eristratus gave us the cerebral nerves and the milk vessels; nay, more, he was the inventor of lithotomy, whatever you may say. Then came another whom I forget; you do somewhat perturb me with your petty exceptions. Then came Ammonius, the author of lithotrity, and here comes Hans with the basin—to stay your volubility. Blow thy chafer, boy, and hand me the basin; 'tis well. Arabians, quotha! What are they but a sect of yesterday, who about the year 1000 did fall in with the writings of those very Greeks, and read them awry, having no concurrent light of their own? for their demi-god, and camel-driver, Mahound, impostor in science as in religion, had strictly forbidden them anatomy, even of the lower animals, the which he who severeth from medicine, *tollit solem e mundo*, as Tully quoth. Nay, wonder not at my fervour, good youth; where the general weal stands in jeopardy, a little warmth is civic, humane, and honourable. Now there is settled of late in this town a pestilent Arabist, a mere empiric, who, despising anatomy, and scarce knowing Greek from Hebrew, hath yet spirited away half my patients; and I tremble for the rest. Put forth thine ankle, and thou, Hans, breathe on the chafer."

Whilst matters were in this posture, in came Denys with the lemons, and stood surprised. "What sport is toward?" said he, raising his brows.

Gerard coloured a little, and told him the learned doctor was going to flebotomise him and cauterise him; that was all.

"Ay! indeed; and yon imp, what bloweth he hot coals for?"

"What should it be for," said the doctor to Gerard, "but to cauterise the vein when opened and the poisonous blood let free? 'Tis the only safe way. Avicenna indeed recommends a ligature of the vein: but how 'tis to be done he saith not, nor knew he himself I wot, nor any of the spawn of Ishmael. For me, I have no faith in such tricksy expedients; and take this with you for a safe principle: 'Whatever an Arab or Arabist says is right, must be wrong.'"

"Oh, I see now what 'tis for," said Denys; "and art thou so simple as to let him put hot iron to thy living flesh? didst ever keep thy little finger but ten moments in a candle? and this will be as many minutes. Art not content to burn in purgatory after thy death? must thou needs buy a foretaste on't here?"

"I never thought of that," said Gerard gravely: "the good doctor spake not of burning, but of cautery; to be sure 'tis all one, but cautery sounds not so fearful as burning."

"Imbecile! That is their art; to confound a plain man with dark words, till his hissing flesh lets him know their meaning. Now listen to what I have seen. When a soldier bleeds from a wound in battle, these leeches say, 'Fever. Blood him!' and so they burn the wick at t'other end too. They bleed the bled. Now at fever's heels comes desperate weakness; then the man needs all his blood to live; but these prickers and burners, having no fore-thought, recking nought of what is sure to come in a few hours, and seeing like brute beasts only what is under their noses, have meantime robbed him of the very blood his hurt had spared him to battle that weakness withal; and so he dies exhausted. Hundreds have I seen so scratched and pricked out of the world, Gerard, and tall fellows too; but lo! if they have the luck to be wounded where no doctor can be had, then they live; this too have I seen. Had I ever outlived that field in Brabant but for my most lucky mischance, lack of chirurgery? The frost choked all my bleeding wounds, and so I lived. A chirurgeon had pricked yet one more hole in this my body with his lance, and drained my last drop out, and my spirit with it. Seeing them thus dis-traught in bleeding of the bleeding soldier, I place no trust in them; for what slays a veteran may well lay a milk-and-water bourgeois low."

"This sounds like common sense," sighed Gerard languidly; "but no need to raise your voice so: I was not born deaf, and just now I hear acutely."

"Common sense! very common sense indeed," shouted the bad listener; "why, this is a soldier; a brute whose business is to kill men, not cure them." He added in very tolerable French, "Woe be to you, unlearned man, if you come between a physician and his patient ; and woe be to you, misguided youth, if you listen to that man of blood."

"Much obliged," said Denys, with mock politeness ; "but I am a true man, and would rob no man of his name. I do somewhat in the way of blood, but not worth mention in this presence. For one I slay, you slay a score ; and for one spoonful of blood I draw, you spill a tubful. The world is still gulled by shows. We soldiers vapour with long swords, and even in war beget two foes for every one we kill ; but you smooth gownsmen, with soft phrases and bare bodkins, 'tis you that thin mankind."

"A sick chamber is no place for jesting," cried the physician.

"No, doctor, nor for bawling," said the patient peevishly.

"Come, young man," said the senior kindly, "be reasonable. *Cuilibet in suâ arte credendum est.* My whole life has been given to this art, I studied at Montpelier ; the first school in France, and by consequence in Europe. There learned I Dririmancy, Scatomancy, Pathology, Therapeusis, and, greater than them all, Anatomy. For there we disciples of Hippocrates and Galen had opportunities those great ancients never knew. Good-bye, quadrupeds and apes, and paganism, and Mohammedanism ; we bought of the churchwardens, we shook the gallows ; we undid the sexton's work o' dark nights, penetrated with love of science and our kind ; all the authorities had their orders from Paris to wink ; and they winked. Gods of Olympus, how they winked ! The gracious king assisted us : he sent us twice a year a living criminal condemned to die, and said, 'Deal ye with him as science asks ; dissect him alive, if ye think fit.'"

"By the liver of Herod and Nero's bowels, he'll make me blush for the land that bore me, an if he praises it any more," shouted Denys at the top of his voice.

Gerard gave a little squawk, and put his fingers in his ears ; but speedily drew them out and shouted angrily, and as loudly, "You great roaring, blaspheming bull of Basan, hold your noisy tongue !"

Denys summoned a contrite look.

"Tush, slight man," said the doctor, with calm contempt, and vibrated a hand over him as in this age men make a pointer dog down charge ; then flowed majestic on. "We seldom or never dissected the living criminal, except in part. We mostly inoculated them with such diseases as the barren time afforded, selecting of course the more interesting ones."

"That means the foulest," whispered Denys meekly.

"These we watched through all their stages to maturity."

"Meaning the death of the poor rogue," whispered Denys meekly.

"And now, my poor sufferer, who best merits your confidence, this honest soldier with his youth, his ignorance, and his prejudices, or a graybeard laden with the gathered wisdom of ages?"

"That is," cried Denys impatiently, "will you believe what a jackdaw in a long gown has heard from a starling in a long gown, who heard it from a jay-pie, who heard it from a magpie, who heard it from a popinjay; or will you believe what I, a man with nought to gain by looking awry, nor speaking false, have seen; not heard with the ears which are given us to gull us, but seen with these sentinels mine eyne, seen, seen; to wit, that fevered and blooded men die, that fevered men not blooded live? stay, who sent for this sang-sue? Did you?"

"Not I. I thought you had."

"Nay," explained the doctor, "the good landlord told me one was 'down' in his house; so I said to myself, 'A stranger, and in need of my art,' and came incontinently."

"It was the act of a good Christian, sir."

"Of a good bloodhound," cried Denys contemptuously. "What, art thou so green as not to know that all these landlords are in league with certain of their fellow-citizens, who pay them toll on each booty? Whatever you pay this ancient for stealing your life-blood, of that the landlord takes his third for betraying you to him. Nay, more, as soon as ever your blood goes down the stair in that basin there, the landlord will see it or smell it, and send swiftly to his undertaker and get his third out of that job. For if he waited till the doctor got downstairs, the doctor would be beforehand and bespeak *his* undertaker, and then *he* would get the black thirds. Say I sooth, old Rouge et Noir? dites!"

"Denys, Denys, who taught you to think so ill of man?"

"Mine eyes, that are not to be gulled by what men say, seeing this many a year what they do, in all the lands I travel."

The doctor with some address made use of these last

words to escape the personal question. "I too have eyes as well as thou, and go not by tradition only, but by what I have seen, and not only seen, but done. I have healed as many men by bleeding as that interloping Arabist has killed for want of it. 'Twas but t'other day I healed one threatened with leprosy; I but bled him at the tip of the nose. I cured last year a quartan ague: how? bled its forefinger. Our curé lost his memory. I brought it him back on the point of my lance; I bled him behind the ear. I bled a dolt of a boy, and now he is the only one who can tell his right hand from his left in a whole family of idiots. When the plague was here years ago, no sham plague, such as empirics proclaim every six years or so, but the good honest Byzantine pest, I blooded an alderman freely, and cauterised the symptomatic buboes, and so pulled him out of the grave; whereas our then chirurgeon, a most pernicious Arabist, caught it himself, and died of it, aha, calling on Rhazes, Avicenna, and Mahound, who, could they have come, had all perished as miserably as himself."

"Oh, my poor ears," sighed Gerard.

"And am I fallen so low that one of your presence and speech rejects my art, and listens to a rude soldier, so far behind even his own miserable trade as to bear an arbalest, a worn-out invention, that German children shoot at pigeons with, but German soldiers mock at since ever arquebusses came and put them down?"

"You foul-mouthed old charlatan," cried Denys, "the arbalest is shouldered by taller men than ever stood in Rhenish hose, and even now it kills as many more than your noisy, stinking arquebus, as the lancet does than all our toys together. Go to! He was no fool who first called you 'leeches.' Sang-sues! va!"

Gerard groaned. "By the holy virgin, I wish you were both at Jericho, bellowing."

"Thank you, comrade. Then I'll bark no more, but at need I'll bite. If he has a lance, I have a sword; if he bleeds you, I'll bleed him. The moment his lance pricks your skin, little one, my sword-hilt knocks against his ribs; I have said it."

And Denys turned pale, folded his arms, and looked gloomy and dangerous.

Gerard sighed wearily. "Now, as all this is about me, give me leave to say a word."

"Ay! let the young man choose life or death for himself."

Gerard then indirectly rebuked his noisy counsellors by contrast and example. He spoke with unparalleled calmness, sweetness and gentleness. And these were the words of Gerard, the son of Eli. "I doubt not you both mean me well; but you assassinate me between you. Calmness and quiet are everything to me; but you are like two dogs growling over a bone.

"And, in sooth, bone I should be, did this uproar last long."

There was a dead silence, broken only by the silvery voice of Gerard, as he lay tranquil, and gazed calmly at the ceiling, and trickled into words.

"First, venerable sir, I thank you for coming to see me, whether from humanity, or in the way of honest gain; all trades must live.

"Your learning, reverend sir, seems great, to me at least, and for your experience, your age voucheth it.

"You say you have bled many, and of these many, many have not died thereafter, but lived, and done well. I must needs believe you."

The physician bowed; Denys grunted.

"Others, you say, you have bled, and—they are dead. I must needs believe you.

"Denys knows few things compared with you, but he knows them well. He is a man not given to conjecture. This I myself have noted. He says he has seen the fevered and blooded for the most part die; the fevered and not blooded live. I must needs believe him.

"Here, then, all is doubt.

"But thus much is certain: if I be bled, I must pay you a fee, and be burnt and excruciated with a hot iron, who am no felon.

"Pay a certain price in money and anguish for a doubtful remedy, that will I never.

"Next to money and ease, peace and quiet are certain goods, above all in a sick-room; but 'twould seem men cannot argue medicine without heat and raised voices; therefore, sir, I will essay a little sleep, and Denys will go forth and gaze on the females of the place, and I will keep you no longer from those who can afford to lay out blood and money in flebotomy and cautery."

The old physician had naturally a hot temper; he had often during this battle of words mastered it with difficulty, and now it mastered him. The most dignified course was silence; he saw this, and drew himself up, and made loftily for the door, followed close by his little boy and big basket.

But at the door he choked, he swelled, he burst. He whirled and came back open-mouthed, and the little boy and big basket had to whisk semicircularly not to be run down, for *de minimis non curat Medicina*—even when not in a rage.

"Ah! you reject my skill, you scorn my art. My revenge shall be to leave you to yourself; lost idiot, take your last look at me, and at the sun. Your blood be on your head!" And away he stamped.

But on reaching the door he whirled and came back; his wicker tail whirling round after him like a cat's.

"In twelve hours at furthest you will be in the secondary stage of fever. Your head will split. Your carotids will thump. Aha! And let but a pin fall, you will jump to the ceiling. Then send for me; and I'll not come." He departed. But at the door-handle gathered fury, wheeled and came flying, with pale, terror-stricken boy and wicker tail whisking after him. "Next will come—CRAMPS of the STOMACH. Aha!

"Then—BILIOUS VOMIT. Aha!

"Then—COLD SWEAT and DEADLY STUPOR.

"Then—CONFUSION OF ALL THE SENSES.

"Then—BLOODY VOMIT.

"And after that nothing can save you, not even I, and if I could I would not, and so farewell!"

Even Denys changed colour at threats so fervent and precise; but Gerard only gnashed his teeth with rage at the noise, and seized his hard bolster with kindling eye.

This added fuel to the fire, and brought the insulted ancient back from the impassable door, with his whisking train.

"And after that—MADNESS!

"And after that—BLACK VOMIT!

"And then—CONVULSIONS!

"And then—THAT CESSATION OF ALL VITAL FUNCTIONS THE VULGAR CALL 'DEATH,' for which thank your own Satanic folly and insolence. Farewell." He went. He came. He roared, "And think not to be buried in any Christian churchyard; for the bailiff is my good friend, and I shall tell him how and why you died: *felo de se! felo de se!* Farewell."

Gerard sprang to his feet on the bed by some supernatural gymnastic power excitement lent him, and, seeing him so moved, the vindictive orator came back at him fiercer than ever, to launch some master-threat the world has unhappily lost; for as he came with his whisking train, and shaking his fist, Gerard hurled the bolster curiously in his face, and knocked him down like a shot, the boy's head cracked under his falling master's, and crash went the dumb-stricken orator into the basket, and there sat wedged in an inverted angle, crushing phial after phial. The boy, being light, was strewed afar, but in a squatting posture; so that they sat in a sequence, like graduated specimens, the smaller howling. But soon the doctor's face filled with horror, and he uttered a far louder and unearthly screech, and kicked and struggled with wonderful agility for one of his age.

He was sitting on the hot coals.

They had singed the cloth and were now biting the man. Struggling wildly but vainly to get out of the basket, he rolled yelling over with it sideways, and lo! a great hissing; then the humane Gerard ran and wrenched off the tight basket not without a struggle. The doctor lay on his face groaning, handsomely singed with his own chafer, and slaked a moment too late by his own villainous compounds, which, however, being as various and even beautiful in colour as they were odious in taste, had strangely diversified his gray robe, and painted it more gaudy than neat.

Gerard and Denys raised him up and consoled him. "Courage, man, 'tis but cautery; balm of Gilead, why, you recommended it but now to my comrade here."

The physician replied only by a look of concentrated spite, and went out in dead silence, thrusting his stomach forth before him in the drollest way. The boy followed him next moment, but in that slight interval he left off whining, burst into a grin, and conveyed to the culprits by an unrefined gesture his accurate comprehension of, and rapturous though compressed joy at, his master's disaster.

CHAPTER XXVII.

THE worthy physician went home and told his housekeeper he was in agony from a "bad burn." Those were the words. For in phlogistic as in other things, we cauterise our neighbour's digits, but burn our own fingers. His housekeeper applied some old woman's remedy mild as milk. He submitted like a lamb to her experience: his sole object in the case of this patient being cure : meantime he made out his bill for broken phials, and took measures to have the travellers imprisoned at once. He made oath before a magistrate that they, being strangers and indebted to him, meditated instant flight from the township.

Alas! it was his unlucky day. His sincere desire and honest endeavour to perjure himself were baffled by a circumstance he had never foreseen nor indeed thought possible.

He had spoken the truth.

And IN AN AFFIDAVIT!

The officers, on reaching "The Silver Lion," found the birds were flown.

They went down to the river, and, from intelligence they received there, started up the bank in hot pursuit.

This temporary escape the friends owed to Denys s good sense and observation. After a peal of laughter, that it was a cordial to hear, and after venting his watchword three times, he turned short grave, and told Gerard Düsseldorf was no place for them. "That old fellow," said he, "went off unnaturally silent for such a babbler : we are strangers here; *the bailiff is his friend;* in five minutes we shall lie in a dungeon for assaulting a Düsseldorf dignity ; are you strong enough to hobble to the water's edge? it is hard by. Once there you have but to lie down in a boat instead of a bed; and what is the odds ? "

"The odds, Denys? untold, and all in favour of the boat. I pine for Rome ; for Rome is my road to Sevenbergen ; and then we shall lie in the boat, but ON the Rhine, the famous Rhine ; the cool, refreshing Rhine. I feel its breezes coming : the very sight will cure a little hop-o'-my-thumb fever like mine ; away, away ! "

Finding his excitable friend in this mood, Denys settled hastily with the landlord, and they hurried to the river. On inquiry they found to their dismay that the public boat was gone this half-hour, and no other would start that day, being afternoon. By dint, however, of asking a great many questions, and collecting a crowd, they obtained an offer of a private boat from an old man and his two sons.

This was duly ridiculed by a bystander. "The current is too strong for three oars."

"Then my comrade and I will help row," said the invalid.

"No need," said the old man. "Bless your silly heart, *he* owns t'other boat."

There was a powerful breeze right astern; the boatmen set a broad sail, and rowing also, went off at a spanking rate.

"Are you better, lad, for the river breeze?"

"Much better. But indeed the doctor did me good."

"The doctor? Why, you would none of his cures."

"No, but I mean—you will say I am nought—but knocking the old fool down—somehow—it soothed me."

"Amiable dove! how thy little character opens more and more every day, like a rosebud. I read thee all wrong at first."

"Nay, Denys, mistake me not, neither. I trust I had borne with his idle threats, though, in sooth, his voice went through my poor ears; but he was an infidel, or next door to one, and such I have been taught to abhor. Did he not as good as say, we owed our inward parts to men with long Greek names, and not to Him, whose name is but a syllable, but whose hand is over all the earth? Pagan!"

"So you knocked him down forthwith—like a good Christian."

"Now, Denys, you will still be jesting. Take not an ill man's part. Had it been a thunderbolt from Heaven, he had met but his due; yet he took but a sorry bolster from this weak arm."

"What weak arm?" inquired Denys, with twinkling eyes. "I have lived among arms, and by Samson's hairy pow never saw I one more like a catapult. The bolster wrapped round his nose and the two ends kissed behind his head, and his forehead resounded, and had he been Goliath, or Julius Cæsar, instead of an old quacksalver, down he had gone. St. Denys guard me from such feeble opposites as thou! and above all from their weak arms—thou diabolical young hypocrite."

The river took many turns, and this sometimes brought the wind on their side instead of right astern. Then they all moved to the weather-side to prevent the boat heeling over too much; all but a child of about five years old, the grandson of the boatman, and his darling; this urchin had slipped on board at the moment of starting, and being too light to affect the boat's trim, was above, or rather below, the laws of navigation.

They sailed merrily on, little conscious that they were pursued by a whole posse of constables armed with the bailiff's writ, and that their pursuers were coming up with them; for if the wind was strong, so was the current.

And now Gerard suddenly remembered that this was a very good way to Rome, but not to Burgundy.

"Oh, Denys," said he, with an almost alarmed look, "this is not your road."

"I know it," said Denys quietly; "but what can I do? I cannot leave thee till the fever leaves thee; and it is on thee still, for thou art both red and white by turns; I have watched thee. I must e'en go on to Cologne, I doubt, and then strike across."

"Thank Heaven," said Gerard joyfully. He added eagerly, with a little touch of self-deception, "'Twere a sin to be so near Cologne and not see it. Oh, man, it is a vast and ancient city, such as I have often dreamed of, but ne'er had the good luck to see. Me miserable, by what hard fortune do I come to it now? Well then, Denys," continued the young man, less warmly, "it is old enough to have been founded by a Roman lady in the first century of grace, and sacked by Attila the barbarous, and afterwards sore defaced by the Norman Lothaire. And it has a church for every week in the year, forbye chapels and churches innumerable of convents and nunneries, and above all, the stupendous minster yet unfinished, and therein, but in their own chapel, lie the three kings that brought gifts to our Lord, Melchior gold, and Gaspar frankincense, and Balthazar the black king, he brought myrrh; and over their bones stands the shrine, the wonder of the world; it is of ever-shining brass brighter than gold, studded with images fairly wrought, and inlaid with exquisite devices, and brave

with colours; and two broad stripes run to and fro, of
jewels so great, so rare, each might adorn a crown or
ransom its wearer at need; and upon it stand the three
kings curiously counterfeited, two in solid silver, richly
gilt; these be bareheaded; but he of Æthiop ebony, and
bareth a golden crown; and in the midst our blessed
Lady, in virgin silver, with Christ in her arms; and at
the corners, in golden branches, four goodly waxen tapers
do burn night and day. Holy eyes have watched and
renewed that light unceasingly for ages, and holy eyes
shall watch them *in sæcula.* I tell thee, Denys, the oldest
song, the oldest Flemish or German legend, found them
burning, and they shall light the earth to its grave. And
there is St. Ursel's church, a British saint's, where lie her
bones and all the other virgins, her fellows; eleven
thousand were they who died for the faith, being put to the
sword by barbarous Moors, on the twenty-third day of
October, two hundred and thirty-eight. Their bones are
piled in the vaults, and many of their skulls are in the
church. St. Ursel's is in a thin golden case, and stands
on the high altar, but shown to humble Christians only
on solemn days."

"Eleven thousand virgins!" cried Denys. "What
babies German men must have been in days of yore.
Well, would all their bones might turn flesh again, and
their skulls sweet faces, as we pass through the gates.
'Tis odds but some of them are wearied of their estate by
this time."

"Tush, Denys!" said Gerard; "why wilt thou, being
good, still make thyself seem evil? If thy wishing-cap be
on, pray that we may meet the meanest she of all those
wise virgins in the next world, and to that end let us
reverence their holy dust in this one. And then there is
the church of the Maccabees, and the caldron in which they
and their mother Solomona were boiled by a wicked king
for refusing to eat swine's flesh."

"Oh, peremptory king! and pig-headed Maccabees! I
had eaten bacon with my pork liever than change places
at the fire with my meat."

"What scurvy words are these? it was their faith."

"Nay, bridle thy choler, and tell me, are there nought
but churches in this thy so vaunted city? for I affect rather
Sir Knight than Sir Priest."

"Ay, marry, there is a university near a hundred years

old; and there is a market-place, no fairer in the world, and at the four sides of it houses great as palaces; and there is a stupendous senate-house all covered with images, and at the head of them stands one of stout Herman Gryn, a soldier, like thyself, lad."

"Ay. Tell me of him! what feat of arms earned him his niche?"

"A rare one. He slew a lion in fair combat, with nought but his cloak and a short sword. He thrust the cloak in the brute's mouth, and cut his spine in twain, and there is the man's effigy and eke the lion's to prove it. The like was never done but by three more, I ween; Samson was one, and Lysimachus of Macedon another, and Benaiah, a captain of David's host."

"Marry! three tall fellows. I would like well to sup with them all to-night."

"So would not I," said Gerard drily.

"But tell me," said Denys, with some surprise, "when wast thou in Cologne?"

"Never but in the spirit. I prattle with the good monks by the way, and they tell me all the notable things both old and new."

"Ay, ay, have not I seen your nose under their very cowls? But when I speak of matters that are out of sight, my words they are small, and the thing it was big; now thy words be as big or bigger than the things; art a good limner with thy tongue; I have said it; and for a saint, as ready with hand, or steel, or bolster—as any poor sinner living; and so, shall I tell thee which of all these things thou hast described draws me to Cologne."

"Ay, Denys."

"Thou, and thou only; no dead saint, but my living friend and comrade true; 'tis thou alone draws Denys of Burgundy to Cologne."

Gerard hung his head.

At this juncture one of the younger boatmen suddenly inquired what was amiss with "little turnip-face?"

His young nephew thus described had just come aft grave as a judge, and burst out crying in the midst without more ado. On this phenomenon, so sharply defined, he was subjected to many interrogatories, some coaxingly uttered, some not. Had he hurt himself? had he over-ate himself? was he frightened? was he cold? was he sick? was he an idiot?

To all and each he uttered the same reply, which English writers render thus, oh ! oh ! oh ! and French writers thus, hi ! hi ! hi ! So fixed are Fiction's phonetics.

"Who can tell what ails the peevish brat?" snarled the young boatman impatiently. "Rather look this way and tell me whom be these after!" The old man and his other son looked, and saw four men walking along the east bank of the river ; at the sight they left rowing awhile, and gathered mysteriously in the stern, whispering and casting glances alternately at their passengers and the pedestrians.

The sequel may show they would have employed speculation better in trying to fathom the turnip-face mystery : I beg pardon of my age : I mean "the deep mind of dauntless infancy."

"If 'tis as I doubt," whispered one of the young men, "why not give them a squeak for their lives ; let us make for the west bank."

The old man objected stoutly. "What," said he, "run our heads into trouble for strangers ! are ye mad? Nay, let us rather cross to the east side ; still side with the strong arm ! that is my rede. What say you, Werter ?"

"I say, please yourselves."

What age and youth could not decide upon, a puff of wind settled most impartially. Came a squall, and the little vessel heeled over ; the men jumped to windward to trim her ; but to their horror they saw in the very boat from stem to stern a ditch of water rushing to leeward, and the next moment they saw nothing, but felt the Rhine, the cold and rushing Rhine.

"Turnip-face" had drawn the plug.

The officers unwound the cords from their waists.

Gerard could swim like a duck ; but the best swimmer, canted out of a boat capsized, must sink ere he can swim. The dark water bubbled loudly over his head, and then he came up almost blind and deaf for a moment ; the next, he saw the black boat bottom uppermost, and figures clinging to it ; he shook his head like a water-dog and made for it by a sort of unthinking imitation ; but ere he reached it he heard a voice behind him cry not loud but with deep manly distress, "Adieu, comrade, adieu !"

He looked, and there was poor Denys sinking, sinking, weighed down by his wretched arbalest. His face was pale, and his eyes staring wide, and turned despairingly on his dear friend. Gerard uttered a wild cry of love and terror, and made for him, cleaving the water madly; but the next moment Denys was under water.

The next, Gerard was after him.

The officers knotted a rope and threw the end in.

CHAPTER XXVIII.

THINGS good and evil balance themselves in a remarkable manner, and almost universally. The steel bow attached to the arbalestrier's back, and carried above his head, had sunk him. That very steel bow, owing to that very position, could not escape Gerard's hands, one of which grasped it, and the other went between the bow and the cord, which was as good. The next moment, Denys, by means of his cross-bow, was hoisted with so eager a jerk that half his body bobbed up out of water.

"Now, grip me not! grip me not!" cried Gerard, in mortal terror of that fatal mistake.

"Pas si bête," gurgled Denys.

Seeing the sort of stuff he had to deal with, Gerard was hopeful and calm directly. "On thy back," said he sharply, and seizing the arbalest, and taking a stroke forward, he aided the desired movement. "Hand on my shoulder! slap the water with the other hand! No—with a downward motion; so. Do nothing more than I bid thee." Gerard had got hold of Denys's long hair, and twisting it hard, caught the end between his side teeth, and with the strong muscles of his youthful neck easily kept up the soldier's head, and struck out lustily across the current. A moment he had hesitated which side to make for, little knowing the awful importance of that simple decision; then seeing the west bank a trifle nearest, he made towards it, instead of swimming to jail like a good boy, and so furnishing one a novel incident. Owing to the force of the current they slanted considerably, and when they had covered near a hundred yards, Denys murmured uneasily, "How much more of it?"

"Courage," mumbled Gerard. "Whatever a duck knows, a Dutchman knows; art safe as in bed."

The next moment, to their surprise, they found themselves

in shallow water, and so waded ashore. Once on terra firma, they looked at one another from head to foot as if eyes could devour, then by one impulse flung each an arm round the other's neck, and panted there with hearts too full to speak. And at this sacred moment life was sweet as heaven to both; sweetest perhaps to the poor exiled lover, who had just saved his friend. Oh, joy to whose height what poet has yet soared, or ever tried to soar? To save a human life; and that life a loved one. Such moments are worth living for, ay, three score years and ten. And then, calmer, they took hands, and so walked along the bank hand in hand like a pair of sweethearts, scarce knowing or caring whither they went.

The boat people were all safe on the late concave, now convex craft, Herr Turnip-face, the "Inverter of things," being in the middle. All this fracas seemed not to have essentially deranged his habits. At least he was greeting when he shot our friends into the Rhine, and greeting when they got out again.

"Shall we wait till they right the boat?"

"No, Denys, our fare is paid; we owe them nought. Let us on, and briskly."

Denys assented, observing that they could walk all the way to Cologne on this bank.

"I fear not to Cologne," was the calm reply.

"Why, whither then?"

"To Burgundy."

"To Burgundy? Ah, no! that is too good to be sooth."

"Sooth 'tis, and sense into the bargain. What matters it to me how I go to Rome?"

"Nay, nay; you but say so to pleasure me. The change is too sudden; and think me not so ill-hearted as take you at your word. Also did I not see your eyes sparkle at the wonders of Cologne? the churches, the images, the relics——"

"How dull art thou, Denys; that was when we were to enjoy them together. Churches! I shall see plenty, go Romeward how I will. The bones of saints and martyrs; alas! the world is full of them; but a friend like thee, where on earth's face shall I find another? No, I will not turn thee farther from the road that leads to thy dear home, and her that pines for thee. Neither will I rob myself of thee by leaving thee. Since I drew thee out of Rhine I love thee better than I did. Thou art my pearl: I fished thee;

and must keep thee. So gainsay me not, or thou wilt bring back my fever; but cry courage, and lead on; and hey for Burgundy!"

Denys gave a joyful caper. "Courage! va pour la Bourgogne. Oh! soyez tranquille! cette fois il est bien décidément mort, ce coquinlà." And they turned their backs on the Rhine.

On this decision making itself clear, across the Rhine there was a commotion in the little party that had been watching the discussion, and the friends had not taken many steps ere a voice came to them over the water. "HALT!"

Gerard turned, and saw one of those four holding out a badge of office and a parchment slip. His heart sank; for he was a good citizen, and used to obey the voice that now bade him turn again to Düsseldorf—the Law's.

Denys did not share his scruples. He was a Frenchman, and despised every other nation, laws, inmates, and customs included. He was a soldier, and took a military view of the situation. Superior force opposed; river between; rear open; why, 'twas retreat made easy. He saw at a glance that the boat still drifted in mid-stream, and there was no ferry nearer than Düsseldorf. "I shall beat a retreat to that hill," said he, "and then, being out of sight, quick step."

They sauntered off.

"Halt, in the bailiff's name!" cried a voice from the shore.

Denys turned round and ostentatiously snapped his fingers at the bailiff, and proceeded.

"Halt! in the archbishop's name."

Denys snapped his fingers at his grace, and proceeded.

"Halt! in the emperor's name."

Denys snapped his fingers at his majesty, and proceeded.

Gerard saw this needless pantomime with regret, and as soon as they had passed the brow of the hill, said, "There is now but one course, we must run to Burgundy instead of walking;" and he set off, and ran the best part of a league without stopping.

Denys was fairly blown, and inquired what on earth had become of Gerard's fever. "I begin to miss it sadly," said he drily.

"I dropped it in Rhine, I trow," was the reply.

Presently they came to a little village, and here Denys

purchased a loaf and a huge bottle of Rhenish wine. "For," he said, "we must sleep in some hole or corner. If we lie at an inn, we shall be taken in our beds." This was no more than common prudence on the old soldier's part.

The official network for catching law-breakers, especially plebeian ones, was very close in that age; though the co-operation of the public was almost null, at all events upon the Continent. The innkeepers were everywhere under close surveillance as to their travellers, for whose acts they were even in some degree responsible, more so it would seem than for their sufferings.

The friends were both glad when the sun set; and delighted, when after a long trudge under the stars (for the moon, if I remember right, did not rise till about three in the morning) they came to a large barn belonging to a house at some distance. A quantity of barley had been lately thrashed; for the heap of straw on one side the thrashing-floor was almost as high as the unthrashed corn on the other.

"Here be two royal beds," said Denys; "which shall we lie on, the mow, or the straw?"

"The straw for me," said Gerard.

They sat on the heap, and ate their brown bread, and drank their wine, and then Denys covered his friend up in straw, and heaped it high above him, leaving him only a breathing-hole: "Water, they say, is death to fevered men; I'll make warm water on't, anyhow."

Gerard bade him make his mind easy. "These few drops from Rhine cannot chill me. I feel heat enough in my body now to parch a kennel, or boil a cloud if I was in one." And with this epigram his consciousness went so rapidly, he might really be said to "fall asleep."

Denys, who lay awake awhile, heard that which made him nestle closer. Horses' hoofs came ringing up from Düsseldorf, and the wooden barn vibrated as they rattled past howling in a manner too well known and understood in the fifteenth century, but as unfamiliar in Europe now as a red Indian's war-whoop.

Denys shook where he lay.

Gerard slept like a top.

It all swept by, and troop and howls died away.

The stout soldier drew a long breath, whistled in a whisper, closed his eyes, and slept like top 2.

In the morning he sat up and put out his hand to wake Gerard. It lighted on the young man's forehead, and found it quite wet. Denys then in his quality of nurse forbore to wake him, "It is ill to check sleep or sweat in a sick man," said he. "I know that far, though I ne'er minced ape nor gallows-bird."

After waiting a good hour he felt desperately hungry; so he turned, and in self-defence went to sleep again.

Poor fellow, in his hard life he had been often driven to this manœuvre. At high noon he was waked by Gerard moving, and found him sitting up with the straw smoking round him like a dunghill. Animal heat *versus* moisture. Gerard called him "a lazy loon." He quietly grinned.

They set out, and the first thing Denys did was to give Gerard his arbalest, etc., and mount a high tree on the road. "Coast clear to the next village," said he, and on they went.

On drawing near the village Denys halted and suddenly inquired of Gerard how he felt.

"What! can you not see? I feel as if Rome was no farther than yon hamlet."

"But thy body, lad; thy skin?"

"Neither hot nor cold; and yesterday 'twas hot one while and cold another. But what I cannot get rid of is this tiresome leg."

"Le grand malheur! Many of my comrades have found no such difficulty."

"Ah! there it goes again; itches consumedly."

"Unhappy youth," said Denys solemnly, "the sum of thy troubles is this: thy fever is gone, and thy wound is —healing. Sith so it is," added he indulgently, "I shall tell thee a little piece of news I had otherwise withheld."

"What is't?" asked Gerard, sparkling with curiosity.

"THE HUE AND CRY IS OUT AFTER US; AND ON FLEET HORSES."

"Oh!"

CHAPTER XXIX.

GERARD was staggered by this sudden communication, and his colour came and went. Then he clenched his teeth with ire. For men of any spirit at all are like the wild boar; he will run from a superior force, owing, perhaps, to his not being an ass; but if you stick to his heels too long, and too close, and, in short, bore him, he will whirl, and come tearing at a multitude of hunters, and perhaps, bore you. Gerard then set his teeth and looked battle. But the next moment his countenance fell, and he said plaintively, "And my axe is in Rhine."

They consulted together. Prudence bade them avoid that village; hunger said, Buy food.

Hunger spoke loudest. Prudence most convincingly. They settled to strike across the fields.

They halted at a haystack and borrowed two bundles of hay, and lay on them in a dry ditch out of sight, but in nettles.

They sallied out in turn and came back with turnips. These they munched at intervals in their retreat until sunset.

Presently they crept out shivering into the rain and darkness, and got into the road on the other side of the village.

It was a dismal night, dark as pitch, and blowing hard. They could neither see, nor hear, nor be seen, nor heard; and for aught I know, passed like ghosts close to their foes. These they almost forgot in the natural horrors of the black tempestuous night, in which they seemed to grope and hew their way as in black marble. When the moon rose they were many a league from Düsseldorf. But they still trudged on. Presently they came to a huge building.

"Courage!" cried Denys, "I think I know this convent. Ay, it is. We are in the see of Juliers. Cologne has no power here."

The next moment they were safe within the walls.

CHAPTER XXX.

HERE Gerard made acquaintance with a monk, who had constructed the great dial in the prior's garden, and a wheel for drawing water, and a winnowing machine for the grain, etc.; and had ever some ingenious mechanism on hand. He had made several psalteries and two dulcimers, and was now attempting a set of regalles, or little organ for the choir.

Now Gerard played the humble psaltery a little: but the monk touched that instrument divinely, and showed him most agreeably what a novice he was in music. He also illuminated finely, but could not write so beautifully as Gerard. Comparing their acquirements with the earnestness and simplicity of an age in which accomplishments implied a true natural bent, Youth and Age soon became like brothers, and Gerard was pressed hard to stay that night. He consulted Denys, who assented with a rueful shrug.

Gerard told his old new friend whither he was going, and described their late adventures, softening down the bolster.

"Alack!" said the good old man, "I have been a great traveller in my day, but none molested me." He then told him to avoid inns; they were always haunted by rogues and roysterers, whence his soul might take harm even did his body escape, and to manage each day's journey so as to lie at some peaceful monastery; then suddenly breaking off and looking as sharp as a needle at Gerard, he asked him how long since he had been shriven? Gerard coloured up and replied feebly—

"Better than a fortnight."

"And thou an exorcist! No wonder perils have overtaken thee. Come, thou must be assoiled out of hand."

"Yes, father," said Gerard, "and with all mine heart;" and was sinking down to his knees, with his hands joined; but the monk stopped him half fretfully—

"Not to me! not to me! not to me! I am as full of the world as thou or any he that lives in't. My whole soul it is in these wooden pipes, and sorry leathern stops, which shall perish—with them whose minds are fixed on such like vanities."

"Dear father," said Gerard, "they are for the use of the Church, and surely that sanctifies the pains and labour spent on them?"

"That is just what the devil has been whispering in mine ear this while," said the monk, putting one hand behind his back and shaking his finger half threateningly, half playfully, at Gerard. "He was even so kind and thoughtful as to mind me that Solomon built the Lord a house with rare hangings, and that this in him was counted gracious and no sin. Oh! he can quote Scripture rarely. But I am not so simple a monk as you think, my lad," cried the good father, with sudden defiance, addressing not Gerard but—Vacancy. "This one toy finished, vigils, fasts, and prayers for me; prayers standing, prayers lying on the chapel floor, and prayers in a right good tub of cold water." He nudged Gerard and winked his eye knowingly. "Nothing he hates and dreads like seeing us monks at our orisons up to our chins in cold water. For *corpus domat aqua.* So now go confess thy little trumpery sins, pardonable in youth and secularity, and leave me to mine, sweet to me as honey, and to be expiated in proportion."

Gerard bowed his head, but could not help saying, "Where shall I find a confessor more holy and clement?"

"In each of these cells," replied the monk simply (they were now in the corridor); "there, go to Brother Anselm, yonder."

Gerard followed the monk's direction, and made for a cell; but the doors were pretty close to one another, and it seems he mistook; for just as he was about to tap, he heard his old friend crying to him in an agitated whisper, "Nay! nay! nay!" He turned, and there was the monk at his cell-door, in a strange state of anxiety, going up and down and beating the air double-handed, like a bottom sawyer. Gerard really thought the cell he was at must be inhabited by some dangerous wild beast, if not by that personage whose presence in the convent had been so distinctly proclaimed. He looked back inquiringly and went on to the next door. Then his old friend nodded his head rapidly, bursting in a moment into a comparatively blissful expression of face, and shot back into his den. He took his hour-glass, turned it, and went to work on his regalloes; and often he looked up, and said to himself, "Well-a-day, the sands how swift they run when the man is bent over earthly toys."

Father Anselm was a venerable monk, with an ample head, and a face all dignity and love. Therefore Gerard in confessing to him, and replying to his gentle though searching questions, could not help thinking, "Here is a head!—O dear! O dear! I wonder whether you will let me draw it when I have done confessing." And so his own head got confused, and he forgot a crime or two. However, he did not lower the bolstering this time, nor was he so uncandid as to detract from the pagan character of the bolstered.

The penance inflicted was this: he was to enter the convent church, and prostrating himself, kiss the lowest step of the altar three times; then kneeling on the floor, to say three paternosters and a credo. "This done, come back to me on the instant."

Accordingly, his short mortification performed, Gerard returned, and found Father Anselm spreading plaster.

"After the soul the body," said he; "know that I am the chirurgeon here, for want of a better. This is going on thy leg; to cool it, not to burn it; the saints forbid."

During the operation, the monastic leech, who had naturally been interested by the Düsseldorf branch of Gerard's confession, rather sided with Denys upon "bleeding." "We Dominicans seldom let blood nowadays; the lay leeches say 'tis from timidity and want of skill; but, in sooth, we have long found that simples will cure most of the ills that can be cured at all. Besides, they never kill in capable hands; and other remedies slay like thunderbolts. As for the blood, the Vulgate saith expressly it is 'the life of a man.' And in medicine or law, as in divinity, to be wiser than the All-wise is to be a fool. Moreover, simples are mighty. The little four-footed creature that kills the poisonous snake, if bitten herself, finds an herb powerful enough to quell that poison, though stronger and of swifter operation than any mortal malady; and we, taught by her wisdom, and our own traditions, still search and try the virtues of those plants the good God hath strewed this earth with, some to feed men's bodies, some to heal them. Only in desperate ills we mix heavenly with earthly virtue. We steep the hair or the bones of some dead saint in the medicine, and thus work marvellous cures."

"Think you, father, it is along of the reliques? for Peter à Floris, a learned leech and no pagan, denies it stoutly."

"What knows Peter à Floris? And what know I? I take not on me to say we can command the saints, and, will they nill they, can draw corporal virtue from their olest remains. But I see that the patient drinking thus in faith is often bettered as by a charm. Doubtless faith in the recipient is for much in all these cures. But so twas ever. A sick woman, that all the Jewish leeches failed to cure, did but touch Christ's garment and was healed in a moment. Had she not touched that sacred piece of cloth she had never been healed. Had she without faith not touched it only, but worn it to her grave, I trow she had been none the better for't. But we do ill to search these things too curiously. All we see around us calls for faith. Have then a little patience. We shall soon know all. Meantime, I, thy confessor for the nonce, do strictly forbid thee, on thy soul's health, to hearken learned lay folk on things religious. Arrogance is their bane; with it they shut heaven's open door in their own faces. Mind, I say, learned laics. Unlearned ones have often been my masters in humility, and may be thine. Thy wound is cared for; in three days 'twill be but a scar. And now God speed thee, and the saints make thee as good and as happy as thou art beautiful and gracious." Gerard hoped there was no need to part yet, for he was to dine in the refectory. But Father Anselm told him, with a shade of regret just perceptible and no more, that he did not leave his cell this week, being himself in penitence; and with this he took Gerard's head delicately in both hands, and kissed him on the brow, and almost before the cell door had closed on him, was back to his pious offices. Gerard went away chilled to the heart by the isolation of the monastic life, and saddened too. "Alas!" he thought, "here is a kind face I must never look to see again on earth; a kind voice gone from mine ear and my heart for ever. There is nothing but meeting and parting in this sorrowful world. Well-a-day! well-a-day!" This pensive mood was interrupted by a young monk who came for him and took him to the refectory; there he found several monks seated at a table, and Denys standing like a poker, being examined as to the towns he should pass through. The friars then clubbed their knowledge, and marked out the route, noting all the religious houses on or near that road; and this they gave Gerard. Then supper, and after it the old monk carried Gerard to his cell, and they had an eager chat, and the friar incidentally revealed the cause of his pantomime in the corridor. "Ye had well-nigh fallen into Brother Jerome's clutches. Yon was his cell."

"Is Father Jerome an ill man, then?"

"An ill man!" and the friar crossed himself; "a saint, an anchorite, the very pillar of this house! He had sent ye barefoot to Loretto. Nay, I forgot, y'are bound for Italy;

the spiteful old—saint upon earth, had sent ye to Canterbory or Compostella. But Jerome was born old and with a cowl; Anselm and I were boys once, and wicked beyond anything you can imagine" (Gerard wore a somewhat incredulous look): "this keeps us humble more or less, and makes us reasonably lenient to youth and hot blood."

Then, at Gerard's earnest request, one more heavenly strain upon the psalterion, and so to bed, the troubled spirit calmed, and the sore heart soothed.

I have described in full this day, marked only by contrast, a day that came like oil on waves after so many passions and perils—because it must stand in this narrative as the representative of many such days which now succeeded to it. For our travellers on their weary way experienced that which most of my readers will find in the longer journey of life, viz., that stirring events are not evenly distributed over the whole road, but come by fits and starts, and as it were, in clusters. To some extent this may be because they draw one another by links more or less subtle. But there is more in it than that. It happens so. Life is an intermittent fever. Now all narrators, whether of history or fiction, are compelled to slur these barren portions of time, or else line trunks. The practice, however, tends to give the unguarded reader a wrong arithmetical impression, which there is a particular reason for avoiding in these pages as far as possible. I invite therefore your intelligence to my aid, and ask you to try and realise that, although there were no more vivid adventures for a long while, one day's march succeeded another ; one monastery after another fed and lodged them gratis with a welcome always charitable, sometimes genial ; and though they met no enemy but winter and rough weather, antagonists not always contemptible, yet they trudged over a much larger tract of territory than that, their passage through which I have described so minutely. And so the pair, Gerard bronzed in the face and travel-stained from head to foot, and Denys with his shoes in tatters, stiff and footsore both of them, drew near the Burgundian frontier.

CHAPTER XXXI.

GERARD was almost as eager for this promised land as
Denys; for the latter constantly chanted its praises, and
at every little annoyance showed him "they did things
better in Burgundy;" and, above all, played on his foible
by guaranteeing clean bed-clothes at the inns of that
polished nation. "I ask no more," the Hollander would
say; "to think that I have not lain once in a naked bed
since I left home! When I look at their linen, instead
of doffing habit and hose, it is mine eyes and nose I
would fain be shut of."

Denys carried his love of country so far as to walk twenty
leagues in shoes that had exploded, rather than buy of a
German churl, who would throw all manner of obstacles
in a customer's way, his incivility, his dinner, his body.

Towards sunset they found themselves at equal distances
from a little town and a monastery, only the latter was off
the road. Denys was for the inn, Gerard for the convent.
Denys gave way, but on condition that once in Burgundy
they should always stop at an inn. Gerard consented to
this the more readily that his chart with its list of convents
ended here. So they turned off the road. And now Gerard
asked with surprise whence this sudden aversion to places
that had fed and lodged them gratis so often. The soldier
hemmed and hawed at first, but at last his wrongs burst
forth. It came out that this was no sudden aversion, but
an ancient and abiding horror, which he had suppressed
till now, but with infinite difficulty, and out of politeness:
"I saw they had put powder in your drink," said he, "so
I forebore them. However, being the last, why not ease
my mind? Know then I have been like a fish out of water
in all those great dungeons. You straightway levant with
some old shaveling, so you see not my purgatory."

"Forgive me! I have been selfish."

"Ay, ay, I forgive thee, little one; 'tis not thy fault: art
not the first fool that has been priest-rid, and monk-bit.
But I'll not forgive *them* my misery." Then, about a
century before Henry VIII.'s commissioners, he delivered
his indictment. These gloomy piles were all built alike.
Inns differed, but here all was monotony. Great gate,
little gate, so many steps and then a gloomy cloister.
Here the dortour, there the great cold refectory, where

you must sit mumchance, or at least inaudible, he who liked to speak his mind out; "and then," said he, "nobody is a man here, but all are slaves, and of what? of a peevish, tinkling bell, that never sleeps. An 'twere a trumpet now, aye sounding alarums, 'twouldn't freeze a man's heart so. Tinkle, tinkle, tinkle, and you must sit to meat with maybe no stomach for food. Ere your meat settles in your stomach, tinkle, tinkle, and ye must to church with may be no stomach for devotion; I am not a hog at prayers, for one. Tinkle, tinkle, and now you must to bed with your eyes open. Well, by then you have contrived to shut them, some uneasy imp of darkness has got to the bell-rope, and tinkle, tinkle, it behoves you say a prayer in the dark, whether you know one or not. If they heard the sort of prayers I mutter when they break my rest with their tinkle! Well, you drop off again and get about an eyeful of sleep; lo, it is tinkle, tinkle for matins."

"And the only clapper you love is a woman's," put in Gerard half contemptuously.

"Because there is some music in that even when it scolds," was the stout reply. "And then to be always checked. If I do but put my finger in the salt-cellar, straightway I hear, 'Have you no knife that you finger the salt?' And if I but wipe my knife on the cloth to save time, then 'tis, 'Wipe thy knife dirty on the bread, and clean upon the cloth!' O small of soul! these little peevish pedantries fall chill upon good fellowship like wee icicles a-melting down from strawen eaves."

"I hold cleanliness no pedantry," said Gerard. "Shouldst learn better manners once for all."

"Nay; 'tis they who lack manners. They stop a fellow's mouth at every word."

"At every other word, you mean; every obscene or blasphemous one."

"Exaggerator, go to! Why, at the very last of these dungeons, I found the poor travellers sitting all chilled and mute round one shaveling, like rogues awaiting their turn to be hanged; so to cheer them up, I did but cry out, 'Courage, tout le monde, le dia——'"

"Connu! what befell?"

"Marry, this. 'Blaspheme not!' quo' the bourreau. 'Plait-il,' say I. Doesn't he wheel and wyte on me in a sort of Alsatian French, turning all the 'P's' into 'B's.' I had much ado not to laugh in his face."

" Being thyself unable to speak ten words of *his* language without a fault."

" Well, all the world ought to speak French. What avail so many jargons except to put a frontier atwixt men's hearts?"

" But what said he?"

" What signifies it what a fool says?"

" Oh, not all the words of a fool are folly, or I should not listen to you."

" Well, then, he said, ' Such as begin by making free with the devil's name, aye end by doing it with all the names in heaven.' ' Father,' said I, ' I am a soldier, and this is but my consigne or watchword.' ' Oh, then, it is just a custom?' said he. I, not divining the old fox, and thinking to clear myself, said, ' Ay, it was.' ' Then that is ten times worse,' said he. ' 'Twill bring him about your ears one of these days. He still comes where he hears his name often called.' Observe ! no gratitude for the tidings which neither his missals nor his breviary had ever let him know. Then he was so good as to tell me, soldiers do commonly the crimes for which all other men are broke on the wheel ; ' à savoir,' murder, rape, and pillage."

" And is't not true?"

" True or not, it was ill manners," replied Denys guardedly. " And so says this courteous host of mine, ' Being the foes of mankind, why make enemies of good spirits into the bargain, by still shouting the names of evil ones?' and a lot more stuff."

" Well, but, Denys, whether you hearken his rede, or slight it, wherefore blame a man for raising his voice to save your soul?"

" How can his voice save my soul, when a keeps turning of his ' P's ' into ' B's '?"

Gerard was staggered : ere he could recover at this thunderbolt of Gallicism, Denys went triumphant off at a tangent, and stigmatised all monks as hypocrites. " Do but look at them, how they creep about and cannot eye you like honest men."

" Nay," said Gerard eagerly, " that modest downcast gaze is part of their discipline, 'tis *custodia oculorum*."

" Cussed toads eating *hoc hac horum?* No such thing ; just so looks a cut-purse. Can't meet a true man's eye. Doff cowl, monk, and behold, a thief ; don cowl, thief, and lo, a monk. Tell me not they will ever be able to look God Almighty in the face, when they can't even look a true man in the face down here. Ah, here it is, black as ink! into the well we go, comrade. Miséricorde, there goes the tinkle already. 'Tis the best of tinkles though; 'tis for dinner: stay, listen! I thought so: the wolf in my stomach cried 'Amen!'" This last statement he confirmed with two oaths, and marched like a victorious gamecock into the convent, thinking by Gerard's silence he had convinced him, and not dreaming how profoundly he had disgusted him.

CHAPTER XXXII.

In the refectory allusion was made, at the table where Gerard sat, to the sudden death of the monk who had undertaken to write out fresh copies of the charter of the monastery, and the rule, etc.

Gerard caught this, and timidly offered his services. There was a hesitation which he mistook. "Nay, not for hire, my lords, but for love, and as a trifling return for many a good night's lodging the brethren of your order have bestowed on me a poor wayfarer."

A monk smiled approvingly; but hinted that the late brother was an excellent penman, and his work could not be continued but by a master. Gerard, on this, drew from his wallet with some trepidation a vellum deed, the back of which he had cleaned and written upon by way of specimen. The monk gave quite a start at sight of it, and very hastily went up the hall to the high table, and bending his knee so as just to touch in passing the fifth step and the tenth, or last, presented it to the prior with comments. Instantly a dozen knowing eyes were fixed on it, and a buzz of voices was heard; and soon Gerard saw the prior point more than once, and the monk came back, looking as proud as Punch, with a savoury crustade ryal, or game pie gravied and spiced, for Gerard, and a silver grace cup full of rich pimentum. This latter Gerard took, and bowing low, first to the distant prior, then to his own company, quaffed, and circulated the cup.

Instantly, to his surprise, the whole table hailed him as a brother: "Art convent bred, deny it not?" He acknowledged it, and gave Heaven thanks for it, for otherwise he had been as rude and ignorant as his brothers, Sybrandt and Cornelis. "But 'tis passing strange how you could know," said he.

"You drank with the cup in both hands," said two monks, speaking together.

The voices had for some time been loudish round a table at the bottom of the hall; but presently came a burst of mirth so obstreperous and prolonged, that the prior sent the very sub-prior all down the hall to check it, and inflict penance on every monk at the table. And Gerard's cheek burned with shame; for in the heart of the unruly merriment his ear had caught the word "courage!" and the trumpet tones of Denys of Burgundy.

Soon Gerard was installed in feu Werter's cell, with wax lights, and a little frame that could be set at any angle, and all the materials of caligraphy. The work, however, was too much for one evening. Then came the question, how could he ask Denys, the monk-hater, to stay longer? However, he told him, and offered to abide by his decision. He was agreeably surprised when Denys said graciously, "A day's rest will do neither of us harm. Write thou, and I'll pass the time as I may."

Gerard's work was vastly admired; they agreed that the records of the monastery had gained by poor Werter's death. The sub-prior forced a rix-dollar on Gerard, and several brushes and colours out of the convent stock, which was very large. He resumed his march warm at heart, for this was of good omen; since it was on the pen he relied to make his fortune and recover his well-beloved. "Come, Denys," said he good-humouredly, "see what the good monks have given me; now, do try to be fairer to them; for to be round with you, it chilled my friendship for a moment to hear even you call my benefactors 'hypocrites.'"

"I recant," said Denys.

"Thank you! thank you! Good Denys."

"I was a scurrilous vagabond."

"Nay, nay, say not so, neither!"

"But we soldiers are rude and hasty. I give myself the lie, and I offer those I misunderstood all my esteem. 'Tis unjust that thousands should be defamed for the hypocrisy of a few."

"Now are you reasonable. You have pondered what I said?"

"Nay, it is their own doing."

Gerard crowed a little, we all like to be proved in the right; and was all attention when Denys offered to relate how his conversion was effected.

"Well then, at dinner the first day a young monk beside me did open his jaws and laughed right out most musically. 'Good,' said I, 'at last I have fallen on a man and not a shorn ape.' So, to sound him further, I slapped his broad back and administered my consigne. 'Heaven forbid!' says he. I stared. For the dog looked as sad as Solomon; a better mime saw you never, even at a Mystery. 'I see war is no sharpener of the wits,' said he. 'What are the clergy for but to fight the foul fiend? and what else are monks for?

"The fiend being dead,
The friars are sped."

You may plough up the convents, and we poor monks shall have nought to do—but turn soldiers, and so bring him to life again.' Then there was a great laugh at my expense. 'Well, you are the monk for me,' said I. 'And you are the crossbowman for me,' quo' he. 'And I'll be bound you could tell us tales of the war should make our hair stand on end.' 'Excusez! the barber has put that out of the question,' quoth I, and then I had the laugh."

"What wretched ribaldry!" observed Gerard pensively.

The candid Denys at once admitted he had seen merrier jests hatched with less cackle. "'Twas a great matter to have got rid of hypocrisy. 'So,' said I, 'I can give you the chaire de poule, if that may content ye.' 'That we will see,' was the cry, and a signal went round."

Denys then related, bursting with glee, how at bed-time he had been taken to a cell instead of the great dortour, and strictly forbidden to sleep; and to aid his vigil, a book had been lent him of pictures representing a hundred merry adventures of monks in pursuit of the female laity; and how in due course he had been taken out bare-footed and down to the parlour, where was a supper fit for the Duke, and at it twelve jolly friars, the roaringest boys he had ever met in peace or war. How the story, the toast, the jest, the wine-cup had gone round, and some had played cards with a gorgeous pack, where

Saint Theresa, and Saint Catharine, etc., bedizened with gold, stood for the four queens; and black, white, gray, and crutched friars for the four knaves; and had staked their very rosaries, swearing like troopers when they lost. And how about midnight a sly monk had stolen out, but had by him and others been as cannily followed into the garden, and seen to thrust his hand into the ivy and out with a rope-ladder. With this he had run up on the wall, which was ten feet broad, yet not so nimbly but what a russet kirtle had popped up from the outer world as quick as he; and so to billing and cooing. That this situation had struck him as rather feline than ecclesiastical, and drawn from him the appropriate comment of a "mew!" The monks had joined the mewsical chorus, and the lay visitor shrieked and been sore discomforted; but Abelard only cried, "What, are ye there, ye jealous miauling knaves? ye shall caterwaul to some tune to-morrow night. I'll fit every man-jack of ye with a fardingale." That this brutal threat had reconciled him to stay another day—at Gerard's request.

Gerard groaned.

Meantime, unable to disconcert so brazen a monk, and the demoiselle beginning to whimper, they had danced caterwauling in a circle, then bestowed a solemn benediction on the two wall-flowers, and off to the parlour, where they found a pair lying dead drunk, and other two affectionate to tears. That they had straightway carried off the inanimate, and dragged off the loving and lachrymose, kicked them all merrily each into his cell—

"And so shut up in measureless content."

Gerard was disgusted, and said so.

Denys chuckled, and proceeded to tell him how the next day he and the young monks had drawn the fish-ponds and secreted much pike, carp, tench, and eel for their own use; and how, in the dead of night, he had been taken shoeless by crooked ways into the chapel, a ghost-like place, being dark, and then down some steps into a crypt below the chapel floor, where suddenly paradise had burst on him.

"'Tis there the holy fathers retire to pray," put in Gerard.

"Not always," said Denys; "wax candles by the dozen were lighted, and princely cheer; fifteen soups maigre, with marvellous twangs of venison, grouse, and hare in them, and twenty different fishes (being Friday), cooked with wondrous art, and each he between two buxom lasses, and each lass between two lads with a cowl, all but me; and to think I had to woo by interpreter. I doubt the knave put in three words for himself and one for me; if he didn't, hang him for a fool. And some of the weaker vessels were novices, and not wont to hold good wine; had to be coaxed ere they would put it to their white teeth; mais elles s'y faisaient; and the story, and the jest, and the cup went round (by the bye, they had flagons made to simulate breviaries); and a monk touched the cittern, and sang ditties with a voice tunable as a lark in spring. The posies did turn the faces of the women folk bright red at first; but elles s'y faisaient." Here Gerard exploded.

"Miserable wretches! Corrupters of youth! Perverters of innocence! but for your being there, Denys, who have been taught no better, oh, would God the church had fallen on the whole gang Impious, abominable hypocrites."

"Hypocrites!" cried Denys, with unfeigned surprise. "Why, that is what I clept them ere I knew them, and you withstood me. Nay, they are sinners; all good fellows are that; but by St. Denys his helmeted skull, no hypocrites, but right jolly roaring blades."

"Denys," said Gerard solemnly, "you little know the peril you ran that night. That church you defiled amongst you is haunted; I had it from one of the elder monks. The dead walk there; their light feet have been heard to patter o'er the stones."

"Miséricorde!" whispered Denys.

"Ay, more," said Gerard, lowering his voice almost to a whisper; "celestial sounds have issued from the purlieus of that very crypt you turned into a tavern. Voices of the dead holding unearthly communion have chilled the ear of midnight, and at times, Denys, the faithful in their nightly watches have even heard music from dead lips; and chords, made by no mortal finger, swept by no mortal hand, have rung faintly, like echoes, deep among the dead in those sacred vaults."

Denys wore a look of dismay. "Ugh! if I had known, mules and wain-ropes had not hauled me thither; and so" (with a sigh) "I had lost a merry time."

Whether further discussion might have thrown any more light upon these ghostly sounds, who can tell? for up came a "bearded brother" from the monastery, spurring his mule, and waving a piece of vellum in his hand. It was the deed between Ghysbrecht and Floris Brandt. Gerard valued it deeply as a remembrance of home : he turned pale at first but to think he had so nearly lost it, and to Denys's infinite amusement not only gave a piece of money to the lay brother, but kissed the mule's nose.

"I'll read you now," said Gerard, "were you twice as ill written ; and—to make sure of never losing you "—here he sat down, and taking out needle and thread, sewed it with feminine dexterity to his doublet—and his mind, and heart, and soul were away to Sevenbergen.

They reached the promised land, and Denys, who was in high spirits, doffed his bonnet to all the females, who curtsied and smiled in return ; fired his consigne at most of the men ; at which some stared, some grinned, some both ; and finally landed his friend at one of the long-promised Burgundian inns.

"It is a little one," said he, "but I know it of old for a good one ; 'Les Trois Poissons.' But what is this writ up ? I mind not this ;" and he pointed to an inscription that ran across the whole building in a single line of huge letters. "Oh, I see. ' Ici on loge à pied et à cheval,'" said Denys, going minutely through the inscription, and looking bumptious when he had effected it.

Gerard did look, and the sentence in question ran thus :

"ON NE LOGE CÉANS À CRÉDIT : CE BON-HOMME EST MORT, LES MAUVAIS PAIEURS L'ONT TUÉ."

CHAPTER XXXIII.

THEY met the landlord in the passage.

"Welcome, messieurs," said he, taking off his cap, with a low bow.

"Come, we are not in Germany," said Gerard.

In the public room they found the mistress, a buxom woman of forty. She curtsied to them, and smiled right cordially. "Give yourself the trouble of sitting ye down, fair sir," said she to Gerard, and dusted two chairs with her apron, not that they needed it.

"Thank you, dame," said Gerard. "Well," thought he, "this *is* a polite nation : the trouble of sitting down !

That will I with singular patience; and presently the labour of eating, also the toil of digestion, and finally, by Hercules his aid, the strain of going to bed, and the struggle of sinking fast asleep.

"Why, Denys, what are you doing? ordering supper for only two?"

"Why not?"

"What, can we sup without waiting for forty more? Burgundy for ever!"

"Aha! Courage, camarade. Le dia——"

"C'est convenu."

The salique law seemed not to have penetrated to French inns. In this one at least wimple and kirtle reigned supreme; doublets and hose were few in number, and feeble in act. The landlord himself wandered objectless, eternally taking off his cap to folk for want of thought; and the women, as they passed him in turn, thrust him quietly aside without looking at him, as we remove a live twig in bustling through a wood.

A maid brought in supper, and the mistress followed her, empty handed.

"Fall to, my masters," said she cheerily; "y'have but one enemy here, and he lies under your knife." (I shrewdly suspect this of formula.)

They fell to. The mistress drew her chair a little toward the table, and provided company as well as meat; gossiped genially with them like old acquaintances; but, this form gone through, the busy dame was soon off and sent in her daughter, a beautiful young woman of about twenty, who took the vacant seat. She was not quite so broad and genial as the elder, but gentle and cheerful, and showed a womanly tenderness for Gerard on learning the distance the poor boy had come, and had to go. She stayed nearly half an hour, and when she left them Gerard said, "This an inn? Why, it is like home."

"Qui fit François, il fit courtois," said Denys, bursting with gratified pride.

"Courteous! nay, Christian; to welcome us like home guests and old friends, us vagrants, here to-day and gone to-morrow. But indeed who better merits pity and kindness than the worn traveller far from his folk? Hola! here's another."

The new-comer was the chambermaid, a woman of about twenty-five, with a cocked nose, a large laughing mouth, and a sparkling black eye, and a bare arm very stout but not very shapely.

The moment she came in, one of the travellers passed a somewhat free jest on her; the next the whole company were roaring at his expense, so swiftly had her practised tongue done his business. Even as, in a passage of arms between a novice and a master of fence, foils clash—novice pinked. On this another, and then another, must break a lance with her; but Marion stuck her great arms upon her haunches, and held the whole room in play. This country girl possessed in perfection that rude and ready humour which looks mean and vulgar on paper, but carries all before it spoken: not wit's rapier; its bludgeon. Nature had done much for her in this way, and daily practice in an inn the rest.

Yet shall she not be photographed by me, but feebly indicated; for it was just four hundred years ago: the raillery was coarse, she returned every stroke in kind, and, though a virtuous woman, said things without winking which no decent man of our day would say even among men.

Gerard sat gaping with astonishment. This was to him almost a new variety of "that interesting species," homo. He whispered Denys, "Now I see why you Frenchmen say 'a woman's tongue is her sword':" just then she levelled another assailant; and the chivalrous Denys, to console and support "the weaker vessel," the iron kettle among the clay pots, administered his consigne, "Courage, ma mie, le——" etc.

She turned on him directly. "How can *he* be dead as long as there is an archer left alive?" (General laughter at her ally's expense.)

"It is 'washing day,' my masters," said she, with sudden gravity.

"Après? We travellers cannot strip and go bare while you wash our clothes," objected a peevish old fellow by the fireside, who had kept mumchance during the raillery, but crept out into the sunshine of commonplaces.

"I aimed not your way, ancient man," replied Marion superciliously. "But *since you ask me*" (here she scanned him slowly from head to foot), "I trow you might take a turn in the tub, clothes and all, and no harm done" (laughter). "But what I spoke for, I thought—this young sire—might like his beard starched."

Poor Gerard's turn had come; his chin crop was thin and silky.

The loudest of all the laughers this time was the traitor Denys, whose beard was of a good length, and singularly stiff and bristly; so that Shakespeare, though he never saw him, hit him in the bull's eye.

> "Full of strange oaths, and bearded like the pard.'
> —*As You Like It.*

Gerard bore the Amazonian satire mighty calmly. He had little personal vanity. "Nay, chambrière," said he, with a smile, "mine is all unworthy your pains; take you this fair growth in hand!" and he pointed to Denys's vegetable.

"Oh, time for that when I starch the besoms."

Whilst they were all shouting over this palpable hit, the mistress returned, and, in no more time than it took her to cross the threshold, did our Amazon turn to a seeming Madonna meek and mild.

Mistresses are wonderful subjugators. Their like I think breathes not on the globe. Housemaids, decide! It was a waste of histrionic ability though; for the landlady had heard, and did not at heart disapprove, the peals of laughter.

"Ah, Marion, lass," said she good-humouredly, "if you laid me an egg every time you cackle, 'Les Trois Poissons' would never lack an omelet."

"Now, dame," said Gerard, "what is to pay?"

"What for?"

"Our supper."

"Where is the hurry? cannot you be content to pay when you go? lose the guest, find the money, is the rule of 'The Three Fish.'"

"But, dame, outside 'The Three Fish' it is thus written—'Ici—on ne loge——'"

"Bah! Let that flea stick on the wall! Look hither," and she pointed to the smoky ceiling, which was covered with hieroglyphics. These were accounts, *vulgo scores;* intelligible to this dame and her daughter, who wrote them at need by simply mounting a low stool, and scratching with a knife so as to show lines of ceiling through the deposit of smoke. The dame explained that the writing on the wall was put there to frighten moneyless folk from the inn altogether, or to be acted on at odd times when a non-paying face should come in and insist on being served.

"We can't refuse them plump, you know. The law forbids us."

"And how know you mine is not such a face?"

"Out, fie! it is the best face that has entered 'The Three Fish' this autumn."

"And mine, dame?" said Denys; "dost see no knavery here?"

She eyed him calmly. "Not such a good one as the lad's; nor ever will be. But it is the face of a true man. For all that," added she drily, "an I were ten years younger, I'd as lieve not meet that face on a dark night too far from home."

Gerard stared. Denys laughed. "Why, dame, I would but sip the night dew off the flower; and you needn't take ten years off, nor ten days, to be worth risking a scratched face for."

"There, our mistress," said Marion, who had just come in, "said I not t'other day you could make a fool of them still, and if you were properly minded?"

"I daresay ye did; it sounds like some daft wench's speech."

"Dame," said Gerard, "this is wonderful."

"What? Oh! no, no, that is no wonder at all. Why, I have been here all my life; and reading faces is the first thing a girl picks up in an inn."

Marion. "And frying eggs the second; no, telling lies; frying eggs is the third, though."

The Mistress. "And holding her tongue the last, and modesty the day after never at all."

Marion. "Alack! Talk of *my* tongue. But I say no more. She under whose wing I live now deals the blow. I'm sped—'tis but a chambermaid gone. Catch what's left on't!" and she staggered and sank backwards on to the handsomest fellow in the room, which happened to be Gerard.

"Tic! tic!" cried he peevishly; "there, don't be stupid! that is too heavy a jest for me. See you not I am talking to the mistress?"

Marion resumed her elasticity with a grimace, made two little bounds into the middle of the floor, and there turned a pirouette. "There, mistress," said she, "I give in; 'tis you that reigns supreme with the men, leastways with male children."

"Young man," said the mistress, "this girl is not so stupid as her deportment; in reading of faces, and frying of omelets, there we are great. 'Twould be hard if we failed at these arts, since they are about all we do know."

"You do not quite take me, dame," said Gerard. "That honesty in a face should shine forth to your experienced eye, that seems reasonable; but how by looking on Denys here could you learn his one little foible, his insanity, his miserable mulierosity?" Poor Gerard got angrier the more he thought of it.

"His mule—his what?" (crossing herself with superstitious awe at the polysyllable).

"Nay, 'tis but the word I was fain to invent for him."

"Invent? What, can a child like you make other words than grow in Burgundy by nature? Take heed what ye do! why, we are overrun with them already, especially bad ones. Lord, these be times. I look to hear of a new thistle invented next."

"But, dame, I found language too poor to paint him. I was fain to invent. You know Necessity is the mother of——"

"Ay, ay, that is old enough, o' conscience."

"Well then, dame, mulierose—that means wrapped up, body and soul, in women. So, prithee, tell me, how did you ever detect the noodle's mulierosity?"

"Alas! good youth, you make a mountain of a molehill. We that are women be notetakers, and out of the tail of our eye see more than most men can glaring through a prospect glass. Whiles I move to and fro doing this and that, my glance is still on my guests, and I did notice that this soldier's eyes were never off the women folk; my daughter, or Marion, or even an old woman like me, all was gold to him, and there a sat glowering; oh, you foolish, foolish man! Now *you* still turned to the speaker, her or him, and that is common sense."

Denys burst into a hoarse laugh. "You never were more out. Why, this silky, smooth-faced companion is a very Turk—all but his beard. He is what d'ye call 'em oser than ere an archer in the Duke's bodyguard. He is more wrapped up in one single Dutch lass called Margaret than I am in the whole bundle of ye, brown and fair."

2   "Man alive, that is just the contrary," said the hostess.

"Yourn is the bane, and hisn the cure. Cling you still to Margaret, my dear. I hope she is an honest girl."

"Dame, she is an angel."

"Ay, ay, they are all that till better acquainted. I'd as lieve have her no more than honest, and then she will serve to keep you out of worse company. As for you, soldier, there is trouble in store for you. Your eyes were never made for the good of your soul."

"Nor of his pouch either," said Marion, striking in; "and his lips, they will sip the dew, as he calls it, off many a bramble bush."

"Overmuch clack, Marion; overmuch clack."

"Ods bodikins, mistress; ye didn't hire me to be one o' your three fishes, did ye?" and Marion sulked thirty seconds.

"Is that the way to speak to our mistress?" remonstrated the landlord, who had slipped in.

"Hold your whisht," said his wife sharply; "it is not your business to check the girl, she is a good servant to you."

"What, is the cock never to crow, and the hens at it all day?"

"You can crow as loud as you like, my man—out o' doors; but the hen means to rule the roost."

"I know a byword to that tune," said Gerard.

"Do ye, now? out wi't then."

"Femme veut en toute saison,
     Estre dame en sa maison."

"I never heard it afore; but 'tis as sooth as gospel. Ay, they that set these bywords a-rolling had eyes and tongues, and tongues and eyes. Before all the world give me an old saw."

"And me a young husband," said Marion. "Now there was a chance for you all, and nobody spoke. Oh! it is too late now, I've changed my mind."

"All the better for some poor fellow," suggested Denys.

And now the arrival of the young mistress, or, as she was called, the little mistress, was the signal for them all to draw round the fire, like one happy family—travellers, host, hostess, and even servants in the outer ring—and tell stories till bedtime. And Gerard in his turn told a tremendous one out of his repertory, a MS. collection of "Acts of the Saints," and made them all shudder deliciously; but soon after began to nod, exhausted by the effort, I should say. The young mistress saw, and gave Marion a look. She instantly lighted a rush, and laying her hand on Gerard's shoulder invited him to follow her. She showed him a room where were two nice white beds, and bade him choose. "Either is paradise," said he. "I'll take this one. Do you know I have not lain in a naked bed once since I left my home in Holland."

"Alack! poor soul!" said she; "well then the sooner my flax and your down (he! he!) come together, the better; so — allons!" and she held out her cheek as business-like as if it had been her hand for a fee.

"Allons? what does that mean?"

"It means 'good-night.' Ahem! What, don't they salute the chambermaid in your part?"

"Not all in a moment."

"What, do they make a business on't?"

"Nay, perverter of words, I mean we make not so free with strange women."

"They must be strange women if they do not think you strange fools then. Here is a coil. Why, all the old greasy graybeards that lie at our inn do kiss us chambermaids; faugh! and what have we poor wretches to set on t'other side the compt but now and then a nice young——? Alack! time flies, chambermaids can't be spared long in the nursery, so how is't to be?"

"An't please you arrange with my comrade for both. He is mulierose; I am not."

"Nay, 'tis the curb he will want, not the spur. Well! well! you shall to bed without paying the usual toll; and oh, but 'tis sweet to fall in with a young man who can withstand these ancient ill customs, and gainsay brazen hussies. Shalt have thy reward."

"Thank you! But what are you doing with my bed?"

"Me? oh, only taking off these sheets, and going to put on the pair the drunken miller slept in last night."

"Oh no! no! You cruel, black-hearted thing! There! there!"

"A la bonne heure! What will not perseverance effect! But note now the frowardness of a mad wench! I cared not for't a button. I am dead sick of that sport this five years. But you denied me; so then forthwith I behoved to have it; belike had gone through fire and water for't. Alas, young sir, we women are kittle cattle; poor perverse toads; excuse us; and keep us in our place, savoir, at arm's length; and so good-night!"

At the door she turned and said, with a complete change of tone and manner, "The Virgin guard thy head, and the holy Evangelists watch the bed where lies a poor young wanderer far from home! Amen!"

And the next moment he heard her run tearing down the stairs, and soon a peal of laughter from the salle betrayed her whereabouts.

"Now that is a character," said Gerard profoundly, and yawned over the discovery.

In a very few minutes he was in a dry bath of cold, clean linen, inexpressibly refreshing to him after so long disuse; then came a delicious glow; and then—Sevenbergen.

In the morning Gerard awoke infinitely refreshed, and was for rising, but found himself a close prisoner. His linen had vanished. Now this was paralysis, for the night-gown is a recent institution. In Gerard's century, and indeed long after, men did not play fast and loose with clean sheets (when they could get them), but crept into them clothed with—their innocence, like Adam: out of bed they seem to have taken most after his eldest son.

Gerard bewailed his captivity to Denys; but that instant the door opened, and in sailed Marion with their linen, newly washed and ironed, on her two arms, and set it down on the table.

"Oh, you good girl," cried Gerard.

"Alack, have you found me out at last?"

"Yes, indeed. Is this another *custom?*"

"Nay, not to take them unbidden; but at night we aye question travellers, are they for linen washed. So I came into you, but you were both sound. Then said I to the little mistress, 'La! where is the sense of waking wearied men, t'ask them is Charles the Great dead, and would they liever carry foul linen or clean, especially this one with a skin like cream?' 'And so he has, I declare,' said the young mistress."

"That was me," remarked Denys, with the air of a commentator.

"Guess once more, and you'll hit the mark."

"Notice him not, Marion, he is an impudent fellow; and I am sure we cannot be grateful enough for your goodness, and I am sorry I ever refused you—anything you fancied you should like."

"Oh, are ye there," said l'espiègle. "I take that to mean you would fain brush the morning dew off, as your bashful companion calls it; well then, excuse me, 'tis *customary*, but not prudent. I decline. Quits with you, lad."

"Stop! stop!" cried Denys, as she was making off victorious; "I am curious to know how many of ye were here last night a-feasting your eyes on us twain."

"'Twas so satisfactory a feast as we weren't half a minute over't. Who? why the big mistress, the little mistress, Janet, and me, and the whole *posse comitatus*, on tiptoe. We mostly make our rounds the last thing, not to get burned down; and in prodigious numbers. Somehow that maketh us bolder, especially where archers lie scattered about."

"Why did not you tell me? I'd have lain awake."

"Beau sire, the saying goes that the good and the ill are all one while their lids are closed. So we said, 'Here is one who will serve God best asleep. Break not his rest!'"

"She is funny," said Gerard dictatorially.

"I must be either that or knavish."

"How so?"

"Because 'The Three Fish' pay me to be funny. You will eat before you part? Good! then I'll go see the meat be fit for such worshipful teeth."

"Denys!"

"What is your will?"

"I wish that was a great boy, and going along with us to keep us cheery."

"So do not I. But I wish it was going along with us as it is."

"Now Heaven forfend! A fine fool you would make of yourself."

They broke their fast, settled their score, and said farewell. Then it was they found Marion had not exaggerated the "custom of the country." The three principal women took and kissed them right heartily, and they kissed the three principal women. The landlord took and kissed them, and they kissed the landlord; and the cry was, "Come back, the sooner the better!"

"Never pass 'The Three Fish'; should your purses be void, bring yourselves: 'le sieur crédit' is not dead for you."

And they took the road again.

They came to a little town, and Denys went to buy shoes. The shopkeeper was in the doorway, but wide awake. He received Denys with a bow down to the ground. The customer was soon fitted, and followed to the street, and dismissed with graceful salutes from the doorstep.

The friends agreed it was Elysium to deal with such a shoemaker as this. "Not but what my German shoes have lasted well enough," said Gerard the just.

Outside the town was a pebbled walk.

"This is to keep the burghers' feet dry, a-walking o' Sundays with their wives and daughters," said Denys.

Those simple words of Denys, one stroke of a careless tongue, painted "home" in Gerard's heart. "Oh! how sweet," said he. "Mercy! what is this? A gibbet! and ugh, two skeletons thereon! Oh, Denys, what a sorry sight to woo by!"

"Nay," said Denys, "a comfortable sight; for every rogue i' the air there is one the less a-foot."

A little farther on they came to two pillars, and between these was a huge wheel closely studded with iron prongs, and entangled in these were bones and fragments of cloth miserably dispersed over the wheel.

Gerard hid his face in his hands. "Oh, to think those patches and bones are all that is left of a man! of one who was what we are now."

"Excusez! a thing that went on two legs and stole; are we no more than that?"

"How know ye he stole? Have true men never suffered death and torture too?"

"None of my kith ever found their way to the gibbet, I know."

"The better their luck. Prithee, how died the saints?"

"Hard. But not in Burgundy."

"Ye massacred them wholesale at Lyons, and that is on Burgundy's threshold. To you the gibbet proves the crime, because you read not story. Alas! had you stood on Calvary that bloody day we sigh for to this hour, I tremble to think you had perhaps shouted for joy at the gibbet builded there; for the cross was but the Roman gallows, Father Martin says."

"The blaspheming old hound!"

"Oh, fie! fie! a holy and a book-learned man. Ay, Denys, y'had read them, that suffered there, by the bare light of the gibbet. 'Drive in the nails!' y'had cried; 'drive in the spear!' Here be three malefactors. Three 'roués.' Yet of those little three one was the first Christian saint, and another was the Saviour of the world which gibbeted him."

Denys assured him on his honour they managed things better in Burgundy. He added, too, after profound reflection, that the horrors Gerard had alluded to had more than once made him curse and swear with rage when told by the good curé in his native village at Eastertide; "but they chanced in an outlandish nation, and near a thousand years agone. Mort de ma vie, let us hope it is not true; or at least sore exaggerated. Do but see how all tales gather as they roll!"

Then he reflected again, and all in a moment turned red with ire. "Do ye not blush to play with your book-craft on your unlettered friend, and throw dust in his eyes, evening the saints with these reptiles?"

Then suddenly he recovered his good humour. "Since your heart beats for vermin, feel for the carrion crows: they be as good vermin as these; would ye send them to bed supperless, poor pretty poppets? Why, these be their larder; the pangs of hunger would gnaw them dead, but for cold cut-purse hung up here and there."

Gerard, who had for some time maintained a dead silence, informed him the subject was closed between them, and for ever. "There are things," said he, "in which our hearts seem wide as the poles asunder, and eke our heads. But I love thee dearly all the same," he added, with infinite grace and tenderness.

Towards afternoon they heard a faint wailing noise on ahead; it grew distincter as they proceeded. Being fast walkers they soon came up with its cause: a score of pikemen, accompanied by several constables, were marching along, and in advance of them was a herd of animals they were driving. These creatures, in number rather more than a hundred, were of various ages, only very few were downright old; the males were downcast and silent. It was the females from whom all the outcry came. In other words, the animals thus driven along at the law's point were men and women.

"Good Heaven!" cried Gerard, "what a band of them! But stay, surely all those children cannot be thieves; why, there are some in arms. What on earth is this, Denys?"

Denys advised him to ask that "bourgeois" with the badge. "This is Burgundy; here a civil question ever draws a civil reply."

Gerard went up to the officer, and removing his cap, a civility which was immediately returned, said, "For our Lady's sake, sir, what do ye with these poor folk?"

"Nay, what is that to you, my lad?" replied the functionary suspiciously.

"Master, I'm a stranger, and athirst for knowledge."

"That is another matter. What are we doing? ahem. Why we—Dost hear, Jacques? Here is a stranger seeks to know what we are doing," and the two machines were tickled that there should be a man who did not know something they happened to know. In all ages this has tickled. However, the chuckle was brief and moderated by their native courtesy, and the official turned to Gerard again. "What we are doing? hum!" and now he hesitated, not from any doubt as to what he was doing, but because he was hunting for a single word that should convey the matter.

"Ce que nous faisons, mon gars?—Mais—dam—NOUS TRANSVASONS."

"You decant? that should mean you pour from one vessel to another."

"Precisely." He explained that last year the town of Charmes had been sore thinned by a pestilence, whole houses emptied and trades short of hands. Much ado to get in the rye, and the flax half spoiled. So the bailiff and aldermen had written to the Duke's secretary, and the Duke he sent far and wide to know what town was too full. "That are we," had the bailie of Toul writ back. "Then send four or five score of your townsfolk," was the order. "Was not this to decant the full town into the empty, and is not the good Duke the father of his people, and will not let the duchy be weakened, nor its fair towns laid waste by sword nor pestilence; but meets the one with pike and arbalest" (touching his cap to the sergeant and Denys alternately), "and t'other with policy? LONG LIVE THE DUKE!"

The pikemen of course were not to be outdone in loyalty, so they shouted with stentorian lungs, "LONG LIVE THE DUKE!" Then the decanted ones, partly because loyalty was an unreasoning sentiment in those days, partly perhaps because they feared some further ill consequence, should they alone be mute, raised a feeble, tremulous shout, "Long live the Duke!"

But at this insulted nature rebelled. Perhaps indeed the sham sentiment drew out the real, for on the very heels of that loyal noise a loud and piercing wail burst from every woman's bosom, and a deep, deep groan from every man's; oh! the air filled in a moment with womanly and manly anguish. Judge what it must have been when the rude pikemen halted unbidden, all confused, as if a wall of sorrow had started up before them.

"En avant," roared the sergeant, and they marched again, but muttering and cursing.

"Ah, the ugly sound," said the civilian, wincing. "Les malheureux!" cried he ruefully, for where is the single man can hear the sudden agony of a multitude and not be moved? "Les ingrats! They are going whence they were *de trop* to where they will be welcome; from starvation to plenty—and they object. They even make dismal noises. One would think we were thrusting them forth from Burgundy."

"Come away," whispered Gerard, trembling; "come away," and the friends strode forward.

When they passed the head of the column, and saw the men walk with their eyes bent in bitter gloom upon the ground, and the women, some carrying, some leading little children, and weeping as they went, and the poor bairns, some frolicking, some weeping because "their mammies" wept, Gerard tried hard to say a word of comfort, but choked and could utter nothing to the mourners; but gasped, "Come on, Denys, I cannot mock such sorrow with little words of comfort." And now, artist-like, all his aim was to get swiftly out of the grief he could not soothe. He almost ran not to hear these sighs and sobs.

"Why, mate," said Denys, "art the colour of a lemon. Man alive, take not other folk's troubles to heart! not one of those whining milksops there but would see thee, a stranger, hanged without winking."

Gerard scarce listened to him.

"Decant them!" he groaned; "ay, if blood were no thicker than wine. Princes, ye are wolves. Poor things! Poor things! Ah, Denys! Denys! with looking on their grief mine own comes home to me. Well-a-day! ah, well-a-day!"

"Ay, now you talk reason. That you, poor lad, should be driven all the way from Holland to Rome is pitiful indeed. But these snivelling curs, where is their hurt? There is six score of 'em to keep one another company; besides, they are not going out of Burgundy."

"Better for them if they had never been in it."

"Méchant, va! they are but going from one village to another, a mule's journey! whilst thou—there, no more. Courage, camarade, le diable est mort."

Gerard shook his head very doubtfully, but kept silence for about a mile, and then he said thoughtfully, "Ay, Denys, but then I am sustained by book-learning. These are simple folk that likely thought their village was the world: now what is this? more weeping. Oh! 'tis a sweet world. Humph! A little girl that hath broke her pipkin. Now may I hang on one of your gibbets but I'll dry somebody's tears," and he pounced savagely upon this little martyr, like a kite on a chick, but with more generous intentions. It was a pretty little lass of about twelve; the tears were raining down her two peaches, and her palms lifted to heaven in that utter, though temporary, desolation which attends calamity at twelve; and at her feet the fatal cause, a broken pot, worth, say the fifth of a modern farthing.

"What, hast broken thy pot, little one?" said Gerard, acting intensest sympathy.

"Hélas! bel gars; as you behold;" and the hands came down from the sky and both pointed at the fragments. A statuette of adversity.

"And you weep so for that?"

"Needs I must, bel gars. My mammy will massacre me. Do they not already" (with a fresh burst of woe) "c-c-call me J-J-Jean-net-on C-c-casse tout? It wanted but this: that I should break my poor pot. Hélas! fallait-il donc, mére de Dieu?"

"Courage, little love," said Gerard; "'tis not thy heart lies broken; money will soon mend pots. See, now, here is a piece of silver, and there, scarce a stone's throw off, is a potter; take the bit of silver to him, and buy another pot, and the copper the potter will give thee keep that to play with thy comrades."

The little mind took in all this, and smiles began to struggle with the tears; but spasms are like waves, they cannot go down the very moment the wind of trouble is lulled. So Denys thought well to bring up his reserve of consolation. "Courage, ma mie, le diable est mort!" cried that inventive warrior gaily. Gerard shrugged his shoulders at such a way of cheering a little girl.

> "What a fine thing
>   Is a lute with one string,"

said he.

The little girl's face broke into warm sunshine.

"Oh, the good news! oh, the good news!" she sang out with such heartfelt joy, it went off into a honeyed whine, even as our gay old tunes have a pathos underneath. "So then," said she, "they will no longer be able to threaten us little girls with him, MAKING OUR LIVES A BURDEN!" And she bounded off "to tell Nanette," she said.

There is a theory that everything has its counterpart; if true, Denys it would seem had found the mind his consigne fitted.

While he was roaring with laughter at its unexpected success and Gerard's amazement, a little hand pulled his jerkin and a little face peeped round his waist. Curiosity was now the dominant passion in that small but vivid countenance.

"Est-ce toi qui l'a tué, beau soldat?"

"Oui, ma mie," said Denys, as gruffly as ever he could, rightly deeming this would smack of supernatural puissance to owners of bell-like trebles. "C'est moi. Çà vaut une petite embrassade—pas?"

"Je crois ben. Aie! aie!"

"Qu'as-tu?"

"Çà pique! çà pique!"

"Quel dommage! je vais la couper."

"Nenni, ce n'est rien; et pisque t'as tué ce méchant. T'es fièrement beau, tout d' même, toi; t'es ben miex que ma grande sœur."

"Will you not kiss me, too, ma mie?" said Gerard.

"Je ne demande par miex. Tiens, tiens, tiens! c'est doulce celle-ci. Ah! que j'aimons les hommes! Des fames, çà ne m'aurait jamais donné l'arjan blanc, plutôt çà m'aurait ri au nez. C'est si peu de chose, les fames. Serviteur, beaulx sires! Bon voiage; et n'oubliez point la Jeanneton!"

"Adieu, petit cœur," said Gerard, and on they marched; but presently looking back they saw the contemner of women in the middle of the road, making them a reverence, and blowing them kisses with little May morning face.

"Come on," cried Gerard lustily. "I shall win to Rome yet. Holy St. Bavon, what a sunbeam of innocence hath shot across our bloodthirsty road! Forget thee, little Jeanneton? not likely, amidst all this slobbering, and gibbeting, and decanting. Come on, thou laggard! forward!"

"Dost call this marching?" remonstrated Denys; "why, we shall walk o'er Christmas Day and never see it."

At the next town they came to, suddenly an arbalestrier ran out of a tavern after them, and in a moment his beard and Denys's were like two brushes stuck together. It was a comrade. He insisted on their coming into the tavern with him, and breaking a bottle of wine. In course of conversation, he told Denys there was an insurrection in the Duke's Flemish provinces, and soldiers were ordered thither from all parts of Burgundy. "Indeed, I marvelled to see thy face turned this way."

"I go to embrace my folk that I have not seen these three years. Ye can quell a bit of a rising without me, I trow."

Suddenly Denys gave a start. "Dost hear, Gerard? this comrade is bound for Holland."

"What then? ah, a letter! a letter to Margaret! but will he be so good, so kind?"

The soldier with a torrent of blasphemy informed him he would not only take it, but go a league or two out of his way to do it.

In an instant out came inkhorn and paper from Gerard's wallet; and he wrote a long letter to Margaret, and told her briefly what I fear I have spun too tediously; dwelt most on the bear, and the plunge in the Rhine, and the character of Denys, whom he painted to the life. And with many endearing expressions bade her be of good cheer; some trouble and peril there had been, but all that was over now, and his only grief left was, that he could not hope to have a word from her hand till he should reach

Rome. He ended with comforting her again as hard as he could. And so absorbed was he in his love and his work, that he did not see all the people in the room were standing peeping to watch the nimble and true finger execute such rare penmanship.

Denys, proud of his friend's skill, let him alone, till presently the writer's face worked, and soon the scalding tears began to run down his young cheeks, one after another, on the paper where he was then writing comfort, comfort. Then Denys rudely repulsed the curious, and asked his comrade with a faltering voice whether he had the heart to let so sweet a love-letter miscarry? The other swore by the face of St. Luke he would lose the forefinger of his right hand sooner.

Seeing him so ready, Gerard charged him also with a short, cold letter to his parents; and in it he drew hastily with his pen two hands grasping each other, to signify farewell. By the bye, one drop of bitterness found its way into his letter to Margaret. "I write to thee alone, and to those who love thee. If my flesh and blood care to hear news of me, they must be kind to thee, and then thou mayest read my letter to them; but not else, and even then let this not out of thy hand, or thou lovest me not. I know what I ask of thee, and why I ask it. Thou knowest not. I am older now by many years than thou art, and I was a month agone. Therefore obey me in this one thing, dear heart, or thou wilt make me a worse wife than I hope to make thee a husband, God willing."

On second thoughts I believe there was something more than bitterness in this. For his mind, young but intense, had been bent many hours every day upon Sevenbergen and Tergou, and speculated on every change of feeling and circumstance that his exile might bring about.

Gerard now offered money to the soldier. He hesitated, but declined it. "No, no! art comrade of my comrade; and may "——(etc.)——"but thy love for the wench touches me. I'll break another bottle at thy charge an thou wilt, and so cry quits."

"Well said, comrade," cried Denys. "Hadst taken money, I had invited thee to walk in the courtyard and cross swords with me."

"Whereupon I had cut thy comb for thee," retorted the other.

"Hadst done thy endeavour, drôle, I doubt not."

They drank the new bottle, shook hands, adhered to custom, and parted on opposite routes.

This delay, however, somewhat put out Denys's calculations, and evening surprised them ere they reached a little town he was making for, where was a famous hotel. However, they fell in with a roadside auberge, and Denys, seeing a buxom girl at the door, said, "This seems a decent inn," and led the way into the kitchen. They ordered supper, to which no objection was raised, only the landlord requested them to pay for it beforehand. It was not an uncommon proposal in any part of the world. Still it was not universal, and Denys was nettled, and dashed his hand somewhat ostentatiously into his purse and pulled out a gold angel. "Count me the change, and speedily," said he. "You tavernkeepers are more likely to rob me than I you."

While the supper was preparing, Denys disappeared, and was eventually found by Gerard in the yard, helping Manon, his plump but not bright decoy duck, to draw water, and pouring extravagant compliments into her dullish ear. Gerard grunted and returned to table, but Denys did not come in for a good quarter of an hour.

"Uphill work at the end of a march," said he, shrugging his shoulders.

"What matters that to you?" said Gerard drily. "The mad dog bites all the world."

"Exaggerator. You know I bite but the fairer half. Well, here comes supper; that is better worth biting."

During supper the girl kept constantly coming in and out, and looking point-blank at them, especially at Denys; and at last in leaning over him to remove a dish, dropped a word in his ear; and he replied with a nod.

As soon as supper was cleared away, Denys rose and strolled to the door, telling Gerard the sullen fair had relented, and given him a little rendezvous in the stable-yard.

Gerard suggested that the cow-house would have been a more appropriate locality. "I shall go to bed, then," said he, a little crossly. "Where is the landlord? out at this time of night? no matter. I know our room. Shall you be long, pray?"

"Not I. I grudge leaving the fire and thee. But what can I do? There are two sorts of invitations a Burgundian never declines."

Denys found a figure seated by the well. It was Manon;

but instead of receiving him as he thought he had a right to expect, coming by invitation, all she did was to sob. He asked her what ailed her? She sobbed. Could he do anything for her? She sobbed.

The good-natured Denys, driven to his wits' end, which was no great distance, proffered the custom of the country by way of consolation. She repulsed him roughly. "Is it a time for fooling?" said she, and sobbed.

"You seem to think so," said Denys, waxing wroth. But the next moment he added tenderly, "and I, who could never bear to see beauty in distress."

"It is not for myself."

"Who then? your sweetheart?"

"Oh, que nenni. My sweetheart is not on earth now, and to think I have not an écu to buy masses for his soul;" and in this shallow nature the grief seemed now to be all turned in another direction.

"Come, come," said Denys, "shalt have money to buy masses for thy dead lad; I swear it. Meantime tell me why you weep."

"For you."

"For me? Art mad?"

"No; I am not mad. 'Tis you that were mad to open your purse before him."

The mystery seemed to thicken, and Denys, wearied of stirring up the mud by questions, held his peace to see if it would not clear of itself. Then the girl, finding herself no longer questioned, seemed to go through some internal combat. At last she said, doggedly and aloud, "I will. The Virgin give me courage! What matters it if they kill me, since he is dead? Soldier, the landlord is out."

"Oh, is he?"

"What, do landlords leave their taverns at this time of night? also see what a tempest! We are sheltered here, but t'other side it blows a hurricane."

Denys said nothing.

"He is gone to fetch the band."

"The band! what band?"

"Those who will cut your throat and take your gold. Wretched man to go and shake gold in an innkeeper's face!"

The blow came so unexpectedly it staggered even Denys, accustomed as he was to sudden perils. He muttered a single word, but in it a volume.

"Gerard!"

"Gerard! What is that? Oh, 'tis thy comrade's name, poor lad. Get him out quick ere they come, and fly to the next town."

"And thou?"

"They will kill me."

"That shall they not. Fly with us."

"'Twill avail me nought; one of the band will be sent to kill me. They are sworn to slay all who betray them."

"I'll take thee to my native place full thirty leagues from hence, and put thee under my own mother's wing, ere they shall hurt a hair o' thy head. But first Gerard. Stay thou here whilst I fetch him!"

As he was darting off, the girl seized him convulsively, and with all the iron strength excitement lends to women. "Stay me not! for pity's sake," he cried; "'tis life or death."

"Sh!—sh!" whispered the girl, shutting his mouth hard with her hand, and putting her pale lips close to him, and her eyes, that seemed to turn backwards, straining towards some indistinct sound.

He listened.

He heard footsteps, many footsteps, and no voices. She whispered in his ear, "They are come."

And trembled like a leaf.

Denys felt it was so. Travellers in that number would never have come in dead silence.

The feet were now at the very door.

"How many?" said he, in a hollow whisper.

"Hush!" and she put her mouth to his very ear.

And who, that had seen this man and woman in that attitude, would have guessed what freezing hearts were theirs, and what terrible whispers passed between them?

"Seven."

"How armed?"

"Sword and dagger; and the giant with his axe. They call him the Abbot."

"And my comrade?"

"Nothing can save him. Better lose one life than two. Fly!"

Denys's blood froze at this cynical advice. "Poor creature, you know not a soldier's heart."

He put his head in his hands a moment, and a hundred thoughts of dangers baffled whirled through his brain.

"Listen, girl! There is one chance for our lives, if thou wilt but be true to us. Run to the town, to the nearest tavern, and tell the first soldier there, that a soldier here is sore beset, but armed, and his life to be saved if they will but run. Then to the bailiff. But first to the soldiers. Nay, not a word, but buss me, good lass, and fly! men's lives hang on thy heels."

She kilted up her gown to run. He came round to the road with her, saw her cross the road cringing with fear, then glide away, then turn into an erect shadow, then melt away in the storm.

And now he must get to Gerard. But how? He had to run the gauntlet of the whole band. He asked himself, what was the worst thing they could do? for he had learned in war that an enemy does not what you hope he will do, but what you hope he will not do. "Attack me as I enter the kitchen! Then I must not give them time."

Just as he drew near to the latch, a terrible thought crossed him. "Suppose they had already dealt with Gerard. Why then," thought he, "nought is left but to kill, and be killed;" and he strung his bow, and walked rapidly into the kitchen. There were seven hideous faces seated round the fire, and the landlord pouring them out neat brandy, blood's forerunner in every age.

"What! company!" cried Denys gaily; "one minute, my lads, and I'll be with you;" and he snatched up a lighted candle off the table, opened the door that led to the staircase, and went up it hallooing, "What, Gerard! whither hast thou skulked to?" There was no answer.

He hallooed louder, "Gerard, where art thou?"

After a moment, in which Denys lived an hour of agony, a peevish half-inarticulate noise issued from the room at the head of the little stairs. Denys burst in, and there was Gerard asleep.

"Thank God!" he said, in a choking voice, then began to sing loud, untuneful ditties. Gerard put his fingers into his ears; but presently he saw in Denys's face a horror that contrasted strangely with his sudden merriment.

"What ails thee?" said he, sitting up and staring.

"Hush!" said Denys, and his hand spoke even more plainly than his lips. "Listen to me."

Denys then pointing significantly to the door, to show Gerard sharp ears were listening hard by, continued his song aloud, but under cover of it threw in short muttered syllables.

"(Our lives are in peril.)

"(Thieves.)

"(Thy doublet.)

"(Thy sword.)

"Aid.

"Coming.

"Put off time." Then aloud—

"Well, now, wilt have t'other bottle ?—Say Nay."

"No, not I."

"But I tell thee, there are half a dozen jolly fellows.— Tired."

"Ay, but I am too wearied," said Gerard. "Go thou."

"Nay, nay!" Then he went to the door and called out cheerfully, "Landlord, the young milksop will not rise. Give those honest fellows t'other bottle. I will pay for't in the morning."

He heard a brutal and fierce chuckle.

Having thus by observation made sure the kitchen door was shut, and the miscreants were not actually listening, he examined the chamber door closely, then quietly shut it, but did not bolt it, and went and inspected the window.

It was too small to get out of, and yet a thick bar of iron had been let in the stone to make it smaller ; and just as he made this chilling discovery, the outer door of the house was bolted with a loud clang.

Denys groaned, "The beasts are in the shambles."

But would the thieves attack them while they were awake ? Probably not.

Not to throw away this their best chance, the poor souls now made a series of desperate efforts to converse, as if discussing ordinary matters, and by this means Gerard learned all that had passed, and that the girl was gone for aid.

"Pray Heaven she may not lose heart by the way," said Denys sorrowfully.

And Denys begged Gerard's forgiveness for bringing him out of his way for this.

Gerard forgave him.

"I would fear them less, Gerard, but for one they call

the Abbot. I picked him out at once. Taller than you, bigger than us both put together. Fights with an axe. Gerard, a man to lead a herd of deer to battle. I shall kill that man to-night, or he will kill me. I think somehow 'tis he will kill me."

"Saints forbid! Shoot him at the door! What avails his strength against your weapon?"

"I shall pick him out; but if it comes to hand fighting, run swiftly under his guard, or you are a dead man. I tell thee neither of us may stand a blow of that axe; thou never sawest such a body of a man."

Gerard was for bolting the door; but Denys with a sign showed him that half the door-post turned outward on a hinge, and the great bolt was little more than a blind. "I have forborne to bolt it," said he, "that they may think us the less suspicious."

Near an hour rolled away thus. It seemed an age. Yet it was but a little hour, and the town was a league distant. And some of the voices in the kitchen became angry and impatient.

"They will not wait much longer," said Denys, "and we have no chance at all unless we surprise them."

"I will do whate'er you bid," said Gerard meekly.

There was a cupboard on the same side as the door, but between it and the window. It reached nearly to the ground, but not quite. Denys opened the cupboard door and placed Gerard on a chair behind it. "If they run for the bed, strike at the napes of their necks! a sword cut there always kills or disables." He then arranged the bolsters and their shoes in the bed so as to deceive a person peeping from a distance, and drew the short curtains at the head.

Meantime Gerard was on his knees. Denys looked round and saw him.

"Ah!" said Denys, "above all, pray them to forgive me for bringing you into this guetapens!"

And now they grasped hands and looked in one another's eyes; oh, such a look! Denys's hand was cold, and Gerard's warm.

They took their posts.

Denys blew out the candle.

"We must keep silence now."

But in the terrible tension of their nerves and very souls they found they could hear a whisper fainter than any man could catch at all outside that door.   They could hear each other's hearts thump at times.

"Good news!" breathed Denys, listening at the door.
"They are casting lots."

"Pray that it may be the Abbot."
"Yes.   Why?"
"If he comes alone I can make sure of him."

"Denys!"
"Ay!"
"I fear I shall go mad if they do not come soon."
"Shall I feign sleep?   Shall I snore?"
"Will that—— ?"
"Perhaps."
"Do then, and God have mercy on us!"
Denys snored at intervals.

There was a scuffling of feet heard in the kitchen, and then all was still.

Denys snored again.   Then he took up his position behind the door.

But he or they who had drawn the lot seemed determined to run no foolish risks.   Nothing was attempted in a hurry.

When they were almost starved with cold, and waiting for the attack, the door on the stairs opened softly and closed again.   Nothing more.

There was another harrowing silence.

Then a single light footstep on the stairs; and nothing more.

Then a light crept under the door; and nothing more.

Presently there was a gentle scratching, not half so loud as a mouse's, and the false door-post opened by degrees, and left a perpendicular space, through which the light streamed in.   The door, had it been bolted, would now have hung by the bare tip of the bolt, which went into the real door-post, but as it was, it swung gently open of itself.   It opened inwards, so Denys did not raise his cross-bow from the ground, but merely grasped his dagger.

The candle was held up, and shaded from behind by a man's hand.

He was inspecting the beds from the threshold, satisfied that his victims were both in bed.

The man glided into the apartment. But at the first step something in the position of the cupboard and chair made him uneasy. He ventured no farther, but put the candle on the floor and stooped to peer under the chair; but as he stooped an iron hand grasped his shoulder, and a dagger was driven so fiercely through his neck that the point came out at his gullet. There was a terrible hiccough, but no cry; and half a dozen silent strokes followed in swift succession, each a death-blow, and the assassin was laid noiselessly on the floor.

Denys closed the door, bolted it gently, drew the post to, and even while he was doing it whispered Gerard to bring a chair. It was done.

"Help me set him up."

"Dead?"

"Parbleu."

"What for?"

"Frighten them! Gain time."

Even while saying this, Denys had whipped a piece of string round the dead man's neck, and tied him to the chair, and there the ghastly figure sat fronting the door.

"Denys, I can do better. Saints forgive me!"

"What? Be quick then, we have not many moments."

And Denys got his cross-bow ready, and, tearing off his straw mattress, reared it before him and prepared to shoot the moment the door should open, for he had no hope any more would come singly when they found the first did not return.

While thus employed, Gerard was busy about the seated corpse, and to his amazement Denys saw a luminous glow spreading rapidly over the white face.

Gerard blew out the candle; and on this the corpse's face shone still more like a glow-worm's head.

Denys shook in his shoes, and his teeth chattered.

"What, in Heaven's name, is this?" he whispered.

"Hush! 'tis but phosphorus, but 'twill serve."

"Away! they will surprise thee."

In fact uneasy mutterings were heard below, and at last a deep voice said, "What makes him so long? is the drôle rifling them?"

It was their comrade they suspected then, not the enemy. Soon a step came softly but rapidly up the stairs; the door was gently tried.

When this resisted, which was clearly not expected, the sham post was very cautiously moved, and an eye no doubt peeped through the aperture; for there was a howl of dismay, and the man was heard to stumble back and burst into the kitchen, where a Babel of voices rose directly on his return.

Gerard ran to the dead thief and began to work on him again.

"Back, madman!" whispered Denys.

"Nay, nay. I know these ignorant brutes; they will not venture here awhile. I can make him ten times more fearful."

"At least close that opening! Let them not see you at your devilish work."

Gerard closed the sham post, and in half a minute his brush made the dead head a sight to strike any man with dismay. He put his art to a strange use, and one unparalleled perhaps in the history of mankind. He illuminated his dead enemy's face to frighten his living foe: the staring eyeballs he made globes of fire; the teeth he left white, for so they were more terrible by the contrast; but the palate and tongue he tipped with fire, and made one lurid cavern of the red depths the chapfallen jaw revealed; and on the brow he wrote in burning letters, "𝕷𝖆 𝕸𝖔𝖗𝖙." And while he was doing it the stout Denys was quaking, and fearing the vengeance of Heaven; for one man's courage is not another's; and the band of miscreants below were quarrelling and disputing loudly, and now without disguise.

The steps that led down to the kitchen were fifteen, but they were nearly perpendicular: there was therefore in point of fact no distance between the besiegers and besieged, and the latter now caught almost every word. At last one was heard to cry out, "I tell ye the devil has got him and branded him with hell-fire. I am more like to leave this cursed house than go again into a room that is full of fiends!".

"Art drunk? or mad? or a coward?" said another.

"Call me a coward, I'll give thee my dagger's point, and send thee where Pierre sits o' fire for ever."

"Come, no quarrelling when work is afoot," roared a tremendous diapason, "or I'll brain ye both with my fist, and send ye where we shall all go soon or late."

"The Abbot," whispered Denys gravely.

He felt the voice he had just heard could belong to no man but the colossus he had seen in passing through the kitchen. It made the place vibrate. The quarrelling continued some time, and then there was a dead silence.

"Look out, Gerard."

"Ay. What will they do next?"

"We shall soon know."

"Shall I wait for you, or cut down the first that opens the door?"

"Wait for me, lest we strike the same and waste a blow. Alas! we cannot afford that."

Dead silence.

Sudden came into the room a thing that made them start and their hearts quiver.

And what was it? A moonbeam.

Even so can this machine, the body, by the soul's action, be strung up to start and quiver. The sudden ray shot keen and pure into that shamble.

Its calm, cold, silvery soul traversed the apartment in a stream of no great volume; for the window was narrow.

After the first tremor Gerard whispered, "Courage, Denys! God's eye is on us even here." And he fell upon his knees with his face turned towards the window.

Ay, it was like a holy eye opening suddenly on human crime and human passions. Many a scene of blood and crime that pure cold eye has rested on, but on few more ghastly than this, where two men, with a lighted corpse between them, waited panting, to kill and be killed. Nor did the moonlight deaden that horrible corpse-light. If anything it added to its ghastliness; for the body sat at the edge of the moonbeam, which cut sharp across the shoulder and the ear, and seemed blue and ghastly and unnatural by the side of that lurid glow in which the face and eyes and teeth shone horribly. But Denys dared not look that way.

The moon drew a broad stripe of light across the door, and on that his eyes were glued. Presently he whispered, "Gerard!"

Gerard looked and raised his sword.

Acutely as they had listened, they had heard of late no sound on the stair. Yet there—on the door-post, at the edge of the stream of moonlight, were the tips of the fingers of a hand.

The nails glistened.

Presently they began to crawl and crawl down towards the bolt, but with infinite slowness and caution. In so doing they crept into the moonlight. The actual motion was imperceptible, but slowly, slowly the fingers came out whiter and whiter, but the hand between the main knuckles and the wrist remained dark. Denys slowly raised his cross-bow.

He levelled it. He took a long steady aim.

Gerard palpitated. At last the cross-bow twanged. The hand was instantly nailed, with a stern jar, to the quivering door-post. There was a scream of anguish. "Cut," whispered Denys eagerly, and Gerard's uplifted sword descended and severed the wrist with two swift blows. A body sank down moaning outside.

The hand remained inside, immovable, with blood trickling from it down the wall. The fierce bolt, slightly barbed, had gone through it and deep into the real door-post.

"Two," said Denys, with terrible cynicism.

He strung his cross-bow, and kneeled behind his cover again.

"The next will be the Abbot."

The wounded man moved, and presently crawled down to his companions on the stairs, and the kitchen door was shut.

There nothing was heard now but low muttering. The last incident had revealed the mortal character of the weapons used by the besieged.

"I begin to think the Abbot's stomach is not so great as his body," said Denys.

The words were scarcely out of his mouth when the following events happened all in a couple of seconds. The kitchen door was opened roughly, a heavy but active man darted up the stairs without any manner of disguise, and a single ponderous blow sent the door not only off its hinges, but right across the room on to Denys's fortification, which it struck so rudely as nearly to lay him flat. And in the doorway stood a colossus with a glittering axe.

He saw the dead man with the moon's blue light on half his face, and the red light on the other half and

the floor spouting blood from back and bosom in two furious jets, and quivered, but breathed no more.

The thieves, smitten with dismay, fell on their knees directly, and the archers bound them, while, above, the rescued ones still stood like statues rooted to the spot, their dripping swords extended in the red torchlight, expecting their indomitable enemy to leap back on them as wonderfully as he had gone.

CHAPTER XXXIV.

"Where be the true men?"

"Here be we. God bless you all! God bless you!"

There was a rush to the stairs, and half a dozen hard but friendly hands were held out and grasped them warmly. "Y'have saved our lives, lads," cried Denys; "y'have saved our lives this night."

A wild sight met the eyes of the rescued pair. The room flaring with torches, the glittering breastplates of the archers, their bronzed faces, the white cheeks of the bound thieves, and the bleeding giant, whose dead body these hard men left lying there in its own gore.

Gerard went round the archers and took them each by the hand with glistening eyes, and on this they all kissed him; and this time he kissed them in return. Then he said to one handsome archer of his own age, "Prithee, good soldier, have an eye to me. A strange drowsiness overcomes me. Let no one cut my throat while I sleep—for pity's sake."

The archer promised with a laugh, for he thought Gerard was jesting; and the latter went off into a deep sleep almost immediately.

Denys was surprised at this, but did not interfere, for it suited his immediate purpose. A couple of archers were inspecting the Abbot's body, turning it half over with their feet, and inquiring, "Which of the two had flung this enormous rogue down from an upper storey like that; they would fain have the trick of his arm."

Denys at first pished and pshawed, but dare not play the braggart, for he said to himself, "That young vagabond will break in and say 'twas the finger of Heaven, and no mortal arm, or some such stuff, and make me look like a fool." But now, seeing Gerard unconscious, he suddenly gave this required information.

"Well, then, you see, comrades, I had run my sword through this one up to the hilt, and one or two more of 'em came buzzing about me, so it behoved me have my sword or die; so I just put my foot against his stomach, gave a tug with my hand and a spring with my foot, and sent him flying to kingdom come! He died in the air, and his carrion rolled in amongst you without ceremony; made you jump, I warrant me. But pikestaves and pillage! what avails prattling of these trifles once they are gone by? buvons, camarades, buvons."

The archers remarked that it was easy to say "buvons" where no liquor was, but not so easy to do it.

"Nay, I'll soon find you liquor. My nose hath a natural alacrity at scenting out the wine. You follow me, and I my nose; bring a torch!" And they left the room, and finding a short flight of stone steps, descended them and entered a large, low, damp cellar.

It smelt close and dank, and the walls were encrusted here and there with what seemed cobwebs, but proved to be saltpetre that had oozed out of the damp stones, and crystallised.

"Oh! the fine mouldy smell," said Denys; "in such places still lurks the good wine; advance thy torch. Diable! what is that in the corner? A pile of rags? No; 'tis a man."

They gathered round with the torch, and lo! a figure crouched on a heap in the corner, pale as ashes, and shivering.

"Why, it is the landlord," said Denys.

"Get up, thou craven heart!" shouted one of the archers.

"Why, man, the thieves are bound, and we are dry that bound them. Up! and show us thy wine, for no bottles see I here."

"What, be the rascals bound?" stammered the pale landlord; "good news. W—w—wine? that will I, honest sirs."

And he rose with unsure joints and offered to lead the way to the wine cellar. But Denys interposed. "You are all in the dark, comrades. He is in league with the thieves."

"Alack, good soldier, me in league with the accursed robbers! Is that reasonable?"

"The girl said so, anyway."

"The girl! What girl? Ah! Curse her, traitress!"

"Well," interposed the other archer, "the girl is not here, but gone on to the bailiff. So let the burghers settle whether this craven be guilty or no: for we caught him not in the act: and let him draw us our wine."

"One moment," said Denys shrewdly. "Why cursed he the girl? If he be a true man, he should bless her, as we do."

"Alas, sir!" said the landlord, "I have but my good name to live by, and I cursed her to you, because you said she had belied me."

"Humph! I trow thou art a thief, and where is the thief that cannot lie with a smooth face? Therefore, hold him, comrades; a prisoner can draw wine an if his hands be not bound."

The landlord offered no objection, but on the contrary said he would with pleasure show them where his little stock of wine was, but hoped they would pay for what they should drink, for his rent was due this two months.

The archers smiled grimly at his simplicity, as they thought it: one of them laid a hand quietly but firmly on his shoulder, the other led on with the torch.

They had reached the threshold when Denys cried "Halt!"

"What is't?"

"Here be bottles in this corner; advance thy light."

The torch-bearer went towards him. He had just taken off his scabbard and was probing the heap the landlord had just been crouched upon.

"Nay, nay," cried the landlord, "the wine is in the next cellar. There is nothing *there*."

"Nothing is mighty hard, then," said Denys, and drew out something with his hand from the heap.

It proved to be only a bone.

Denys threw it on the floor; it rattled.

"There is nought there but the bones of the house," said the landlord.

"Just now 'twas nothing. Now that we have found something, 'tis nothing but bones. Here's another. Humph! look at this one, comrade; and you come too and look at it, and bring yon smooth knave along."

The archer with the torch, whose name was Philippe, held the bone to the light and turned it round and round.

"Well?" said Denys.

"Well, if this was a field of battle, I should say 'twas the shankbone of a man; no more, no less. But 'tisn't a battlefield, nor a churchyard; 'tis an inn."

"True, mate; but yon knave's ashy face is as good a light to me as a field of battle. I read the bone by it. Bring yon face nearer, I say. When the chine is amissing, and the house dog can't look at you without his tail creeping between his legs, who was the thief? Good brothers mine, my mind it doth misgive me. The deeper I thrust, the more there be. Mayhap if these bones could tell their tale they would make true men's flesh creep that heard it."

"Alas! young man, what hideous fancies are these! The bones are bones of beeves, and sheep, and kids, and not, as you think, of men and women. Holy saints preserve us!"

"Hold thy peace! thy words are air. Thou hast not got burghers by the ear, that know not a veal knuckle from their grandsire's ribs, but soldiers—men that have gone to look for their dear comrades, and found their bones picked as clean by the crows as these I doubt have been by thee and thy mates. Men and women, saidst thou? And prithee, when spake I a word of women's bones? Wouldst make a child suspect thee. Field of battle, comrade! Was not this house a field of battle half an hour agone? Drag him close to me: let me read his face: now then, what is this, thou knave?" and he thrust a small object suddenly in his face.

"Alas! I know not."

"Well, I would not swear neither; but it is too like the thumb bone of a man's hand; mates, my flesh it creeps. Churchyard! how know I this is not one?"

And he now drew his sword out of the scabbard and began to rake the heap of earth and broken crockery and bones out on the floor.

The landlord assured him he but wasted his time. "We poor innkeepers are sinners," said he; "we give short measure and baptise the wine: we are fain to do these things, the laws are so unjust to us; but we are not assassins. How could we afford to kill our customers? May Heaven's lightning strike me dead if there be any bones there but such as have been used for meat. 'Tis the kitchen wench flings them here: I swear by God's holy mother, by holy Paul, by holy Dominic, and Denys my patron saint——ah ! "

Denys held out a bone under his eye in dead silence. It was a bone no man, however ignorant, however lying, could confound with those of sheep or oxen. The sight of it shut the lying lips, and palsied the heartless heart.

The landlord's hair rose visibly on his head like spikes, and his knees gave way as if his limbs had been struck from under him. But the archers dragged him fiercely up, and kept him erect under the torch, staring fascinated at the dead skull which, white as the living cheek opposed, but no whiter, glared back again at its murderer, whose pale lip now opened and opened, but could utter no sound.

" Ah ! " said Denys solemnly, and trembling now with rage, " look on the sockets out of which thou hast picked the eyes, and let them blast thine eyes, that crows shall pick out ere this week shall end. Now, hold thou that while I search on. Hold it, I say, or here I rob the gallows——" and he threatened the quaking wretch with his naked sword, till with a groan he took the skull and held it, almost fainting.

Oh ! that every murderer, and contriver of murder, could see him, sick, and staggering with terror, and with his hair on end, holding the cold skull, and feeling that his own head would soon be like it. And soon the heap was scattered, and alas ! not one nor two, but many skulls were brought to light, the culprit moaning at each discovery.

Suddenly Denys uttered a strange cry of distress to come from so bold and hard a man, and held up to the torch a mass of human hair. It was long, glossy, and golden. A woman's beautiful hair. At the sight of it the archers instinctively shook the craven wretch in their hands, and he whined.

" I have a little sister with hair just so fair and shining as this," gulped Denys. " Jesu ! if it should be hers ! There, quick, take my sword and dagger, and keep them from my hand, lest I strike him dead and wrong the gibbet. And thou, poor innocent victim, on whose head this most lovely hair did grow, hear me swear thus, on bended knee, never to leave this man till I see him broken to pieces on the wheel even for thy sake."

He rose from his knee. " Ay, had he as many lives as here be hairs, I'd have them all, by God," and he put the hair into his bosom. Then in a sudden fury seized the landlord fiercely by the neck, and forced him to his knees, and foot on head ground his face savagely among the bones of his victims, where they lay thickest; and the assassin first yelled, then whined and whimpered, just as a dog first yells, then whines, when his nose is so forced into some leveret or other innocent he has killed.

"Now lend me thy bowstring, Philippe!" He passed it through the eyes of a skull alternately, and hung the ghastly relic of mortality and crime round the man's neck, then pulled him up and kicked him industriously into the kitchen, where one of the aldermen of the burgh had arrived with constables, and was even now taking an archer's deposition.

The grave burgher was much startled at sight of the landlord driven in bleeding from a dozen scratches inflicted by the bones of his own victims, and carrying his horrible collar. But Denys came panting after, and in a few fiery words soon made all clear.

"Bind him like the rest," said the alderman sternly. "I count him the blackest of them all."

While his hands were being bound, the poor wretch begged piteously that "the skull might be taken from him."

"Humph!" said the alderman. "Certes I had not ordered such a thing to be put on mortal man; yet being there, I will not lift voice nor finger to doff it. Methinks it fits thee truly, thou bloody dog. 'Tis thy ensign, and hangs well above a heart so foul as thine."

He then inquired of Denys if he thought they had secured the whole gang, or but a part.

"Your worship," said Denys, "there are but seven of them, and this landlord. One we slew upstairs, one we trundled down dead, the rest are bound before you."

"Good! go fetch the dead one from upstairs, and lay him beside him I caused to be removed."

Here a voice like a guinea-fowl's broke peevishly in. "Now, now, now, where is the hand? that is what I want to see." The speaker was a little pettifogging clerk.

"You will find it above, nailed to the door-post by a cross-bow bolt."

"Good!" said the clerk. He whispered his master, "What a goodly show will the *pièces de conviction* make!" and with this he wrote them down, enumerating them in separate squeaks as he penned them. Skulls—Bones—A woman's hair—A thief's hand—1 axe—2 carcasses—1 cross-bow bolt. This done, he itched to search the cellar himself: there might be other invaluable morsels of evidence, an ear, or even an earring. The alderman assenting, he caught up a torch and was hurrying thither, when an accident stopped him, and indeed carried him a step or two in the opposite direction.

The constables had gone up the stair in single file.

But the head constable no sooner saw the phosphorescent corpse seated by the bedside, than he stood stupefied; and next he began to shake like one in an ague, and terror gaining on him more and more, he uttered a sort of howl and recoiled swiftly. Forgetting the steps in his recoil, he tumbled over backward on his nearest companion; but *he*, shaken by the shout of dismay, and catching a glimpse of something horrid, was already staggering back, and in no condition to sustain the head constable, who, like most head constables, was a ponderous man. The two carried away the third, and the three the fourth, and they streamed into the kitchen, and settled on the floor, overlapping each other like a sequence laid out on a card-table. The clerk coming hastily with his torch ran an involuntary tilt against the fourth man, who, sharing the momentum of the mass, knocked him instantly on his back, the ace of that fair quint; and there he lay kicking and waving his torch, apparently in triumph, but really in convulsion, sense and wind being driven out together by the concussion.

"What is to do now, in Heaven's name?" cried the alderman, starting up with considerable alarm. But Denys explained, and offered to accompany his worship. "So be it," said the latter. His men picked themselves ruefully up, and the alderman put himself at their head and examined the premises above and below. As for the prisoners, their interrogatory was postponed till they could be confronted with the servant.

Before dawn, the thieves, alive and dead, and all the relics and evidences of crime and retribution, were swept away into the law's net, and the inn was silent and almost deserted. There remained but one constable, and Denys and Gerard, the latter still sleeping heavily.

CHAPTER XXXV.

GERARD awoke, and found Denys watching him with some anxiety.

"It is you for sleeping! Why, 'tis high noon."

"It was a blessed sleep," said Gerard; "methinks Heaven sent it me. It hath put as it were a veil between me and that awful night. To think that you and I sit here alive and well. How terrible a dream I seem to have had!"

"Ay, lad, that is the wise way to look at these things when once they are past; why, they are dreams, shadows. Break thy fast, and then thou wilt think no more on't. Moreover, I promised to bring thee on to the town by noon, and take thee to his worship."

"What for?"

"He would put questions to thee; by the same when he was for waking thee to that end, but I withstood him earnestly, and vowed to bring thee to him in the morning."

"Thou shalt not break troth for me."

Gerard then sopped some rye bread in red wine and ate it to break his fast, then went with Denys over the scene of combat, and came back shuddering, and finally took the road with his friend, and kept peering through the hedges, and expecting sudden attacks unreasonably, till they reached the little town. Denys took him to "The White Hart."

"No fear of cut-throats here," said he. "I know the landlord this many a year. He is a burgess, and looks to be bailiff. 'Tis here I was making for yestreen. But we lost time, and night o'ertook us—and——"

"And you saw a woman at the door, and would be wiser than la Jeanneton; she told us they were nought."

"Why, what saved our lives if not a woman? ay, and risked her own to do it."

"That is true, Denys; and though women are nothing to me, I long to thank this poor girl, and reward her, ay, though I share every doit in my purse with her. Do not you?"

"Parbleu."

"Where shall we find her?"

"Mayhap the alderman will tell us. We must go to him first."

The alderman received them with a most singular and inexplicable expression of countenance. However, after a moment's reflection, he wore a grim smile, and finally proceeded to put interrogatories to Gerard, and took down the answers. This done, he told them that they must stay in the town till the thieves were tried, and be at hand to give evidence, on peril of fine and imprisonment. They looked very blank at this.

"However," said he, "'twill not be long, the culprits having been taken red-handed." He added, "And you know, in any case you could not leave the place this week."

Denys stared at this remark, and Gerard smiled at what he thought the simplicity of the old gentleman in dreaming that a provincial town of Burgundy had attraction to detain him from Rome and Margaret.

He now went to that which was nearest both their hearts. "Your worship," said he, "we cannot find our benefactress in the town."

"Nay, but who is your benefactress?"

"Who? why the good girl that came to you by night and saved our lives at peril of her own. Oh, sir, our hearts burn within us to thank and bless her; where is she?"

"Oh, *she* is in prison."

CHAPTER XXXVI.

"IN prison, sir! good lack, for what misdeed?"

"Well, she is a witness, and may be a necessary one."

"Why, Messire Bailiff," put in Denys, "you lay not all your witnesses by the heels, I trow."

The alderman, pleased at being called bailiff, became communicative. "In a case of blood we detain all testimony that is like to give us leg bail and so defeat justice, and that is why we still keep the women folk; for a man at odd times bides a week in one mind, but a woman, if she do her duty to the realm o' Friday, she shall undo it afore Sunday, or try. Could you see yon wench now, you should find her a-blubbering at having betrayed five males to the gallows. Had they been females, we might have trusted to a subpœna, for they despise one another: and there they show some sense!

But now I think on't, there were other reasons for laying this one by the heels. Hand me those depositions, young sir." And he put on his glasses. "Ay! she was implicated; she was one of the band."

A loud disclaimer burst from Denys and Gerard at once.

"No need to deave me," said the alderman. "Here 'tis in black and white. 'Jean Hardy (that is one of the thieves), being questioned, confessed that'—humph! Ay, here 'tis. 'And that the girl Manon was the decoy, and her sweetheart was Georges Vipont, one of the band, and hanged last month; and that she had been deject ever since, and had openly blamed the band for his death, saying if they had not been rank cowards, he had never been taken, and it is his opinion she did but betray them out of very spite, and——' "

"His opinion," cried Gerard indignantly; "what signifies the opinion of a cut-throat, burning to be revenged on her who has delivered him to justice? And an you go to that, what avails his testimony? Is a thief never a liar? Is he not aye a liar? and here a motive to lie? Revenge! why, 'tis the strongest of all the passions. And oh, sir, what madness to question a detected felon and listen to him lying away an honest life—as if he were a true man swearing in open day, with his true hand on the Gospel laid!"

"Young man," said the alderman, "restrain thy heat in presence of authority! I find by your tongue you are a stranger. Know then that in this land we question all the world. We are not so weak as to hope to get at the truth by shutting either our left ear or our right."

"And so you would listen to Satan belying the saints!"

"Ta! ta! The law meddles but with men and women, and these cannot utter a story all lies, let them try ever so. Wherefore we shut not the barn-door (as the saying is) against any man's grain. Only having taken it in, we do winnow and sift it. And who told you I had swallowed the thief's story whole like fair water? Not so. I did but credit so much on't as was borne out by better proof."

"Better proof?" and Gerard looked blank. "Why, who but the thieves would breathe a word against her?"

"Marry, herself."

"Herself, sir? what, did you question her too?"

"I tell you we question all the world. Here is her deposition; can you read? Read it yourself, then."

to her, and keep her a prisoner without letting her feel it, the friends went out; and lo! as they stepped into the street they saw two processions coming towards them from opposite sides. One was a large one, attended with noise and howls and those indescribable cries by which rude natures reveal at odd times that relationship to the beasts of the field and forest, which at other times we succeed in hiding. The other, very thinly attended by a few nuns and friars, came slow and silent.

The prisoners going to exposure in the market-place. The gathered bones of the victims coming to the churchyard.

And the two met in the narrow street nearly at the inn door, and could not pass each other for a long time, and the bier that bore the relics of mortality got wedged against the cart that carried the men who had made those bones what they were, and in a few hours must die for it themselves. The mob had not the quick intelligence to be at once struck with this stern meeting; but at last a woman cried, "Look at your work, ye dogs!" and the crowd took it like wildfire, and there was a horrible yell, and the culprits groaned and tried to hide their heads upon their bosoms, but could not, their hands being tied. And there they stood, images of pale hollow-eyed despair, and oh, how they looked on the bier, and envied those whom they had sent before them on the dark road they were going upon themselves! And the two men who were the cause of both processions stood and looked gravely on, and even Manon, hearing the disturbance, crept to the window, and, hiding her face, peeped tremblingly through her fingers, as women will.

This strange meeting parted Denys and Gerard. The former yielded to curiosity and revenge, the latter doffed his bonnet, and piously followed the poor remains of those whose fate had so nearly been his own. For some time he was the one lay mourner; but when they had reached the suburbs, a long way from the greater attraction that was filling the market-place, more than one artisan threw down his tools, and more than one shopman left his shop, and touched with pity or a sense of our common humanity, and perhaps decided somewhat by the example of Gerard, followed the bones bareheaded, and saw them deposited with the prayers of the Church in hallowed ground.

After the funeral rites Gerard stepped respectfully up to the curé, and offered to buy a mass for their souls.

Gerard, son of Catherine, always looked at two sides of a penny, and he tried to purchase this mass a trifle under the usual terms, on account of the pitiable circumstances. But the good curé gently but adroitly parried his ingenuity, and blandly screwed him up to the market price.

In the course of the business they discovered a similarity of sentiments. Piety and worldly prudence are not very rare companions; still it is unusual to carry both so far as these two men did. Their collision in the prayer market led to mutual esteem, as when knight encountered knight worthy of his steel. Moreover, the good curé loved a bit of gossip, and finding his customer was one of those who had fought the thieves at Domfront, would have him into his parlour and hear the whole from his own lips. And his heart warmed to Gerard, and he said, "God was good to thee. I thank Him for't with all my soul. Thou art a good lad." He added drily, "Shouldst have told me this tale in the churchyard. I doubt I had given thee the mass for love. However," said he (the thermometer suddenly falling), "'tis ill luck to go back upon a bargain. But I'll broach a bottle of my old Medoc for thee; and few be the guests I would do that for." The curé went to his cupboard, and, while he groped for the choice bottle, he muttered to himself, "At their old tricks again!"

"Plait-il?" said Gerard.

"I said nought. Ay, here 'tis."

"Nay, your reverence; you surely spoke: you said, 'At their old tricks again!'"

"Said I so in sooth?" and his reverence smiled. He then proceeded to broach the wine, and filled a cup for each. Then he put a log of wood on the fire, for stoves were none in Burgundy. "And so I said 'At their old tricks!' did I? Come, sip the good wine, and, whilst it lasts, story for story, I care not if I tell you a little tale."

Gerard's eyes sparkled.

"Thou lovest a story?"

"As my life."

"Nay, but raise not thine expectations too high, neither. 'Tis but a foolish trifle compared with thine adventures."

THE CURÉ'S TALE.

"Once upon a time, then, in the kingdom of France, and in the duchy of Burgundy, and not a day's journey from the town where now we sit a-sipping of old Medoc, there lived—a curé. I say he lived; but barely. The parish was small, the parishioners greedy, and never gave their curé a doit more than he could compel. The nearer they brought him to a disembodied spirit by meagre diet, the holier should be his prayers in their behalf. I know not if this was their creed, but their practice gave it colour.

"At last he pickled a rod for them.

"One day the richest farmer in the place had twins to baptise. The curé was had to the christening dinner as usual; but ere he would baptise the children, he demanded, not the christening fees only, but the burial fees. 'Saints defend us, parson,' cried the mother; 'talk not of burying! I did never see children liker to live.' 'Nor I,' said the curé, 'the praise be to God. Natheless, they are sure to die, being sons of Adam, as well as of thee, dame. But die when they will, 'twill cost them nothing, the burial fees being paid and entered in this book.' 'For all that 'twill cost them something,' quoth the miller, the greatest wag in the place, and as big a knave as any; for which was the biggest God knoweth, but no mortal man, not even the hangman. 'Miller, I tell thee nay,' quo' the curé. 'Parson, I tell you ay,' quo' the miller. ''Twill cost them their lives.' At which millstone conceit was a great laugh; and in the general mirth the fees were paid and the Christians made.

"But when the next parishioner's child, and the next after, and all, had to pay each his burial fee, or lose his place in heaven, discontent did secretly rankle in the parish. Well, one fine day they met in secret, and sent a churchwarden with a complaint to the bishop, and a thunderbolt fell on the poor curé. Came to him at dinner-time a summons to the episcopal palace, to bring the parish books and answer certain charges. Then the curé guessed where the shoe pinched. He left his food on the board, for small his appetite now, and took the parish books and went quaking.

"The bishop entertained him with a frown, and exposed the plaint. 'Monseigneur,' said the curé right humbly, 'doth the parish allege many things against me, or this one only?' 'In sooth, but this one,' said the bishop, and softened a little. 'First, monseigneur, I acknowledge the fact.' ''Tis well,' quoth the bishop; 'that saves time and trouble. Now to your excuse, if excuse there be.' 'Monseigneur, I have been curé of that parish seven years, and fifty children have I baptised, and buried not five. At first I used to say, "Heaven be praised, the air of this village is main healthy;" but on searching the register book I found 'twas always so, and on probing the matter, it came out that of those born at Domfront, all, but here and there one, did go and get hanged at Aix. But this was to defraud not their curé only, but the entire Church of her dues, since "pendards" pay no funeral fees, being buried in air. Thereupon, knowing by sad experience their greed, and how they grudge the Church every sou, I laid a trap to keep them from hanging; for greed against greed, there be of them that will die in their beds like true men ere the Church shall gain those funeral fees for nought.' Then the bishop laughed till the tears ran down, and questioned the churchwarden, and he was fain to confess that too many of the parish did come to that unlucky end at Aix. 'Then,' said the bishop, 'I do approve the act, for myself and my successors; and so be it ever, till they mend their manners and die in their beds.' And the next day came the ringleaders crestfallen to the curé, and said, 'Parson, ye were ever good to us, barring this untoward matter: prithee let there be no ill blood anent so trivial a thing.' And the curé said, 'My children, I were unworthy to be your pastor could I not forgive a wrong; go in peace, and get me as many children as may be, that by the double fees the curé you love may miss starvation.'

"And the bishop often told the story, and it kept his memory of the curé alive, and at last he shifted him to a decent parish, where he can offer a glass of old Medoc to such as are worthy of it. Their name it is not legion."

A light broke in upon Gerard; his countenance showed it.

"Ay!" said his host, "I am that curé: so now thou canst guess why I said 'At their old tricks.' My life on't they have wheedled my successor into remitting those funeral fees. You are well out of that parish. And so am I."

The curé's little niece burst in, " Uncle, the weighing— la ! a stranger ! " And burst out.

The curé rose directly, but would not part with Gerard.

" Wet thy beard once more, and come with me."

In the church porch they found the sexton with a huge pair of scales, and weights of all sizes. Several humble persons were standing by, and soon a woman stepped forward with a sickly child and said, " Be it heavy, be it light, I vow, in rye meal of the best, whate'er this child shall weigh, and the same will duly pay to Holy Church, an if he shall cast his trouble. Pray, good people, for this child, and for me his mother hither come in dole and care ! "

The child was weighed, and yelled as if the scale had been the font.

" Courage ! dame," cried Gerard. " This is a good sign. There is plenty of life here to battle its trouble."

" Now, blest be the tongue that tells me so," said the poor woman. She hushed her ponderling against her bosom, and stood aloof watching, whilst another woman brought her child to scale.

But presently a loud, dictatorial voice was heard, " Way there, make way for the seigneur ! "

The small folk parted on both sides like waves ploughed by a lordly galley, and in marched in gorgeous attire, his cap adorned by a feather with a topaz at its root, his jerkin richly furred, satin doublet, red hose, shoes like skates, diamond-hilted sword in velvet scabbard, and hawk on his wrist, " the lord of the manor." He flung himself into the scales as if he was lord of the zodiac as well as the manor : whereat the hawk balanced and flapped ; but stuck ; then winked.

While the sexton heaved in the great weights, the curé told Gerard, " My lord had been sick unto death, and vowed his weight in bread and cheese to the poor, the Church taking her tenth."

" Permit me, my lord ; if your lordship continues to press with your lordship's staff on the other scale, you will disturb the balance."

His lordship grinned and removed his staff, and leaned on it. The curé politely but firmly objected to that too.

" Mille diables ! what am I to do with it, then ? " cried the other.

" Deign to hold it out so, my lord, wide of both scales."

When my lord did this, and so fell into the trap he had laid for Holy Church, the good curé whispered to Gerard, "Cretensis incidit in Cretensem!" which I take to mean, "Diamond cut diamond." He then said with an obsequious air, "If that your lordship grudges Heaven full weight, you might set the hawk on your lacquey, and so save a pound."

"Gramercy for thy rede, curé," cried the great man reproachfully. "Shall I for one sorry pound grudge my poor fowl the benefit of Holy Church? I'd as lieve the devil should have me and all my house as her, any day i' the year."

"Sweet is affection," whispered the curé.

"Between a bird and a brute," whispered Gerard.

"Tush!" and the curé looked terrified.

The seigneur's weight was booked, and Heaven I trust and believe did not weigh his gratitude in the balance of the sanctuary.

For my unlearned reader is not to suppose there was anything the least eccentric in the man, or his gratitude to the Giver of health and all good gifts. Men look forward to death, and back upon past sickness with different eyes. Item, when men drive a bargain, they strive to get the sunny side of it; it matters not one straw whether it is with man or Heaven they are bargaining. In this respect we are the same now, at bottom, as we were four hundred years ago: only in those days we did it a grain or two more naïvely, and that naïveté shone out more palpably, because, in that rude age, body prevailing over mind, all sentiments took material forms. Man repented with scourges, prayed by bead, bribed the saints with wax tapers, put fish into the body to sanctify the soul, sojourned in cold water for empire over the emotions, and thanked God for returning health in 1 cwt. 2 stone 7 lb. 3 oz. 1 dwt. of bread and cheese.

Whilst I have been preaching, who preach so rarely and so ill, the good curé has been soliciting the lord of the manor to step into the church, and give order what shall be done with his great-great-grandfather.

"Ods bodikins! what, have you dug him up?"

"Nay, my lord, he never was buried."

"What, the old dict was true after all?"

"So true that the workmen this very day found a skeleton erect in the pillar they are repairing. I had sent to my lord at once, but I knew he would be here."

"It is he! 'Tis he!" said his descendant, quickening his pace. "Let us go see the old boy. This youth is a stranger, I think."

Gerard bowed.

"Know then that my great-great-grandfather held his head high, and being on the point of death, revolted against lying under the aisle with his forbears for mean folk to pass over. So, as the tradition goes, he swore his son (my great-grandfather), to bury him erect in one of the pillars of the church" (here they entered the porch). "For, quoth he, 'NO BASE MAN SHALL PASS OVER MY STOMACH.' Peste!" and, even while speaking, his lordship parried adroitly with his stick a skull that came hopping at him, bowled by a boy in the middle of the aisle, who took to his heels yelling with fear the moment he saw what he had done. His lordship hurled the skull furiously after him as he ran, at which the curé gave a shout of dismay, and put forth his arm to hinder him, but was too late.

The curé groaned aloud. And, as if this had evoked spirits of mischief, up started a whole pack of children from some ambuscade, and unseen, but heard loud enough, clattered out of the church like a covey rising in a thick wood.

"Oh! these pernicious brats," cried the curé. "The workmen cannot go to their nonemete but the church is rife with them. Pray Heaven they have not found his late lordship; nay, I mind, I hid his lordship under a workman's jerkin, and—saints defend us! the jerkin has been moved."

The poor curé's worst misgivings were realised: the rising generation of plebeians had played the mischief with the haughty old noble. "The little ones had jockeyed for the bones oh," and pocketed such of them as seemed adapted for certain primitive games then in vogue amongst them.

"I'll excommunicate them," roared the curé, "and all their race."

"Never heed," said the scapegrace lord, and stroked his hawk; "there is enough of him to swear by. Put him back! put him back!"

"Surely, my lord, 'tis your will his bones be laid in hallowed earth, and masses said for his poor prideful soul?"

The noble stroked his hawk.

"Are ye there, Master Curé?" said he. "Nay, the business is too old: he is out of purgatory by this time, *up or down*. I shall not draw my purse-strings for him. Every dog his day. Adieu, messires, adieu, ancestor;" and he sauntered off whistling to his hawk and caressing it.

His reverence looked ruefully after him.

"Cretensis incidit in Cretensem," said he sorrowfully. "I thought I had him safe for a dozen masses. Yet I blame him not, but that young ne'er-do-weel which did trundle his ancestor's skull at us: for who could venerate his great-great-grandsire and play football with his head? Well it behoves us to be better Christians than he is." So they gathered the bones reverently, and the curé locked them up, and forbade the workmen, who now entered the church, to close up the pillar, till he should recover by threats of the Church's wrath every atom of my lord. And he showed Gerard a famous shrine in the church. Before it were the usual gifts of tapers, etc. There was also a wax image of a falcon, most curiously moulded and coloured to the life, eyes and all. Gerard's eye fell at once on this, and he expressed the liveliest admiration. The curé assented. Then Gerard asked, "Could the saint have loved hawking?"

The curé laughed at his simplicity. "Nay, 'tis but a statuary hawk. When they have a bird of gentle breed they cannot train, they make his image, and send it to this shrine with a present, and pray the saint to work upon the stubborn mind of the original, and make it ductile as wax: that is the notion, and methinks a reasonable one, too."

Gerard assented. "But alack, reverend sir, were I a saint, methinks I should side with the innocent dove, rather than with the cruel hawk that rends her."

"By St. Denys you are right," said the curé. "But, que voulez-vous? the saints are débonair, and have been flesh themselves, and know man's frailty and absurdity. 'Tis the Bishop of Avignon sent this one."

"What! do bishops hawk in this country?"

"One and all. Every noble person hawks, and lives with hawk on wrist. Why, my lord abbot hard by, and his lordship that has just parted from us, had a two years' feud as to where they should put their hawks down on that very altar there. Each claimed the right hand of the altar for his bird."

"What desecration!"

"Nay! nay! thou knowest we make them doff both glove and hawk to take the blessed eucharist. Their jewelled gloves will they give to a servant or simple Christian to hold; but their beloved hawks they will put down on no place less than the altar."

Gerard inquired how the battle of the hawks ended.

"Why, the abbot he yielded, as the Church yields to laymen. He searched ancient books, and found that the left hand was the more honourable, being in truth the right hand, since the altar is east, but looks westward. So he gave my lord the *soi-disant* right hand, and contented himself with the real right hand, and even so may the Church still outwit the lay nobles and their arrogance, saving your presence."

"Nay, sir, I honour the Church. I am convent bred, and owe all I have and am to Holy Church."

"Ah, that accounts for my sudden liking to thee. Art a gracious youth. Come and see me whenever thou wilt."

Gerard took this as a hint that he might go now. It jumped with his own wish, for he was curious to hear what Denys had seen and done all this time. He made his reverence and walked out of the church; but was no sooner clear of it than he set off to run with all his might; and, tearing round a corner, ran into a large stomach, whose owner clutched him to keep himself steady under the shock; but did not release his hold on regaining his equilibrium.

"Let go, man," said Gerard.

"Not so. You are my prisoner."

"Prisoner?"

"Ay."

"What for, in Heaven's name?"

"What for? Why, sorcery."

"SORCERY?"

"Sorcery."

CHAPTER XXXVII.

THE culprits were condemned to stand pinioned in the market-place for two hours, that should any person recognise them or any of them as guilty of other crimes, they might depose to that effect at the trial.

They stood, however, the whole period, and no one advanced anything fresh against them. This was the less remarkable that they were night birds, vampires who preyed in the dark on weary travellers, mostly strangers.

But just as they were being taken down, a fearful scream was heard in the crowd, and a woman pointed at one of them, with eyes almost starting from their sockets; but ere she could speak she fainted away.

Then men and women crowded round her, partly to aid her, partly from curiosity. When she began to recover they fell to conjectures.

" 'Twas at him she pointed."

" Nay, 'twas at this one."

" Nay, nay," said another, " 'twas at yon hangdog with the hair hung round his neck."

All further conjecture was cut short. The poor creature no sooner recovered her senses than she flew at the landlord like a lioness. "My child! Man! man! Give me back my child." And she seized the glossy golden hair that the officers had hung round his neck, and tore it from his neck, and covered it with kisses; then, her poor confused mind clearing, she saw even by this token that her lost girl was dead, and sank suddenly down shrieking and sobbing so over the poor hair, that the crowd rushed on the assassin with one savage growl. His life had ended then and speedily, for in those days all carried death at their girdles. But Denys drew his sword directly, and shouting " A moi, camarades!" kept the mob at bay. " Who lays a finger on him dies." Other archers backed him, and with some difficulty they kept him uninjured, while Denys appealed to those who shouted for his blood.

" What sort of vengeance is this? would you be so mad as rob the wheel, and give the vermin an easy death?"

The mob was kept passive by the archers' steel rather than by Denys's words, and growled at intervals with flashing eyes. The municipal officers seeing this collected round, and with the archers made a guard, and prudently carried the accused back to gaol.

The mob hooted them and the prisoners indiscriminately. Denys saw the latter safely lodged, then made for "The White Hart," where he expected to find Gerard.

On the way he saw two girls working at a first-floor window. He saluted them. They smiled. He entered into conversation. Their manners were easy, their complexion high.

He invited them to a repast at "The White Hart." They objected. He acquiesced in their refusal. They consented. And in this charming society he forgot all about poor Gerard, who meantime was carried off to gaol; but on the way suddenly stopped, having now somewhat recovered his presence of mind, and demanded to know by whose authority he was arrested. "By the vice-bailie's!" said the constable.

"The vice-bailie! Alas! what have I, a stranger, done to offend a vice-bailie? For this charge of sorcery must be a blind. No sorcerer am I; but a poor true lad far from his home."

This vague shift disgusted the officer. "Show him the capias, Jacques," said he.

Jacques held out the writ in both hands about a yard and a half from Gerard's eye; and at the same moment the large constable suddenly pinned him; both officers were on tenter-hooks lest the prisoner should grab the document, to which they attached a superstitious importance.

But the poor prisoner had no such thought. Query whether he would have touched it with the tongs. He just craned out his neck and read it, and, to his infinite surprise, found the vice-bailiff who had signed the writ was the friendly alderman. He took courage and assured his captor there was some error. But finding he made no impression, demanded to be taken before the alderman.

"What say you to that, Jacques?"

"Impossible. We have no orders to take him before his worship. Read the writ!"

"Nay, but good kind fellows, what harm can it be? I will give ye each an écu."

"Jacques, what say you to that?"

"Humph! I say we have no orders not to take him to his worship. Read the writ!"

"Then say we take him to prison round by his worship."

It was agreed. They got the money; and bade Gerard observe they were doing him a favour. He saw they wanted a little gratitude as well as much silver. He tried to satisfy *this* cupidity, but it stuck in his throat. Feigning was not his forte.

He entered the alderman's presence with his heart in his mouth, and begged with faltering voice to know what he had done to offend since he left that very room with Manon and Denys.

"Nought that I know of," said the alderman.

On the writ being shown him, he told Gerard he had signed it at daybreak. "I get old, and my memory faileth me; a discussing of the girl I quite forgot your own offence; but I remember now. All is well. You are he I committed for sorcery. Stay! ere you go to gaol, you shall hear what your accuser says; run and fetch him, you."

The man could not find the accuser all at once. So the alderman, getting impatient, told Gerard the main charge was that he had set a dead body a burning with diabolical fire, that flamed, but did not consume. "And if 'tis true, young man, I'm sorry for thee, for thou wilt assuredly burn with fire of good pine logs in the market-place of Neufchasteau."

"Oh, sir, for pity's sake let me have speech with his reverence the curé."

The alderman advised Gerard against it. "The Church was harder upon sorcerers than was the corporation."

"But, sir, I am innocent," said Gerard, between snarling and whining.

"Oh, if *you*—*think*—you are *innocent*—officer, go with him to the curé; but see he 'scape you not. Innocent, quotha?"

They found the curé in his doublet repairing a wheelbarrow. Gerard told him all, and appealed piteously to him. "Just for using a little phosphorus—in self-defence —against cut-throats they are going to hang."

It was lucky for our magician that he had already told his tale in full to the curé; for thus that shrewd personage had hold of the stick at the right end. The corporation held it by the ferule. His reverence looked exceedingly grave and said, "I must question you privately on this untoward business." He took him into a private room and made the officer stand outside and guard the door, and be ready to come if called. The big constable stood outside the door, quaking, and expecting to see the room fly away and leave a stink of brimstone. Instantly they were alone the curé unlocked his countenance and was himself again.

"Show me the trick on't," said he, all curiosity.

"I cannot, sir, unless the room be darkened."

The curé speedily closed out the light with a wooden shutter. "Now then."

"But on what shall I put it?" said Gerard. "Here is no dead face. 'Twas that made it look so dire." The curé groped about the room. "Good; here is an image; 'tis my patron saint."

"Heaven forbid! That were profanation."

"Pshaw! 'twill rub off, will't not?"

"Ay, but it goes against me to take such liberty with a saint," objected the sorcerer.

"Fiddlestick!" said the divine.

"To be sure my putting it on his holiness will show your reverence it is no Satanic art."

"Mayhap 'twas for that I did propose it," said the curé subtly.

Thus encouraged, Gerard fired the eyes and nostrils of the image and made the curé jump. Then lighted up the hair in patches; and set the whole face shining like a glow-worm's.

"By'r Lady," shouted the curé, "'tis strange, and small my wonder that they took you for a magician, seeing a dead face thus fired. Now come thy ways with me!"

He put on his gray gown and great hat, and in a few minutes they found themselves in presence of the alderman. By his side, poisoning his mind, stood the accuser, a singular figure in red hose and red shoes, a black gown with blue bands, and a cocked hat.

After saluting the alderman, the curé turned to this personage and said good-humouredly, "So, Mangis, at thy work again, babbling away honest men's lives! Come, your worship, this is the old tale; two of a trade can ne'er agree. Here is Mangis, who professes sorcery, and would sell himself to Satan to-night, but that Satan is not so weak as buy what he can have gratis; this Mangis, who would be a sorcerer, but is only a quack-salver, accuses of magic a true lad, who did but use in self-defence a secret of chemistry well known to me and to all churchmen."

"But he is no churchman, to dabble in such mysteries," objected the alderman.

"He is more churchman than layman, being convent bred, and in the lesser orders," said the ready curé. "Therefore, sorcerer, withdraw thy plaint without more words!"

"That will I not, your reverence," replied Mangis stoutly. "A sorcerer I am, but a white one, not a black one. I make no pact with Satan, but, on the contrary, still battle him with lawful and necessary arts. I ne'er profane the sacraments, as do the black sorcerers, nor turn myself into a cat and go sucking infants' blood, nor e'en their breath, nor set dead men o' fire. I but tell the peasants when their cattle and their hens are possessed, and at what time of the moon to plant rye, and what days in each month are lucky for wooing of women, and selling of bullocks, and so forth: above all, it is my art and my trade to detect the black magicians, as I did that whole tribe of them who were burnt at Dol but last year."

"Ay, Mangis. And what is the upshot of that famous fire thy tongue did kindle?"

"Why, their ashes were cast to the wind."

"Ay; but the true end of thy comedy is this. The parliament of Dijon have since sifted the matter, and found they were no sorcerers, but good and peaceful citizens; and but last week did order masses to be said for their souls, and expiatory farces and mysteries to be played for them in seven towns of Burgundy; all which will not of those cinders make men and women again. Now 'tis our custom in this land, when we have slain the innocent by hearkening false knaves like thee, not to blame our credulous ears, but the false tongue that gulled them. Wherefore bethink thee that, at a word from me to my lord bishop, thou wilt smell burning pine nearer than e'er knave smelt it and lived, and wilt travel on a smoky cloud to him whose heart thou bearest (for the word devil in the Latin it meaneth 'false accuser'), and whose livery thou wearest."

And the curé pointed at Mangis with his staff.

"That is true i'fegs," said the alderman, "for red and black be the foul fiendys colours."

By this time the white sorcerer's cheek was as colourless as his dress was fiery. Indeed the contrast amounted to pictorial. He stammered out, "I respect Holy Church and her will; he shall fire the churchyard, and all in it, for me : I do withdraw the plaint."

"Then withdraw thyself," said the vice-bailiff.

The moment he was gone the curé took the conversational tone, and told the alderman courteously that the accused had received the chemical substance from Holy Church, and had restored it her, by giving it all to him.

"Then 'tis in good hands," was the reply; "young man, you are free. Let me have your reverence's prayers."

"Doubt it not! Humph! Vice-bailie, the town owes me four silver franks, this three months and more."

"They shall be paid, curé, ay, ere the week be out."

On this good understanding Church and State parted. As soon as he was in the street Gerard caught the priest's hand, and kissed it.

"Oh, sir! Oh, your reverence. You have saved me from the fiery stake. What can I say, what do? what——"

"Nought, foolish lad. Bounty rewards itself. Natheless —Humph!—I wish I had done't without leasing. It ill becomes my function to utter falsehoods."

"Falsehood, sir?" Gerard was mystified.

"Didst not hear me say thou hadst given me that same phosphorus? 'Twill cost me a fortnight's penance, that light word." The curé sighed, and his eye twinkled cunningly.

"Nay, nay," cried Gerard eagerly. "Now Heaven forbid! That was no falsehood, father: well you knew the phosphorus was yours, is yours." And he thrust the bottle into the curé's hand. "But alas, 'tis too poor a gift : will you not take from my purse somewhat for Holy Church?" and now he held out his purse with glistening eyes.

"Nay," said the other brusquely, and put his hands quickly behind him; "not a doit. Fie! fie! art pauper et exul. Come thou rather each day at noon and take thy diet with me; for my heart warms to thee;" and he went off very abruptly with his hands behind him.

They itched.

But they itched in vain.

Where there's a heart there's a Rubicon.

Gerard went hastily to the inn to relieve Denys of the anxiety so long and mysterious an absence must have caused him. He found him seated at his ease, playing dice with two young ladies whose manners were unreserved, and complexion high.

Gerard was hurt. "N'oubliez point la Jeanneton!" said he, colouring up.

"What of her?" said Denys, gaily rattling the dice.

"She said, 'Le peu que sont les femmes.'"

"Oh, did she? And what say you to that, mesdemoiselles?"

"We say that none run women down, but such as are too old, or too ill-favoured, or too witless to please them."

"Witless, quotha? Wise men have not folly enough to please them, nor madness enough to desire to please them," said Gerard loftily; "but 'tis to my comrade I speak, not to you, you brazen toads, that make so free with a man at first sight."

"Preach away, comrade. Fling a byword or two at our heads. Know, girls, that he is a very Solomon for bywords. Methinks he was brought up by hand on 'em."

"Be thy friendship a byword!" retorted Gerard. "The friendship that melts to nought at sight of a farthingale."

"Malheureux!" cried Denys, "I speak but pellets, and thou answerest daggers."

"Would I could," was the reply. "Adieu."

"What a little savage!" said one of the girls.

Gerard opened the door and put in his head. "I have thought of a byword," said he spitefully—

> "'Qui haute femmes et dez
> Il mourra en pauvretez.'

There." And having delivered this thunderbolt of antique wisdom, he slammed the door viciously ere any of them could retort.

And now, being somewhat exhausted by his anxieties, he went to the bar for a morsel of bread and a cup of wine. The landlord would sell nothing less than a pint bottle. Well then he would have a bottle; but when he came to compare the contents of the bottle with *its* size, great was the discrepancy: on this he examined the bottle keenly, and found that the glass was thin where the bottle tapered, but towards the bottom un-naturally thick. He pointed this out at once.

The landlord answered superciliously that he did not make bottles; and was nowise accountable for their shape.

"That we will see presently," said Gerard. "I will take this thy pint to the vice-bailiff."

"Nay, nay, for Heaven's sake," cried the landlord, changing his tone at once. "I love to content my customers. If by chance this pint be short, we will charge it and its fellow three sous, instead of two sous each."

"So be it. But much I admire that you, the host of so fair an inn, should practise thus. The wine, too, smacketh strongly of spring water."

"Young sir," said the landlord, "we cut no travellers' throats at this inn, as they do at most. However, you know all about that. 'The White Hart' is no lion, nor bear. Whatever masterful robbery is done here, is done upon the poor host. How then could he live at all if he dealt not a little crooked with the few who pay?"

Gerard objected to this system root and branch. Honest trade was small profits, quick returns; and neither to cheat nor be cheated.

The landlord sighed at this picture. "So might one keep an inn in Heaven, but not in Burgundy. When foot soldiers going to the wars are quartered on me, how can I but lose by their custom? Two sous per day is their pay, and they eat two sous' worth, and drink into the bargain. The pardoners are my good friends, but palmers and pilgrims, what think you I gain by them? Marry, a loss. Minstrels and jongleurs draw custom, and so claim to pay no score, except for liquor. By the secular monks I neither gain nor lose, but the black and gray friars have made vow of poverty, but not of famine; eat like wolves and give the poor host nought but their prayers; and mayhap not them: how can he tell? In my father's day we had the weddings; but now the great gentry let their houses and their plates, their mugs and their spoons, to any honest couple that want to wed, and thither the very mechanics go with their brides and bridal train. They come not to us: indeed we could not find seats and vessels for such a crowd as eat and drink and dance the week out at the homeliest wedding now. In my father's day the great gentry sold wine by the barrel only; but now they have leave to cry it, and sell it by the galopin, in the very market-place. How can we vie with them? They grow it. We buy it of the grower. The coroner's quests we have still, and these would bring goodly profit, but the meat is aye gone ere the mouths be full."

"You should make better provision," suggested his hearer.

"The law will not let us. We are forbidden to go into the market for the first hour. So, when we arrive, the burghers have bought all but the refuse. Besides, the law forbids us to buy more than three bushels of meal at a time: yet market-day comes but once a week. As for the butchers, they will not kill for us unless we bribe them."

"Courage!" said Gerard kindly, "the shoe pinches every trader somewhere."

"Ay; but not as it pinches us. Our shoe is trode all o' one side as well as pinches us lame. A savoir, if we pay not the merchants we buy meal, meat, and wine of, they can cast us into prison and keep us there till we pay or die. But we cannot cast into prison those who buy those very victuals of us. A traveller's horse we may keep for his debt; but where, in Heaven's name? In our own stable, eating his head off at our cost. Nay, we may keep the traveller himself; but where? In gaol? Nay, in our own good house, and there must we lodge and feed him gratis. And so fling good silver after bad? Merci! no: let him go with a wanion. Our honestest customers are the thieves. Would to Heaven there were more of them. They look not too close into the shape of the canakin, nor into the host's reckoning: with them and with their purses 'tis lightly come, and lightly go. Also they spend freely, not knowing but each carouse may be their last. But the thief-takers, instead of profiting by this fair example, are for ever robbing the poor host. When noble or honest travellers descend at our door, come the Provost's men pretending to suspect them, and demanding to search them and their papers. To save which offence the host must bleed wine and meat. Then come the excise to examine all your weights and measures. You must stop their mouths with meat and wine. Town excise. Royal excise. Parliament excise. A swarm of them, and all with a wolf in their stomachs and a sponge in their

Gerard was dumbfoundered.

"What? You offered her what?"

"Marriage. Is that such a mighty strange thing to offer a wench?"

"'Tis a strange thing to offer to a strange girl in passing."

"Nay, I am not such a sot as you opine. I saw the corn in all that chaff. I knew I could not get her by fair means, so I was fain to try foul. 'Mademoiselle,' said I, 'marriage is not one of my habits, but struck by your qualities I make an exception: deign to bestow this hand on me.'"

"And she bestowed it on thine ear."

"Not so. On the contrary she—Art a disrespectful young monkey. Know that here, not being Holland or any other barbarous state, courtesy begets courtesy. Says she, a colouring like a rose, 'Soldier, you are too late. He is not a patch on you for looks; but then—he has loved me a long time.'

"'He? who?'

"'T'other.'

"'What other?

"'Why, he that was not too late.' Oh, that is the way they all speak, the loves, the she-wolves. Their little minds go in leaps. Think you they marshal their words in order of battle? Their tongues are in too great a hurry. Says she, 'I love him not; not to say love him; but he does me, and dearly; and for that reason I'd sooner die than cause him grief, I would.'"

"Now I believe she did love him."

"Who doubts that? Why, she said so, round about, as they always say these things, and with 'nay' for 'ay.' 'I hope you will be happy together,' said I.

"Well, one thing led to another, and at last, as she could not give me her hand, she gave me a piece of advice, and that was to leave part of my money with the young mistress. Then, when bad company had cleaned me out, I should have some to travel back with, said she. I said I would better her advice, and leave it with her. Her face got red. Says she, 'Think what you do. Chambermaids have an ill name for honesty.' 'Oh, the devil is not so black as he is painted,' said I. 'I'll risk it;' and I left fifteen gold pieces with her."

Gerard sighed. "I wish you may ever see them again.

It is wondrous in what esteem you do hold this sex, to trust so to the first comer. For my part I know little about them; I never saw but one I could love as well as I love thee. But the ancients must surely know; and they held women cheap. 'Levius quid fœminâ,' said they, which is but la Jeanneton's tune in Latin, 'Le peu que sont les femmes.' Also do but see how the graybeards of our own day speak of them, being no longer blinded by desire: this alderman, to wit."

"Oh, novice of novices," cried Denys, "not to have seen why that old fool rails so on the poor things! One day, out of the millions of women he blackens, one did prefer some other man to him: for which solitary piece of bad taste, and ten to one 'twas good taste, he doth bespatter creation's fairer half, thereby proving what? Le peu que sont les hommes."

"I see women have a shrewd champion in thee," said Gerard, with a smile. But the next moment inquired gravely why he had not told him all this before.

Denys grinned. "Had the girl said 'Ay,' why then I had told thee straight. But 'tis a rule with us soldiers never to publish our defeats; 'tis much if after each check we claim not a victory."

"Now that is true," said Gerard. "Young as I am, I have seen this: that after every great battle the generals on both sides go to the nearest church, and sing each a Te Deum for the victory; methinks a Te Martem, or Te Bellonam, or Te Mercurium, Mercury being the god of lies, were more fitting."

"Pas si bête," said Denys approvingly. "Hast a good eye; canst see a steeple by daylight. So now tell me how thou hast fared in this town all day."

"Come," said Gerard, "'tis well thou hast asked me; for else I had never told thee." He then related in full how he had been arrested, and by what a providential circumstance he had escaped long imprisonment or speedy conflagration.

His narrative produced an effect he little expected or desired. "I am a traitor," cried Denys. "I left thee in a strange place to fight thine own battles, while I shook the dice with those jades. Now take thou this sword and pass it through my body forthwith."

"What for, in Heaven's name?" inquired Gerard.

"For an example," roared Denys. "For a warning to all false loons that profess friendship and disgrace it."

"Oh, very well," said Gerard. "Yes. Not a bad notion. Where will you have it?"

"Here, through my heart; that is, where other men have a heart, but I none, or a Satanic false one."

Gerard made a motion to run him through, and flung his arms round his neck instead. "I know no way to thy heart but this, thou great silly thing."

Denys uttered an exclamation, then hugged him warmly; and quite overcome by this sudden turn of youthful affection and native grace, gulped out in a broken voice, "Railest on women—and act—like them—with thy pretty ways. Thy mother's milk is in thee still. Satan would love thee, or—le bon Dieu would kick him out of hell for shaming it. Give me thy hand! Give me thy hand! May" (a tremendous oath) "if I let thee out of my sight till Italy."

And so the stanch friends were more than reconciled after their short tiff.

The next day the thieves were tried. The *pièces de conviction* were reduced in number, to the great chagrin of the little clerk, by the interment of the bones. But there was still a pretty show. A thief's hand struck off *flagrante delicto*, a murdered woman's hair, the Abbot's axe, and other tools of crime. The skulls, etc., were sworn to by the constables who had found them. Evidence was lax in that age and place. They all confessed but the landlord. And Manon was called to bring the crime home to him. Her evidence was conclusive. He made a vain attempt to shake her credibility by drawing from her that her own sweetheart had been one of the gang, and that she had held her tongue so long as he was alive. The public prosecutor came to the aid of his witness, and elicited that a knife had been held to her throat, and her own sweetheart sworn with solemn oaths to kill her should she betray them, and that this terrible threat, and not the mere fear of death, had glued her lips.

The other thieves were condemned to be hanged, and the landlord to be broken on the wheel. He uttered a piercing cry when his sentence was pronounced.

As for poor Manon, she became the subject of universal criticism. Nor did opinion any longer run dead in her favour; it divided into two broad currents. And, strange to relate, the majority of her own sex took her part, and the males were but equally divided; which hardly happens once in a hundred years. Perhaps some lady will explain the phenomenon. As for me, I am a little shy of explaining things I don't understand. It has become so common. Meantime, had she been a lover of notoriety, she would have been happy, for the town talked of nothing but her. The poor girl, however, had but one wish; to escape the crowd that followed her, and hide her head somewhere where she could cry over her " pendard," whom all these proceedings brought vividly back to her affectionate remembrance. Before he was hanged he had threatened her life; but she was not one of your fastidious girls, who love their male divinities any the less for beating them, kicking them, or killing them, but rather the better, provided these attentions are interspersed with occasional caresses; so it would have been odd indeed had she taken offence at a mere threat of that sort. He had never threatened her with a rival. She sobbed single-mindedly.

Meantime the inn was filled with thirsters for a sight of her, who feasted and drank to pass away the time till she should deign to appear. When she had been sobbing some time, there was a tap at her door, and the landlord entered with a proposal. " Nay, weep not, good lass, your fortune it is made an you like. Say the word, and you are chambermaid of 'The White Hart.'"

" Nay, nay," said Manon, with a fresh burst of grief. " Never more will I be a servant in an inn. I'll go to my mother."

The landlord consoled and coaxed her; and she became calmer, but none the less determined against his proposal.

The landlord left her. But ere long he returned and made her another proposal. Would she be his wife, and landlady of " The White Hart ? "

" You do ill to mock me," said she sorrowfully.

" Nay, sweetheart. I mock thee not. I am too old for sorry jests. Say you the word, and you are my partner for better for worse."

She looked at him, and saw he was in earnest; on this she suddenly rained hard to the memory of " le pendard "; the tears came in a torrent, being the last; and she gave her hand to the landlord of " The White Hart," and broke a gold crown with him in sign of plighted troth.

"We will keep it dark till the house is quiet," said the landlord.

"Ay," said she; "but meantime prithee give me linen to hem, or work to do, for the time hangs on me like lead."

Her betrothed's eye brightened at this housewifely request, and he brought her up two dozen flagons of various sizes to clean and polish.

She gathered complacency as she reflected that by a strange turn of fortune all this bright pewter was to be hers.

And this mighty furbishing up of pewter reminds me that justice requires me to do a stroke of the same work.

Well then, the deposition, read out in the alderman's room as Manon's, was not so exact as such things ought to be. The alderman had condensed her evidence. Now there are in every great nation about three persons capable of condensing evidence without falsifying it; but this alderman was not one of that small band. In the first part of the deposition he left out as unimportant these words, "My mother advised me to keep out of his way till his wrath should cool."

Between the words "jealous of me" and "the reason" Manon had said, "My master was aye at my heels: so I told my mistress, and said I would rather go than be cause of mischief." This the alderman suppressed as mere babble: whereas it was a worthy trait. He also let slip the word "afterwards" in the next sentence. Manon had said the reason they gave *afterwards*, *i.e.*, "when I was no longer there to contradict them." And so on all through the deposition.

Sometimes the deponent suffered as many a one does nowadays, in the newspaper and other reports, by the mere suppression of the question. For instance, this is what actually was said:—

The Alderman. "Come now, should you have interfered if this soldier had had no beard?"

Manon. "How can I tell what I *should* have done?"

Now this was merely a sensible answer to a monstrous question no magistrate had a right to put. But, under the condensing process, behold her saddled with a volunteer statement of a very damaging character.

Finally she had said, "I am sorry I told, if I am to be hanged for it."

This the old boy condensed *ut supra*, p. 237, anticipating as far as possible the tuneful Sinclair.*

Whilst Manon and I were cleaning, she her coming, I my parting, pewter, the landlord went downstairs, and falling in with our friends drew them aside into the bar.

He then addressed Denys with considerable solemnity. "We are old acquaintances, and you want not for sagacity : now advise me in a strait. My custom is somewhat declining : this girl Manon is the talk of the town ; see how full the inn is to-night. She doth refuse to be my chambermaid. I have half a mind to marry her. What think you ? shall I say the word ? "

Denys in reply merely opened his eyes wide with amazement.

The landlord turned to Gerard with a half-inquiring look.

"Nay, sir," said Gerard ; "I am too young to advise my seniors and betters."

"No matter. Let us hear your thought."

"Well, sir, it was said of a good wife by the ancients, 'bene quæ latuit, bene vixit,' that is, she is the best wife that is least talked of ; but here 'male quæ patuit' were as near the mark. Therefore, an you bear the lass good-will, why not club purses with Denys and me and convey her safe home with a dowry ? Then mayhap some rustical person in her own place may be brought to wive her."

"Why so many words ? " said Denys. "This old fox is not the ass he affects to be."

"Oh ! that is your advice, is it ? " said the landlord testily. "Well then we shall soon know who is the fool, you or me, for I *have* spoken to her as it happens ; and what is more, she has said Ay, and she is polishing the flagons at this moment."

"Oho !" said Denys drily, "'twas an ambuscade. Well, in that case, my advice is, run for the notary, tie the noose, and let us three drink the bride's health, till we see six sots a-tippling."

"And shall. Ay, now you utter sense."

---

* Sinclair was a singer ; and complained to the manager that in the operatic play of "Rob Roy" he had a multitude of mere words to utter between the songs. "Cut, my boy, cut !" said the manager. On this vox et p. n. cut Scott, and doubtless many of his cuts would not have discredited the condensers of evidence. But only one of his master-strokes has reached posterity. His melodious organs had been taxed with this sentence : " Rashleigh is my cousin ; but, for what reason I cannot divine, he is my bitterest enemy." This he condensed and delivered thus : " Rashleigh is my cousin, but for what reason I cannot divine."

In ten minutes a civil marriage was effected upstairs before a notary and his clerk and our two friends.

In ten minutes more the white hind, dead sick of seclusion, had taken her place within the bar, and was serving out liquids, and bustling, and her colour rising a little.

In six minutes more she soundly rated a careless servant-girl for carrying a nipperkin of wine awry and spilling good liquor.

During the evening she received across the bar eight offers of marriage, some of them from respectable burghers. Now the landlord and our two friends had in perfect innocence ensconced themselves behind a screen, to drink at their ease the new couple's health. The above comedy was thrown in for their entertainment by bounteous fate. They heard the proposals made one after another, and uninventive Manon's invariable answer —"Serviteur; you are a day after the fair." The landlord chuckled and looked good-natured superiority at both his late advisers, with their traditional notions that men shun a woman "quæ patuit," *i.e.*, who has become the town talk.

But Denys scarce noticed the spouse's triumph over him, he was so occupied with his own over Gerard. At each municipal tender of undying affection, he turned almost purple with the effort it cost him not to roar with glee; and driving his elbow into the deep-meditating and much-puzzled pupil of antiquity, whispered, "Le peu que sont les hommes."

The next morning Gerard was eager to start, but Denys was under a vow to see the murderers of the golden-haired girl executed.

Gerard respected his vow, but avoided his example.

He went to bid the curé farewell instead, and sought and received his blessing. About noon the travellers got clear of the town. Just outside the south gate they passed the gallows; it had eight tenants: the skeleton of Manon's late wept, and now being fast forgotten, lover, and the bodies of those who had so nearly taken our travellers' lives. A hand was nailed to the beam. And hard by on a huge wheel was clawed the dead landlord, with every bone in his body broken to pieces.

Gerard averted his head and hurried by. Denys lingered, and crowed over his dead foes. "Times are changed, my lads, since we two sat shaking in the cold awaiting you seven to come and cut our throats."

"Fie, Denys! Death squares all reckonings. Prithee pass on without another word, if you prize my respect a groat."

To this earnest remonstrance Denys yielded. He even said thoughtfully, "You have been better brought up than I."

About three in the afternoon they reached a little town with the people buzzing in knots. The wolves, starved by the cold, had entered, and eaten two grown-up persons overnight, in the main street: so some were blaming the eaten—"None but fools or knaves are about after night-fall;" others the law for not protecting the town, and others the corporation for not enforcing what laws there were.

"Bah! this is nothing to us," said Denys, and was for resuming their march.

"Ay, but 'tis," remonstrated Gerard.

"What, are we the pair they ate?"

"No; but we may be the next pair."

"Ay, neighbour," said an ancient man, "'tis the town's fault for not obeying the ducal ordinance, which bids every shopkeeper light a lamp o'er his door at sunset, and burn it till sunrise."

On this Denys asked him somewhat derisively, "What made him fancy rush dips would scare away empty wolves? Why, mutton fat is all their joy."

"'Tis not the fat, vain man, but the light. All ill things hate light; especially wolves and the imps that lurk, I ween, under their fur. Example—Paris city stands in a wood like, and the wolves do howl around it all night: yet of late years wolves come but little in the streets. For why, in that burgh the watchmen do thunder at each door that is dark, and make the weary wight rise and light. 'Tis my son tells me. He is a great voyager, my son Nicholas."

In further explanation he assured them that previously to that ordinance no city had been worse infested with wolves than Paris; a troop had boldly assaulted the town in 1420, and in 1438 they had eaten fourteen persons in a single month between Montmartre and the gate St. Antoine, and that not a winter month even, but September; and as for the dead, which nightly lay in the streets slain in midnight brawls, or assassinated, the wolves had used to devour them, and to grub up the fresh graves in the churchyards and tear out the bodies.

Here a thoughtful citizen suggested that probably the wolves had been bridled of late in Paris, not by candle-lights, but owing to the English having been driven out of the kingdom of France. "For those English be very wolves themselves for fierceness and greediness. What marvel, then, that under their rule our neighbours of France should be wolf-eaten?" This logic was too suited to the time and place not to be received with acclamation. But the old man stood his ground. "I grant ye those islanders are wolves; but two-legged ones, and little apt to favour their four-footed cousins. One greedy thing loveth it another? I trow not. By the same token, and this too I have from my boy Nicole, Sir Wolf dare not show his nose in London city, though 'tis smaller than Paris, and thick woods hard by the north wall, and therein great store of deer, and wild boars rife as flies at midsummer."

"Sir," said Gerard, "you seem conversant with wild beasts, prithee advise my comrade here and me: we would not waste time on the road, an if we may go forward to the next town with reasonable safety."

"Young man, I trow 'twere an idle risk. It lacks but an hour of dusk, and you must pass nigh a wood where lurk some thousands of these half-starved vermin, rank cowards single; but in great bands bold as lions. Wherefore I rede you sojourn here the night; and journey on betimes. By the dawn the vermin will be tired out with roaring and rampaging; and mayhap will have filled their lank bellies with flesh of my good neighbours here, the unteachable fools."

Gerard hoped not; and asked could he recommend them to a good inn.

"Humph! there is 'The Tête d'Or.' My granddaughter keeps it. She is a mijaurée, but not so knavish as most hotel-keepers, and her house indifferent clean."

"Hey, for 'The Tête d'Or,'" struck in Denys, decided by his ineradicable foible.

On the way to it, Gerard inquired of his companion what a "mijaurée" was?

Denys laughed at his ignorance. "Not know what a mijaurée is? why, all the world knows that. It is neither more nor less than a mijaurée."

As they entered "The Tête d'Or," they met a young lady

richly dressed, with the velvet chaperon on her head, which was confined by law to the nobility. They unbonneted and louted low, and she curtsied, but fixed her eye on vacancy the while, which had a curious rather than a genial effect. However, nobility was not so unassuming in those days as it is now. So they were little surprised. But the next minute supper was served, and lo! in came this princess and carved the goose.

"Holy St. Bavon," cried Gerard. "'Twas the landlady all the while."

A young woman cursed with nice white teeth and lovely hands: for these beauties being misallied to homely features, had turned her head. She was a feeble carver, carving not for the sake of others but herself, *i.e.*, to display her hands. When not carving she was eternally either taking a pin out of her head or her body, or else putting a pin into her head or her body. To display her teeth, she laughed indifferently at gay or grave, and from ear to ear. And she "sat at ease" with her mouth ajar.

Now there is an animal in creation of no great general merit; but it has the eye of a hawk for affectation. It is called "a boy." And Gerard was but a boy still in some things; swift to see, and to loathe, affectation. So Denys sat casting sheep's eyes, and Gerard daggers, at one comedian.

Presently, in the midst of her minauderies, she gave a loud shriek and bounded out of her chair like hare from form, and ran backwards out of the room uttering little screams, and holding her farthingale tight down to her ankles with both hands. And, as she scuttled out of the door, a mouse scuttled back to the wainscot in a state of equal, and perhaps more reasonable, terror. The guests, who had risen in anxiety at the principal yell, now stood irresolute awhile, then sat down laughing. The tender Denys, to whom a woman's cowardice, being a sexual trait, seemed a lovely and pleasant thing, said he would go comfort her and bring her back.

"Nay! nay! nay! for pity's sake let her bide," cried Gerard earnestly. "Oh, blessed mouse! sure some saint sent thee to our aid."

Now at his right hand sat a sturdy middle-aged burgher, whose conduct up to date had been cynical. He had never budged nor even rested his knife at all this fracas. He now turned on Gerard and inquired haughtily whether he really thought that "grimacière" was afraid of a mouse.

"Ay; she screamed hearty."

"Where is the coquette that cannot scream to the life? These she tavern-keepers do still ape the nobles. Some princess or duchess hath lain here a night, that was honestly afeard of a mouse, having been brought up to it. And this ape hath seen her, and said, 'I will start at a mouse, and make a coil.' She has no more right to start at a mouse than to wear that fur on her bosom, and that velvet on her monkey's head. I am of the town, young man, and have known the mijaurée all her life, and I mind when she was no more afeard of a mouse than she is of a man." He added that she was fast emptying the inn with these "singeries." "All the world is so sick of her hands, that her very kinsfolk will not venture themselves anigh them." He concluded with something like a sigh, "'The Tête d'Or' was a thriving hostelry under my old chum her good father; but she is digging its grave tooth and nail."

"Tooth and nail? good! a right merry conceit and a true," said Gerard. But the right merry conceit was an inadvertence as pure as snow, and the stout burgher went to his grave and never knew what he had done: for just then attention was attracted by Denys returning pompously. He inspected the apartment minutely, and with a high official air: he also looked solemnly under the table; and during the whole inquisition a white hand was placed conspicuously on the edge of the open door, and a tremulous voice inquired behind it whether the horrid thing was quite gone.

"The enemy has retreated, bag and baggage," said Denys; and handed in the trembling fair, who, sitting down, apologised to her guests for her foolish fears, with so much earnestness, grace, and seeming self-contempt that, but for a sour grin on his neighbour's face, Gerard would have been taken in as all the other strangers were. Dinner ended, the young landlady begged an Augustine friar at her right hand to say grace. He delivered a longish one. The moment he began, she clapped her white hands piously together, and held them up joined for mortals to admire; 'tis an excellent pose for taper white fingers; and cast her eyes upward towards heaven, and felt as thankful to it as a magpie does while cutting off with your thimble.

After supper the two friends went to the street-door and eyed the market-place. The mistress joined them, and pointed out the town-hall, the borough jail, St. Catharine's Church, etc. This was courteous, to say the least. But the true cause soon revealed itself; the fair hand was poked right under their eyes every time an object was indicated; and Gerard eyed it like a basilisk, and longed for a bunch of nettles. The sun set, and the travellers, few in number, drew round the great roaring fire, and, omitting to go on the spit, were frozen behind though roasted in front. For if the German stoves were oppressively hot, the French *salles à manger* were bitterly cold, and above all, stormy. In Germany men sat bareheaded round the stove, and took off their upper clothes, but in Burgundy they kept on their hats, and put on their warmest furs to sit round the great open chimney-places, at which the external air rushed furiously from door and ill-fitting window. However, it seems their mediæval backs were broad enough to bear it : for they made themselves not only comfortable but merry, and broke harmless jests over each other in turn. For instance, Denys's new shoes, though not in direct communication, had this day exploded with twin-like sympathy and unanimity. "Where do you buy your shoon, soldier ?" asked one.

Denys looked askant at Gerard, and not liking the theme, shook it off. "I gather 'em off the trees by the roadside," said he surlily.

"Then you gathered these too ripe," said the hostess, who was only a fool externally.

"Ay, rotten ripe," observed another, inspecting them.

Gerard said nothing, but pointed the circular satire by pantomime. He slily put out both his feet, one after another, under Denys's eye, with their German shoes, on which a hundred leagues of travel had produced no effect. They seemed hewn out of a rock.

At this, "I'll twist the smooth varlet's neck that sold me mine," shouted Denys, in huge wrath, and confirmed the threat with singular oaths peculiar to the mediæval military. The landlady put her fingers in her ears, thereby exhibiting the hand in a fresh attitude. "Tell me when he has done his orisons, somebody," said she mincingly. And after that they fell to telling stories.

Gerard, when his turn came, told the adventure of Denys and Gerard at the inn in Domfront, and so well, that the hearers were rapt into sweet oblivion of the very existence of mijaurée and hands. But this made her very uneasy, and she had recourse to her grand coup. This misdirected genius had for a twelvemonth past practised yawning, and could do it now at any moment so naturally as to set all creation gaping, could all creation have seen her. By this means she got in all her charms. For first she showed her teeth, then, out of good-breeding, you know, closed her mouth with three taper fingers. So the moment Gerard's story got too interesting and absorbing, she turned to and made yawns, and "croix sur la bouche."

This was all very fine; but Gerard was an artist, and artists are chilled by gaping auditors. He bore up against the yawns a long time; but finding they came from a bottomless reservoir, lost both heart and temper, and suddenly rising in mid narrative, said, "But I weary our hostess, and I am tired myself: so good-night!" whipped a candle off the dresser, whispered Denys, "I cannot stand her," and marched to bed in a moment.

The mijaurée coloured and bit her lips. She had not intended her byplay for Gerard's eye; and she saw in a moment she had been rude, and silly, and publicly rebuked. She sat with cheek on fire, and a little natural water in her eyes, and looked ten times comelier and more womanly and interesting than she had done all day. The desertion of the best narrator broke up the party, and the unassuming Denys approached the meditative mijaurée, and invited her, in the most flattering terms, to gamble with him. She started from her reverie, looked him down into the earth's centre with chilling dignity, and consented, for she remembered all in a moment what a show of hands gambling admitted.

The soldier and the mijaurée rattled the dice. In which sport she was so taken up with her hands that she forgot to cheat, and Denys won an "écu au soleil" of her. She fumbled slowly with her purse, partly because her sex do not burn to pay debts of honour, partly to admire the play of her little knuckles peeping between their soft white cushions. Denys proposed a compromise. "Three silver franks I win of you, fair hostess. Give me now three kisses of this white hand, and we'll e'en cry quits."

"You are malapert," said the lady, with a toss of her head; "besides, they are so dirty. See! they are like ink!" and to convince him she put them out to him and turned them up and down. They were no dirtier than cream fresh from the cow. And she knew it: she was eternally washing and scenting them.

Denys read the objection like the observant warrior he was, seized them and mumbled them.

Finding him so appreciative of her charm, she said timidly, "Will you do me a kindness, good soldier?"

"A thousand, fair hostess, an you will."

"Nay, I ask but one. 'Tis to tell thy comrade I was right sorry to lose his most thrilling story, and I hope he will tell me the rest to-morrow morning. Meantime I shall not sleep for thinking on't. Wilt tell him that—to pleasure me?"

"Ay, I'll tell the young savage. But he is not worthy of your condescension, sweet hostess. He would rather be aside a man than a woman any day."

"So would—ahem. He is right: the young women of the day are not worthy of *him*, 'un tas des mijaurées.' He has a good, honest, and right comely face. Anyway, I would not guest of mine should think me unmannerly, not for all the world. Wilt keep faith with me and tell him?"

"On this fair hand I swear it; and thus I seal the pledge."

"There; no need to melt the wax, though. Now go to bed. And tell him ere you sleep."

The perverse toad (I thank thee, Marion, for teaching me that word) was inclined to bestow her slight affections upon Gerard. Not that she was inflammable: far less so than many that passed for prudes in the town. But Gerard possessed a triple attraction that has ensnared coquettes in all ages. 1. He was very handsome. 2. He did not admire her the least. 3. He had given her a good slap in the face.

Denys woke Gerard and gave the message. Gerard was not enchanted. "Dost wake a tired man to tell him that? Am I to be pestered with 'mijaurées' by night as well as day?"

"But I tell thee, novice, thou hast conquered her: trust to my experience: her voice sank to melodious whispers; and the cunning jade did in a manner bribe me to carry thee her challenge to Love's lists! for so I read her message."

Denys then, assuming the senior and the man of the world, told Gerard the time was come to show him how a soldier understood friendship and camaraderie. Italy was now out of the question. Fate had provided better; and the blind jade Fortune had smiled on merit for once. "The Head of Gold" had been a prosperous inn, would be again with a man at *its* head. A good general laid far-sighted plans; but was always ready to abandon them, should some brilliant advantage offer, and to reap the full harvest of the unforeseen; 'twas chiefly by this trait great leaders defeated little ones, for these latter could do nothing not cut and dried beforehand.

"Sorry friendship that would marry me to a mijaurée," interposed Gerard, yawning.

"Comrade, be reasonable; 'tis not the friskiest sheep that falls down the cliff. All creatures must have their fling soon or late; and why not a woman? What more frivolous than a kitten? what graver than a cat?"

"Hast a good eye for Nature, Denys," said Gerard, "that I proclaim."

"A better for thine interest, boy. Trust then to me; these little doves they are my study day and night; happy the man whose wife taketh her fling before wedlock, and who trippeth up the altar-steps instead of down 'em. Marriage it always changeth them for better or else for worse. Why, Gerard, she is honest when all is done; and he is no man, nor half a man, that cannot mould any honest lass like a bit of warm wax, and she aye aside him at bed and board. I tell thee in one month thou wilt make of this coquette the matron the most sober in the town, and of all its wives the one most docile and submissive. Why, she is half tamed already. Nine in ten meek and mild ones had gently hated thee like poison all their lives, for wounding of their hidden pride. But she for an affront proffers affection. By Joshua his bugle a generous lass, and void of petty malice. When thou wast gone she sat a-thinking and spoke not. A sure sign of love in one of her sex; for of all things else they speak ere they think. Also her voice did sink exceeding low in discoursing of thee, and murmured sweetly; another infallible sign. The bolt hath struck and rankles in her; oh, be joyful! Art silent? I see; 'tis settled. I shall go alone to Remiremont, alone and sad. But, pillage and poleaxes! what care I for that, since my dear comrade will stay here, landlord of 'The Tête d'Or,' and safe from all the storms of life? Wilt think of me, Gerard, now and then by thy warm fire, of me camped on some windy heath, or lying in wet trenches, or wounded on the field and far from comfort? Nay" (and this he said in a manner truly noble), "not comfortless. For cold, or wet, or bleeding, 'twill still warm my heart to lie on my back and think that I have placed my dear friend and comrade true in 'The Tête d'Or,' far from a soldier's ills."

"I let you run on, dear Denys," said Gerard softly, "because at each word you show me the treasure of a good heart. But now bethink thee, my troth is plighted there where my heart it clingeth. You so leal, would you make me disloyal?"

"Perdition seize me, but I forgot that," said Denys.

"No more then, but hie thee to bed, good Denys. Next to Margaret I love thee best on earth, and value thy *cœur d'or* far more than a dozen of these 'Têtes d'Or.' So prithee call me at the first blush of rosy-fingered morn, and let's away ere the woman with the hands be stirring."

They rose with the dawn, and broke their fast by the kitchen fire.

Denys inquired of the girl whether the mistress was about.

"Nay; but she hath risen from her bed: by the same token I am carrying her this to clean her withal;" and she filled a mug with boiling water, and took it upstairs.

"Behold," said Gerard, "the very elements must be warmed to suit her skin; what had the saints said, which still chose the coldest pool? Away, ere she come down and catch us."

They paid the score, and left "The Tête d'Or," while its mistress was washing her hands.

CHAPTER XXXVIII.

OUTSIDE the town they found the snow fresh trampled by innumerable wolves every foot of the road.

"We did well to take the old man's advice, Denys."

"Ay did we. For now I think on't, I did hear them last night a-scurrying under our window, and howling and whining for man's flesh in yon market-place. But no fat burgher did pity the poor vagabonds and drop out o' window."

Gerard smiled, but with an air of abstraction.

And they plodded on in silence.

"What dost meditate so profoundly?"

"Thy goodness."

Denys was anything but pleased at this answer. Amongst his oddities you may have observed that he could stand a great deal of real impertinence; he was so good-humoured. But would fire up now and then where not even the shadow of a ground for anger existed.

"A civil question merits a civil reply," said he very drily.

"Alas, I meant no other," said Gerard.

"Then why pretend you were thinking of my goodness, when you know I have no goodness under my skin?"

"Had another said this, I had answered, 'Thou liest.' But to thee I say, 'Hast no eye for men's qualities, but only for women's.' And once more I do defy thy unreasonable choler, and say I was thinking on thy goodness of overnight. Wouldst have wedded me to 'The Tête d'Or,' or rather to the 'tête de veau dorée,' and left thyself solitary."

"Oh, are ye there, lad?" said Denys, recovering his good-humour in a moment. "Well, but to speak sooth, I meant that not for goodness; but for friendship and true fellowship, no more. And let me tell you, my young master, my conscience it pricketh me even now for letting you turn your back thus on fortune and peaceful days. A truer friend than I had ta'en and somewhat hamstrung thee. Then hadst thou been fain to lie smarting at 'The Tête d'Or' a month or so : yon skittish lass had nursed thee tenderly, and all had been well. Blade I had in hand to do't, but remembering how thou hatest pain, though it be but a scratch, my craven heart it failed me at the pinch." And Denys wore a look of humble apology for his lack of virtuous resolution when the path of duty lay so clear.

Gerard raised his eyebrows with astonishment at this monstrous but thoroughly characteristic revelation; however, this new and delicate point of friendship was never discussed, viz., whether one ought in all love to cut the tendon Achilles of one's friend. For an incident interposed.

"Here cometh one in our rear a-riding on his neighbour's mule," shouted Denys.

Gerard turned round. "And how know ye 'tis not his own, pray?"

"Oh, blind! Because he rides it with no discretion."

And in truth the man came galloping like a fury. But what astonished the friends most was that on reaching them the rustic rider's eyes opened saucer-like, and he drew the rein so suddenly and powerfully, that the mule stuck out her fore-legs, and went sliding between the pedestrians like a four-legged table on castors.

"I trow ye are from 'The Tête d'Or'?" They assented. "Which of ye is the younger?"

"He that was born the later," said Denys, winking at his companion.

"Gramercy for the news."

"Come, divine then!"

"And shall. Thy beard is ripe, thy fellow's is green; he shall be the younger; here, youngster." And he held him out a paper packet. "Ye left this at 'The Tête d'Or,' and our mistress sends it ye."

"Nay, good fellow, methinks I left nought." And Gerard felt his pouch, etc.

"Would ye make our burgess a liar," said the rustic reproachfully; "and shall I have no pourboire?" (still more reproachfully); "and came ventre à terre."

"Nay, thou shalt have pourboire," and he gave him a small coin.

"A la bonne heure," cried the clown, and his features beamed with disproportionate joy. "The Virgin go with ye; come up, Jenny!" and back he went "stomach to earth," as his nation is pleased to call it.

Gerard undid the packet: it was about six inches square, and inside it he found another packet, which contained a packet, and so on. At the fourth he hurled the whole thing into the snow. Denys took it out and rebuked his petulance. He excused himself on the ground of hating affectation.

Denys attested, "'The great toe of the little daughter of Herodias' there was no affectation here, but only woman's good wit. Doubtless the wraps contained something which out of delicacy, or her sex's lovely cunning, she would not her hind should see her bestow on a young man; thy garter, to wit."

" I wear none."

" Her own then ; or a lock of her hair. What is this ? A piece of raw silk fresh from the worm. Well, of all the love tokens ! "

" Now who but thee ever dreamed that she is so naught as send me love tokens ? I saw no harm in her—barring her hands."

" Stay, here is something hard lurking in this soft nest. Come forth, I say, little nestling ! Saints and pikestaves ! look at this ! "

It was a gold ring, with a great amethyst glowing and sparkling, full coloured, but pure as crystal.

" How lovely ! " said Gerard innocently.

" And here is something writ ; read it thou ! I read not so glib as some, when I know not the matter beforehand."

Gerard took the paper. " ' 'Tis a posy, and fairly enough writ." He read the lines, blushing like a girl. They were very naïve, and may be thus Englished :—

> " Youth, with thee my heart is fledde,
>   Come back to the 'golden Hedde !'
> Wilt not ? yet this token keepe
> Of hir whŏ dŏĕth thy goeing weepe.
> Gyf the world prove harṣh and cold,
> Come back to ' the Hedde of gold.' "

" The little dove ! " purred Denys.

" The great owl ! To go and risk her good name thus. However, thank Heaven she has played this prank with an honest lad that will ne'er expose her folly. But oh, the perverseness ! Could she not bestow her nauseousness on thee ? " Denys sighed and shrugged. " On thee that art as ripe for folly as herself ? "

Denys confessed that his young friend had harped his very thought. 'Twas passing strange to him that a damsel with eyes in her head should pass by a man, and bestow her affections on a boy. Still he could not but recognise in this the bounty of Nature. Boys were human beings after all, and but for this occasional caprice of women, their lot would be too terrible ; they would be out of the sun altogether, blighted, and never come to anything ; since only the fair could make a man out of such unpromising materials as a boy. Gerard interrupted this flattering discourse to beg the warrior-philosopher's acceptance of the lady's ring. He refused it flatly, and insisted on Gerard going back to "The Tête d'Or" at once, ring and all, like a man, and not letting a poor girl hold out her arms to him in vain.

"Her hands, you mean."

"Her hand, with 'The Tête d'Or' in it."

Failing in this, he was for putting the ring on his friend's finger. Gerard declined. "I wear a ring already."

"What, that sorry gimcrack? why, 'tis pewter, or tin at best; and this virgin gold, forbye the jewel."

"Ay, but 'twas Margaret gave me this one; and I value it above rubies. I'll neither part with it nor give it a rival," and he kissed the base metal, and bade it fear nought.

"I see the owl hath sent her ring to a goose," said Denys sorrowfully. However, he prevailed on Gerard to fasten it inside his bonnet. To this, indeed, the lad consented very readily. For sovereign qualities were universally ascribed to certain jewels; and the amethyst ranked high among these precious talismans.

When this was disposed of, Gerard earnestly requested his friend to let the matter drop, since speaking of the other sex to him made him pine so for Margaret, and almost unmanned him with the thought that each step was taking him farther from her. "I am no general lover, Denys. There is room in my heart for one sweetheart, and for one friend. I am far from my dear mistress; and my friend, a few leagues more, and I must lose him too. Oh, let me drink thy friendship pure while I may, and not dilute with any of these stupid females."

"And shalt, honey-pot, and shalt," said Denys kindly. "But as to my leaving thee at Remiremont, reckon thou not on that! For" (three consecutive oaths) "if I do. Nay, I shall propose to thee to stay forty-eight hours there, while I kiss my mother and sisters, and the females generally, and on go you and I together to the sea."

"Denys! Denys!"

"Denys not me! 'Tis settled. Gainsay me not! or I'll go with thee to Rome. Why not? his Holiness the Pope hath ever some little merry pleasant war toward, and a Burgundian soldier is still welcome in his ranks."

On this Gerard opened his heart. "Denys, ere I fell in with thee, I used often to halt on the road, unable to go farther, my puny heart so pulled me back; and then, after a short prayer to the saints for aid, would I rise and drag my most unwilling body onward. But since I joined company with thee, great is my courage. I have found the saying of the ancients true, that better is a bright comrade on the weary road than a horse-litter; and, dear brother, when I do think of what we have done and suffered together! Savedst my life from the bear, and from yet more savage thieves; and even poor I did make shift to draw thee out of Rhine, and somehow loved thee double from that hour. How many ties tender and strong between us! Had I my will, I'd never, never, never, never part with my Denys on this side the grave. Well-a-day! God His will be done."

"No, my will shall be done this time," shouted Denys. "Le bon Dieu has bigger fish to fry than you or me. I'll go with thee to Rome. There is my hand on it."

"Think what you say! 'Tis impossible. 'Tis too selfish of me."

"I tell thee, 'tis settled. No power can change me. At Remiremont I borrow ten pieces of my uncle, and on we go; 'tis fixed; irrevocable as fate."

They shook hands over it. Then Gerard said nothing, for his heart was too full; but he ran twice round his companion as he walked, then danced backwards in front of him, and finally took his hand, and so on they went hand in hand like sweethearts, till a company of mounted soldiers, about fifty in number, rose to sight on the brow of a hill.

"See the banner of Burgundy," said Denys joyfully; "I shall look out for a comrade among these."

"How gorgeous is the standard in the sun," said Gerard; "and how brave are the leaders with velvet and feathers, and steel breastplates like glassy mirrors!"

When they came near enough to distinguish faces, Denys uttered an exclamation: "Why, 'tis the Bastard of Burgundy, as I live. Nay, then; there is fighting a-foot since he is out; a gallant leader, Gerard, rates his life no higher than a private soldier's, and a soldier's no higher than a tomtit's; and that is the captain for me."

"And see, Denys, the very mules with their great brass frontlets and trappings seem proud to carry them; no wonder men itch to be soldiers;" and in the midst of this innocent admiration the troop came up with them.

"Halt!" cried a stentorian voice. The troop halted. The Bastard of Burgundy bent his brow gloomily on

Denys: "How now, arbalestrier, how comes it thy face is turned southward, when every good hand and heart is hurrying northward?"

Denys replied respectfully that he was going on leave, after some years of service, to see his kindred at Remiremont.

"Good. But this is not the time for't; the duchy is disturbed. Ho! bring that dead soldier's mule to the front; and thou mount her and forward with us to Flanders."

"So please your highness," said Denys firmly, "that may not be. My home is close at hand. I have not seen it these three years; and, above all, I have this poor youth in charge, whom I may not, cannot leave, till I see him shipped for Rome."

"Dost bandy words with me?" said the chief, with amazement, turning fast to wrath. "Art weary o' thy life? Let go the youth's hand, and into the saddle without more idle words."

Denys made no reply; but he held Gerard's hand the tighter, and looked defiance.

At this the Bastard roared, "Jarnac, dismount six of thy archers, and shoot me this white-livered cur dead where he stands—for an example."

The young Count de Jarnac, second in command, gave the order, and the men dismounted to execute it.

"Strip him naked," said the Bastard, in the cold tone of military business, "and put his arms and accoutrements on the spare mule. We'll maybe find some clown worthier to wear them."

Denys groaned aloud, "Am I to be shamed as well as slain?"

"Oh, nay! nay! nay!" cried Gerard, awaking from the stupor into which this thunderbolt of tyranny had thrown him. "He shall go with you on the instant. I'd liever part with him for ever than see a hair of his dear head harmed. Oh, sir, oh, my lord, give a poor boy but a minute to bid his only friend farewell! he will go with you. I swear he shall go with you."

The stern leader nodded a cold, contemptuous assent. "Thou, Jarnac, stay with them, and bring him on alive or dead. Forward!" And he resumed his march, followed by all the band but the young Count and six archers, one of whom held the spare mule.

Denys and Gerard gazed at one another haggardly. Oh, what a look!

And after this mute interchange of anguish, they spoke hurriedly, for the moments were flying by.

"Thou goest to Holland: thou knowest where she bides. Tell her all. She will be kind to thee for my sake."

"Oh, sorry tale that I shall carry her! For God's sake go back to 'The Tête d'Or.' I am mad."

"Hush! Let me think: have I nought to say to thee, Denys? my head! my head!"

"Ah! I have it. Make for the Rhine, Gerard! Strasbourg. 'Tis but a step. And down the current to Rotterdam. Margaret is there: I go thither. I'll tell her thou art coming. We shall all be together."

"My lads, haste ye, or you will get us into trouble," said the Count firmly, but not harshly now.

"Oh, sir, one moment! one little moment!" panted Gerard.

"Cursed be the land I was born in! cursed be the race of man! and he that made them what they are!" screamed Denys.

"Hush, Denys, hush! blaspheme not! Oh, God forgive him, he wots not what he says. Be patient, Denys—be patient: though we meet no more on earth, let us meet in a better world, where no blasphemer may enter. To my heart, lost friend; for what are words now?" He held out his arms, and they locked one another in a close embrace. They kissed one another again and again, speechless, and the tears rained down their cheeks. And the Count Jarnac looked on amazed, but the rougher soldiers, to whom comrade was a sacred name, looked on with some pity in their hard faces. Then at a signal from Jarnac, with kind force and words of rude consolation, they almost lifted Denys on to the mule; and putting him in the middle of them, spurred after their leader. And Gerard ran wildly after (for the lane turned) to see the very last of him; and the last glimpse he caught, Denys was rocking to and fro on his mule, and tearing his hair out. But at this sight something rose in Gerard's throat so high, so high, he could run no more nor breathe, but gasped, and leaned against the snow-clad hedge, seizing it, and choking piteously.

The thorns ran into his hand.

After a bitter struggle he got his breath again; and now began to see his own misfortune. Yet not all at once to realise it, so sudden and numbing was the stroke. He staggered on, but scarce feeling or caring whither he was going; and every now and then he stopped, and his arms fell and his head sank on his chest, and he stood motionless: then he said to himself, "Can this thing be? This must be a dream. 'Tis scarce five minutes since we were so happy, walking handed, faring to Rome together: and we admired them and their gay banners and helmets—oh, hearts of hell!"

All Nature seemed to stare now as lonely as himself. Not a creature in sight. No colour but white. He, the ghost of his former self, wandered alone among the ghosts of trees, and fields, and hedges. Desolate! desolate! desolate! All was desolate.

He knelt and gathered a little snow. "Nay, I dream not; for this *is* snow: cold as the world's heart. It is bloody, too: what may that mean? Fool! 'tis from thy hand. I mind not the wound. Ay, I see: thorns. Welcome! kindly foes: I felt ye not, ye ran not into my heart. Ye are not cruel like men."

He had risen, and was dragging his leaden limbs along, when he heard horses' feet and gay voices behind him. He turned with a joyful but wild hope that the soldiers had relented and were bringing Denys back. But no, it was a gay cavalcade. A gentleman of rank and his favourites in velvet and furs and feathers; and four or five armed retainers in buff jerkins.

They swept gaily by.

Gerard never looked at them after they were gone by: certain gay shadows had come and passed; that was all. He was like one in a dream. But he was rudely wakened; suddenly a voice in front of him cried harshly, "Stand and deliver!" and there were three of the gentleman's servants in front of him. They had ridden back to rob him.

"How, ye false knaves," said he quite calmly; "would ye shame your noble master? He will hang ye to the nearest tree;" and with these words he drew his sword doggedly, and set his back to the hedge.

One of the men instantly levelled his petronel at him.

But another, less sanguinary, interposed. "Be not so hasty! And be not thou so mad! Look yonder!"

Gerard looked, and scarce a hundred yards off the noble-man and his friends had halted, and sat on their horses, looking at the lawless act, too proud to do their own dirty work, but not too proud to reap the fruit, and watch lest their agents should rob them of another man's money.

The milder servant then, a good-natured fellow, showed Gerard resistance was vain ; reminded him common thieves often took the life as well as the purse, and assured him it cost a mint to be a gentleman; his master had lost money at play overnight, and was going to visit his leman, and so must take money where he saw it.

"Therefore, good youth, consider that we rob not for ourselves, and deliver us that fat purse at thy girdle without more ado, nor put us to the pain of slitting thy throat and taking it all the same."

"This knave is right," said Gerard calmly, aloud but to himself. "I ought not to fling away my life ; Margaret would be so sorry. Take then the poor man's purse to the rich man's pouch ; and with it this ; tell him, I pray the Holy Trinity each coin in it may burn his hand, and freeze his heart, and blast his soul for ever. Begone and leave me to my sorrow !" He flung them the purse.

They rode away muttering ; for his words pricked them a little, a very little ; and he staggered on, penniless now as well as friendless, till he came to the edge of a wood. Then, though his heart could hardly feel this second blow, his judgment did ; and he began to ask himself what was the use going farther ? He sat down on the hard road, and ran his nails into his hair, and tried to think for the best—a task all the more difficult that a strange drowsiness was stealing over him. Rome he could never reach without money. Denys had said, "Go to Strasbourg, and down the Rhine home." He would obey Denys. But how get to Strasbourg without money ?

Then suddenly seemed to ring in his ears—

"Gyf the world prove harsh and cold,
Come back to the hedde of gold."

"And if I do I must go as her servant ; I who am Margaret's. I am a-weary, a-weary. I will sleep, and dream all is as it was. Ah me, how happy were we an hour agone, we little knew how happy. There is a house : the owner well-to-do. What if I told him my wrong, and prayed his aid to retrieve my purse, and so to Rhine? Fool! is he not a man, like the rest? He would scorn me and trample me lower. Denys cursed the race of men. That will I never; but oh, I 'gin to loathe and dread them. Nay, here will I lie till sunset: then darkling creep into this rich man's barn, and take by stealth a draught of milk or a handful o' grain, to keep body and soul together. God, who hath seen the rich rob me, will peradventure forgive me. They say 'tis ill sleeping on the snow. Death steals on such sleepers with muffled feet and honey breath. But what can I? I am a-weary, a-weary. Shall this be the wood where lie the wolves yon old man spoke of? I must e'en trust them: they are not men; and I am so a-weary."

He crawled to the roadside, and stretched out his limbs on the snow, with a deep sigh.

"Ah, tear not thine hair so! teareth my heart to see thee."

"Mar—garet. Never see me more. Poor Mar—ga—ret."

And the too tender heart was still.

And the constant lover, and friend of antique mould, lay silent on the snow; in peril from the weather, in peril from wild beasts, in peril from hunger, friendless and penniless, in a strange land, and not half way to Rome.

CHAPTER XXXIX.

RUDE travel is enticing to us English. And so are its records; even though the adventurer be no pilgrim of love. And antique friendship has at least the interest of a fossil. Still, as the true centre of this story is in Holland, it is full time to return thither, and to those ordinary personages and incidents whereof life has been mainly composed in all ages.

Jorian Ketel came to Peter's house to claim Margaret's promise; but Margaret was ill in bed, and Peter, on hearing his errand, affronted him and warned him off the premises, and one or two that stood by were for ducking him; for both father and daughter were favourites, and the whole story was in every mouth, and the Sevenbergens

you say such a word to me? And I rede you never mention
that hussy's name in this house, that she has laid bare.
She is the ruin of my poor boy, the flower of all my flock.
She is the cause that he is not a holy priest in the midst of
us, but is roaming the world, and I a desolate, broken-
hearted mother. There, do not cry, my girl, I do ill to
speak harsh to you. But oh, Kate! you know not what
passes in a mother's heart. I bear up before you all; it
behoves me swallow my fears: but at night I see him in
my dreams, and still some trouble or other near him:
sometimes he is torn by wild beasts; other times he is in
the hands of robbers, and their cruel knives uplifted to
strike his poor, pale face, that one should think would move
a stone. Oh! when I remember that, while I sit here in
comfort, perhaps my poor boy lies dead in some savage
place, and all along of that girl: there, her very name is
ratsbane to me. I tremble all over when I hear it."

"I'll not say anything, nor do anything to grieve you
worse, mother," said Kate tenderly; but she sighed.

She whose name was so fiercely interdicted in this house
was much spoken of, and even pitied, elsewhere. All
Sevenbergen was sorry for her, and the young men and
maidens cast many a pitying glance, as they passed, at
the little window where the beauty of the village lay
"dying for love." In this familiar phrase they underrated
her spirit and unselfishness. Gerard was not dead, and
she was too loyal herself to doubt his constancy. Her
father was dear to her and helpless; and, but for bodily
weakness, all her love for Gerard would not have kept
her from doing her duties, though she might have gone
about them with drooping head and heavy heart. But
physical and mental excitement had brought on an attack
of fever so violent, that nothing but youth and constitution
saved her. The malady left her at last, but in that terrible
state of bodily weakness in which the patient feels life a
burden.

Then it is that love and friendship by the bedside are
mortal angels with comfort in their voices, and healing
in their palms.

But this poor girl had to come back to life and vigour
how she could. Many days she lay alone, and the heavy
hours rolled like leaden waves over her. In her enfeebled
state existence seemed a burden, and life a thing gone by.
She could not try her best to get well. Gerard was gone.

She had not him to get well for. Often she lay for hours quite still, with the tears welling gently out of her eyes.

One day, waking from an uneasy slumber, she found two women in her room. One was a servant, the other by the deep fur on her collar and sleeves was a person of consideration: a narrow band of silvery hair, being spared by her coiffure, showed her to be past the age when women of sense conceal their years. The looks of both were kind and friendly. Margaret tried to raise herself in the bed, but the old lady placed a hand very gently on her.

"Lie still, sweetheart; we come not here to put you about, but to comfort you, God willing. Now cheer up a bit, and tell us, first, who think you we are?"

"Nay, madam, I know you, though I never saw you before: you are the demoiselle Van Eyck, and this is Reicht Heynes. Gerard has oft spoken of you, and of your goodness to him. Madam, he has no friend like you near him now," and at this thought she lay back, and the tears welled out of her eyes in a moment.

The good-natured Reicht Heynes began to cry for company; but her mistress scolded her. "Well, you are a pretty one for a sick-room," said she; and she put out a world of innocent art to cheer the patient, and not without some little success. An old woman, that has seen life and all its troubles, is a sovereign blessing by a sorrowful young woman's side. She knows what to say, and what to avoid. She knows how to soothe her and interest her. Ere she had been there an hour, she had Margaret's head lying on her shoulder instead of on the pillow, and Margaret's soft eyes dwelling on her with gentle gratitude.

"Ah! this is hair," said the old lady, running her fingers through it. "Come and look at it, Reicht!"

Reicht came and handled it, and praised it unaffectedly. The poor girl that owned it was not quite out of the reach of flattery; owing, doubtless, to not being dead.

"In sooth, madam, I did use to think it hideous; but *he* praised it, and ever since then I have been almost vain of it, saints forgive me. You know how foolish those are that love."

"They are greater fools that don't," said the old lady sharply.

Margaret opened her lovely eyes, and looked at her for her meaning.

This was only the first of many visits. In fact, either